SNOW WOMAN

SNOW WOMAN

LEENA LEHTOLAINEN

Translated by Owen F. Witesman

amazon crossing

Text copyright © 1996 by Leena Lehtolainen
English translation copyright © 2014 Owen F. Witesman
All rights reserved.

Previously published as *Luminainen* by Tammi Publishers, Finland, in 1996. Translated from Finnish by Owen F. Witesman and first published in English by AmazonCrossing in 2014. Published by agreement with Tammi Publishers and Elina Ahlbäck Literary Agency, Helsinki, Finland.

Published by AmazonCrossing, Seattle
www.apub.com

Amazon, the Amazon logo, and AmazonCrossing are trademarks of Amazon.com, Inc., or its affiliates.

Lyrics from "A Farewell to Arms" ("Jäähyväiset aseille") reprinted by permission of Jyrki Siukonen.

ISBN-13: 9781477826515
ISBN-10: 1477826513

Cover design by Cyanotype Book Architects

Library of Congress Control Number: 2014910532

Printed in the United States of America

CAST OF CHARACTERS

THE COPS

Maria Kallio .... Espoo Violent Crime Unit (VCU) detective
Pekka Koivu .... Maria's old partner
Juhani Palo .... Espoo VCU detective
Pihko .... Espoo VCU detective
Ville "Dennis the Menace" Puupponen ..... Espoo VCU detective
Pertti Ström .... Espoo VCU detective
Jyrki Taskinen .... Head of Espoo VCU
Minna Rautamaa .... Oulu police officer
Akkila .... Espoo patrol officer
Haikala .... Espoo patrol officer
Jäämaa .... County police commissioner
Koskivuori .... Ministry of the Interior police captain
Lähde .... Espoo police administrator

THE WOMEN

Tarja Kivimäki .... Reporter, Elina's friend
Heidi Kuusinen .... Niina's mother
Niina Kuusinen .... Music teacher, Elina's patient
Kirsti Jensen .... Antti's coworker
Eva Jensen .... Therapist, Elina's former patient, Kirsti's wife
Milla Marttila .... Stripper, Elina's patient
Elina Rosberg .... Therapist, owner of Rosberga Manor
Aira Rosberg .... Elina's aunt, Rosberga caretaker
Anna Säntti .... Johanna's daughter

THE MEN

SUPPORTING CAST

PROLOGUE

I wasn't sure who was more nervous, the judge or me. My college friend Riina had never performed a wedding before, and I could see her cheeks tremble as she started the ceremony. But then, I had never gotten married before either. My knees were like jelly, and my hand, squeezing Antti's, was probably dripping sweat onto the parquet floor of the Villa Elfvik dining room.

"Do you, Maria Kristiina Kallio, take this man, Antti Johannes Sarkela . . . "

I had forgotten that a civil ceremony used the same familiar lines. I could barely get the two-word response out of my mouth. Antti glanced at me, probably thinking I was going to back out. Faintly I stuttered my assent. As if in alarm, Antti blurted out his response so loudly it made Riina jump. Later, when asked, our guests diplomatically claimed they had noticed nothing strange about our vows.

Riina proclaimed us husband and wife, and we turned toward the audience to kiss each other and accept their congratulations. We had wanted as informal a wedding as possible, and as Antti didn't belong to the church, a civil ceremony seemed natural. My own relationship with religion was confused enough that I wasn't concerned about a Lutheran priest's blessing.

In the receiving line, the hugging seemed to go on forever. Parents, siblings, and then friends. My friend and old partner, Koivu, lifted me into the air and then, only half kidding, told Antti he'd better take good care of me.

The delegation from work, however, was strangely taciturn. My boss, Detective Lieutenant Jyrki Taskinen, head of the Espoo Police Violent Crime and Repeat Offender Unit, congratulated us nicely enough, but the two officers chosen to represent the rank and file, Juhani Palo and Pertti Ström, seemed almost resentful about being there. It was as if they thought getting married would make me a worse cop. To top it off, Taskinen's phone started ringing just as he shook Antti's hand.

I groaned and said to Palo, "Hopefully nobody's been raped. I'm a little tied up at the moment."

One of Antti's colleagues from the university was next in the receiving line. Overhearing these words, she looked at me, startled.

Taskinen excused himself to take the call, and I continued shaking hands. Out of the corner of my eye I saw him return to the wedding reception. Apparently it was nothing that required the head of the unit to be on scene. I swallowed my curiosity and turned my attention back to our guests. It was not as though the work sitting on my desk would go away while I was on my honeymoon.

As a little girl I daydreamed about white weddings just like everyone else, but I quickly discovered there were bigger goals in life to shoot for than a veil and a rich husband. From the age of fifteen to about thirty, I was a confirmed bachelorette, and even now I was a bit mystified by what had convinced me to accept Antti's proposal. It wasn't that I didn't love Antti, I just loved my freedom more—and I rather liked my erratic work schedule as well.

"Are you still a Kallio?" Antti's sister asked me when she gave me a hug in the receiving line.

"We both kept our names," Antti hurried to say.

Antti's black hair, which fell to his shoulders, was in stark contrast to the formality of his tuxedo. The cut of the elegant suit made him look taller and thinner than usual. My wedding outfit was less traditional. Although long and ivory colored, my dress was adorned with garlands of crimson silk roses, one of which continued up into my hair. My gloves and shoes were also a riotous red. Maybe ten-year-old Maria wouldn't have liked my bridal gown, but the wedding guests seemed to approve.

"It's nice seeing you in something besides jeans or that same old pantsuit," Palo said with a wry grin when Antti and I sat down at my coworkers' table while making our rounds. Ström smirked, probably remembering me while I was wearing a leather miniskirt and fishnet stockings during a murder investigation a few years earlier.

"Did you leave that case report on my desk?" Ström asked, but before I had time to answer, Taskinen interrupted sharply.

"Ström, no shoptalk now. This is Maria's wedding."

"If I don't have that report, I'll have to bother her on her honeymoon," Ström snapped back.

"Don't worry, it's on your desk," I said, my voice dripping honey. Ström was always lurking around, waiting for me to slip up. I wondered how he had ended up at my wedding. We moved to the next table.

The food tasted great—of course it would, since I hadn't eaten anything all day. Our fathers and friends gave their speeches, repeating every possible wedding cliché, from balls and chains to two rivers running together. Even the first waltz went well—or as well as could be expected when a six-foot-five man dances with a five-foot-three woman.

I was dancing with Palo when Ström butted in.

"Raitio just got collared at Turku Airport."

That was all Ström needed to say. Raitio was the ringleader of a drug gang we'd been tracking for months. He'd gone to ground a few weeks earlier, and we'd been sure he'd made it out of the country.

"Put off the wedding night and come to Turku with us to pick him up. It's not like you're going to be doing anything new," Ström added. It was crude even for him.

"Sure, but it's the first time I'll get to do it legally," I shot back.

"Time to go," Taskinen said, joining us at the edge of the dance floor. I wished them a pleasant journey, and Taskinen shook my hand and Palo gave me an awkward hug.

Ström, however, leaned over and whispered in my ear, "Enjoy it while it lasts. Cops and marriage don't mix. Admit it. You're at your wedding and you still want to come with us. There's no man alive who'll put up with that."

"Thank you for your kind words, Pertti," I replied sweetly and left a smudge of red lipstick on his cheek. Ström fled, blushing, but my smile faded as I wondered whether he might be right. Luckily Antti chose that moment to drag me back onto the dance floor, and I forgot my doubts for the rest of the night.

1

Wind buffeted my tiny Fiat, whipping snow against the windshield. Even this far south, December had been unusually wintry. It was only three o'clock but already almost dark. Although I visited Nuuksio, a rural suburb north of Espoo, relatively often, in the dark the road suddenly seemed unfamiliar. I remembered the directions I'd been given: turn right a little before the curve at the lake and then take the next two lefts. The last road would be narrow and possibly blocked by snow. Fortunately I had a shovel in the trunk.

In the end, I didn't have to stop once to use it. Someone had already plowed the lane to Rosberga Manor. The lights of the main house shone from high on a hill. Someone had even spread gravel on a steep stretch that led to the reddish-brown stone gates. Rosberga was probably a beautiful place in the summer, but in winter the rosebushes surrounding the walls jutted out like spikes.

The gate was closed, and the sign attached to it wasn't terribly friendly: "No Men Allowed" it proclaimed in simple black letters. A few years ago, when the Rosberga Women's Education Institute was founded and the sign appeared, it had caused quite a fuss. A cat-sized bear statue skulking atop the gate looked significantly more welcoming.

Elina Rosberg, owner of Rosberga Manor and director of the Rosberga Women's Education Institute, didn't let any men onto the grounds. The therapy groups and self-defense courses she hosted were meant only for women. Rumor had it that she even insisted on hiring female plumbers and painters to do work on the home. And when she wanted the police to come talk at an emotional self-defense course, she requested a female officer.

The Espoo Police Department had been emphasizing external outreach for the last few years. We gave schoolkids trading cards featuring the department's local cops and our octopus mascot, and we were encouraged to attend any events that could provide opportunities for us to talk about our work. So no one but Ström had laughed when Elina Rosberg requested a female officer to come to the manor and talk about violence against women and relations between women and the police.

"That's a perfect job for Kallio," he said. "If you want to get those feminazis to trust the police, you have to send one of their own."

"It's too bad they won't let you in. I could take you along as Male Chauvinist Pig Exhibit Number One," I tossed back.

"Who, Ström, a chauvinist pig? Come on. Remember, he did let his wife get a job. Of course, we all know how that turned out," Palo said and then ducked under the table to avoid the swing of Ström's fist that perhaps wasn't as playful as he tried to make it seem. Even after a few years, Ström's divorce was a sore spot.

I was happy to provide a realistic picture of the work of a female officer and discuss women's interactions with the police. But I wasn't sure what kind of audience I'd be addressing. Some in the media had labeled the Rosberga Institute a hotbed of feminist extremism, especially because they offered courses in cooperation with the Finnish Feminist Association and LGBTI Rights Finland. I was a member of both, and I knew how many different kinds of women belonged to them. I imagined I'd have to defend my profession, which would be a little different from the senior centers and homemaking club meetings I usually spoke at.

The department liked sending me to represent the force because I didn't fit the traditional image of a cop. Not only was I female, I was also shorter than average. I had tousled red hair—natural but amped up a bit via the hair salon—a snub nose, and freckles, which thankfully disappeared in the winter. I was in good shape, my body was naturally curvy, and I tended to dress a bit young. Although I was over thirty, cashiers at the liquor store still asked for my ID.

For the visit to Rosberga Manor, I'd thrown a blazer over my jeans and polo shirt and put on makeup. Hopefully the combination gave an impression of maturity.

I couldn't see a bell or knocker on the gate, but just as I was getting out of the car to have a closer look, the gate opened. I drove into a courtyard filled with the same spiky rosebushes shriveled by the cold. The gate closed behind me with a clang that sounded strangely threatening.

Rosberga Manor was painted a rosy pink, and withered rose vines grew up the walls. I recalled the inevitable jokes about Sleeping Beauty's castle that had made the rounds when the institute was closed to men. "Feminists still waiting for Prince Charming's kiss?" one tabloid headline inquired. Apparently Elina Rosberg's great grandmother had planted the roses.

When I reached the manor, Elina Rosberg stood in the white-framed door. She shook my hand firmly. She was several inches taller than me, slender, but with broad shoulders and large breasts. The wind blew her short blond hair up, and the side lighting emphasized her narrow nose and high cheekbones. Even wearing Levi's and a shearling coat, she looked like a chatelaine. Her voice was low and pleasant, as though on the verge of laughing.

"Would you like a cup of tea before your presentation?" Elina asked. "We still have a relaxation exercise going on in the meeting room."

As I followed Elina into a spacious farmhouse-style kitchen, I asked her what the Emotional Self-Defense audience would be like.

"It's one of our larger groups. Around twenty women. This is the first time we're offering the course, but they're a talkative bunch and not without their conflicts."

In the corner of the cozy kitchen an older woman, probably in her seventies, sat near a tiled masonry baking oven that radiated heat. I couldn't help but look for a cat curled up somewhere near the hearth.

"Aira, would you mind fetching Sergeant Kallio a cup of tea? I'm going to peek in and see how the session is going."

Rosberg left the room, and the woman stood up and introduced herself as Aira Rosberg.

"Elina's aunt," she added.

Even without the clarification, I would have known they were family. Aira was nearly as tall as her niece, with the same erect posture. She also had the same long, narrow nose, pale-blue eyes, and high cheekbones. Only their hair was strikingly different: Aira's had grayed to an elegant steel.

Sitting down in an armchair in a corner of the kitchen with a mug of hot black currant tea, I declined Aira's offer of bread. I tried to run through my presentation in my mind, but my eyes kept wandering back to Aira, who was moving dishes from the dishwasher to the cupboard in her gray-striped Marimekko apron. Was she the cook at Rosberga? Aira's movements were methodical and quick, and she worked undisturbed by my presence, only stopping once to ask if I wanted more tea.

Time seemed to move slowly here in the warm kitchen, but when Elina returned, I looked at the clock and saw that only seven minutes had passed.

"We're ready when you are."

I followed her into a wide hall with an ornate stairway. Double doors opened into what must have been the manor's former drawing room. Rose-patterned paper covered the walls, but the furniture consisted of utilitarian folding tables and chairs assembled in rows like a school classroom. Elina showed me to a table with a projector at the front of the room and introduced me to the women.

I began my presentation a little nervously but quickly found my feet. Elina sat in the front row listening, her blue sweater reflecting more color into her light eyes. Her long legs were shoved awkwardly under her chair, and I noticed that one of her gray wool socks had been darned hastily with violet yarn. After a few minutes Aira slipped into the back row. She had removed her apron and looked angular in her gray flannel shirt and navy velvet pants.

The women listened quietly, with surprising interest; one of them even took notes. They were exactly the kind of women I'd imagined attended Rosberga Institute courses: average age around thirty-five, casually dressed, and at least half with red-tinted hair. Traditional Finnish Kalevala jewelry hung from almost every ear. Many were wearing the same little Moon Goddess design I wore. I fit in perfectly.

There were two class members who did stand out though. The younger woman had extremely short hair with purple and black stripes. She wore more makeup than all the other course participants combined and had on a black minidress that barely covered her buttocks and slightly plump curves, a black leather jacket, and high-heeled purple suede boots. Although it seemed obvious she was trying to add years with her makeup, she didn't appear to be older than twenty. Looking bored, she stared at her dark-purple nails and unconsciously grimaced every time I said the word "police."

The other woman was so gaunt she could have been doing hard labor her entire life. Her vaguely blond hair was held back in a tight bun, and her cloudy-gray eyes seemed to stare into the middle distance. It was hard to pin down her age; her grandmotherly brown cardigan and brown checked dress would make anyone look old. She sat stock-still in a little bubble that seemed to separate her from the rest of the world.

While most of the women in the audience smiled at my stories or occasionally touched their neighbor on the arm or exchanged glances, these two sat alone in the crowded room—one loudly restless and the other in oppressive silence.

When I finished my presentation and moved on to questions, I wasn't surprised that the women asked about the increase in sexual harassment on the streets.

"The police just say we shouldn't be out alone after dark," one woman said indignantly. "I don't know about anybody else, but I have to exercise when I can, which means running when my husband is home and the kids are asleep. I'm not the criminal, so why should I have to time my life according to these dirtbags?"

"I totally agree, you shouldn't have to," I said. "But it also makes sense to avoid unnecessary risks. Where do you run?"

I knew the feeling that sometimes came over you running alone in the dark. When you started listening for every little rustle, worrying there might be a murderer lurking in the bushes.

One of the women described getting away from an attacker by biting him, and another related a story about her coworker, who put an abrupt end to a Christmas party when she told the hostess that her husband had been coming on to her. I quickly found myself acting as a sort of therapeutic sounding board for the women's diverse stories. I couldn't help feeling irritated. I was there to talk about my work, not play life coach. Apparently Rosberga really was the fortress of man-bashing the media had wrung its hands about.

When one of the women angrily started describing an incident involving a male police officer, I was relieved to be back on topic. Apparently he'd automatically assumed she was responsible for a collision at an intersection and joked that her husband was going to have a fit when he found out she'd wrecked his car. She'd bought the car with her own money, she added indignantly. At least I could give her some practical advice about dealing with the police. But just as I began outlining some options, the young woman with the striped hair sitting in the back, who'd been focused on her nails throughout the presentation, jumped up.

"Your problems are fucking pathetic!" she yelled. "Oh, your car got dented. Oh me oh my! Is that why you need emotional self-defense, or don't you have the guts to talk about your real problems? Huh?"

She walked quickly up the aisle toward me. Her perfume was musky, and sweat beaded the thick coat of powder on her forehead.

"I've been raped so many times in my life I can't even count them all. Incest first, of course, and then a pack of other guys.

Most of the time I was so drunk I barely even remember it. But I remember the last time. I might be a sex worker, but I'm not a whore. Look down on me if you want to, but I just dance for money—that's it. A guy in my building came to watch me a bunch of times, and then one night he grabbed me in the basement when I was getting a bag of potatoes out of my storage unit. He thought since I dance naked he could do whatever he wanted to me. He did it right there on the concrete floor. Apparently that was a turn-on for him."

Her strangely pale eyes, surrounded by nearly a quarter inch of black eyeliner, stared accusingly at me. The nostrils of her tiny pierced nose trembled like an enraged animal's.

"Did you file a police report?" I asked when I couldn't think of anything else to say.

"Of course not! Do you think those pigs would treat me any different than my neighbor did? But I sent the asshole a letter telling him I have HIV." Then, as if out of some strange social compunction, she added, "I don't really, unless I got it from him."

"What exactly is it you're hoping to get from this course, Milla?" Elina Rosberg intervened. I was relieved that I wouldn't have to continue the conversation.

"What do I want? I don't have any idea. I keep wondering what the hell I'm doing here." Milla turned to me again. "But you, are you some kind of feminist cop or something? What would you have said to me if I'd reported him to you? Would you have taken me seriously?"

"Of course," I answered.

"And you wouldn't have given me some kind of sermon about being a stripper?"

"We aren't in the habit of giving sermons on morality in situations like that." I was trying to be friendly, but it didn't take. I could feel the antagonism ooze from the girl like smoke from dry ice.

"But not filing a police report is accepting being a victim!" said a heavy woman sitting in the front row. She had been diligently taking notes throughout my talk. "Your behavior ensured that you and, through you, any woman can be raped because there aren't any consequences. When did this happen? Maybe you can still file a report."

"Not interested," Milla said. "The creep hasn't shown his face in the club since."

"About the incest . . ." Elina began with the calm, empathetic tone of a person accustomed to dealing with sensitive issues. "Is there anything you'd like to speak with a police officer about? I think it makes sense for us to stick to police issues since we have Sergeant Kallio here tonight."

Milla snorted. "That's all ancient history. Statute of limitations, you know. And there's no point talking about my issues. Just talk about your car accidents and lost cats or whatever. I'm going for a smoke." Milla turned on her heel and walked out the door, swaying her hips fetchingly.

Elina look confused, as though she was surprised the situation had momentarily slipped out of her control. She glanced at the class members and then at me, waiting for someone to say something. Stiffly I started going through the steps of filing a police report. I was off balance too, but not so much from Milla's behavior as Elina's. Elina Rosberg was a familiar figure to me. When I was in high school, my younger sister had subscribed to a teen magazine in which Elina wrote a column. While I'd considered myself too old for the magazine in general, I read her column on a regular basis. I liked that she didn't moralize or belittle the problems teenagers faced. She just answered questions directly.

I guess I considered her something of a role model. When I was trying to get into the police academy, I'd hoped I could discharge my duty, especially with female crime victims, by showing the same simple understanding Elina Rosberg did. While my illusions about police work were shattered pretty quickly, I'd always assumed Elina had continued her work with the same competence and enthusiasm she'd conveyed when she was thirty. And in a way, that was what the Rosberga Women's Institute was all about, allowing her to focus on the cases that interested her most—psychiatric conditions common to women, such as eating disorders.

No one seemed to want to ask any more questions, and I was already gathering my papers into my backpack when the gaunt woman with the bun suddenly stood up. She opened her mouth, closed it, and then looked to Elina as if for help. When Elina nodded, she opened her mouth again.

"Can a person be prevented from seeing her children?" Her voice quivered and cracked like an instrument being played too loud, and her face flushed red. Saying those nine words seemed to have required tremendous effort.

"What kind of situation are we talking about? It's hard for me to say anything specific without the details," I replied.

Clearly frightened, the woman lowered her head.

Elina answered for her: "Johanna moved away from her husband and children and filed for divorce. They both want the children, but her ex-husband is preventing Johanna from seeing them."

"He certainly doesn't have any legal right to do that if there isn't a court order barring you from your children." I looked at the woman. She cringed at the words "court order."

"Why won't your husband let you see your children?" I asked.

This time she answered almost defiantly, but her voice broke near the end. "Because I killed our last baby."

It was as if the whole audience instantly turned to snow women, cold and frozen. After a quick communal intake of breath, no one moved, but every eye was glued to Johanna. Her face had turned from red back to gray. I also stared at her, taking in her bowed head and the clothing that hung too loosely from her shriveled body. Had she been in prison? Was that why she looked so worn-out? Again Elina's calm voice broke the silence.

"I think we've had a little misunderstanding. I doubt anyone here considers abortion murder, especially when the pregnancy and birth would have been life threatening for both Johanna and the baby. She already has nine children and nearly died giving birth to her previous one."

"Well, couldn't the doctors tie your tubes or give you an IUD?" yelled the same woman who had accused Milla of making herself a victim.

"Our church does not approve of birth control. It is contrary to God's will." Johanna's voice repeated the rote phrases without expression.

"What are you, a Catholic or something?" the same woman barked.

"Johanna belongs to one of the stricter conservative Laestadian sects," Elina replied.

"Does she have a lawyer?" I directed my question to Elina, even though talking around Johanna as if she were some sort of half-wit irritated me.

Instead of answering my question, Elina turned to the assembled women and said in an authoritative tone, "If no one else has any questions for Sergeant Kallio, let's thank her for her visit and wrap things up. This was a very interesting lecture."

Elina began to applaud, and the rest of the bewildered group joined in weakly. We watched the women trickle out, and then Elina turned to me. "We still need to address your honorarium. And if you have time, I'd like you to talk to Johanna a little more."

I did have time, and I was curious to hear Johanna's story. With the others gone, Johanna walked toward my table. As Elina turned to close the door, Johanna raised her eyes to me for the first time. In them was a contagious anxiety so powerful I had to fight not to avert my own gaze.

"How old are your children?" I asked lamely when I couldn't come up with anything else. I wasn't good at things like this. How was I supposed to understand a woman longing for her children when I'd only just begun to even consider having my own sometime in the distant future?

"Johannes, my oldest, is fourteen, and the youngest, Maria, is one and a half." Johanna's voice grew more confident when she talked about her children. This was clearly her territory.

"Maria . . . just like me. And my husband's middle name is Johannes," I said with a smile, desperately trying to lighten the mood. "Why does your husband want to prevent you from seeing your children? Just because of the abortion? Or because you left him?"

"For us, a husband's word is law and procreation is a gift from God." Johanna's voice contained not the slightest hint of irony. "If God wants me to die giving birth, that is his will."

"But you have nine children you'd be leaving behind! How could any God want that?" I was too furious at her answer to maintain my professionalism. Johanna turned her face away, and Elina strode over as if to protect her.

I took a deep breath. Wasn't I ever going to learn to control myself? "I'm sorry. I shouldn't question your church doctrines.

Let's focus on practicalities. Is your husband physically preventing you from seeing your children?"

"Johanna lives in a small northern Ostrobothnian village where seventy percent of the people are Laestadians, including the doctor and all the police except for one," Elina answered for Johanna. She explained that the children weren't allowed to talk to their mother on the phone and that her husband had confiscated Johanna's letters before ordering the post office not to deliver them anymore. When Johanna last tried to see the children in person, the father called the police, who escorted Johanna out of town.

I had to count to ten more than once, and even then I still felt like kicking something. The whole thing just sounded so incredible. How could something like this happen in modern-day Finland? There had been Laestadians and Jehovah's Witnesses where I grew up too, but the most noticeable difference between them and the other kids was that they couldn't participate in any music programs, not even marching along with a tambourine, and they couldn't watch educational shows on the school TV. They did grow up to have their own huge packs of kids, but I'd never heard of any of them dying giving birth.

"Those police officers broke the law unless you were behaving violently. You should call the one who isn't a member of the church and negotiate with him. I'd also contact the county police. What's your husband's name and occupation?"

"Leevi Säntti. He's a minister," Johanna replied, and I almost started laughing. It sounded so unbelievable.

"So he's some sort of town bigwig?"

"Our church's lay pastor."

"He's a pretty famous preacher, actually," Elina added, and both of them looked at me expectantly.

I wasn't quite sure what they wanted from me. I asked again whether Johanna had a lawyer, and the answer was also complicated. The town's legal aid counsel was a Laestadian, and Johanna didn't have the money to hire anyone else.

I kicked myself in the mental shins to prevent myself from promising her anything. In addition to my police qualifications, I had gone to law school and worked in a law firm for almost a year before it went belly up. Sometimes I got the itch to practice my other profession, but when was I going to find time for that? My desk was already piled high with unsolved cases. And even though Johanna did live far away from Espoo, I wasn't completely sure of the ethical dimensions of this case. Maybe a policewoman shouldn't do legal gigs on the side.

"I know someone who might be able to help," I finally said. Leena was a friend from law school who sometimes volunteered on the Feminist Association's legal hotline. "I'll give you the number. You should call her. And I can check with the county police. I may know someone there. Have you officially filed for divorce?"

"Not yet," Johanna whispered.

"As far as I can tell, you aren't insane or an alcoholic. And you haven't been with any other men yet, right?"

Johanna shook her head quickly, as if appalled by my question.

"It would be really strange if the court gave the children to your husband." I tried to sound comforting, although I knew a lot depended on the judge. Just then my beeper went off.

"I'm sorry, I need to use my phone. I'm on call."

"The kitchen is quiet, and Aira can handle the paperwork there too. I don't imagine you could stay for dinner?"

"I don't think so. But keep me up to date about this situation," I said as I scribbled Leena's phone number on a piece of paper and handed it to Johanna.

Aira was busy cooking in the kitchen. Based on the smell, she was making some sort of vegetable casserole. I filled out my pay slip as I punched in the phone number for the station. When Ström picked up, he growled that a woman had stabbed her husband in Suvela. For some reason he thought that was right up my alley. I promised to head straight there.

I didn't speak to Elina or Johanna again before leaving. Walking to my car, I saw the group of women through a window chattering happily around a long, candlelit table. Elina was just sitting down at the head, and Aira was carrying in baskets of bread. Johanna was nowhere to be seen.

Just as I was turning the key in the ignition, the front door of the house opened. Milla's purple-striped head was briefly framed in the light from the hall, then the door closed, and after a few seconds I saw the glow of a cigarette. I drove toward the gate, which opened automatically and then closed silently behind me, leaving Rosberga trapped within its walls, far removed from the rest of the world.

2

I stared out my office window at the Turku Highway, where cars glided by at long intervals despite it being a weekday afternoon. An inexplicable fatigue had me in its grip. My head kept nodding and the sofa on the other side of the room seemed to mock me.

Maybe it was because of Christmas. It was December 27, the day after Boxing Day. Antti and I had spent the holidays mostly lounging around reading in our new home in Henttaa, a neighborhood near Espoo Central Park. Working between Christmas and New Year's had seemed like a good idea. It gave us a good excuse not to travel to Antti's parents' place in Inkoo or to my parents' in Northern Karelia. But now I wished I'd taken a few more days off so I could keep sitting in front of the fireplace, Einstein curled in my lap, reading Agatha Christie's *A Holiday for Murder* and eating chocolate.

No, no chocolate. Yuck. Suddenly the thought of anything sweet made my stomach turn. I must have eaten too much over Christmas.

With a sigh, I opened a new document on my computer and started typing a report about the interview I'd just completed. Plenty of people in Espoo hadn't enjoyed nearly as peaceful a

Christmas as Antti and I had. As usual, the holidays had increased the incidence of domestic violence. Returning from my vacation, I found several assaults and one fatal stabbing waiting for me at the station. No wonder so many of my colleagues took a cynical view of family life and marriage. Half the cops in our unit were divorced; Palo was on marriage number three.

What the hell was making me so tired? I hadn't been doing anything special. Due to the cold snap, our daily cross-country ski outings had been short and relaxed.

Antti and I were living in a run-down little house that had been owned by Antti's coworker's late brother. The family was having a hard time selling the house because it was located right along the future route of the Ring II beltway. The windows offered a view of fallow fields where rabbits jumped and moles rooted, but when the road was done, the landscape would be just asphalt and noise. Strangely, the impermanence of our abode didn't bother me. Maybe I needed the possibility of change now that I had a permanent job and a husband. Before this I'd had a hard time staying happy in a job, so temporary gigs and substitute postings had fit me just fine. Even dating Antti for two and a half years had been quite an accomplishment for me. I wondered whether I'd only found the courage to get married because divorce was so easy nowadays.

Antti, on the other hand, had become attached to the bucolic scene outside our windows and mourned its impending loss. He'd even joined the No to Ring II opposition group, but the fight seemed hopeless; although no one else seemed to see any need for a new road, whatever the Public Roads Administration and Espoo bureaucrats got into their heads seemed inevitable. Antti was already despondent over the West Highway expansion destroying so many of the places he remembered from his childhood in Tapiola. He blamed the change in that landscape for his parents' decision to finally sell their home and move permanently to their summer cabin in Inkoo.

In fact, Antti had become so anti-road and environmentally conscious that I half-seriously thought he'd run for local council on the Green ticket in the next elections.

"Actually, you should infiltrate the Social Democrats or National Coalition. They're the most enthusiastic road builders," I'd jokingly suggested.

Antti clearly needed something new to do other than work. I, on the other hand, was content jogging, hitting the gym, and visiting the department firing range. I'd been forced to use my weapon for the first time in my career the summer before and had found that my marksmanship needed a lot of work. Since then I'd been visiting the range regularly. My technique was getting better, but I truly hoped I'd never have to use that skill in the field again.

My phone rang. On the other end of the line was Dispatch, who notified me of an incoming call from Aira Rosberg. It took me a moment to remember her and my visit to the Rosberga Institute a few weeks ago. I'd heard nothing more about Johanna's case, and with all the rush around the holidays, I'd forgotten my promise to see if I knew any police in the district where she lived.

Aira's voice sounded strangely hesitant when Dispatch connected the call. "I don't really know whether this is the sort of thing to bother the police about, Maria, but . . . Elina is missing."

"Missing? What do you mean?"

"No one's seen her since last night. It doesn't look like she slept in her bed, and we can't find her nightgown or bathrobe anywhere. And the clothes she laid out for today are still in her room. It's as if she went somewhere in her nightgown."

"When did you last see her?"

"Last night around ten o'clock. She'd just come in from an evening walk and was going to her room. We've had a small group of women here celebrating Christmas. Four in addition to me and Elina. No one remembers seeing her after that."

"And she didn't leave any kind of message?"

"No."

Was that misgiving in Aira's voice when she replied?

"Is there any place Elina could have gone? Who are her closest friends?"

"I called Joona right away . . . Joona Kirstilä. He's Elina's boyfriend. But Elina wasn't there."

"You mean the poet Joona Kirstilä?" I asked curiously. Elina was in the press relatively often, and Kirstilä was well known, but I'd never heard any rumors of a romantic relationship.

"Yes, that's him. They've been seeing each other for a couple of years. Elina spends the night at Joona's now and then, so I thought maybe she was there."

"Is there any particular reason to be concerned about Elina's disappearance? Did anything happen over Christmas, maybe an argument? Who else is there with you at the house?"

"You met Johanna Säntti and Milla Marttila when you came. They've basically lived here since that course at the beginning of December. Tarja Kivimäki is an old friend of Elina's; she also spent Christmas here. And Niina Kuusinen arrived on Christmas Day. She's a therapy patient who attended Elina's courses too."

I was shocked to hear Milla was still at the manor, remembering how much she had seemed to dislike being there. And Johanna . . . Wasn't she able to see her children even at Christmas?

I didn't want to think about Johanna, so I continued my questioning. "Was Elina in the habit of disappearing without prior warning?"

"No! This is very strange. If you could—"

"She hasn't been missing for twenty-four hours," I interrupted gently, "and since she's an adult, the police won't initiate a search yet. Does Elina have any friends or relatives she might have gone to see?"

Aira replied in the negative once again. She didn't seem to want to end the call. People disappeared with no explanation all the time, and they usually turned up in one piece. But I didn't think saying so would comfort Aira. Besides, Elina Rosberg's sudden disappearance sounded strange to me too.

"Aira, if you haven't heard anything from Elina by tomorrow morning, call me again," I finally said. Addressing a woman I barely knew and who was forty years my senior by her first name felt strange, but she had called me by my first name too. I guess that's how they did things at the Rosberga Institute. "And even if she does come back, please give me a call." Although I knew I shouldn't, I gave Aira my home number. I tried to rationalize that I was just curious, but I knew that was a lie. I was worried.

After hanging up, I went back to typing my report. Before leaving work, I called and asked Antti to wax my skis. It had been snowing heavily all day, and the fields near the house were covered with a thick layer of white. Now that the sky was clearing and everything was freezing up, the conditions were good for skiing. One of the benefits of our temporary living arrangement was that we could ski right from our yard. Breaking trail would be a pleasant change from jogging.

As I was leaving my office, I ran into Ström in the hallway. Ström had worked straight through Christmas. His ex-wife and her new husband had taken the children to the Canary Islands. Ström looked even more sullen than usual. The skin on his face with its large pores was drawn tight in a frown and his thinning brown hair was plastered to his head. He looked like he'd been sweating. Broken more than once, his nose glowed red on his pale face. I wondered if he was coming down with a cold.

"I spent the whole day with those goddamn shooters from Perkkaa, and supposedly nobody remembers anything," Ström snapped in response to my greeting. "I bet they went and got stoned after they shot that guy just so they could claim they didn't remember anything and no one could be charged."

He looked at me and changed gears: "So how did the blushing bride's Christmas go? Plenty of binge eating and screwing?"

I'd gotten used to Ström's rough manner when we were in the same class at the police academy, so I just nodded and smiled. Besides, Ström was right—although I might have expressed our activities a little differently.

"So do you have a bun in the oven yet?" Ström continued, looking me up and down.

"That's none of your business," I hissed, "but since you're so interested, it isn't in the plans. I have an IUD." I pushed open the door before Ström could whip out any more smart-ass remarks. I wasn't in the mood for a verbal jousting match, and our conversations almost always turned into arguments. We just didn't get along.

Although I'd heard he was the one who recommended I be asked to join the unit, I had worried about coming to work in Espoo with him here. A few years before, when I was working for a law firm in Tapiola, Ström and I had had a serious confrontation over a murder investigation. I was legal counsel for an innocent man whom Ström had arrested. In the end, I solved the case by basically going over the heads of the police. Ström had had a hard time swallowing this. Later I heard that he'd been right in the middle of his divorce at the time and that this had affected his work. Of course, he never talked about his breakup, but Palo's third wife knew Ström's ex, and Palo had no qualms about gossiping about Ström's personal life.

When I finally left the station, I was met with falling snow. The snow and the Christmas lights burning on the houses along Lower Henttaa Road created a postcard scene. Even our own run-down red cottage looked homey. Antti had lit the candle lantern to welcome me home and was shoveling when I pulled up.

He waited while I went in to throw on my ski gear and quickly eat a banana. The fresh air washed away my tiredness, and once we were on the trail, I began to enjoy the sound of the snow under my skis, simultaneously familiar yet new to me every winter.

But my mind kept wandering back to Elina Rosberg. Where on earth could she be? Although I knew Elina Rosberg only from her media image, she didn't seem the kind of person who did anything on a whim. She was a regular guest on talk shows where issues related to sexuality and gender roles were discussed, and while the other participants tended to lose their cool and shout at each other, Elina always remained maddeningly calm. Usually it was her voice that made the others eventually settle down and listen. No, Elina was not the kind of person to jump on a train for a last-minute visit to a girlfriend in another city. Not without telling anyone and especially not when she had Christmas guests.

After a couple miles of skiing, my strange exhaustion returned. My legs felt lethargic and weak, as if they no longer wanted to propel the skis forward. Antti was moving along at a steady clip ahead of me, and I had to ask him to slow down.

"What's up, snow woman?" Antti asked, laughing.

I shook the powder out of my hair before answering.

"My legs are tired. They feel really weird. I think I might be coming down with something. Or maybe my period is starting. That could be it."

"Maybe we should turn back," Antti suggested.

I managed to turn around on my Jell-O legs. Trying not to think about how weak I felt, I concentrated on Antti's back gliding along ahead of me. His green anorak glowed against the snow, his shadow looking impossibly tall and thin. His large, aquiline nose looked even more prominent than usual when he turned back to ask whether the speed was OK. I was relieved when I finally saw the house lights and glad to know a hot sauna was waiting. The thought of getting warm and crawling into bed with Einstein curled up on my feet after his evening meal was heavenly.

But even when I was finally lying in bed listening to him purr, my thoughts kept turning to Elina. She wouldn't leave me alone in my dreams either. I saw her walking along a lake of ice, wearing a flowing white nightgown. Suddenly the wind took hold of the nightgown and lifted Elina into the air, twirling her higher . . . higher . . . higher . . . until finally she was nothing but a speck disappearing in a swirl of snowflakes.

In the morning, I'd barely made it into my office before Aira Rosberg phoned. Still no sign of Elina. I explained that I'd have to connect her with Patrol. Without any evidence of a crime, a disappearance didn't fall under our unit's responsibilities.

"I'm so sorry to impose on you, but . . . I was hoping that . . . that you could come here." Aira sounded concerned and confused. "If I call the regular police, they're sure to send a man here, and I know Elina wouldn't approve of that."

"There are plenty of women in that department these days, but I'll see what I can do." I put down the handset and quickly checked my schedule. My afternoon wasn't booked solid, so I had time to swing by Nuuksio. "I'll come around two. Call me back if you hear anything from Elina."

Just then Taskinen opened the door and summoned me to the interrogation room. In addition to all the Christmas assaults, we were in the middle of a complicated money laundering investigation that fell jointly to us and the Finance Unit. One of the main perpetrators was an MBA type who'd started his career in bankruptcy fraud sometime back in the 1970s and had organized this new operation from prison. Today we were interviewing the suspect's brother-in-law, who was one of the key stockholders in the front company.

Taskinen and I thought that if we bombarded him with quick cross-examination questions, we might be able to put him off balance, at least momentarily. We badgered him for close to three hours before we were satisfied. He had contradicted himself several times and made so many little slips that we decided we had enough to file charges. We'd been plugging away at the case since the summer, and it felt fantastic to finally have some movement on it.

"Do you have time for lunch?" Taskinen asked as we were leaving the interrogation room.

"Actually I have something to talk to you about." On our way down to the cafeteria I explained Elina Rosberg's strange disappearance and asked permission to go have a look—informally, of course—to see whether I could find any evidence of a crime.

Truth be told, I'd already made up my mind to go whether I had permission or not.

"I have a feeling Aira Rosberg isn't telling me the real reason why she's concerned enough about Elina to turn to the police," I said.

We started loading food on our trays. Taskinen chose skim milk and didn't take any butter for his bread. I squirted ketchup all over my cheesy macaroni casserole and poured thick garlic dressing on my salad. Taskinen shook his head in amusement when he looked at my plate. He waited until we were settled at our table before saying anything about Elina's disappearance.

"You can go. But tell Aira Rosberg to make an official missing persons report if it looks like anything fishy is going on. And check to see if her niece might have left the country. These are tough cases, adult disappearances. If I were you, I'd have a talk with the boyfriend too."

"I was thinking the same." I shoved a big forkful of macaroni in my mouth and watched Taskinen as he mashed slices of rye bread into little balls with his fingers before eating them.

Detective Lieutenant Jyrki Taskinen was a neat, meticulous man. He was a little over five feet ten and had straight blond hair that looked as if it had been parted with a ruler. There were never stray hairs or dandruff on the shoulders of his blue suit, and his fingernails were always trimmed short. Everything about Taskinen's face was narrow and straight. Even his teeth lay in flawless white lines. His body was also slim, wiry like a marathoner's. I'd heard that even at fifty Taskinen could run a 10K in under forty minutes. The only exception to his narrow lines was an almost half-inch-wide polished gold wedding band.

Based on his appearance, you could easily take Taskinen for a tight ass, but in fact he was easy to get along with. He handled his work extremely well and encouraged the same in others. He always knew how to express exactly what he wanted and was clear about what pleased him and what didn't. On occasion he was irritated by my habit of bending police procedures a bit, but we'd never had any other problems. After my previous bosses— an alcoholic at the Helsinki PD and a shifty lawyer—working with Taskinen was a breeze.

I hardly knew anything about his personal life, but if I remembered right, his wife was a day-care administrator for the city of Espoo. He also had a teenage daughter who was one of the best figure skaters in the country in her age division. Except for Ström, I got along well with all of my coworkers—despite being the only woman in the unit. Fortunately our neighboring units and the Patrol Division had a few female officers with whom I'd become friends. We even played volleyball once a week. Nowadays, with those other women in the building, I didn't feel like such a freak. During my police academy days and right after graduation it had seemed I was the only representative of any kind of minority on the force.

After lunch Taskinen and I worked on putting together the paperwork on the money laundering investigation. The sun was already setting by the time I turned my Fiat toward Nuuksio. After Antti and I had moved to the cottage, we'd given in and bought a used car. During the summer my commute was a breeze by bike, or even walking if I wasn't in a hurry, and Antti didn't mind walking half a mile to the bus stop or even having to transfer once to get to the math department at the university. But trips to the store and things like that were difficult enough that we'd decided to drop a few thousand on the ancient black Italian job. It clearly wasn't made for slick roads. The back swung nastily as I slid down the curving hills of Nuuksio on my way to Rosberga.

The gate was shut tight again, and this time it didn't open on its own. Aira had to walk down and unlock it. The last rays of the sun struck Rosberga Manor at an angle, painting the delicate pink walls the color of a blazing-red rose garden. Milla was outside smoking. In her black clothes and heavy makeup, she looked significantly more like Maleficent than Sleeping Beauty.

"The sergeant returns. Did you come to look for Elina's body?" she asked derisively.

Aira recoiled at Milla's words, as did I, but when I looked closely at Milla, I thought I detected genuine concern.

"Hopefully not," I said, stepping past Milla into the entryway. Muffled piano music was coming from somewhere. It was the same Satie piece Antti sometimes practiced for fun.

"Let's go have a look at Elina's room. Then maybe you'll understand my concern." Aira gestured toward the door leading to the kitchen.

"The estate's rooms are divided so the right side of the downstairs is public space, the dining room, lecture hall, and library. The kitchen is here in the middle, next to the stairs. Upstairs are the guest rooms where we house course participants. Our rooms are on the other side of the kitchen."

"How many can stay here at one time?"

"Around twenty women. We have eight bedrooms upstairs. Our rooms are here," Aira said, opening a narrow blue door to the left of the kitchen. "This is my room."

The room gave the impression of old-fashioned servants' quarters. The furnishings were spare and plain: a bed, a desk, and a loveseat with a small television facing it on a bookshelf. A second door led directly into the kitchen. Above the bed hung a print of a guardian angel helping a little girl and boy over a bridge. Aira closed the door.

"And these are Elina's rooms. Although we both use the parlor." Aira motioned me into the next room, and I swallowed a gasp of surprise. Appointed with romantic flower motifs, lace curtains, and little tables with doilies, the room fit with the pink manor, but I had a hard time connecting it to my picture of Elina Rosberg. I had imagined her room decorated cleanly, full of Artek or Kukkapuro design pieces. Aira must have noticed my confused expression.

"This was my mother's room—Elina's grandmother. Mother lived out her last decades here because she couldn't climb the stairs anymore. And she also liked the view."

I glanced out the large window, but all I could make out were silhouettes in the darkness. On this side of the house, the ground fell away and the walls surrounding the manor were low enough not to block the view down into the valley. I imagined that the white open space dimly visible in the distance was Lake Pitkäjärvi.

"Elina wanted to preserve this room the way it was. The bedroom is more her own style though."

Aira opened the room's other door. I stepped into the bedroom, which also didn't match my expectations. Although the furniture was modern and simple, the color palette was too bright: red, yellow, and light blue. A double bed dominated the room. The bedspread had been turned down, but no one had slept in the bed since it was last made. Next to the window was an uncomfortable-looking armchair with a triangular ottoman. On the desk was a computer, and on the bookshelf next to it was a collection of psychiatry books. Carefully laid out on the chair in front of the desk were violet corduroy pants, a white blouse, and a sweater in a smoky shade of gray.

"She wore those clothes the day before yesterday, but she usually wears the same ones several days in a row unless they're dirty. And if she left those clothes on the chair instead of putting them in the dirty hamper, then . . ." Aira went silent. "She kept her nightgown on her pillow, but there's nothing here. Her robe is usually in the bathroom, but I can't find it," Aira said finally.

"Are her winter coat and boots here?"

"She keeps them in the side entry so they won't get mixed up with course participants'. Follow me."

Aira went back into the entry and from there to a side entrance that led from the kitchen to the backyard. A collection of women's coats hung on a row of hooks.

"These are mine," Aira said, pointing to an old-fashioned Persian lamb coat and a dark-blue, hip-length blazer. The shearling coat I'd seen Elina wearing hung next to them, as did a shorter purple quilted jacket that was more appropriate for taking a walk. A smart dark-gray Ulster coat was carefully hung on a wooden hanger.

"Elina doesn't have any winter coats besides these. And all her shoes are here too. Winter boots, rubber boots, and hiking shoes."

"Could she have borrowed something from one of the other women?"

"You'd have to ask them. No one has mentioned anything missing. But let's go back to Elina's room. The most important sign that things aren't right is in her bathroom."

The bathroom attached to Elina's bedroom had been carefully restored. There was a claw-foot bathtub and a toilet with a wooden lid. A small dressing table full of bottles and tins also fit into the room. On the wall hung an electric toothbrush.

"Elina takes very good care of her face, but all of her cleansing gels and creams are here."

I carefully examined the expensive skin care products.

"Couldn't she have used travel sizes? A lot of brands offer those. And it's easy enough to buy new bottles of whatever you forget."

"But she wouldn't have left her antibiotics! Elina had an upper respiratory infection, and she only started her course of medicine the day before yesterday. She had a bad cough and almost lost her voice. The bottle is right here, look!"

On the edge of the dressing table was a small white plastic bottle that said "Erasis 400 Mg." The label instructed Elina Rosberg to take one pill three times a day for ten days. I opened the bottle, which still contained a few dozen tablets.

"Strange. But she could get more of these too. Elina must know a lot of doctors."

Although Aira seemed very sure that there was something suspicious about Elina's disappearance and clearly wanted us to open an official investigation, I had the feeling she wasn't telling me everything she knew.

"When did you last see Elina?"

"On Boxing Day, around ten o'clock that night. She was just coming in from a walk. I thought she was foolish to go out in the cold when she was sick, but she said she wanted some time alone. I made her a cup of tea afterward, and she took it to her room. She seemed perfectly normal other than being tired because her cough had been keeping her up at night. There was no sign that she was going out again."

"Was she alone on her walk?"

Aira seemed to consider this. "I think she was with Joona, but I can't be sure. She never asks him in when they meet. We don't allow men here at Rosberga, as you know."

"Where do they meet then?"

Although Elina's ban on allowing even her own boyfriend onto the grounds seemed logical, I was certain it caused them a number of practical difficulties.

"Usually at Joona's apartment." Aira's voice betrayed her disapproval of Elina's relationship with Joona Kirstilä. "And in the little house."

"Little house? What's that?"

"The old sauna building on the west side of the estate," Aira said a little uneasily. "Elina had a power line run out to it a few years ago. I think she meets Joona there sometimes, even though theoretically no men are allowed inside the walls at all."

"I'd like to see that. But let's continue here. You're sure you didn't hear Elina go out again?"

Aira looked embarrassed, even guilty. "I'd been sleeping poorly too because of Elina's coughing. I took a sleeping pill and put in earplugs. I didn't wake up until nine o'clock when Niina started clattering around in the kitchen making breakfast."

I asked to interview the other women on the premises. Hopefully someone would be able to tell me more. Aira said that Tarja Kivimäki, Elina's friend, had already left the estate for Tapiola because this was a workday for her.

Tarja Kivimäki . . . Where did I know that name from?

"I hear Niina playing piano in the library," Aira said. "Would you like to speak with her?"

Aira led me through the dining room, and I asked her whether Johanna had contacted the lawyer I'd mentioned on my first visit. I'd remembered to call the police in Johanna's home county that morning too, but unfortunately nothing had come of it: I didn't know anyone in the department there.

"Johanna has been terribly depressed," Aira said. "Spending Christmas away from her children . . . I know Elina spoke with a lawyer, but I think she's mostly been focused on helping Johanna cope with her guilt."

"Guilt? Over the abortion?"

"And leaving the children."

We went into the library, where a Chopin etude was being played furiously. The pianist was obviously good. Antti wasn't a beginner by any means, yet he never made it through the piece's tricky middle passages that well.

The young woman playing the piano was so engrossed in her music that she didn't notice our arrival. At first I could only see her back. Her straight brown hair extended to her waist and swayed with the rhythm of the music. A blue-and-white-striped shirt covered her slender back, and she was wearing jeans and combat boots. From the rear, Niina Kuusinen looked almost like a teenager, somehow too delicate and frail for the dark tones of the room. With its heavy furniture and walls of books, the 1920s feel of the space was broken only by the television in one corner.

"Niina!" Aira said loudly when the etude ended. "This is Sergeant Kallio from the Espoo Police. She'd like to ask you some questions."

Niina turned on the piano stool so quickly that her sheet music flew to the floor and the piano lid banged shut. From the front, she seemed older than from the back. Her startled almond-shaped eyes and small mouth did seem childlike, but her nose was long and narrow, giving her otherwise doll-like face an adult appearance. I guessed Niina was around twenty-four.

"Have you heard anything new from Elina?" Niina asked anxiously. Her long fingers, which were adorned with several silver Kalevala rings, nervously twisted the tips of her hair.

"No. That's why I wanted to chat. But this isn't a formal interview. When did you see her last?"

"At dinner on Boxing Day . . . around eight o'clock. When the rest of us came in here to watch a movie on TV, Elina insisted on going for a walk. After that, I didn't see her again."

Niina looked distressed, and she turned her eyes away from me as if to block out the possibility that something had happened to Elina. I imagined that as a police officer I represented a threat because law enforcement didn't generally intervene in people's lives when things were peaceful.

"You must have known Elina well since you were here for Christmas?"

Niina flinched, and I realized I'd used the past tense in referring to Elina. I didn't correct myself though.

"Well, not really. I attended a couple of her courses, and I started therapy with her at the beginning of the month. I didn't have anyone else to spend Christmas with. My mom is dead, my dad lives in France, and I don't have any siblings." Her voice trembled.

"Do you have any idea where Elina might have gone?"

"I tried looking at her chart, but I couldn't quite make anything out," said Niina.

"Chart, what chart?"

"Astrology chart. There are pretty strong influences from Saturn and Pluto, which would indicate self-destructiveness. And conflict with someone close to her, like a family member . . ." Niina glanced quickly at Aira.

Every once in a while during tricky cases we got calls at the station from astrologers, fortune-tellers, and clairvoyants offering to help. I always refused to take them seriously, and if the call reached me, I ended the conversation as quickly as possible with a few deprecating remarks. I didn't actually know anything about astrology other than that my sign was Pisces, which meant I was supposed to be sensitive, emotional, changeable, and creative. Although newspaper horoscopes were amusing to read, I had a hard time seeing myself in them. Most of my boyfriends, including Antti, had been the same sign—Sagittarius. Perhaps that meant something after all?

I asked Niina for her contact information in case I needed to ask any follow-up questions. She didn't know how much longer she'd be staying at Rosberga but gave me her address and phone number. I thought I detected relief in her expression when we left the library in search of the other women.

Milla was sitting in the lecture hall playing computer solitaire. Black and red cards swarmed on the screen, bouncing on top of each other as the mouse clicked furiously. I was glad my work computer didn't have any games. I definitely would have turned into an addict. When I addressed Milla, she lifted her eyes from the screen in irritation and then shut down the machine with a sigh.

"Is it time for the third degree already? And I can't even fucking smoke in here!" Milla sounded surprisingly similar to my colleague Ström—although both definitely would have taken umbrage at the comparison. Amused by this observation, I found myself softening toward her.

"You don't have to answer my questions. This isn't a formal interview. But if you liked Elina enough to want to spend Christmas with her, I'm sure you'll want to help find her."

"Blah, blah, blah! I don't know anything about Elina. I wasn't even here the night before last," said Milla.

Aira seemed surprised. "Where were you then? There isn't any way out of here at night."

"No shit!" replied Milla. "I slogged through the snow and goddamn freezing cold to the road and hitched a ride into the city. I caught the first bus back in the morning. Everyone was still asleep except Johanna. I saw her in the hall, but she's so afraid of me she didn't dare ask where I'd been."

Milla's look was a challenge. Her eye makeup was, if possible, even thicker and blacker than the first time I'd seen her, and her lips were orange.

"What the hell are you staring at? I can leave, can't I? This isn't a prison camp."

"Why did you want to go to Helsinki?" Aira's voice was like a boarding school headmistress's interrogating a problem child.

"I was starting to miss men and booze. And speaking of men, I did see Elina as I was wading toward the road. She was walking down the hill with that poet boyfriend of hers."

"At what time? What was Elina wearing?" I asked.

"I guess it was sometime after nine. I wasn't really paying attention."

"And you didn't come back until the next morning?"

"Yep. I was at this guy's apartment in Kulosaari. I didn't ask his name, but if I really tried, I might be able to remember where he lives. He wasn't the kind of guy you'd want to have your morning coffee with, but he had money."

"Nothing's happened here that anyone needs an alibi for yet. But where can I get hold of you if we find a reason to follow up?" I said.

"I'm supposed to be at work tonight. Fanny Hill on Helsinginkatu. We put on a nice show. You should come watch. I live right next to the club on the corner."

Milla added, "I can guess what happened to Elina though. She was going to dump her poet boy, and he couldn't take it, so he lured her over to his place and then killed her and himself. Probably thought that would put him in the history books with all the other great poets. A little like Sid Vicious, you know?"

From the look on Aira's face, the punk legend's name was a total mystery to her, but Milla's theory almost made me laugh.

"As far as we know, Joona Kirstilä is still alive. Where is Johanna, by the way?" I asked.

Aira was quiet for a second and then asked that I not interview Johanna quite yet, adding that she was sure Johanna hadn't seen Elina after Boxing Day. I agreed, recalling how fragile Johanna had seemed the first time I met her. It would be kinder not to confront her unless I had a reason to.

But there were still two people I needed to find who might know something about Elina's whereabouts. Tarja Kivimäki was the last of the women who had been at the house, and Aira had given me her phone number and address in Tapiola. I'd also have to track down the boyfriend. Aira had called him yesterday, but having a chat with him myself might prove more productive.

The old wooden sauna building was a grayish-rose color. It seemed to crouch near the wall to the west of the manor. Aira had said the key would be in the door. Aira had already been out to check it, so I didn't expect to find Elina there—but maybe there was something else.

The air inside was rank with stale cigarette smoke. Maybe Milla had been coming here to escape the cold while she smoked.

Inside, the dressing room was perhaps sixty degrees, but the sauna proper was only a few degrees above freezing. Apparently only part of the building had been wired for electricity. The furnishing was sparse, just a single chair and a small, cloth-covered table with an empty flower vase, a couple of wine glasses, and a half-full ashtray. There were also a narrow bed with just enough space that two lovers could manage to sleep the odd night away, a washed-out blue terry cloth bathrobe and a few towels hung over the chair, and in the drawers under the table I found a couple of toothbrushes, a tube of face cream, and an unopened bottle of red wine. The bed was clumsily made. I peeked under the blanket and found a single black hair on one of the pillows.

Maybe along with smoking here, Milla used the space to take naps.

After my brief inspection of the sauna, I returned to Elina's room, where I looked at the calendar on her desk. The only meeting for next week was an entry marked "RFT," which had been crossed out. I had heard of radical feminist therapy, but I didn't really know what it entailed. I wondered whether to take the calendar and address book with me, but decided to leave them. Elina might return at any moment, and then this whole thing would seem like an embarrassing overreaction.

The dark road back to the highway was slick. The temperature had risen again. I decided to call the station from the car and ask someone to check the passenger lists for any flights or ships that had left the county, although the idea of Elina taking a sudden trip still didn't seem very plausible. I thought of the old police rule of thumb: the longer a person was missing, the more unlikely it was they would be found alive.

3

After I called the station, I tried Tarja Kivimäki's number, but she didn't answer her phone. I was secretly relieved, because now I wouldn't have to drive all the way to Tapiola. Since nothing particularly important was waiting for me at the station, I headed home to regroup before trying to track down Elina's boyfriend.

Antti was still at the university. During the holidays it was quiet there, which meant he could concentrate on his research, which was good. Antti was working on a couple of articles he needed to publish in order to beef up his CV, and the deadlines were approaching. An assistant professorship was opening in the math department, and Antti intended to apply.

"If you get the job, I'll be a professor's wife. That sounds pretty damn fabulous," I'd said teasingly when Antti told me about it.

"I don't have a very good shot. Kirsti Jensen is the strongest candidate. But it's good practice to at least apply."

I was tired again. Maybe I had a vitamin deficiency. I felt like crawling into bed and calling Antti to cheer me up. But I'd promised Aira I would visit Joona Kirstilä. Boiling a pot of super strong coffee, I washed off my work makeup and changed my clothes. This refreshed me a little, although there was something strange about the coffee, a sort of metallic flavor.

I tried one more time to get Tarja Kivimäki on the phone. This time her answering machine picked up and announced that if I had urgent business, I could try to reach her at her work number at the Finnish Broadcasting Company. Then something clicked in my mind, and I knew why her name was familiar. Kivimäki was the political correspondent for the news on FBC. Unlike her colleagues, Kivimäki never appeared in front of the camera. Viewers only heard her husky, often aggressive voice, sometimes seeing a flash of a hand with long fingers and no rings thrusting a microphone at an interviewee. Kivimäki rarely let people off easy, and I always enjoyed watching her leave even slick operators like the Minister of Finance flustered and tongue-tied. I tried in vain to remember what Tarja Kivimäki looked like. I wasn't sure I'd actually ever seen her.

I dialed the number the answering machine had given but still didn't get through. According to the receptionist, Kivimäki was in the editing room working on a report that had to be ready for the evening broadcast. I left a request that she call me back at my work number in the morning, threw The Ramones' debut album on the record player, cranked it up to eleven, and then started redoing my makeup. When Antti called, I told him I was going to try to find Joona Kirstilä downtown, and we agreed to meet for a beer at the Ruffe Pub afterward.

The thought of a strong, dark Belgian beer was inviting, but first I had work to do. I didn't want to warn Kirstilä that I was coming. If for some incomprehensible reason Elina was holed up in his apartment, I wanted to surprise her there and catch her off guard in order to question her. Maybe the reason for her disappearance from Rosberga was simple. Maybe Elina had just grown tired of her flood of Christmas guests and wanted to spend the rest of the holidays in peace.

Wet snow dripped from the sky as I slogged to the bus stop. I nearly fell asleep in the warm bus. As I waited for the next one at the transfer station in Tapiola, the icy wind woke me up again.

Joona Kirstilä lived in an apartment above the Kabuki Restaurant, just east of the main Helsinki cemetery. He was home. I heard him pad to the door, and then there was a moment of silence as he looked through the peephole. Finally he opened the door just a crack, leaving the chain in place.

"What do you want?" he asked brusquely. Maybe admirers of his poetry banged on his door every night.

"Sergeant Kallio, Espoo Police. Good evening." I flashed my badge through the crack. "I'd like to talk to you about Elina Rosberg."

"Why are the police interested in Elina?" Kirstilä sounded incredulous.

"Elina Rosberg is missing. I thought Aira Rosberg told you."

"Aira called me yesterday, but . . . What do you mean missing? What's this all about?"

"If you let me in, I'll tell you. Or if you'd prefer to talk somewhere else, we can go to a café."

He hesitated but finally unfastened the door chain. "Ignore the mess. I haven't had time to do much cleaning lately."

Joona Kirstilä's home was a small one-bedroom apartment. A partially opened door off the living room revealed a chaotic-looking bedroom. Next to the bedroom was the cramped kitchenette, with barely space enough for a hotplate, microwave, and an ancient, whirring refrigerator. But the high ceilings of the old building lent the main room, with its piles of papers and books, a certain charm. It resembled Antti's old digs before I moved in.

Only the piano was missing. A black typewriter, at least as old as the poet himself, sat on the desk beside a slick-looking laptop.

Kirstilä shifted a stack of papers off the couch and motioned for me to sit. He sat on the floor and lit a cigarette. When I'd seen him on TV and in the tabloids, I'd always suspected he played the stereotypical poet deliberately. His dark, wavy hair was worn below his ears and occasionally fell in front of his eyes, triggering a compulsive gesture to sweep it away. His skin was pale, and he had large, long-lashed brown eyes that seemed to burn intensely. His nose was straight and narrow, his lips slightly downturned at the corners. It was just the sort of face you assumed a poet would have. Although he was in his early thirties, Kirstilä looked younger. He was short, barely over five foot six, and very thin. His standard outfit of tight jeans and a thick black sweater—with protruding wrist bones poking out of the sleeves and small, artistic hands—heightened the impression of delicacy. His fingers were long and thin, as if made to hold a quill pen. I'd read some of his poetry collections and admired his unique use of language, although the general mood of the romantic poems was a bit too masculine for my tastes.

"What do you mean Elina is missing?" Kirstilä asked again, blowing streams of smoke at me. Before I could answer, the books on top of the nearest bookcase started shaking strangely. I just managed to get out of the way before they fell, nearly landing on my head.

"Pentti, stop it!" Kirstilä snapped at a cat with dun-colored stripes and a white breast. Pentti nimbly jumped from one shelf to another, bounced onto the floor, and rushed to sniff my shoes, probably smelling Einstein.

"His name is Pentti? I assume for Pentti Saarikoski?"

"Yeah. At least one of us should be a famous poet. I'm sorry. He's too curious sometimes. But about Elina . . ."

Kirstilä's worry seemed genuine, and it increased when I told him that no one had seen or heard from Elina in days. He lit a new cigarette immediately after putting out the first, and Pentti retreated to the kitchen looking annoyed after receiving a face full of smoke.

"I don't have a clue where she is!" Kirstilä stood and walked to the window. Stubbing out his cigarette on the wide windowsill, he leaned his forehead on the pane for a moment. His dark eyes shone in the glass's reflection as if in a mirror.

"You don't talk every day?"

"Not usually," Kirstilä said, still leaning against the glass. "When I'm writing, I don't want to know anything about the rest of the world. And Elina has her courses. We arranged to meet sometime before New Year's. Elina's coming over here then . . ." Kirstilä's voice faded again. I wondered whether he always left his sentences unfinished.

"When did you last see Elina?"

Kirstilä's reply was surprising: "When did Elina disappear?"

"On Boxing Day. The night before last."

"It was the day before Christmas Eve," Kirstilä said. "In the afternoon, a little before I left on the train to see my parents in Hämeenlinna."

I wondered why he was lying. Aira had been all but convinced that Elina had been out walking with him, and Milla had claimed she'd actually seen the two of them together. But I wasn't investigating a crime, just trying to determine Elina's location, so I didn't accuse Kirstilä of lying yet. Instead, I asked when he had returned from Hämeenlinna. Kirstilä claimed he'd arrived home early the previous morning.

"So Aira Rosberg called right after you got home?" I asked.

"I'd just gone to sleep. I'd been up all night drinking with old friends. That's probably why I didn't even realize Aira was saying Elina was missing. Usually I'm the one who does the disappearing act."

Despite his delicate appearance, Kirstilä was known for upholding the legendary boozing traditions of Finnish poets. He seemed an unlikely choice as a lover for a woman like Elina Rosberg, but I guess human emotions aren't always about logic. If I'd let logic rule my life, I never would have married Antti—or anyone else, for that matter.

I left Kirstilä shaking his head in bewilderment and set off for the Ruffe Pub to meet Antti. I was annoyed. So far all I'd succeeded in doing was scaring people. I'd found no clues as to Elina's whereabouts.

Antti was sitting at a table near the window trying to read by the light of a candle. The shadows cast by the flickering flame made his features look thinner than ever. When I knocked on the window above him, a wide, boyish smile spread across his face.

"What are you drinking?" he asked when I came in.

I looked with interest at the bulbous glass in front of him, which was graced by a red heart and a chubby little man.

"Belgian Oerbier," Antti explained. "It's a real winner."

I tasted it but decided to stick with my standard, Old Peculier. The cigarette smoke in the pub seemed thicker than normal and made it difficult to breathe, and for some reason my beer didn't taste as full-bodied as usual. We chatted about Joona Kirstilä's poetry for a bit, but then I began to feel tired and asked if Antti minded heading home. Was I getting old?

At home I passed out, and the next morning I woke up with a hangover despite only drinking two beers the night before.

At work a new case was waiting for me: a restaurant break-in during the night looked professional enough that Palo and I got on the computer and started searching for backsliders. We had narrowed it down to a few possible candidates when Taskinen appeared at the door.

"Someone found the body of an approximately forty-year-old woman in the forest in Nuuksio. In a nightgown. Interested in having a look, Maria?"

Actually, the answer was no. I wasn't interested in seeing Elina Rosberg or any other woman dead. After a moment, I rose wordlessly from my chair and started pulling on my warm outer clothes. Palo said he'd stay behind to fight with the computer.

"Ström's downstairs checking out a car. I'll get my coat," Taskinen said as I went down the hall to tell Dispatch I was leaving.

Ström was just turning the ignition in the department's most presentable Saab when I reached the motor pool garage. I climbed into the front seat—Taskinen could sit in back. Someone on the radio was calling Forensics.

"Nuuksio . . . The same road that goes out to the nature center?" Ström asked.

"I don't know where they found the body yet. Ask Taskinen," I said.

Taskinen got in the car lugging a large duffel bag. "Nuuksio Road to the turnoff for Rosberga Manor. We can't get anywhere close by car, so I brought boots. The ones I got for you are probably too big, Maria," he said.

"What do you mean we can't get there by car? Where the hell is the carcass then?" Ström growled in his usual sweet way.

"Next to a ski track about half a mile from the road," said Taskinen. "A skier found her and called the police from the nearest house."

"From Rosberga?" I asked. Aira and the others would have known immediately who the body was.

"No, another neighbor," Taskinen said. "The skier rang the bell at Rosberga's gate, but no one answered."

"So it's one of those goddamn lesbians who bunk there?" Ström angrily wheeled the cruiser onto the street, spraying slush on the sidewalk and onto an old man walking by. From the corner of my eye, I saw Taskinen's mouth tighten. He didn't like Ström's driving any more than he liked his way of speaking.

"The owner of the estate, Elina Rosberg, has been missing for a couple of days," answered Taskinen, his even tone betraying none of his irritation. Grabbing his phone, he dictated driving directions to Forensics.

"We should've brought skis," Ström muttered. "Now we're going to be wading up to our asses in goddamn snowdrifts."

The skier who had found the body was waiting for us in the lane leading to Rosberga. In his bright-blue cross-country ski bibs and with ultramodern skate skis strapped to his feet, he looked like he'd dropped in from Mercury. I felt sorry for him. He'd obviously been sprinting and was now freezing just standing in the cold. And then Ström started taking his information in his usual friendly fashion. I turned away, disgusted, and surveyed the terrain. The sight of the deep drifts surrounding the skier's tracks didn't make me particularly happy, but there was nothing to be done about it. Ström was right—we should have brought skis.

"It's easier once you move farther into the forest. The rain last night melted a lot of the snow," the skier said, sensing my trepidation.

Pulling on my boots, I was relieved I'd decided to wear my thigh-length down coat rather than my long Ulster. I tried to keep up with the skier, Ström, and Taskinen, but the competition was stacked against me. Ström was over six feet tall, Taskinen was a marathoner, and the skier had on skis. I wasn't in bad shape, but I was much shorter and my legs were feeling unusually weak.

Only a couple inches of snow lay in the more thickly forested areas, but it was frozen and slick. And in the clearings, the snow was deeper than our boots. The wind made me grimace, and the fir needles slapped my cheeks, leaving tiny scratches.

Because of the ski tracks, our destination was easy to find. The body was lying on the top of a tiny knoll, under a dense spruce tree. Only bare, slender legs protruded. They must have been covered by snow before, but last night's rain had melted it. Ström was the first one to carefully part the branches of the tree. I heard his deep intake of breath, and then I stepped up to take my turn.

The body was unquestionably Elina Rosberg. She wore a delicate pink satin robe, and the hem of her matching pink nightgown, no longer frozen solid with ice because of the runoff from the tree, moved when I recoiled instinctively. Frostbite covered her bare legs and feet, but her face with its high cheekbones was calm, almost smiling. But still dead.

Her eyes were closed, the eyelids bluish. There were no apparent external signs of violence. It was as if she had calmly lain down under the tree and fallen asleep like Sleeping Beauty. But the kind of prince who could wake her only existed in fairy tales.

"It's Elina Rosberg," I said, nodding to Taskinen as he moved in to look. My feet were icy cold, and a strange pain scratched in my throat. Ström talked with the skier in hushed tones. It was as if finding Elina's body had tempered his crude bluster for once. The forest around us was silent until a clattering started from the road and Taskinen's cell phone rang. Forensics was on their way.

The routine was comfortingly familiar. Photographs, measurements, the futile search for Elina's footprints. It looked as though Elina had died from exposure, but we couldn't confirm that until the autopsy.

"I think that's about it," Taskinen sighed after the forensics team informed him they had found no evidence of anyone else being under the tree with Elina. "Maria, do you know who the next of kin are?"

"Elina's aunt lives at the estate. I don't think she had a husband or children. I'm pretty sure her parents are dead."

"Well then, on to Rosberga Manor," he said grimly.

With that Taskinen trudged away toward the road. Forensics had tramped a wide path, and their sleds, loaded with heavy equipment, had compacted the snow. The walk back to the cruiser was almost too quick for me because I was trying to think of what I would say to Aira.

"Are we supposed to stay here in the car and wait since those broads won't let us in?" Ström asked as our car spun out trying to make it up the hill to the manor. Ström seemed to have a good understanding of the rules of the house.

"I don't see much sense in that," I said.

When we reached the gate, I got out of the car and rang the bell. Aira must have seen us on the security camera because she opened the gate remotely instead of coming down herself. As our car glided up the drive, I wondered if Taskinen and Ström were the first men to enter Rosberga Manor this decade.

Aira opened the front door. Her face had aged since I last saw her, and her shoulders slumped when she looked at us. She knew why we were there.

"You found Elina. Where?"

Taskinen told her where the body was found, emphasizing that we didn't have any idea yet how Elina had ended up under the tree or whether a crime was involved. Aira stared somewhere past Taskinen into the distance. Her eyes were free of tears.

"Can I see her?" Aira finally asked, and I told her that we did need an official identification.

"Would you like to come now, or would you prefer tomorrow?" I asked. "We'll have to interview you again anyway, along with everyone else who was here that night."

Aira was about to answer when a shriek came from upstairs. A door slammed and Niina Kuusinen charged down the stairs, screaming hysterically. She rushed at Ström, who stood nearest to her: "No men allowed!"

Niina tried to shove Ström toward the front door, but her attempt was useless. Although she was tall, Ström was much too big for her. I dragged Niina off Ström, mostly because I didn't want him to hurt her.

"Niina!" Aira's voice cut the air, as thin and sharp as a spear. "These are police officers. They found Elina."

Niina froze in my arms. Aira didn't leave room for questions, continuing in her new, pointed tone, "Elina is dead."

Niina went suddenly limp and collapsed on the floor, bursting into inconsolable sobs. I was surprised by the speed of her reaction: usually people took a while to realize what had happened.

Wrapping her arms around Niina, Aira murmured something comforting. It struck me that Aira was the one who
most needed consoling words, but she came across as the kind
of woman who always put the needs of others before her own.
She would no doubt cry her own tears later in the privacy of her
bedroom.

I almost started crying myself, but managed to fend off the
tears by focusing on my job. "Is anyone else still here who was
at the house on the night of the twenty-sixth?" My own voice
sounded cold and sharp, like the screech of the rails under a
braking train.

Aira momentarily cut her eyes from Niina to me. "Johanna
is upstairs, Sergeant," she said. "Would you like to take her the
news yourself?"

It was a spiteful question, its bite made worse by the shift
back to my formal title. I didn't have any idea how to handle
Johanna under normal circumstances. I always felt uncomfortable around religious believers. Maybe I feared some type of
fanaticism I recognized in myself. And I was afraid of the broken look in Johanna's eyes, that gaze that led somewhere I never
wanted to go.

"I can do that," I said briskly. "What about identifying the
body?"

"If I can have a couple of hours first." Aira's voice was com-
bative. "Niina and Johanna need me right now."

Niina's outburst had subsided to pathetic whimpering, and
she raised her face from Aira's shoulder. "Where did you find
Elina?"

I told her, answering as many questions as I could and promising to share more information as soon as we received the results

of the autopsy. Then a bang from the top of the stairs made us all look up.

Pale and expressionless, Johanna stared down at us. I wondered if she'd been napping; she wore a carelessly belted blue-gray bathrobe. A lock of drab blond hair had escaped its tight bun and curled down to frame her face. I hadn't noticed before that her hair was naturally curly.

Her words came from above like a proclamation from a pulpit. "Suicide is a sin! Those who take their own lives will be barred from heaven's gate! I asked Leevi if it wouldn't be a sin if I continued the tenth pregnancy knowing full well we would both probably die? Wouldn't that be suicide and murder too? But Leevi said it was God's will."

I saw the growing panic in Ström's eyes. He clearly wanted to get away from these crazy women. I tried to catch Taskinen's attention, to shift the decision to continue the interviews to him. Slowly Johanna descended the stairs and wrapped her arms around Aira and Niina with the sudden self-assurance of a mother accustomed to tending a brood of children. When Johanna closed her eyes and allowed her face to relax, she almost looked like a young girl. With surprise I realized that she probably wasn't more than a few years older than me. She must have started having babies in her teens.

"We'd really like to speak with all of you. What time can you come to the police station?" Taskinen phrased this as a question, but it was clear the women were expected to comply.

We arranged a meeting for the following morning. It would mean working on Saturday again, but there was no avoiding it. With any luck, I could skip Antti's coworker's family's New Year's party too.

On the way back to the station, I related what I already knew about Elina's disappearance to Ström and Taskinen. As I suspected he would, Taskinen asked me to handle the preliminary interrogations if the autopsy justified them.

"The only question may end up being why she went out in the middle of the night in the freezing cold and walked half a mile in her nightgown." Taskinen shrugged. "Maybe we'll find a natural explanation for that too. I should have asked if she was a sleepwalker. Will you also look up any other next of kin in the population registry?"

"Rosberg was rich," said Ström. "That house is worth millions, and she had to sell part of her forest to the state when they set up the Nuuksio National Park. Who gets the money? The aunt? Or some club for man-haters?"

"Yeah, probably the Castration Army," I snapped, although Ström had actually made an interesting point. Elina Rosberg had been rich. In what industry had the Rosberg family made their fortune? Wasn't it timber? My first order of business would be putting together a better biography of Elina Rosberg.

Back in my office, I logged in to the Population Register Center database and waited a few seconds while the server executed the search for Elina Rosberg. From the wall, my friends' bachelorette party present smiled down at me: "THE ONES THAT GOT AWAY!" the poster screamed, with photographs of Geir Moen, Hugh Grant, Mick Jagger, Valentin Kononen. The collage frequently elicited crabby comments from my male coworkers, but of course that was the best reason for keeping it on the wall. No one had accused me of sexual harassment yet, not even Ström. Because I rarely handled official interviews in my office, I also never worried that the silly poster would undermine my image.

As I switched on my printer, I read through the search results on the screen. Rosberg, Elina Katrina, b. Espoo, Finland, November 26, 1954. Parents Kurt Johannes Rosberg, b. 1914, occupation: estate owner, and Sylva Katrina Rosberg, née Kajanus, b. 1920. No spouse, no children. No other entries.

I looked her up in the criminal database as well, although I was fairly certain her record would be clean. Surprisingly, there was one arrest, from a demonstration against the shah of Iran in 1970. And then twenty-five years of nothing. What else? Where would I find her medical degree? Did the database include psychotherapists? I clicked around some more and then found what I was looking for. Elina Rosberg, high school graduation, 1973, Lycée Franco-Finlandais d'Helsinki, master in psychology, 1979, Helsinki University, psychotherapy certification, 1981. Founded Rosberga Women's Education Institute, 1990, previously worked for Helsinki University Central Hospital youth psychiatric clinic and Lapinlahti Hospital. Hobbies: hiking and reading.

Nothing out of the ordinary there either. Elina had an unusually small extended family. She was an only child, her mother hadn't had any siblings, and Kurt and Aira's two other brothers had both died during the Continuation War with Russia. Other than Aira, the closest people to Elina had been Joona Kirstilä and Tarja Kivimäki. Maybe they could tell me who murdered Elina, leaving her this melted snow woman.

Murder? Why was I even thinking that? So far, nothing about Elina's death indicated a crime. It could just as easily have been an accident or suicide.

A strange, heavy feeling sat in my gut. My period was probably about to start. When had it started last month? For years I'd tracked it by the rhythm of the monthly package of pills, but now, with the IUD, I'd stopped counting. My breasts were starting to feel tender too. I was just looking for backup tampons in my desk drawer when someone knocked at the door.

"Come in!" I assumed it was one of my coworkers, probably Taskinen, because few others would have bothered knocking.

Instead, a strange woman stood in the doorway. Maybe a couple of years older than me, though it was difficult to tell her precise age. She was about my height and had a pale, unremarkable face. Her careful makeup—a women's magazine would call it natural—did little to counter her lack of personality. Her brown hair curled at the ends and fell just below her ears. The curls were pulled back from her forehead with a black suede headband. Her unripe-blueberry-colored eyes stared at me through stylish glasses. The brown pantsuit she wore was straight out of the Successful Female Professional catalog.

"You must be Sergeant Kallio. I came to speak with you about Elina Rosberg," the woman said. Her voice was immediately familiar. She had to be Tarja Kivimäki.

She confirmed this and shook my hand firmly but briefly. Her nails were carefully painted an inconspicuous beige.

"Aira Rosberg called me and said Elina was dead. She said suicide was a possibility." Kivimäki sat down on the sofa of my cramped office and crossed her legs. Her calves were very attractive, clearly those of an athlete. I wondered what her sport was. My guess was boxing or fencing.

"I came here to tell you that Elina would never do that. If she was so depressed that she was planning suicide, she would have sought professional help." Kivimäki's voice was calm, but I detected the same sharpness and indignation familiar from her political reporting. That was her MO: maintaining a placid exterior while an unpleasant question lurked under the surface, ready to explode and confound any politician within its blast radius.

"Until the results of the autopsy come back, we're really just speculating." I found myself taking up a battle position—mostly because I didn't want to say anything that would make Tarja Kivimäki see me as a stupid cop. She might tongue-tie the prime minister, but Maria Kallio was made of sterner stuff.

"Where are you in the investigation?" she asked.

"There really isn't an investigation unless something in the autopsy points to a crime. But while you're here, I'd like to ask when you last saw Elina. You were at her house on Boxing Day. Is that correct?"

"I spent all of Christmas there. I left for work the morning after Boxing Day, on the twenty-seventh. I had a shift."

It seemed odd that Kivimäki wasn't more upset. According to Aira, Kivimäki and Elina had been close friends for years. You'd think she'd be devastated by the news of Elina's death. But the woman sitting across from me was as cool as she would be reporting on the friendly conclusion of a government-mediated union contract negotiation.

"Did anything happen over Christmas that could explain Elina turning up dead in the forest?" I asked.

Now Kivimäki looked uncomfortable—clearly she didn't like being the interviewee.

"There was a lot of tension in the air," she answered slowly. "Originally it was supposed to be only Aira, Elina, and me. Then Johanna and Milla decided to just hang around after one of Elina's seminars. Elina collected charity cases like other people take in stray cats. Niina's a good example. There's nothing wrong with her other than a massive case of selfishness. She had no reason not to go home after the seminar. Milla's the same way. Why would she give up Rosberga Manor for a dismal apartment? The only one with a real problem who might be justified in staying is

Johanna. And all she has to do is file for divorce and demand her children back. Simple as that."

"How long have you known Elina Rosberg?" I asked.

"About six years. I used to report for *Studio A* and did a program about child sexual abuse. It was a hot topic at the time, and I interviewed Elina and we hit it off. We seemed to speak the same language. She gave a good interview."

"I remember that program." I'd been in law school, and our criminal law professor used one of the incest cases from the program as an example of how difficult family court cases could be: the adult daughters of an American couple had accused their father of rape, but their mother and their brother refused to testify against him. Remembering that case still made me angry.

"Elina was a very sensible person," said Kivimäki. "She would never go out in the cold without a coat, especially with that terrible cough. She must have been in really serious distress. And besides, no outsider could even get into Rosberga. The gates were always locked."

"Why were they locked?"

"Elina didn't want interlopers, especially men. She wanted at least one place in Espoo where women could be safe from men's harassment. Every once in a while a group of drunks would wander up from the sports institute down the road or teenagers out hiking in the national park would make noise at the gate. Men always get really irritated when they're barred from any place."

"OK, but let's get back to that night," I said. "When did you last see Elina?"

"Aira and I were in the library. Niina was probably there too. We were watching TV, an old Marilyn Monroe movie, I think, something sentimental and fun. Elina stuck her head in to say she was going out for some fresh air. We tried to stop her because she had such a bad cold, but she went anyway. Elina was like that. Once she decided something, trying to talk her out of it was useless.

"I had an early morning, so I went to bed as soon as the movie ended. Before I left around six, I stopped at her door thinking that if she was awake I'd say good-bye and thank her for Christmas, but I didn't see a light on. I had the code to the gate, so I let myself out and headed for the TV station in Pasila."

"Who else knows the gate code?" I asked.

"Aira, of course, and probably Johanna since she's been there so long. Elina usually didn't give it out. She wanted to avoid uninvited guests."

My phone rang and Kivimäki stood up, taking advantage of the interruption to end our conversation. I asked the caller to wait a moment and stood up to shake Kivimäki's hand. I promised to be in touch when we had more information. Hopefully I wouldn't need to interview her again.

As she left, Kivimäki glanced in amusement at my beefcake poster. "Nice choices!" she said in a surprisingly girlish tone. "Although Hugh Grant has been slipping lately."

I smiled in response and picked up the phone. It was the pathologist who was examining Elina's body. He was already sure of one thing.

Elina's back, buttocks, and thighs all had scratches and bruises caused when she was still alive but presumably unconscious. The pathologist and forensic technicians had concluded that someone had dragged her through the forest and left her under the tree. The pathologist couldn't say yet why Elina was unconscious but promised lab results by morning.

When I hung up the phone, I tasted bile rising in my throat. Dragged through the forest. So it was at least manslaughter. Or worse. If this was a murder, it was going to be complicated. I already had a long list of suspects. Again.

4

"I'm sure it was her boyfriend she was walking with that night," Milla Marttila said over the phone. A deep yawn followed. It was a little past nine on Saturday morning, the day before New Year's Eve. My call had woken Milla, whose work shift had ended at four in the morning. Apparently she wasn't alone in her apartment. I could hear muffled snoring in the background.

"Have you ever met Joona Kirstilä?" I asked.

"He's been to the club a few times. I doubt he ever told Elina that. I'd know him anywhere, he's so small and thin. He looked like a dwarf next to Elina. And he always has that stupid red scarf so everyone'll know he's a poet. Like Edith Södergran."

"What? Oh, you mean he thinks poets are supposed to wear red capes or something. Do you like Södergran's poems?"

"You think a stripper can't know anything about poetry? Can we be done now? I just want to go back to sleep."

"Come to the police station at one," I said. "I need an official statement from you that you saw Elina with Kirstilä on the night she . . . disappeared."

"The Espoo police station? Where the fuck is that even?" Milla asked.

I tried to give her directions, but she yelled that she wasn't going to go searching for it in BFE, so finally I offered to send a car to pick her up.

With Milla coming at one, I thought it best to interview Kirstilä right after that. Aira would be meeting me in the lobby in an hour so that we could identify Elina together. The thought of going to the morgue made me feel sick again and my head ached. Exhaustion wavered behind my eyes like a thin shroud. I had slept in snatches the night before, dreaming first of Elina and then of trying to take a pregnancy test at work but not being able to get into the bathroom.

While driving home from work last night, pregnancy had popped into my mind as a possible reason for my constant tiredness. At home I'd checked my calendar—six weeks had passed since my last period. Then I'd looked at the instructions that came with the IUD and saw that, no, it wasn't a hundred percent reliable.

I needed to swing by the pharmacy to buy the test.

I'd tried not to think about it; it was just a suspicion. All the same, I'd skipped my beer the night before, despite really wanting one after dealing with Elina's death all day. In some ways, thinking about murder was easier than thinking about the possibility of being pregnant. For me, murders were something to be solved. When the case was over, it would no longer affect my life. But a child was forever.

Ström pushed my office door open just as I was about to call Joona Kirstilä. Without asking, he collapsed on the sofa under my shrine to masculinity and put his feet on the table.

"So it looks like this death is turning out to be murder. That's your favorite kind of job, right, Kallio? And you get to interview a whole bunch of feminazis too."

"What makes you think murder investigations are my favorite jobs?" I asked.

"Well, you're just so damn efficient. Once you get started on one, it's all you think about—even if that means doing something stupid and almost getting yourself killed. Come to think of it, you're already looking pale. Maybe you should cut back on the honeymooning every night."

"Could you get lost?" I said. "I'm kind of busy. I have to get these interviews going, and I've got a trip to the morgue in a few minutes."

"I know, hon. I'm your bad cop today." Ström's expression was nauseatingly self-satisfied.

About a year before, our unit had adopted a practice of rotating investigative duties rather than relying on seniority. Whoever Taskinen assigned to head up a case acted as independently as possible, and everyone took turns playing support roles as necessary. Even Taskinen had sat in as a witness for some of my interviews. The purpose was to break down the strict police hierarchy and prevent people from getting sick of always doing the same jobs.

"I thought Pihko was my number two on this case. Isn't he on shift today?" I asked.

"He flew up to Lapland to do some skiing. You'll have to settle for spending the holiday with me."

"OK, but just remember who's doing what. I'm asking the questions. You keep your mouth shut. You don't even have to record the interview. You just have to be there."

Ström just smiled.

"Oh, by the way, do you know anyone on the force up in Karhumaa or Ii?" I was still trying to track down a cop from

Johanna's hometown that someone in my department knew. But my goal was no longer just to help her out in her custody dispute.

"Not that I can think of. Why?"

"One of our witnesses is from there. If you could check, I'd appreciate it. Now get lost. I need to get this work done. Or maybe you want to come to the morgue?" I smiled unpleasantly.

A disdainful expression flashed across his face. None of us liked looking at corpses, but Ström would never admit that. The rest of us agreed that you got used to it, but you never liked it. At least Elina Rosberg's body was in one piece, with no blood.

"I have a couple of things to do too," he said quickly. "Call when you need me in the interrogation room."

Instead of picking up the phone after Ström left, I thought about my own situation again. Was it dangerous to get pregnant when the IUD was still in? If I was pregnant, I should probably contact my gynecologist right away. Damn. I'd have to squeeze in time for a pharmacy run between Aira's and Milla's interviews.

The air in the room suddenly seemed stuffy, so I opened the postage-stamp-sized ventilation window. Immediately my nipples felt painfully cold.

The phone rang. It was Dr. Kervinen, the pathologist doing Elina's autopsy.

"Do you know whether Rosberg was on a course of antibiotics when she disappeared?"

"Yes, she was," I said. Aira had said that Elina's leaving her pill bottle behind was a clear indication that something was wrong.

"Do you happen to remember the brand or what it was prescribed for?" he asked.

"Something that started with *e-r*, and it was prescribed for a respiratory infection. She had a bad cough."

"That fits well. We found erythromycin in her system, which is often used to treat things like bronchitis. The bottle would be useful. I'd like to know who was treating her. Apparently her doctor forgot to warn her that erythromycin inhibits the metabolism of benzodiazepines."

"Metabolism of benzo . . . what?"

"Rosberg had a high dose of benzodiazepines—sedatives—and a few servings of alcohol in her system. Erythromycin increases the effects of benzodiazepines on the body and causes them to remain in the system longer. Together these substances could have left her comatose long enough for her to freeze to death."

I thought feverishly. Antibiotics, sedatives, liquor. Was Elina's death an accident? If so, why had she been walking around in the snow in just her nightgown?

"Were there enough sedatives and booze in her system that she would have passed out without the antibiotic?" I asked.

"Maybe for a little while, but probably not long enough for her to freeze to death. But it's hard to say. The interaction of these drugs isn't well known, and reported cases have involved comas, not death. The effects of alcohol on drugs are also very individual, and you have to take the cold into consideration. The temperatures around Christmas were quite low, and she disappeared at night, right?"

"Yes . . ."

The case was becoming stranger by the hour. Had Elina simply been trying to sleep and took the sedatives not knowing the danger posed by the antibiotics? Or had someone else given her the mixture?

"Listen," I said. "I'm coming down there in about half an hour for the ID. Rosberg's aunt is coming with me. I'll ask her about the medicine and the doctor. But don't say anything to her about a specific cause of death."

"Is she a suspect?" Kervinen asked enthusiastically. Most of us in law enforcement did various things to distance ourselves from our cases. Kervinen did so not by telling horrible corpse jokes or trying to shock people with coarse language like some of our colleagues. Instead, he treated victims like curiosities that had never really been living people. And he seemed to genuinely enjoy playing the detective sidekick.

"Yes, you could say that. Hey, can I ask you one more question? A personal one. Is it dangerous to get pregnant with an IUD in?"

An embarrassed cough came from the other end of the line. "Dammit, Kallio, I'm a pathologist, not a gynecologist. But yeah . . . You should probably see a doctor. I mean . . ." Kervinen laughed nervously, clearly tongue-tied.

I suspected that he had no children himself and that everything he knew about pregnancy and childbirth was gleaned from chapters in a textbook long forgotten once he focused his medical education more on the dead than the living.

"Yeah, I guess so. Well, I'll see you in a little while. I have to go meet the aunt."

When I entered the police station lobby, I found both Aira Rosberg and Johanna Säntti waiting. Next to Johanna, who looked haggard and shrunken, Aira stood tall and broad-shouldered, but the sorrow on both of their faces was the same—immovable and desolate. Aira was wearing the black Persian lamb coat I had seen at the manor. A hat made of the same material was pulled over her forehead. Johanna wore a dark sack-like coat with a black-and-gray-patterned scarf tied around her head.

"I brought Johanna along. She said she had a matter to discuss with the police," Aira explained.

"Would you like to wait for me here?" I asked. "We won't be long. Or would you prefer to come and wait there?"

It bothered me that everyone always spoke for Johanna, first Elina and now Aira. At least during her interview Johanna would have a chance to speak for herself.

"I'll come along." Her voice was exasperatingly nervous and small, but at least she was talking. I led them to the car, which I'd parked in front of the building, and they both sat in back. We drove through the dusk toward the Turku Highway and from there to the Institute of Forensic Medicine.

As I drove, I glanced into the backseat. "This is only a formality since we already know it's Elina." I kept my voice as calm and comforting as possible.

It had started drizzling, and the radio was predicting a thaw in Southern Finland that would probably melt all of the snow that had fallen during December. A passing van threw the slush collected in the ruts in the road onto our windshield, leaving me blind for a couple of seconds before it occurred to me to turn on the wipers. The van was speeding, but I didn't have the energy to care.

"Don't worry. I was at both of my parents' deathbeds, and Elina's parents' too." A dry amusement was audible in Aira Rosberg's tone. "And I was a nurse. I retired just a few years before Elina founded the therapy center. I worked in nursing homes for years. But you haven't told us the cause of death. Was it . . . messy? Is she hard to look at?"

"No." My cheeks burned with embarrassment and irritation. Aira seemed to deflect every attempt I made at showing empathy. OK, I wouldn't try anymore.

At the forensic medical center, we left Johanna in the waiting room. She sat at the end of a sofa, back straight, legs tightly pressed together like a little girl whose mommy had told her to behave while she went into the store. How could a person who seemed so weak and servile have nine children?

I checked in at the information desk, and a nurse led us to the morgue door, where Kervinen met us. The nurse stood at the door, apparently poised to rush in to lend assistance if one of us fainted or had a hysterical fit.

Identifying bodies was like a strange, ritualized dance around a wheeled bed draped in white. We walked to the gurney, and Kervinen lifted the sheet momentarily. I looked at Elina's chilled face one more time before I raised my eyes to Aira, who nodded.

"Frozen to death," she said softly. I nodded and asked Aira for her signature on the necessary forms, and then inquired about the medicine Elina had taken. She told me both the brand name and the doctor who prescribed it. I glanced at Kervinen, who nodded.

"If you'll go and wait with Johanna, I'll be out in just a minute," I said to Aira.

When Aira reached the door, the nurse approached her to inquire whether she was all right. I didn't hear the answer. They walked together into the bright fluorescent lights of the hallway while I turned back to Kervinen. I suddenly noticed the stench of disinfectant and the nauseating way Kervinen's unusually feminine floral-smelling aftershave mixed with it.

"Erasis, the drug she mentioned, fits perfectly with my erythromycin theory," said Kervinen. "It would certainly increase the effect of the alcohol and benzodiazepines. If she'd been found in her bed, you'd think she just wanted to guarantee herself a good night's sleep by taking a double dose of benzos and booze. You might also suspect suicide. But how did she get outside, and what would explain the scrapes on her back and buttocks? They were fresh and they bled, so they occurred before she died, presumably after she lost consciousness."

"Could she have dragged herself there? Maybe the medicine paralyzed her or—"

"No. I'll look at the ankles again carefully though. That might give us an answer," said Kervinen.

"Like what?"

"Depressions or broken tissue could show someone dragged her under the tree or wherever it was you found her. Were there any marks on the ground?"

I shook my head. "The rain softened the snow so much it was hard to tell anything. Show me her back."

Kervinen handled the dead flesh with nonchalant professionalism. I tried not to look at the long cuts the autopsy tools had made in Elina's skin—or the minimal stitching that patched them up. Next to the autopsy incisions, the scratches on her back looked insignificant.

"Based on my examination, she was a healthy, fit woman. She doesn't appear to have smoked or drunk more than usual, and she had good muscle tone," Kervinen said while I made a mental note to ask who had undressed Elina's body and what her robe and nightgown had revealed. They would be ripped in the back if she'd been dragged through the forest. "There was one strange thing though. I didn't find any explanation in her records for the cervix."

I stared at Kervinen. "Cervix? What do you mean?"

"According to her records, Rosberg never had children or any uterine surgeries. The orifice of a woman's uterus who hasn't given birth is sort of round and tight, but Rosberg's was stretched like a woman who'd had at least one child."

"Are you saying she gave birth?" I asked.

Kervinen's embarrassed gaze wandered the room, avoiding mine. "As I said before, I'm not a gynecologist. The stretching could have come from something else, such as surgery. If you think it's important, I can call in a specialist to have a look."

"Yes, do that," I said. "I don't know what's going to be important. Maybe it was a miscarriage."

"That should show in her medical records too," Kervinen pointed out.

I would have liked to continue speculating with Kervinen, but Aira and Johanna were waiting, and I had other things to do. As I stepped into the corridor, the cold, artificial light of the institute enveloped me and dispelled the thought that had momentarily popped into my mind. Elina couldn't have had a child. That would have shown up in the population registry too. And why did Kervinen act so embarrassed when he talked about pregnancy? He was a doctor! Most doctors I knew were either emphatically businesslike or flippant when the subject came up. Kervinen was the only one I knew who got nervous.

Aira was sitting in the lobby staring into space, and Johanna was nowhere to be seen. I sat down next to Aira, searching her face for any signs of shock. She was obviously upset, but I didn't detect anything abnormal.

"Did Johanna go to the restroom?" I asked.

"Johanna." Aira said the name as if it meant nothing to her. "Oh yes, Johanna. She wasn't here when I came back."

So Aira wasn't as strong as she seemed outwardly. She was upset. But where on earth was Johanna? I wanted to get back to the police station and start my interviews. This was going to be a busy day even without delays. But we couldn't just leave Johanna. She had no way of getting back to the Espoo Police Station, and I wanted to interview her too.

"Wait here. I'll find her."

I looked for Johanna in the nearest women's restroom and then the other one, with no success. Crap. I knew there was a café. Maybe Johanna had gone there. I wandered in what I thought was the right direction, but after five minutes I became hopelessly lost. I finally asked directions from an amused orderly. I was grateful violent crime detectives didn't have to wear uniforms; there was something tragically comic about a police officer lost in a forensic medical center. I hated revealing my ignorance by asking for directions.

When I finally made the turn into the hallway leading to the café, I saw Johanna standing near the entrance staring at a painting hung on the wall. I walked up to her, but she didn't seem to notice me. I turned to the painting. The stylized näivist image depicted a happy brood of children frolicking in a flowery meadow. Tears streamed from Johanna's eyes, and the collar of her gray coat was completely wet with them. When I placed my hand on her shoulder, she didn't react. My voice finally snapped her out of her obvious misery.

"Time to go, Johanna. Nice picture." Nice picture. That sounded so stupid! When would I learn how to deal with people who were hurting? Why couldn't I just say how sorry I was for her loss? I could handle hard-bitten repeat offenders and slick white-collar criminals, but comforting someone in pain was beyond me. Grief left me mute and shy, irrationally fumbling for words and running away instead of moving closer.

Fortunately Johanna obediently accompanied me down the hall. She was clearly accustomed to following orders. Aira was waiting where I'd left her, and we silently marched out to the car in the rain and drove back to the station.

When we arrived, I asked Johanna whether she wanted to be interviewed first as she'd waited so long at the morgue.

"Waiting doesn't bother me," she said quietly. Then a little more loudly, "It's nice having time to just sit and be."

Although the Espoo Police Station was new, the interrogation rooms were bleak, sterile white boxes. At least the chairs were comfortable. I was setting up the interview recorder's microphones when Ström walked in, shoving the last piece of a meat turnover into his mouth. My stomach growled. I asked Aira whether she wanted coffee. She asked for a glass of water instead.

To begin, I recited the date and time of the interview for the recorder and asked Aira to provide her basic information.

"Aira Elina Rosberg, born February second, 1925. Profession: nurse, retired. Unmarried." Reeling off her official information for the recorder almost seemed to amuse Aira.

"Elina was named after you?" I asked.

"It's a common name in my mother's family, and I am . . . I was Elina's godmother." Aira's steady voice cracked. "Talking about her in the past tense is going to take some getting used to."

"Do you know who will inherit Elina's property? Did she leave a will?"

"I believe so, yes. You should ask the family lawyer, Juha Saario. The firm's name is Saario and Ståhlberg. You can find them in the phone book." Aira barely seemed aware of what she was saying; her mind was so far away.

I wrote down the name of the law office and started running through the events of Boxing Day again. Aira didn't have anything new to add. But after half an hour of questioning, she awoke suddenly from her daze. Opening her handbag, she interrupted me.

"There's something I need to show you, Maria. When Elina disappeared, we didn't find any kind of note from her. But I found this in my purse this morning." She pulled out a white envelope with "Aira" printed on it in blue ballpoint pen. I reached to take it, but Aira squeezed it tight.

"I only carry a purse when I go out, and I haven't left home since Christmas. I didn't open it until I got in the car this morning. That's when I found this. Look!"

Aira handed the envelope to me. Inside was a handwritten note that read: "Dear Aira, after everything I've heard, I can't go on with this. I'm sorry for all the trouble I caused. Elina." It looked like a suicide note.

I read it again. "After everything I've heard, I can't go on with this." What had Elina heard that was so damaging it made her commit suicide? My thoughts returned to Joona Kirstilä, whom both Aira and Milla claimed Elina met that night. Could Elina have committed suicide because Kirstilä said he was leaving her? That was hard to imagine.

"What do you think this letter means? Do you think it's a suicide note?" I asked. "What did Elina hear? It sounds like she expects you to know what she's referring to."

Aira shook her head impatiently. "Joona . . ."

"Did Kirstilä intend to leave her?" I realized I was putting words in Aira's mouth when Ström made a warning sound next to me. I had forgotten he was even there. Aira nodded, looking uncomfortable.

"Did you see Elina again after she came in from that walk?" I asked.

"I already told you I didn't! But before Christmas she'd talked about the relationship ending."

"But that's a classic cause of depression!" I said. "Why didn't you mention this from the beginning?"

"I didn't want to blame Joona." Aira's voice was both sad and hollow. She began crying, the tears bursting out as though from a faucet that was suddenly twisted on. I just sat in my chair and watched while Ström sat next to me staring at the floor. Only when Aira had cried for a couple of minutes did I have the sense to ask whether she wanted anything, a tissue or another glass of water. She shook her head and pulled a handkerchief out of her purse.

"I'm sorry. I'm so sorry," she repeated mechanically as she dried her eyes. I mumbled an attempt at something consoling. Ström pushed his chair back with a clatter and said he would get Aira another glass of water. At that point, I turned off the recorder. I tried not to watch as Aira forced herself to calm down. When I asked, she said haltingly that she would prefer to end the interview unless it was imperative we continue.

"Someone can bring Johanna back to Rosberga if you'd like to go home now," I said.

"I think I'll take a little walk while I wait for her. I don't think I should be driving in this state." In a couple of quick gulps, Aira drank the water Ström brought. Her hands were shaking.

I sent Ström to fetch Johanna for her interview. I watched as the women exchanged a few words in the hallway. It was almost twelve, and Milla was supposed to be at the station by one. I was never going to have time to eat between interviews, let alone stop at the pharmacy. Crap.

Johanna removed her coat and scarf. The dress she revealed was so outdated that in a few years it would be back in style. A couple of curls were trying to escape her drab blond bun, which wasn't pulled as tight today. I had heard that natural curls usually straightened after a woman had a baby, but nine pregnancies had done nothing to tame Johanna's.

Again I started the interview by asking for personal information. Johanna's birth date made me swallow; she really was only a year and a half older than me.

"You were eighteen when you had your oldest child?" I asked.

"I was nineteen. Leevi and I got married two weeks after I graduated from high school. Johannes came the next March."

"Have you been in contact with your children recently?"

For a moment joy flashed in Johanna's eyes, its light washing away the deep furrows in her face.

"Anna, my oldest daughter, called me yesterday. She ran away and called from the phone booth in the village. She said they all miss me, except, of course, Johannes, who only listens to his father." Her face seemed to shrivel again, but her voice remained strong and warm.

"Anna is a good girl. Only thirteen but so independent. The poor thing has always had to help me with her younger siblings and the house, and now she's taking care of so much with me gone. Leevi's mother doesn't have much energy anymore."

Ström shifted restlessly. I knew he thought I was wasting time on small talk. But I wanted to get Johanna to relax before I brought up the subject of Elina. Besides, her life story interested me. It was unbelievable that a man could seriously believe that his wife, the mother of his nine children, dying in childbirth was the will of God. Didn't that sort of thing happen only in faraway places where women wore veils and didn't even own their own bodies? This was Finland!

"How did you end up at Rosberga Institute? Did you already know Elina?" I asked.

"Where would I have met a person like her in my little village? I gave birth to Maria, my youngest, here in Helsinki, at the Women's Hospital. It was a high-risk pregnancy too. They had a magazine there with an interview with Elina, and then one night I was watching television—" Johanna blushed as if revealing a transgression, and I remembered that fundamentalist Laestadians considered television sinful. "Elina was on a talk show. She was so . . . so calm and safe, and she said that every woman had the right to control her own body."

A snort came from Ström's direction. I knew he was anxious for me to get to the point.

"Actually it was Elina who gave me the courage to terminate my pregnancy," continued Johanna softly. "I looked up her phone number and asked her for advice. She invited me to Rosberga if I needed a place to rest after the . . . procedure."

To my horror I heard Ström actually clearing his throat.

"Did you go to Rosberga right after the abortion?" I glared at Ström, who opened his mouth but then closed it when he saw the look in my eyes.

"No. I went home. But Leevi knew what I had done and hit me . . . pretty hard. He told the children I was a murderer."

As Johanna struggled with her tears, rage welled inside me. I caught myself grinding my teeth. Ström was the one who opened his mouth first.

"You filed a police report about him hitting you, right?" he asked.

The question so surprised Johanna that she was able to swallow her sobs. "I committed a sin. Hitting me was a just punishment."

"Are you a goddamn Muslim or something?" Ström's roar made Johanna shrink back in her chair. She looked quickly at the floor.

"Mrs. Säntti is a Laestadian," I said. "Her husband is a preacher." I hoped Ström would hear the unspoken "shut your trap" in my words. But then I realized in irritation that I was doing the same thing Elina and Aira had, speaking on Johanna's behalf. I wanted to teach Johanna to fight, not silence her.

"And after that beating you went to Rosberga?" I said.

"Leevi ordered me to leave. He gave me some money for a train ticket because I used all my savings from my allowance on the trip to the hospital."

I could hardly believe my ears. An allowance? With nine children, Johanna had to be receiving thousands in benefits from the government. Where was that going? Into Leevi Säntti's pockets, I presumed.

"Elina picked me up at the train station. She said not to worry, together we could get the children away from Leevi. And Elina would have done it. She knew the right people. That was probably why Leevi killed her."

"What?" I didn't know which of us yelled this louder, me or Ström.

"Leevi said on the phone to Elina that God would punish her because she encouraged me to commit infanticide and she was trying to take his children away. And Leevi considers himself an instrument in God's hands. He killed Elina. I know it."

5

When Johanna finally left, Ström and I stared at each other in amazement. Johanna had stated over and over that her husband had killed Elina. She'd even claimed it was Leevi, not Joona Kirstilä, who'd been walking with Elina the night of her disappearance. However, Johanna had offered no real evidence for her allegation. It seemed more like wishful thinking. If her husband killed Elina, Johanna would get the kids.

Kids . . . That reminded me I hadn't asked Aira Rosberg whether Elina had ever been pregnant or had gynecological surgery that might not have shown up in her medical records. I had been too thrown by the suicide note. I would have to remember to ask about that.

"Let's go eat," Ström finally said. I glanced at the clock. Quarter to one.

"No time. Marttila will be here at one."

"Then she can goddamn wait!"

My stomach was growling so loud you could have heard it fifteen feet away.

I was about to give in when the phone rang. It was Haikala from Patrol, calling from Helsinki. Milla Marttila wasn't home. At least, she hadn't answered her door or picked up the phone.

"What do we do now?" Haikala sounded irritated. He thought pickups were a waste of time when there wasn't an arrest involved.

"Is there a super?" I asked.

"There's a number for a maintenance man hanging on the wall downstairs, but we don't have a search warrant."

"No, you don't. But . . . Hang out there a little while. Didn't you tell her you'd be there to get her at twenty till? Maybe she just ran out for a few minutes."

Suddenly the hollowness in my stomach wasn't just hunger. First Elina had disappeared and now Milla. Or could she have fled? Maybe Milla had killed Elina, dragging her through the woods before leaving the house, and now she had fled.

And then done something to herself.

"I'm not going to hang around waiting for anyone," Ström growled. "If that bitch did a runner, so what? Or was she your prime suspect?"

"No. At least not yet. She's mostly a witness for Rosberg's boyfriend's movements," I said.

"So get the boyfriend. Come on, let's eat. Bring your beeper."

"No, I'm going into the city."

Which would give me plenty of time to drop by a pharmacy on my way to Milla's apartment. Ström shrugged and stalked out.

Instead of taking a police cruiser, I drove my personal car to the Tapiola pharmacy. As I picked out the pregnancy test that claimed to be the most reliable and paid at the self-service check-out, I felt as if everyone in the store was staring at me. I wanted to go straight home to do the test, but instead I pointed the Fiat toward the Ring I beltway.

While I was stopped at a red light before the bridge into Helsinki, Haikala called again.

"We still haven't seen Marttila, and I'm not really sure, but I think I smell gas coming under the door."

"Oh shit! Get the maintenance guy. I'm already on my way!"

My flippin' Fiat didn't have a siren, but I still sped over the bridges that hopped from island to island across the bay and then turned south into Helsinki, just squeaking through a yellow light. The sky had started dumping sleet again, and I found myself behind a snowplow clearing the road and backing up traffic. As I swung recklessly around it on the streetcar tracks, I realized how senseless it was for me to rush. If Milla had decided to stick her head in the oven, what was I going to do about it?

Haikala's patrol car was parked in front of an old yellow stucco building. No ambulance yet at least. I pulled up behind him and hurried inside. I heard pounding on a door somewhere above. The elevator was in use, so I trotted up the narrow stairs to the fourth floor. There I found Officers Haikala and Akkila watching with interest as a man in a blue jumpsuit tried to insert his master key into Milla's apartment door. His hangover was epic. He seemed to be sweating beer, and you could have measured the shaking of his hands on the Richter scale.

Eventually Akkila noticed me, and that seemed to give him courage. He grabbed the key out of the maintenance man's hand.

"Let me do it."

The lock was turned almost instantly, and the sharp, nauseating smell of gas rolled over us. My stomach felt like an icy snowball had been thrown in it. I shouted Milla's name as I struggled in vain to squeeze through the small gap left by the security chain. Then I stopped to listen. Was that a muffled voice coming from somewhere inside?

"Do you have bolt cutters?" Akkila asked the maintenance man.

He didn't seem to register the question immediately. "Think I left the toolbox at home," he finally said, coughing. The smell of gas was getting stronger.

"Let me try," Haikala said.

Knowing that he practiced both karate and kickboxing, I got out of the way.

"I'll try to kick the screws out," he said as he took a fighting stance in front of the door. Rapidly bringing his leg back, he let out a yell and sprang.

But as it turned out, Milla was quicker, throwing the chain off and the door open just as Haikala launched into a jump kick. As it swung out, the door floored Haikala, who took the maintenance man down with him, howling in pain as the emergency beer bottle in his jacket pocket broke and slashed his side. Akkila and I were lucky to make it out of the way.

"What the hell is going on out here?" Milla yelled.

She had obviously come straight out of the shower, evidenced by the towel wrapped around her head and the short, bright-red lace robe she was wearing. Without makeup, her round face looked babyish and soft, but the expression in her eyes was hard.

I tried to explain as Haikala picked himself up off the floor and Akkila bent to inspect the groaning maintenance man's injuries. When I reached the part about the gas, Milla screamed, "Fucking Asikainen!" and ran back inside.

I hurried after her into the dim entryway. The kitchen was somewhere at the end of the hall, and as I moved toward it, the stench of gas worsened.

"That goddamn meathead made oatmeal and then left the gas on. What the fuck? Lucky I didn't light a cigarette." Turning off the burner with one hand, she opened the window with the other.

"Asikainen who?"

"Oh, he's nobody. Just here for the night. What the fuck are you doing barging in here anyway? Wasn't I supposed to be in Espoo at three?"

"One," I said. "And didn't you hear the doorbell or the phone?"

"I turned the ringer off after you called so no other idiots would wake me up. I was working until four in the fucking morning. Who in their right mind calls at nine?"

"Was the doorbell turned off too?"

"I never open the door unless I know who it is. There's way too many goddamn Jehovah's Witnesses and rapists running around here. Besides, I was in the shower."

I suspected Milla had arranged the whole incident on purpose to avoid the trip to Espoo, but I didn't bother arguing about it. I could just as easily interview her here since I had two other officers with me. Then on the way back to Espoo I could pick up Kirstilä and bring him to the station.

The bleeding maintenance man had hobbled inside with the help of the officers. In addition to being cut, he had bumped his head badly when he fell. Poor old guy. I asked Akkila to take him to the emergency room.

"Am I some kind of effing ambulance now?" he groused, running his eyes over Milla in her skimpy outfit. Haikala, on the other hand, didn't object at all when I suggested he help me conduct Milla's interview in the meantime.

"Take your time getting dressed," I told Milla. "This isn't a matter of life and death."

I dialed Joona Kirstilä's number and arranged to pick him up in a couple of hours. Hopefully he wouldn't take off before I got there. Kirstilä's voice was pathetic, almost weepy. I wasn't looking forward to meeting with him.

When I got off the phone, Milla was still in the kitchen making no moves toward getting dressed. She was clearly enjoying the way Haikala didn't quite know where to rest his eyes. Milla's body was more *Some Like it Hot*-era Marilyn Monroe than the current thin and trim female ideal. Curvy in the lace negligee that barely covered her buttocks, she flounced around the kitchen without any inhibitions, putting on coffee and fishing a package of cereal out of the cupboard.

"I haven't had time to eat anything. Want some?" she asked.

The smell of gas lingering in the kitchen made the bile rise in my throat again, and I knew that coffee on an empty stomach would only make it worse. But I couldn't very well go munching Milla's cereal either. For a second I considered just putting the interview off, but I thought it important to question Milla before meeting with Joona Kirstilä.

Looking around, I guessed Milla's apartment had once been a second kitchen and servant's room attached to a larger apartment. Apparently the kitchen now also served as a living room. In addition to a small table and two chairs, there was a battered sofa, an armchair, and a dresser with a TV on top. Haikala sat on the sofa and set up the recorder. I sat across from Milla at the table and tried to position the microphone so it would record both of our voices clearly.

"Milla Susanna Marttila, born November eighth, 1975, erotic dancer." The latter item she tossed straight at Haikala in a suggestive voice. Her seductress image broke down, however, as soon as she stuffed her mouth with cereal.

"How long have you known Elina Rosberg?" I asked.

"Since that emotional self-defense course where you came to talk," answered Milla.

"Why did you attend the course?" This didn't really have anything to do with the interview. I was just curious.

Milla glanced at Haikala and then at me. "I guess I didn't understand the emotional part. I was just thinking about self-defense. A lot of times when I leave work there are weird guys hanging around."

Milla didn't say anything about the rape she had mentioned at the course. Damn it. She was clearly trying to play the hard-boiled stripper for Haikala. Keeping up that role was apparently more important to her than answering my questions.

"At the self-defense course I got the impression you didn't really like the Rosberga Institute. But Aira Rosberg said you've been living there since the course. What made you stay?"

Milla swallowed a mouthful of cereal and glared at me. "What does that have to do with Elina's death?"

"It indicates how involved you were with Elina," I answered. "For example, we still can't rule out the possibility of suicide. Maybe you noticed a change in Elina or someone close to her while you were staying at Rosberga."

A violent rumbling from my stomach accompanied this last sentence. It was loud enough that the tape recorder probably picked it up. Milla pushed the cereal package toward me. I shook my head even though the extracrunchy chocolate flakes, which according to the advertisement would give me the power of a tiger, were tempting. Chewing loudly, Milla finished hers off and drank the cocoa-colored milk from the bowl. The way she licked the milk mustache from her upper lip was clearly intended for Haikala.

Milla lit a cigarette before finally answering my question. Instead of looking at either of us, she stared fixedly at the steel microphone. "I went to the course two days after that neighbor guy raped me. I called the rape crisis hotline, and they said it might help. Of course I'd already heard of Elina. I read her articles in women's magazines, and when I was a kid I read the psychology column she used to do in *Fan Fave*."

Milla pulled her legs under her on the chair, curling up as if to protect herself. "I couldn't go to work, I was so bruised and scratched up everywhere. I tried to cover it with makeup, but Rami, the club owner, said he didn't want me there looking like that. He told me to come back after Christmas once I healed up. Of course that pissed me off since it was the middle of the Christmas party season, and there's always lots of demand for private dances, but I couldn't do anything about it."

"So you went on sick leave?" I asked.

Milla grimaced. "Well, I guess you could say that. I have a fixed-term contract, and that means no sick leave. At least he promised to take me back. You don't need to say he's a shithead. I know he is."

She paused and then continued. "I guess I just stayed at Rosberga because . . . because . . . because I was afraid of my neighbor, damn it! I still want to throw up when I think I might run into him. I think Elina knew that, even though she kept bugging me to report him to the police. Before Christmas she helped me install that chain on my door."

"What made you come home again then?" I asked.

"After Elina disappeared, I couldn't stand being there anymore! All during Christmas that Kivimäki bitch stared at me like I was cheap meat, Johanna was wandering around sighing about her brats, and that other one, Niina, was always banging that classical shit on the piano or blabbering about horoscopes. Apparently I'm a triple Scorpio, which is why I'm such a fuckup. I guess it makes things easier for her to explain away everything with some freaking star chart. No one seemed too concerned when I left."

"So the last time you saw Elina was on the night of Boxing Day?" I asked.

"Yeah, that's what I said. Do we have to go over that again?" Milla raised her eyes from the microphone, and I saw from her expression how difficult it had been for her to talk about the rape. I wondered about her experiences with incest. What kind of life had she had? Milla seemed like a little girl to me despite her tough exterior. I'm not sure why. Maybe it was the childish way she talked.

"We have some slightly contradictory information about who Elina was walking with that night. You said before that you saw her with Joona Kirstilä," I continued.

Milla nodded. "I saw and heard them. I noticed them coming toward me on the road, and I didn't want Elina to start lecturing me about where I was going, so I hid behind some trees. They were so into their conversation they didn't notice me."

"And you're completely sure it was Kirstilä with Elina?" I said.

"Absolutely! I saw him! Short guy with dark, curly hair, dressed in black with a red scarf. I'd know him anywhere. Sort of a magazine cover type."

"What were Elina and Kirstilä talking about?" I asked.

"They weren't talking, they were arguing. I think it was about moving in together. Elina was saying something about how she couldn't even think about it in the situation she was in. Then Joona asked what situation, but I didn't hear the answer."

I thought it was interesting that Milla referred to Kirstilä as "Joona." How well did she know him? She'd said he was an occasional customer at Fanny Hill. My runaway imagination instantly dreamed up a scenario in which Milla and Joona murdered Elina together. But what would their motive be?

"Let's forget Kirstilä for now," I said. "Where did you go after you left the estate?"

"I told you, I hitched a ride from Nuuksio to Espoo and then took the train to Helsinki. I spent some time barhopping, and then at Kaarle's I met . . . what was his name? I don't remember. Does it matter?"

It did. Determining Elina's precise time of death was impossible, but she had probably succumbed to the cold sometime in the early morning hours of the twenty-seventh. Milla could be lying. Maybe she didn't go to Helsinki at all. I quizzed her about who gave her a ride—apparently a man who lived near the estate—the bars she had been to, and the man she spent the night with. Milla couldn't remember anything other the man's nickname, Jorkka, and an apartment building near the Kulosaari metro station.

Just as we finished the interview, Akkila returned from his trip to the hospital.

"Go with Akkila to see if you can track down this Jorkka character," I said to Haikala. "Take Marttila along. We'll see if he'll corroborate her alibi and—"

My phone interrupted me. Sounding even more testy than usual, Ström asked where the hell I was. Between my hunger, my anxiety about the pregnancy test, and my general irritation with Ström, I suddenly erupted. Ström was a perfect person to vent at.

"Don't you have any goddamn thing better to do than call people and interrupt them when they're working?" I shouted into the phone. "I'm picking up Kirstilä, and I'll be at the station in an hour—if Your Majesty can see fit to wait that long. Remember, you volunteered to work with me on this!"

"You're in no position to be giving me orders, Kallio," Ström retorted. He was right. Ström was technically above me in the police hierarchy. But in our unit's organization we were equal—neither of us was the other's boss. Sometimes I thought a clear line of authority one way or the other would be easier than our current back-and-forth, always trying to have the last word.

The guys from Patrol had listened to me scream with their mouths hanging open. At least Milla was in the other room changing her clothes.

After I hung up, I filled a glass of water from the tap and drank it. Then I gave Haikala and Akkila more instructions. They glanced at each other, grinning like embarrassed teenagers. Obviously they found it titillating to track down Milla's one-night stand. And I had no doubt Milla would enjoy further embarrassing the young officers. But I didn't have time to hang around to play chaperone. I wanted to find out why Joona Kirstilä had lied to me.

"Hey, Kallio, or whatever your name is," Milla suddenly yelled from the bedroom. "Come in here a sec!"

Milla's room was a high, narrow box that barely had space for the wide bed, which was draped with a black satin bedspread. Both the black satin and the dim red lighting made the room look more like a turn-of-the-century Paris bordello than a woman's bedroom.

Milla was dressed in black tights and a top resembling a corset. Her mounded breasts looked like two handballs. Her black eye shadow and dark-brown lips gave her the look of a rebellious teenager.

Milla added another layer of color to her lashes before addressing me. "Um . . . How have Aira and Johanna taken Elina's death?"

"How does anybody take the death of a friend? They're in shock. They cry a lot. How are you taking it?" I said.

"I wasn't that close to her." Milla's tone was defensive. She wrapped a bright-red chiffon scarf around her neck and then wrinkled her nose at her reflection in the mirror.

"You don't have to be family to mourn," I said.

"What makes you think I'm mourning?" Milla pulled a pair of black boots with chunky high heels out from under the bed and put them on. "The whole thing is a pain in the ass. I mean, I've got cops in my apartment. And please, don't ever call me before two again. I have to sleep or I won't have the energy to do my job."

Milla clacked past me and in an artificially seductive voice told the officers she was ready to go. The hall outside smelled like beer. Unlocking my car, I decided to stop at a McDonald's on the way to Kirstilä's place. My brain was going to shut down if I didn't eat something soon. I inhaled a double cheeseburger and a large order of fries in less than two minutes. It wasn't until I was devouring the last bites that it occurred to me that if I were pregnant I should start living more healthily. But was I? I glanced at my watch. The test promised results in minutes. What if I just snuck into the bathroom here?

I laughed to myself at the thought. A pregnancy test at McDonald's? Maybe I just needed to forget my own life for a few more hours and focus on Elina's death and questioning Joona Kirstilä. The case had made the cover of both Helsinki tabloids today. The content of the stories was the same: famous feminist psychologist found dead under suspicious circumstances. Police investigation underway. One tabloid hinted salaciously about a lack of clothing on the body, as if Elina had been caught in the middle of an orgy.

Kirstilä was waiting for me at the front door of his apartment building. He looked small and fragile in his black coat. The ubiquitous red scarf flapped as a gust of wind blew from the bay. Kirstilä's face was even paler than usual, and he avoided my eyes as he climbed into the Fiat's passenger seat. We made it all the way to the highway before he opened his mouth.

"What exactly do you want from me?"

"Elina Rosberg was your girlfriend," I said. "With unexplained deaths we always interview everyone close to the victim."

"Aira said Elina froze to death. I don't understand how that could be possible."

The agony in Kirstilä's voice sounded genuine, but I stayed impassive. I've always had a weakness for beautiful men, and there was no denying Kirstilä was that. Maybe a bit too short and delicate for my taste, but still very handsome. He gave you the impression that even a harsh word could knock him to the ground. His poetry was at odds with his appearance, and maybe that was what made him so interesting. His poems had a modern masculine sexuality to them while retaining romantic echoes of the nineteenth century. He was like a Byron for the new millennium.

"We'll get into the details at the station. For investigative reasons we can't tell you much at this point." I didn't want to talk with Kirstilä before we were in the interrogation room with Ström present and the recorder running.

"But I loved Elina!" Kirstilä burst out like a five-year-old who thinks repeating his argument will move his intractable parents.

Instead of answering, I focused on getting into the left lane so I could pass the semi crawling in front of us. I wished I were driving a police car. Getting into the other lane would have been significantly easier in the modern Saab than in my rattletrap Fiat. To top it all off, I seemed to be out of wiper fluid. Fortunately we made it back to the police station in one piece.

I requested that Dispatch send Ström to interrogation room three and asked Kirstilä whether he wanted coffee or water. Kirstilä barely shook his head; he had disappeared into his own impenetrable world. As we walked to the interrogation room, he seemed to be staring somewhere beyond the walls, as if he didn't really understand where he was.

I grabbed a cup of coffee from the vending machine in the hall. When we got to the interrogation room, Ström was waiting for us. Next to Kirstilä with his delicate frame and pale complexion, Ström looked even more red-faced and hulking than usual. The poet didn't bother taking off his coat, just collapsed into the chair I indicated, looking chilled and confused.

"Mind if I smoke?" he asked, already groping for his pack of cigarettes.

"This is a smoke-free building," I said a little apologetically and pointed to the sign on the wall. We did on occasion bend the rules if an interviewee was in serious nicotine withdrawal and we thought the shared tobacco ritual might make him trust us enough to relax and let something slip.

"Of course." Kirstilä shoved his hands deep into his coat pockets. He looked like a teenage kid dragged in for robbing a newspaper stand. As I asked him his personal information, I noticed in his file that he had a criminal record, although it was all petty stuff from a long time ago: a couple of drunk and disorderlies years before and a broken shop window in Hämeenlinna when he was seventeen.

"We last talked informally a few days ago," I said. "You told me then that the last time you saw Elina Rosberg was before Christmas. Can you repeat now what you were doing on the evening of Rosberg's disappearance?"

Kirstilä's voice contained no hint of hesitation as he told the recorder that he had been out drinking with old friends that night.

"Could you tell me these friends' names?"

"OK, who was it now? At least Esa Kinnunen and Tinde Hatakka . . . Timo, I mean. And Bulla . . . what the hell is his real name? Let me think." Kirstilä sounded so sure that I wondered if maybe he had simply mixed up the days. But no—it would be impossible to lose track of what day it was so close to Christmas.

"Tell me your drinking buddies' addresses, if you know them, and the bars you visited," I said. "I ask because we've been told that you were actually in Nuuksio out walking with Elina Rosberg on the night after Christmas."

Kirstilä quickly glanced at me and then at Ström. I could almost hear the gears turning in his head as he considered how to answer. Finally he decided to counter with his own question. "Who says? Aira?"

"That doesn't actually matter. Do you have anything to say?"

Kirstilä's small hands shook and his eyes scanned the walls as if he were searching for a hole to escape through.

Ström's gaze flashed with interest. He smelled a lie and a possible murderer. I wasn't terribly surprised when Kirstilä again denied being at Rosberga Manor on Boxing Day.

"Fine. We'll check that with the friends you were out with. So tell us about your relationship with Elina Rosberg. How long had you been dating?" I asked.

Kirstilä suddenly looked irritated. "Dating... That sounds so juvenile. I dated girls in high school. I didn't date Elina Rosberg. We were lovers."

His Byron eyes looked at me, half-angry, half-pleading. Apparently Kirstilä had decided to appeal to his interrogator's feminine empathy. I did feel sorry for him. Losing a lover is tragic. I just wasn't sure he was innocent.

"I know you want to hear how long we'd known each other and so forth," Kirstilä said. "The police and the tabloids. You're all interested in the same things. Elina and I never advertised our relationship, but today some society reporter called and basically asked me to write a poem in her memory." Kirstilä's delicate mouth contorted in scorn. "Apparently they think they can draw me into their vulgarity."

Ström had had enough of Kirstilä's evasion. "Tell us about your relationship with Rosberg already," he snapped.

I was pissed. Ström's demand sounded exactly the way he intended it to: the lady cop couldn't rein in this blabbermouth so a man had to step in.

"OK." Kirstilä groped for a cigarette again and then stopped in frustration. He dug out a match, which he put in his mouth and started gnawing.

"We met a couple of years ago in Kouvola at a seminar on masculinity. Of course we disagreed about everything, but after the seminar we continued our conversation in the dining car on the train and then at a restaurant in the train station in Helsinki. Elina didn't feel like taking a taxi back to Nuuksio and ended up staying the night at my place. That was when it started." Kirstilä bit the matchstick in half and then dug out another.

"Neither of us was looking for a relationship, but somehow it just sort of ended up being one. Elina had the institute, which was a lot of work, and she had private patients too. The last thing she needed in her life was a man." Kirstilä wrinkled his brow in a weird birdlike way, and it took me a minute to realize he was trying to keep from crying.

I wondered how psychiatrists felt, how Elina Rosberg felt, when a patient sobbed while telling them the sordid details of their lives. Had Elina sat unmoved and neutral or did the patients' feelings sweep her along? She hadn't belonged to the most clinical school of psychology. In my understanding of feminist-oriented psychiatry, the therapist got to feel too. But did a police officer?

I usually tried to make my face a mask whenever a subject started to cry or freak out. Too many suspects tried to avoid difficult questions by bursting into tears or thought that by acting pathetic they could appeal to the sympathy hidden behind my badge. Aira Rosberg had succeeded—and some questions had gone unasked when she broke down. I didn't intend to fall into the same trap with Kirstilä.

"But your relationship continued," I said. "How was it developing recently? Was it cooling off or were you thinking about getting more serious, getting married maybe?"

"Developing . . ." Kirstilä looked perplexed. "Why would our relationship have been changing? We were happy the way things were."

"Where did you see each other?"

"Usually at my place. Sometimes in Nuuksio. Not in the main house, of course. In the old sauna house—the little house. But you can't tell anyone."

The cigarette butts and dark hair on the pillow . . . When had Kirstilä last spent the night in Nuuksio? I didn't have time to ask before Ström opened his mouth again.

"Didn't it bother you that Elina was eight years older than you?"

Ström's graceless question made Kirstilä's eyes open wide.

"What a stupid question. You wouldn't ask something like that if I was eight years older than Elina," Kirstilä said. He nodded toward me: "She wouldn't have asked something like that."

But Ström wasn't silenced so easily. "So you didn't have your sights on something a little younger that made you want to get rid of Elina? Do you know anything about her will? She was rich. Maybe she left something to you."

Ström's crude attempt to turn up the heat worked far better to make me sympathetic toward the subject than Kirstilä's agonized glances and furrowed brow.

"Young women and money, that's what every man wants, isn't it?" Kirstilä had taken up a battle position. "Well, I'm not interested. Elina was smart and sexy and didn't want a full-time relationship either. And why are you talking about getting rid of Elina? You haven't even said how she died. Did someone kill her?"

"Did someone have a reason to kill Elina?" I shot back. Kirstilä sounded convincing, but there were two things I couldn't get out of my head: Milla's tip that Kirstilä was a customer at Fanny Hill and Aira's claim that he was leaving Elina.

Kirstilä sat back in his seat and seemed to consider my question.

"She did have some pretty unbalanced patients. Who knows what one of them could have done? And Elina's opinions irritated plenty of people. She even had what you might call enemies in the psychology world. But murder . . . I don't know."

"What about suicide?" Kirstilä didn't seem to understand my question, so I clarified. "Could Elina have killed herself?"

Although Aira's story about finding the letter from Elina in her purse seemed suspicious, we couldn't ignore it. Perhaps there was a logical explanation for the scrapes on Elina's back and thighs, or maybe someone had found Elina and, thinking she was dead, dragged her body under the tree and was now afraid of being blamed for killing her.

Kirstilä contemplated the idea in complete silence for at least thirty seconds and then flatly rejected the idea. "The only reason I could imagine Elina killing herself would be a terminal illness. But she wasn't sick, unless you count that terrible head cold."

"True," I said. "So she hadn't been more depressed than usual lately?"

"Actually something was weighing on her," Kirstilä admitted, "some problem she seemed to be having a hard time solving. But it was related to work. She wouldn't tell me the details."

I was about to move the conversation back to Kirstilä's alibi when Ström's beeper went off. He hurried to his office to check on it, and I was forced to pause the formal interview.

"Pretty big shithead," Kirstilä observed in a conversational tone. Much as I agreed with him, I couldn't answer in the affirmative. I just grinned lamely.

"I got arrested once when I was a kid," he continued. "We were drunk and kind of got out of control. One of the cops was a zit-scarred bully just like that. I wasn't even resisting arrest, but when he dragged me to the car he managed to yank my arm back so hard it still hurts sometimes. I don't like pigs."

I didn't know why Kirstilä was trying to be so chummy now that we were alone. Was it because I was a woman and he thought he could charm me or because he knew I'd known Elina? Admittedly the first time we met at his apartment, the interaction was more like acquaintances who were worried about a common friend.

Well, two could play at that game. I switched off the recorder and leaned forward empathetically. "That isn't an excuse for lying," I said softly.

"What do you mean by that?" he asked.

My approach was working. Kirstilä's tone was questioning rather than defensive.

"You were at Rosberga that night, weren't you?"

Or maybe not working so well. Kirstilä again denied being there.

When Ström reentered the room moments later, Kirstilä was giving me his parents' telephone number. They could confirm his whereabouts on Boxing Day, he said.

"You're getting off easy, Kirstilä," Ström growled. "We've got to go to Mankkaa. But don't worry, we'll check your alibi."

"What's up in Mankkaa?" I asked once we'd directed Kirstilä to the bus stop and were headed for the motor pool to get a car.

"Another popsicle. Probably not as nice to look at as Rosberg though. Some wino, at the dump. Apparently he's missing some entrails."

My stomach did a nasty somersault. If anyone else had been walking next to me in the parking garage, I would have said I couldn't go because I still needed to schedule interviews with Tarja Kivimäki and Niina Kuusinen. But I couldn't show any hesitation with Ström.

At the garage, I turned toward the staff parking area. "I'll take my own car. I need to head home after this."

The sight awaiting us across town was just as appalling as I'd feared. The dead man's face was etched into agelessness by booze, and since he'd been beaten to death a few days earlier, the birds had pecked out his frozen innards. I only looked once because I had to. I was thankful the cold prevented him from stinking any worse than he did. A lovely start to the New Year's holiday. The Rosberga case interviews would have to wait on ice for a while.

The narrow road home was slick. The house was dark, and Antti's skis were missing from the porch. Einstein greeted me by butting my legs gently in the entryway, almost making me lose my balance.

Pulling the pregnancy test out of my bag, I went in the bathroom and sat on the toilet. Suddenly the idea of taking the test terrified me. What if I really was pregnant? The image of the corpse lying in the dump in Mankkaa flashed into my mind, and I barely kept down the vomit that heaved toward my throat. At least I wouldn't have to look at dead bodies for a while.

Should I wait for Antti? But I had to pee now. Opening the test box, I read the instructions through once and then got down to business. Wet stick and insert into tube. Wait one minute. If a blue line appears in the test window, you're pregnant.

One minute . . . Instead of sitting there staring at the tube like an idiot, I marched into the bedroom to look for the instructions that came with my IUD.

"If you suspect you might be pregnant, contact your physician immediately," the label read.

OK. And what if I didn't? Would the baby die?

Finally a minute had passed. The trip back to the bathroom felt too short, and I could barely force myself to open the door and turn on the light. Bite the bullet, baby. Open your eyes and look.

A blue line as bright as the Finnish flag stared back at me from the test window. I was already on my way to the kitchen for a shot of whiskey before I realized that wasn't going to work now either.

6

When Antti came home, I was dozing on the living room couch with Einstein lying on top of me. When Antti turned on the lamp, the light penetrated my eyelids and snapped me out of my slumber.

"Oh, you're here. Hard day?" Antti asked.

"Not as bad as it could've been. Ström was just getting on my nerves. Are you going to shower?"

"I've got the sauna heating. Want me to get you a beer?"

"No thanks."

His outing in the snow had tangled the curls of his dark hair into a damp clump that flopped over his forehead. He looked surprised. "What, no beer? Are you sick? Or do you still have to drive somewhere?"

I shook my head and marched after him to the sauna. Antti smelled like wet wool and ski wax. I considered how to phrase what I had to tell him and wondered what his reaction would be. We stripped off our clothes in silence. When we climbed onto the benches and the water hit the hissing rocks, I remembered my sauna companion from the summer before last, my uncle Pena's cat, Mikko, who had always liked the heat. Einstein wouldn't go anywhere near the sauna.

We sat quietly in the darkness of the wood-paneled room. I stared at my belly button and lower abdomen curving toward my pubic hair. There was someone in there, a tiny bundle of cells who wasn't even really a person yet. I looked at Antti's huge nose and then felt my own little snub, wondering how they would combine on our offspring's face.

Antti threw a large ladleful of water onto the rocks, and the rush of stinging steam sent me into a crouch. I had to squeeze my eyes shut. My breasts felt hard and heavy against my knees. When I straightened up and looked at Antti's face, I decided to talk. Straight to the point and without any preparation, the way I always did.

"Antti, listen. I'm pregnant."

"What?" The expression on my husband's face was even more confused than when I had turned down that beer. Nor was there the slightest hint of amusement.

"Well, my period didn't start, and so today I took a test."

"But the IUD . . ." he said.

"They don't always work."

"You know what I think," Antti said with a smile and pulled me onto his lap. His skin smelled of winter and sweat, and his vacation stubble scratched my cheek. Antti had wanted to have kids from the start, but he'd promised not to pressure me until I was ready. Antti had assured me he'd be as involved as possible when we did have a child, but he knew I was the one who'd be carrying the child and pushing it into the world.

"What happens now?" he whispered into my hair.

"I have to get it taken out," I said.

Antti released his embrace, his expression disbelieving. "The baby?"

"The IUD. Otherwise it can cause problems."

Antti's eyes relaxed, but a hint of alarm remained. For a moment I sensed what it must have been like for Johanna when she told her husband that she'd aborted her child to save her life. I felt alone and abandoned. Antti so clearly wanted this child. I didn't know what I wanted, and no one had asked me yet. This child had just appeared inside me despite my plans. For years I'd bounced from place to place, from one city and job to another. Now a child was going to shake everything up again, like a hand turning a kaleidoscope.

"As long as the baby's healthy, there's no way I'd have an abortion," I said, leaning into Antti's almost hairless chest again. "But I need time before I'm going to be happy about it. I'm still in shock."

"Of course. What's the due date?"

"Sometime in August. Thank goodness nature set this up so we have time to get used to it."

We stayed up late into the night marveling at our new situation. Antti was clearly trying not to show how excited he was, but a couple of times I caught him staring eagerly at my belly. When I finally yawned so wide you could fit a whole orange in my mouth, Antti started fussing about how I needed to sleep more.

"Don't you go nannying me now or I'll kick your ass," I snapped. I despised all the mollycoddling and pink softness associated with motherhood. Based on what my sisters had told me, the reality was something else entirely. Eeva was already expecting her second; Saku would be a big brother in April. And Helena had Janina, who had just turned one.

"At what point in the pregnancy do you start craving pickles and ice cream?" Antti asked. I decided to retreat upstairs, thankful for the excuse of an increased need for sleep. I didn't have to fake the intense exhaustion that glued me between the mattress and blanket.

The next day we were still stunned by the sudden change in our lives, and so in the end I was grateful that Antti's friends, the Jensens, had invited us over for New Year's Eve. It would take our minds off the pregnancy. Because I wouldn't be drinking more than half a glass of wine and could be the designated driver, we took the car. The Jensens lived about a mile and a half east of us in a newish-looking duplex. One of the mail slots read "40A, Jukka and Lauri Jensen" and the other read "40B, Eva and Kirsti Jensen." I wondered which mail slot the three Jensen children's mail went through, but maybe it didn't matter.

We knocked at the door of 40B, because it was Kirsti Jensen, Antti's coworker, who had invited us over. Although Antti had been to the house before, I had been forced to cancel because I was busy with work—as I remembered, I had collared a serial rapist that night. Antti and Kirsti shared an office at the university, so Antti didn't have much choice when it came to learning the ins and outs of Jensen family life.

In addition to the four adults and three children, two golden retrievers greeted us in the entryway, doing their best to knock me down. Eva, who was in her third trimester, shooed the dogs back inside. Meanwhile Jukka appeared wearing an apron and carrying a tray of drinks while Kirsti comforted the smallest of the children, who had been jostled by the dogs and all the adult legs. The noise was incredible, but it wasn't aggressive. It was homey.

I tasted my drink and then handed the rest of the glass off to Antti. Lauri Jensen, an architect by trade, took me on a tour of the house while Eva and Jukka put the finishing touches on dinner. The middle child, four-year-old Kanerva, came with us.

Although the Jensens' home had two entrances, for all intents and purposes it was a single household. Each couple had their own bedroom and study in their half of the house, along with a separate kitchen. In the middle were a shared dining room, living room, and library. The children's bedrooms were clustered around the living room. The cellar contained storage space, a large sauna with two bathtubs, and a pair of washing machines. The house was roomy and bright; the furnishings carefully selected but still casual and made for use.

"Did you plan this from the ground up, or is it a remodel?" I asked Lauri.

"When we bought it, it was sort of a standard seventies duplex, but the footprint was just what we needed," Lauri said. "When our oldest, Juri, was born, we were living in neighboring apartments, but that arrangement didn't really work. We were constantly running in and out."

"Dad, let's show Maria me and Juri's bikes," Kanerva demanded, so we went outside to see the shed too. The children had built a small snow fort in the backyard.

"Is Eva the only original Jensen?" I asked once we'd finished the tour and were seated at the table eating wild mushroom soup.

"I'm a Jensen too," Lauri said with a laugh. "No relation though, as far as we know. Eva and I met at a pride event in the early eighties. We thought it was funny we had the same last name. Then we just got along and became friends. When Eva and Kirsti decided to have a baby, I knew they would ask me to be the dad."

Antti had told me a lot about the Jensens, but I was still curious about a few things.

"So Juri is your and Eva's son?" I asked Lauri. I thought I could make out Lauri's large brown eyes and Eva's wide, smiling mouth in the six-year-old's face.

Kirsti laughed. "Yes, but in practice all of the children are everybody's. All of them have a dad, a daddy, a mom, and a mommy," she said. "But biologically, Kanerva and Kerkko are mine. Jukka is Kanerva's dad and Lauri is Kerkko's."

"And this new arrival is mine and Jukka's," Eva explained, touching her beach ball belly. I looked at my own belly, which was still flat enough to fit into even my tightest jeans and thought about what it would feel like at the end of the summer when my stomach was as big as Eva's was now. I dropped my soup spoon into the bowl with a clatter. Was I already accepting the idea of being pregnant?

"So now we've tried all of the genetic combinations," Kirsti said, laughing as she began clearing the bowls from the table with Juri and Kanerva helping. "The biological parents are always listed as the children's guardians on all the official paperwork, but we're raising them together. And it's so handy since everyone has the same last name. Jukka and I had to fight a bit with the county government before they'd put our name changes through. Apparently they felt it was setting a strange precedent."

"Four parents sounds like a good system," I said. "You probably don't have much trouble finding child care."

"We all have pretty flexible schedules. Architect, restaurateur, researcher, and psychiatrist," Eva explained. "Although my office hours have been more regular the last couple of years. Speaking of work . . . I know it's probably confidential, but are you investigating Elina Rosberg's death? We were all so shocked!

Do you know anything? The tabloids are saying it was suicide, but we just can't believe that."

"I'm on the case," I admitted. From the other side of the table, Antti's eyes telegraphed that I shouldn't get into police business. I shoveled a serving of roast beef onto my plate before adding that we didn't know anything for certain yet.

"Did you know Elina well?" I couldn't help asking.

"She was my therapist during school," said Eva, "and we've stayed friends. She was here visiting just three weeks ago."

"Did she say anything that—" I started, but when Antti's eyes gave me the equivalent of a swift kick in the shins, I stopped myself. "Sorry, no shoptalk now. Eva, do you think we could meet to talk about this more? You were Elina's colleague and friend, so your insight might be useful."

"Just name the time. I'm already on maternity leave," said Eva.

We agreed that I'd give her a call after the holiday.

Watching the Jensens' harmonious domestic hullabaloo made me both wistful and hesitant. I had a hard time imagining myself putting up with the noise, the insane mess a one-year-old learning to eat made under his high chair, or the constant questioning of a four-year-old. And yet a few moments—one-year-old Kerkko's strawberry sorbet-stained cheek pressed against my own, Kanerva's and Juri's boundless enthusiasm as the first fireworks blasted into the crisp, clear night sky, or Kerkko's drowsy snuffling on the couch—gave me a glimpse of the rosy side of life with children. It did exist. I still felt things were moving too fast, but I also found myself worrying whether the IUD would hurt my baby and hoping I'd get in to see the doctor right after New Year's.

The chaos waiting when I returned to work after the holidays was comforting in its familiarity. I was used to the callback requests and stacks of paperwork, and I was prepared for the New Year's Eve beatings and stabbings that would keep us busy after we cleared the pile still left over from Christmas. And I wasn't even surprised at the news from the county penitentiary that "Madman" Markku Malmberg had fled prison two days before New Year's. Malmberg had been convicted in the fall of three armed bank robberies and two assaults in the Espoo area. He had only been out on parole from his previous convictions for a few weeks before the holdups started. Palo and I had tracked him down using American law enforcement profiling techniques. The unusual approach made serious waves in Finland, and although it might have brought to mind some sort of *Silence of the Lambs* scenario, with supercops chasing supervillains, in Malmberg's case, it had worked.

Because Malmberg had threatened to kill Palo and me when he got out, the prison called to warn us. Why they hadn't called sooner was anyone's guess. I didn't know how seriously to take the threat, but I remembered how enraged Malmberg had been that one of the officers who caught him was a woman. Violence toward women was central to his profile. While his bank jobs were otherwise fast and efficient, he always took time to attack at least one female bank employee. In addition, one of his other assaults was a rape.

After thinking for a few minutes, I called the front desk and asked them to keep a closer eye than usual on everyone entering the building. Then I went to see Palo, who was so nervous I wondered if I should take the threat more seriously too.

"I'm keeping my service weapon with me until we catch him again," Palo said. "That guy's nuts."

I went back to my office pondering whether to do the same, but didn't have much time to think about Madman Malmberg because Tarja Kivimäki finally returned my call just as I sat down at my desk.

"I could meet at twelve o'clock," she said coolly. "I'll have to sacrifice my lunch hour since I'm booked solid."

Twelve o'clock didn't work for me at all. I had a doctor's appointment at twelve thirty. As I tried to think of a solution, it dawned on me that this was my new normal. Balancing work and family, and choosing which was most important at any given time, was going to be a constant source of stress. Maybe thinking about a homicidal fugitive wasn't so bad after all . . .

In the end I talked Kivimäki into meeting me near the Government Palace at eleven thirty so I would have time to make it uptown to the doctor's office by twelve thirty.

Next I tried to find Niina Kuusinen. She wasn't answering her phone, so I left a message and concentrated on other tasks until Palo and Ström suddenly showed up in my office. Flopping down in the chair facing me, Ström tossed a series of pictures of the body from the Mankkaa dump on my desk.

"Take a look at this, Kallio. The doc's stumped about the murder weapon. What do you think?"

Although the pictures lacked the smell, the images of the mangled face and frozen entrails pecked by birds against the pure-white snow were still nauseating.

"You don't make a hole like that with a knife. It had to be something bigger. I was thinking a saw," Ström suggested.

Ström's aftershave had a cloying smell, a little like cherry wine left out too long in a hot room. My morning coffee suddenly decided to come back up, and sweat ran from my neck to the small of my back. I didn't have time to say anything. I just ran for the nearest toilet, never mind that it was in the men's rest-room. The vomiting wracked my entire body, and I was instantly covered in sweat—under my breasts, on my thighs, even between my toes.

After the nausea passed, I rinsed my mouth with water and pilfered some toothpaste from Taskinen's tube—I skipped bor-rowing a toothbrush though.

"Bad hangover?" Palo asked sympathetically when I dragged myself back to my office.

"A couple of shots too many, I guess. I'll be OK." I tried to sound casual.

"Want some motion sickness pills?" Palo was already reach-ing into his pocket, which contained his legendary miniature pharmacy. "Take this and a couple of B vitamins and you'll be good as new."

"Thanks, but I don't think my stomach can handle it," I said.

Ström was looking at me just a little too carefully, and I real-ized he suspected this wasn't a hangover.

"Have we identified the victim?" I asked before Ström could open his mouth.

"Yep . . ." Palo leafed through the papers he was holding. "Pentti Olavi Lindström, born 1940, a ninety-niner. His drink-ing buddies ID'd him."

Around the department we called people without a perma-nent residence ninety-niners because they had to drag themselves to Election District 99 if they wanted to cast a ballot. Apparently Lindström had been crashing in a transient camp near the Mankkaa dump.

"Record?" I asked.

"Little things," said Palo. "Moonshining and petty theft. One DUI when he was younger."

"Looks like a classic booze brawl." I shrugged. "Why did you bring this to me? Ström, weren't you going to handle this with Lähde?"

"Lindström just happened to be Madman Malmberg's dad. Maybe that's why he jumped the fence. . ." Palo said.

"What the hell?" I looked at Palo. "Are you telling me he heard about this in lockup before we did and busted out to get revenge?"

Palo looked hesitant, but Ström nodded. "Let's start looking for Lindström's killer, and I bet we'll nail Markku Malmberg too. I suggest the first thing we do is pull in this whole crew of winos just to keep them out of the crossfire."

I couldn't count the number of times I'd listened to Ström bellyaching about drunks living on the dole, drinking away the tax money he earned by the sweat of his brow. So this was probably less about wanting to be a Good Samaritan and more about wanting to use his nightstick on certain people when they resisted. Personally I didn't have much interest in protecting anyone who sawed a person open, although I figured it probably happened while the killer was having some sort of drunken hallucination. On the other hand, it was probably better that society meted out the punishment and not Madman Malmberg.

"I guess we should be glad someone besides us is first on the hit list," I said to Palo with a grin. "Let's get Patrol to start rounding up winos. I'm available this afternoon too."

"Taskinen asked me to tell you to watch your back," Ström tossed out as they left, and then he added, "For two reasons I guess."

Goddamn Ström. Of course he'd be the first to figure out I was pregnant. I stuck my tongue out at his back and then returned to the rape report I'd been working on. But concentrating wasn't easy. My mind kept wandering back to Madman Malmberg, Elina Rosberg's frozen corpse, and the tiny creature swimming around inside of me. I remembered how Malmberg's eyes had looked when we arrested him, strangely pale and unmoving, as big and round as a child's. When eyes like that filled with unbridled fury, the effect was downright terrifying. As if a monster from an old science fiction movie was looking out of his eyes. And yet his psychiatric tests showed he was perfectly competent. Malmberg even had a therapist, some kind of "astropsychologist," who, with a straight face, had explained to the judge that Malmberg's violent tendencies were a result of crossed stars and a domineering mother.

Shaking my head to snap myself back to the task at hand, I continued reading.

"In his statement, the accused reported dancing with the victim, Raija Kolehmainen, several times during the evening. According to him, the victim appeared amenable to 'getting to know him better' and agreed to the accused's offer to take her home. However, in the car Kolehmainen rebuffed the accused's advances. At this, the accused lost his temper and attacked Kolehmainen."

I remembered how angry Taskinen had been when Ström asked the victim what she had been wearing. I was already worried that Kolehmainen wouldn't press charges so the case could go to trial. She was a forty-year-old single mother who now had to explain to her teenage son exactly why a stranger had attacked her. Ström's insensitivity had no doubt increased her reluctance to pursue the matter.

Before leaving for downtown Helsinki, I ate a cup of instant soup and then, after thinking about it for a few seconds, walked over to our gun safe. But even as I tucked the revolver under my arm, I wondered what help a sidearm would be if Malmberg ambushed me coming around a corner. His style was more knives and fists. Still, the revolver was a decent choice of weapon and I was a good shot again, but I didn't feel comfortable carrying a gun. Few of us carried all the time, and although the arming of police was becoming more common, we rarely had guns hanging on our hips.

Down in the garage, I met my partner for the day, Officer Pihko, who took the passenger seat while I drove. It occurred to me that I'd need to send him back to Espoo after we interviewed Kivimäki. Pihko just nodded when I mentioned it. He didn't talk much in general, and as soon as we turned onto the Turku Highway, he pulled out his criminal law textbook. Lately we'd been calling him "the Brain" because he was always studying. A double major in law and political science while trying to hold down a full-time job opened a person up to that. No one was surprised when he was the first in line to sign up when the Ministry of the Interior announced plans to create a doctoral training program for police officers.

Personally I liked working with Pihko. He never acted out of turn. Sometimes I wondered what his school grind was about. Maybe he'd slacked off in high school and only realized after the academy that he could set his sights a little higher than spending the rest of his life as a beat cop. I'd thought about the doctoral program too, but now I'd have to put off any plans like that for a few years.

A barricade of television cameras was piled in front of the Government Palace, with reporters and photographers shoving each other to get to the front. The Minister of the interior, Martti Sahala, was making some sort of statement in the center of the swarm. I had glanced at the morning paper long enough to know that the scandal of the day had to do with a dustup at a border station on New Year's Day when a bunch of Bosnian Croats carrying guns had tried to cross the border and apply for asylum. That only one border guard was injured was a miracle. The government had called an emergency meeting, and now I picked out Tarja Kivimäki's bright-yellow trench coat in the middle of the gaggle of reporters; she was practically shoving her microphone in Sahala's mouth. I couldn't see her expression, but I was sure she wasn't letting him off easy.

Martti Sahala seldom experienced this sort of media siege even though rumor had it he was something of an *éminence grise* of the current government, with more power than the voting public understood. Sahala was only in his forties, and many considered him a serious contender for the 2006 presidential election. From a policing perspective, Sahala had been a fairly active Minister of the interior. For example, he'd drawn up new police district lines during his term. On the other hand, he was one of those "never leave a man behind" types who always interfered with investigations of his cronies if there was the slightest justification. Sahala's intervention had extricated more than one CEO from hot water.

The reporters dispersed as Sahala pushed his way to his car. Tarja Kivimäki exchanged a few words with her cameraman and then turned to look for me. I suddenly realized I hadn't thought at all about where to conduct the interview. In our cold police car?

"What exactly is it you want?" Kivimäki asked after shaking hands.

"I'd like to get what you told me a couple of days ago on the record," I said. "The car is a little uncomfortable for this sort of thing, so maybe we can find a café somewhere close."

"How about the university library," Pihko suggested. "There's no one there this time of day."

"That's fine, since I need to be at Parliament by twelve thirty," Kivimäki said. "Can I eat during official police questioning?"

"Yes, but I have to admit it's a bit out of the ordinary for us to conduct this kind of interview in a student café," I said. Talking with Kivimäki made me feel a little like a fencer, one not quite in control of her weapon. Like me, Kivimäki was a professional talker, actually an interrogator, and being a respondent wasn't a particularly natural role for her. As she had the first time we met, she wanted to ask the questions and immediately began pressing us about Elina's cause of death.

"The investigation is ongoing," I parried.

"You already know something," persisted Kivimäki. "Aira used the phrase "freezing to death" and said Elina had been out wandering through the forest in her nightgown. Is that accurate?"

I just nodded as I opened the heavy door of the university library. During my years as a student, I'd spent a lot of time in its café. I'd never felt at home in the Porthania Building, where most students tended to hang out, and there were always too many people I knew in the main building. At the library café I could count on being left alone.

The back room was empty. Pihko grabbed us coffee while I set up the tape recorder. Kivimäki set a cup of tea and a bowl of vegetable stew down with a clatter. Maybe eating would distract her enough for me to fling a few of my own questions at her. To begin, I asked for her basic information. Hearing that she was originally from Tuusniemi, twenty miles from my own hometown, was a surprise. Any hint of the regional accent was gone. She had doubtless erased it intentionally. At thirty-three, she had probably lived in the capital for over ten years now. I wanted to know more about Kivimäki's background, to get past her polished, aggressive outer shell, but standard interview protocol only allowed for the usual birth date and address type of stuff. Then we went over what we'd discussed previously. Kivimäki still thought suicide was out of the question.

"I can't image any explanation for Elina wandering around in the forest in nothing but her nightgown and robe either. Or maybe . . ." Kivimäki stopped and seemed to think. Then she put another forkful of stew in her mouth to buy more time to ponder. My coffee tasted like the bottom of a pot. Of course Pihko hadn't put milk in it. "Maybe one of Elina's stray cats lured her out into the woods. Maybe she thought she was just stepping out for a second. Otherwise she would have taken a coat."

It suddenly occurred to me that Elina could have been wearing a coat and shoes when she went out, even though Aira had said they were all accounted for. Maybe someone had taken them off her and brought them back to the house. That opened up any number of new scenarios . . .

"Last time you talked about strays too. Why was she looking out for all of you?" I asked a little too brusquely, trying to break down Kivimäki's authoritative wall.

"I wasn't her pet." Kivimäki's voice was icy, but its volume and pitch remained steady. "I was her friend, not some hanger-on. What does our relationship have to do with any of this?"

I didn't answer, which clearly irritated Kivimäki, because she went on without prompting.

"I know you're going to repeat the old cliché that because this is a murder investigation, everything you ask is critical. But I didn't murder Elina. Maybe you think I'm cold because my best friend just died and I'm not blubbering. But what do you know about me? You don't know how I mourn when I'm alone, and this isn't going to screw up my life."

"So you were Elina Rosberg's best friend?" I said. "Do you know whether she was ever pregnant? Did she ever have an abortion or a miscarriage? Had she ever had major gynecological surgery?"

"You should ask her doctor for her medical history."

"I need this information from you," I said.

"Why? I never heard of Elina being pregnant. I always got the idea she didn't want children. We were the same that way."

"Who was her doctor?" I asked.

"Eira Lehtovaara had been her gynecologist forever, but she retired a couple of years ago. Elina saw someone else at the same clinic after that. Aira would know more." Kivimäki sipped the last of her tea and looked at me expectantly, as if hoping I'd ask a brilliant question this time instead of more trivialities.

This woman was really starting to get on my nerves. I doubted she went into interviews hoping for surly retorts either. And as she had said herself, her best friend was dead. I'd have thought she'd want to know the truth about that as much as she wanted to know about the government's latest budget cuts.

"I can't tell you anything more about what happened," said Kivimäki as she began to collect her things. "I've tried to think of an explanation for Elina's disappearance, and the only reason I can come up with is that someone asked her to help them. Or pretended to."

I muttered something about a possible follow-up interview, and then I turned to Pihko and told him I was staying in the city.

"You go ahead and take the car," Pihko said, his boyish face flushing with embarrassment as he added that he had something to take care of at the university. It was almost as if he were talking about something illicit. I didn't quiz him about where he was going. Instead, I offered to drop Tarja Kivimäki off at the parliament building.

"Umm, it'll seem strange if I arrive in a police car." Kivimäki's voice contained a new note of irony when she continued. "Although I suppose I wouldn't be the first person to get a ride to that building from the police."

Pulling out of the parking spot, we almost immediately got stuck at a red light on the Esplanade. Seeing the time, I realized I was going to be late for my doctor's appointment. To cover my anxiety, I asked Kivimäki another question.

"You must not have any close family, since you spent Christmas at Rosberga?"

Kivimäki glanced at me quickly, and I expected another snippy comment about inappropriate questions, but to my surprise she answered. "I have plenty of relatives. They're all still up on the family farm in Tuusniemi and thereabouts, my parents and three brothers and their families. I imagine they all gathered around the Christmas table like always, eight adults and ten children. I think it was Juha's turn to play Santa Claus this time. Only the black sheep of the family was missing from the circus."

The light turned green. This time I made it to the City Center Building with its sausage-shaped belt of a parking level before we got stuck again.

"What do you mean, 'black sheep'?" I asked. I was curious. I'd often felt like the family outcast myself due to my unusual profession and general aversion to traditional femininity. "You're such an accomplished woman."

"Well, at first my parents were thrilled because I work on television and meet government ministers and celebrities," she said. "I guess they're a little disappointed I'm not more visible, that they can't actually see my face on screen or in the tabloids. The job itself doesn't matter to them. Who cares that I'm the only one of their kids with a college degree? All that matters is whether a woman has a husband and children."

Kivimäki's tone could have punctured a car tire, but her face was still impassive. I was so surprised I didn't notice the green light until someone behind me screwed up the courage to honk at a police car. Tarja Kivimäki was the last person I would've pegged as being scarred by her childhood.

"And I can't stand their questions either," she continued. "What is the prime minister like in real life? Is the president really as fat as he looks on TV? They talk about the people who lead our nation as if they were characters on *The Bold and the Beautiful*."

The inklings of sympathy I was beginning to feel toward Tarja Kivimäki evaporated, even though I realized her arrogance was just a self-defense mechanism. I sped through greens the rest of the way to the senate building. As she opened the door, Kivimäki looked me straight in the eyes.

"Elina was right," she said. "You two are alike in some ways. I don't usually hang out my dirty laundry for perfect strangers."

The door slammed shut, and I sat wondering whether her last statement had been genuine or a warning not to take her too seriously. I was ten minutes late to my doctor's appointment, but I still had to wait. I distracted myself by reading a health magazine.

When the gynecologist confirmed my pregnancy with a blood test and said she would take out the IUD immediately to prevent any danger to me or the baby, my main emotion was relief. Finally someone else was going to take part of the responsibility for my body and the raisin growing inside it now. The gynecologist seemed apologetic on behalf of the entire medical community for the IUD's failure and asked whether we wanted to abort.

It was my last chance. They wouldn't ask again. How easy it would be—a few minutes of waiting and then I could go on like before. Instead, I muttered no and walked behind the screen to take off my clothes.

Pulling the apparently useless gadget out of me hurt, but I endured it, thinking that in just over eight months I'd be in for something much more painful. August 25 was the due date. So much for our hiking vacation in Corsica, the City Marathon . . .

When I got up to dress, bloody and light-headed, the doctor yelled over the screen, "Your job can be dangerous sometimes. You might want to ask for a transfer to something a little less exciting."

"Mostly I just sit behind a desk and talk to people or write reports. But are there specific things I can't do now?" I asked.

"Do everything that feels good," she replied. "Your body will tell you what's too much. I don't know that much about police work . . . I mean, I've never seen someone in uniform in her third trimester."

"I work in street clothes," I said, "and I mostly just need my brain. Pregnancy isn't going to affect that, is it?"

As I drove along the slush-choked roads back to Espoo, I decided not to tell anyone at the department about my pregnancy until I had to, even though Ström seemed to have guessed. It was no one else's business. I could just imagine how Palo would fuss and Ström would bitch and moan if I made even a single mistake.

After work I headed to the gun range. It was as far removed as possible from the pastel-pink image I had of pregnancy. But however rebellious I felt about the role of motherhood now being thrust upon me, I still didn't go out for a beer after emptying my ten clips.

7

When I returned to the station, I found that Niina Kuusinen had replied to my message, leaving both her home number and the number for the Espoo Music Institute, where she apparently worked. No one answered at either, and the machine at the music institute said they would be starting classes again after Epiphany on January 6.

After calling Elina's lawyer to ask about her will—she promised to send me the main points by tomorrow morning—I decided to head back to Nuuksio. I wanted to look at the land and walk in Elina's footsteps. Maybe that would help me figure out how and why she ended up in the forest. My doctor had ordered me to take it easy for the rest of the day, but even though blood was trickling between my thighs and my head was still spinning a bit, I decided to stay at work. At home my thoughts would just keep circling around the fetus floating inside me, and I couldn't bear that. It wasn't as easy to deal with my personal life rationally as it was my work.

I called Rosberga Manor to verify that Aira was at home. When I ran into Palo in the hall, I asked him to go with me.

Fortunately Ström was gone; otherwise he would've forced himself on us just to piss me off.

Palo had spent the morning with Taskinen in Mankkaa following up some leads in the dump corpse case, but there was no sign of Madman Malmberg. Palo said Ström was making the rounds of all the drunk tanks in the metro area, gathering information about Malmberg's father's final days. Although I already knew that Palo was taking Malmberg's threats more seriously than I was, it still surprised me to notice he was carrying his pistol on his belt rather than in a shoulder holster. When I looked closer, I discovered he was wearing a vest under his sweater too.

"Oh, Nuuksio . . ." Palo seemed hesitant. "That's a good idea. Being there is the best way to figure out how Rosberg could have ended up in the forest. But is it smart for you and me to be together? I mean . . ."

"You mean that Malmberg might come after me first and then go looking for you?" I said a little more ill-temperedly than necessary. Of course Palo had every right to be afraid. I was probably the one being stupid.

"I'm not your boss," I continued more softly. "I was just really hoping you'd go with me. Malmberg isn't going to follow us to Nuuksio. They might have already caught him anyway."

Palo stared at the floor. His short, straight brown hair had plenty of gray in it, and his otherwise slender body spread into a soft tire around his belly. Palo needed glasses for more than reading and driving, but for some reason he wouldn't wear them, and the constant squinting made his gray-blue eyes red and watery and gave him wrinkles around his eyes and in his cheeks. Palo had been working for the Espoo Police Department for more than twenty-five years, and he knew every petty crook and professional thug in town. He had a wide network of informers and an excellent memory. As a coworker, he was a reliable foot sol-dier, not someone who was ever going to think of anything new, but he did his job and was rarely difficult.

"How's that hangover doing?" Palo finally asked, trying to make peace.

"I'm fit as a fiddle now. And look." Dramatizing a bit, I patted my shoulder holster. "I'm taking precautions too."

Palo suggested that I drive. He wanted to keep an eye on the roadway. I threw some high boots in the trunk for tromping through the snow, although skis probably would've been better.

"We can continue questioning Aira Rosberg too," I said as I drove, "but the most important thing is to get out in that forest and walk to the place where Elina's body turned up and think about how she ended up there. We don't have a lot of time before it gets dark, but that might be good since that's when she disap-peared. Things look different at night."

"That'll put me into overtime again," Palo said. "But the wife is working the night shift, and our youngest is with a babysitter, so why not."

The children from Palo's previous two marriages lived with their mothers, and some of them might have even moved out and had their own families by now. Wife number three was fifteen years younger than Palo, and the guys in the unit claimed his vitamin habit was less about longevity and more about keeping up with his youthful bride.

The light was already dusky, and the forest along the road to Nuuksio was an impenetrable green-black. The lights of an oncoming car blinded me for a second, almost making me miss the turnoff for Rosberga Manor. The manor was dark but for a single window upstairs. Not even the front porch light was burn-ing. I got out of the car and was fumbling with the buttons for the intercom in the inadequate beam of my headlights when the gate opened. A moment later the porch light switched on.

Aira stood at the front door and showed us in without comment. I got the feeling Aira wasn't really with us. She was just a shell of a person with the heart and thoughts missing, perhaps gone to the same place Elina was. The silence in the large, empty house was deafening. In the entryway, I stomped the snow from my boots and talked to Palo louder than I needed to, although I knew it wouldn't diffuse the heavy sense of grief in the home. Sorrow had carved new grooves in Aira's face, flattening her gray hair and slumping her wide shoulders.

She opened the door to Elina's rooms for us. I stood and looked out through the lacy frills of the living room curtains and then went and lifted the blinds in the bedroom. The landscape outside the windows was almost pure darkness. You could just catch a glimpse of the shore of Lake Pitkäjärvi. When I turned off the overhead light, the darkness outside began taking on shapes. The lights shining from Aira's room and the kitchen reflected off the snow, giving definition to the wall and forest beyond.

"Palo, go outside," I said. "First inside the wall and then on the other side. I want to know how well I can see someone moving around outside."

The slowness of Palo's steps showed how little he wanted to go outside alone. I understood. I didn't want to go out either, but I'd opened my mouth first.

"Could you hear Elina's phone from your room?" I asked Aira after Palo left.

"In general, yes, but not that night. As I said before, I took a sleeping pill and wore earplugs so I could finally rest." Aira didn't even have the energy to sound irritated.

"Elina had her own personal number separate from the main house phone, right?"

"Yes. It was unlisted, and she rarely gave it out. Elina usually turned on the answering machine for the house phone at night."

"Which number did people call to reach you?" I asked.

"Me?" Aira smiled faintly. "No one calls for me. A couple of old work friends keep in touch a few times a year, but otherwise my life is here."

I jumped when Palo knocked on the bedroom window. It was easy to see him from the lit room when he pressed his nose against the glass. I tried different lighting alternatives as Palo walked around the yard, glancing constantly from side to side as if he thought Malmberg might jump over the wall any second. Watching events in the yard had been easy for Elina, even with all the lights on. But beyond the wall, all I could see was the beam of Palo's flashlight. When he turned it off, the darkness swallowed him. But had the moon been visible that night? With a moon, the landscape might look different than on a cloudy night like this.

Palo had no trouble getting the gate open with the code. When he came back in, I sent him to look at the rooms upstairs—mostly for outside visibility and possible egress points such as balconies or fire escapes. If Elina had seen something from the window that lured her outside, it had to have been inside the wall. And who besides those in the house itself could get onto the grounds? But if Elina had received a phone call that lured her into the forest, the possibilities were endless.

This clowning around wasn't really getting us anywhere. We still had to go into the forest. I had to *be* Elina. I had to know why she'd gone out wandering in her nightgown in the bitter cold.

Remembering Elina's scarred cervix, I asked Aira whether Elina had ever been pregnant.

Aira looked shocked. "Elina, pregnant? Not to my knowledge. Do you mean she was pregnant now?" Aira's eyes started fluttering with anxiety.

"No, I don't mean that," I hurried to say. "The shape of her cervix indicated she might have given birth or had a miscarriage, but we couldn't find any notes in her medical records."

Aira's expression relaxed again, but the underlying sorrow still showed behind the relief.

"That must be that old thing. I'd almost forgotten about it. When she was in her twenties, Elina spent six months in India. While she was there she had a bleeding disorder caused by a growth in her uterus. Some local quack performed surgery on her, and the scars must have stayed. I don't remember the exact chain of events, but it took Elina's hormones a couple of years before they were normal again. Her gynecologist should be able to tell you more."

So this oddity had a perfectly reasonable explanation. No out-of-wedlock pregnancies or tragic abortions. What had I been expecting? That Elina had seen the ghost of her abandoned child outside the window and gone out chasing it?

"Have you made any progress?" Aira asked.

Glumly I shook my head.

Palo's footfalls echoed heavily on the stairs. It was as if they were only accustomed to the light tread of women. Once Palo's size nine boots tromped the rest of the way down, he just shrugged to indicate he hadn't found anything.

"It's pretty damn dark out there. If someone was in the forest without a light, you'd never see it inside," Palo said. I wondered whether he'd been trying to spy Madman Malmberg out in the forest.

"Let's go out anyway," I said with a sigh.

Aira started pulling her coat on as if to come with us, but I said no. Aira was one of our suspects, after all, and I was certain she was hiding something from us.

Outside the gate, a stiff wind coming up from Lake Pitkäjärvi assaulted us immediately. By the time we reached the top of the hill, the wind could have pushed us over. I stopped to tighten my bootstraps and shove the ends of my scarf more securely under my coat to protect my breasts. Slogging through the snow criss-crossed by the shadows of trees was no fun. The shortest path to the location of the body was across an overgrown field ending at the forest's edge. Another option was to walk along the road for a while and then turn into the forest and follow the ski track. There'd been a lot of snow on Boxing Day, and as far as we could tell, Elina was wearing no shoes, so maybe she had taken the shorter way across the field, despite its steep ascent.

Resigned, I started tramping uphill with Palo. After a while we could see the lights of a neighboring house, the one from which the skier had called the police after finding Elina's body. An occasional light glimmered along the shore of the lake, but otherwise the landscape was windswept and empty. Palo walked with his face scrunched up, glancing around furtively even though we would've heard Madman Malmberg coming from a long way off. The frozen snow crunched loudly under our feet.

"I don't know . . . Maybe Elina Rosberg just accidentally took some Dormicum with a whiskey chaser while she was on the erythromycin, and that put her into a state of confusion and she went wandering? Then she sat down in the snow and passed out.

It might be that simple." I was talking more to myself than to Palo.

"Then where did the scratches on her back come from?" Palo replied, sweeping the beam of his flashlight across the closely set fir trees at the edge of the forest. They didn't look the least bit inviting, especially in the dark. I tried to see a break in the trees where Elina might have passed through, but not a single limb was broken. They looked impenetrable, as if no one had gone that way in ages.

"Let's go back and try the ski track," I suggested. "Maybe someone found her and started dragging her under cover and then got frightened when they realized she was dead? Someone completely unrelated?"

Backtracking across the field was at least easy, and walking on the road was nothing compared to slogging through the heavy snow. There was a path of sorts running along the ski track as well, making the going even easier.

Inside the forest, the wind only blew the tops of the trees. It didn't reach us at ground level. Our lights distorted the shapes of the trees, and branches grabbed at my hair. Tripping on a spruce seedling, I only avoided landing on my rear end by holding on to a scrubby birch tree. Then I spotted a pink piece of satin snagged on a branch.

"Shine your light over here, Palo!"

The scrap of fabric was small, maybe one by three inches. Carefully I broke off the whole branch and pulled a small plastic bag out of my pocket. I dropped the fabric into the bag. I was almost certain it was torn from Elina's robe. Pink satin wasn't a particularly common material for ski clothing. Of course the forensics lab would provide the final verdict.

Maybe knowing Elina's route would help us keep moving. We proceeded more slowly now, peering between the trees and at the ground. Suddenly Palo froze. The beam of his flashlight started shaking.

"What's that?" he breathed.

From the forest to the left came a thumping and breaking of branches. Someone was coming through the woods—fast. Immediately I envisioned Madman Malmberg charging through the trees like Rambo carrying an assault rifle with a knife between his teeth and the glint of murder in his pale, babylike eyes. Palo pulled his revolver. Seeing the panic in his face, I realized just how afraid of Malmberg he was.

After my own initial panic subsided, I recognized the sound coming through the trees. Even though I wasn't frightened anymore, I also didn't have any interest in mixing it up with an angry moose. Based on the noise, there were two of them. Hopefully they'd be too afraid of us to come any closer.

"Put your gun away. Hunting season is over," I said, trying for a lighthearted tone. Moose didn't frighten me, and the pounding of their hooves was already fading in the darkness. But what did frighten me was the panic in Palo's eyes and how fast he had grabbed his gun. The chance for a miscalculation was huge. I'd heard stories about cops in similar states of mind—and of the accidents that uncontrolled fear could lead to. Fear was beginning to creep into me, but I wasn't afraid of Madman Malmberg. I was afraid of Palo. And *for* him.

"They were moose," I said again when he kept aiming his weapon. "Holster your gun and let's keep going. The body was found right up here. We'll take a look and then get out of this forest."

The darkness concealed Palo's face, but his posture conveyed some degree of embarrassment as he inserted his pistol in his hip holster and turned back up the hill along the ski track.

The crime scene was the same as before: almost out of sight of the ski track at the top of a small rise was a large fir tree with weeping branches, the kind of tree we pretended was a cave when we were kids.

This case still made no sense.

"But Rosberg was a doctor," Palo said as I contemplated the crime scene. "She should have known about the drug interaction."

"Actually Elina wasn't a doctor. She was a psychologist who studied some psychiatry. She didn't have an MD or prescription privileges."

I remembered the pathologist saying the danger of interactions between erythromycin and sleeping pills like Dormicum and Halcion had been discovered only recently. Although the instructions for erythromycin now contained appropriate warnings, how often do people actually read the label on a medication?

I tried to remember how Dormicum tasted. Did it taste like anything? Now I wouldn't even be able to test that because acetaminophen was about the only drug allowed during pregnancy. But could you drink a large amount of Dormicum mixed into something like whiskey, which I'd heard Elina enjoyed, without detecting the taste?

"OK, theory number two. Someone wanted Elina to sleep and served her whiskey laced with Dormicum without knowing about Elina's antibiotics," I said. "Elina ended up delirious and basically went sleepwalking. Whoever gave her the whiskey didn't mean to kill her but is afraid to tell us because she thinks we'll charge her with murder."

"Could be." Palo was watching me intently the whole time, but I could tell he was also listening to the forest. He kept scanning for movement in the trees and jumping at any strange sound. I continued thinking out loud, trying not to feel the cold, which sneaked into every opening of my coat and through the worn rubber of my boots.

"I have two candidates for that theory: Milla Marttila and Aira Rosberg. Milla could have given Elina the laced whiskey so she wouldn't hear her sneaking out that night. And Aira admitted she took a sleeping pill so Elina's coughing wouldn't keep her up. Maybe Aira took a big swig and then gave the rest to Elina so they could both sleep."

"But Marttila left earlier in the evening," Palo pointed out.

"Yeah. Maybe she took the medicine earlier. Then again, Dormicum is pretty fast acting." I shook my head. "I don't know. This is pointless. Let's go!"

We slogged back the same way we came. The moon was nearly full and was now peeking out from behind a cloud. The forest was still very dark. On Boxing Day it would have been barely half full, so it wouldn't have been a particularly good light source. We hadn't found a flashlight on Elina, but of course someone could have taken it. I would have to ask Aira whether any flashlights were missing.

More lights were shining in the house by now, as if Aira had lit the lamps to guide us back. Enclosed within its walls, the house looked inviting and warm, a refuge where neither frost nor Madman Malmberg could threaten us. But that was only an illusion. Evil had slipped through the walls of Rosberga Manor and had somehow lured Elina into the forest to die.

"Flashlights? I hadn't thought of that," Aira said as we sat in the kitchen holding cups of tea. Palo stared dubiously at his.

Maybe my theory about Aira and the whiskey had put him on guard. I let the warmth soak from the ceramic cup into my hands, occasionally pressing my numb cheek against it too.

"We have several flashlights so course participants can go out for walks. I don't know exactly how many, but I could collect them all and see if any seem to be missing."

"You said you took a sleeping pill that night. Did you wash it down with whiskey?" I asked.

"Whiskey?" Aira sounded dismayed. "I don't really drink alcohol. Sometimes a glass of wine or a drop of cognac, but I've only tasted whiskey once."

"Did Elina drink whiskey?" I asked.

"She did like whiskey, but she was particular about her brands. Only Scottish whiskeys and preferably malt. Sometimes I'd buy her a bottle of Laphroaig."

"Did she have any tucked away at the time?"

"Certainly. I bought her a bottle for Christmas. Just a moment." Aira rose and opened an upper cabinet. Inside were a few bottles of wine, a half-drunk Meukow, and an almost-full Laphroaig. I could almost taste its deep, smoky flavor on my tongue, but guilt immediately followed the illusion of pleasure. Delicacies like that would be off-limits until August—or longer if I intended to nurse.

"Who'll drink the rest of this now?" Aira said to herself. "Elina had a glass with Tarja Kivimäki on Christmas Eve. Maybe she'd like it."

Aira put the bottle back in the cupboard and sat down again. "I've been writing letters and making telephone calls all day canceling the spring courses. No one could ever replace Elina. I don't know what'll happen to Rosberga."

"Unless Elina stated otherwise in her will, then I assume you'll inherit all of this," I said more pointedly than I really intended.

"Yes," said Aira. She seemed unperturbed by my statement. "It would feel strange to move away. Other than a few years, I've lived here my whole life. After nursing school I worked at Meilahti Hospital for a while, but then my father got sick, and then my mother. I cared for them, and then Elina's mother, who suffered from leukemia for years. My brother, Elina's father I mean, never would have survived alone. When he died ten years ago, Elina and I sold most of the farmland. I worked for a few years before retiring—Elina found me a position at a private rest home in north Espoo so I could easily commute from here. I was born in this house and would prefer to die here too. But—"

The banging of the front door interrupted Aira's musings. Footsteps sounded, and at first I didn't recognize the woman who walked into the room. Johanna Säntti was wearing jeans, and her hair was down. From a distance, she looked like a schoolgirl. But the eyes that looked into my own in greeting were still the eyes of an old woman, surrounded by a web of wrinkles.

"Johanna is leaving tomorrow to visit her children," Aira said.

"It's good I bumped into you," I said. "Will you be staying there long?"

"I doubt it. The closest hotel is in Oulu, and I'll have to take the bus back and forth to Karhumaa." There was something new in Johanna's voice, something that sounded like indignation.

"Couldn't you stay at home?" I asked.

"Leevi will likely refuse to allow it, especially when I tell him I filed for divorce. My parents don't want to see me either. My little sister, Maija-Leena, is living in my house watching the children. Maybe Leevi will marry her now." It was impossible to mistake the tone in her voice; the anger and sarcasm were palpable. Johanna Säntti was no shrinking violet. Why had I ever thought so? Transgressing against everything she had ever learned by seeking an abortion must have required immense courage.

"I met with the lawyer you recommended today, Maria. She convinced me there isn't any way Leevi can keep me from my children. Some of them might decide not to see me, but at least I'll see Anna and the little ones." Johanna's defiant voice trembled a bit, and I realized that she wasn't quite as brave as she appeared. I imagined what it would be like to know your entire village was doing its best to turn your children against you, but I couldn't.

"Do you mind telling me a little about your life, Johanna?" I asked. "I'm curious, not so much as a police officer but as a woman. I've never met someone with nine children before."

A sigh came from Palo's direction. Apparently the patience that had enabled him to stretch out his workday had just come to an end. Fortunately Johanna ignored him.

"What's there to tell? Praying and making babies. I don't really know how to talk about it. Elina told me to write an auto-biography. She said it would help me understand my life better. And I did."

"Could I read it?" I asked.

"Why would you want to?" Johanna looked straight at me. A lock of hair fell over her face as she did so, and she brushed it away clumsily, like a woman who had spent her life wearing her hair up. "If I give you what I wrote, will you tell me about your life? You're the first female police officer I've met."

I had a strong feeling that Johanna was laughing at me, but the expression in her eyes was almost childlike in its innocence.

"It's a deal," I replied.

When Johanna went to get her manuscript, I said to Aira, "She's obviously better."

"Only because she keeps telling herself that her husband killed Elina," Aira answered dryly. "If he's guilty, she thinks she'll get the children for herself."

Johanna returned and handed me a stack of neatly printed pages.

"Milla taught me to use the computer," she said enthusiastically. "You can keep it. I can print a new version anytime."

I wondered at the echo of triumph in her voice. Maybe Aira was right. Maybe Johanna's new confidence really was a result of self-deception. I thought of Leevi Säntti, whom I had never met but implicitly detested. Now *there* was a culprit I could accept.

As we left, I wished Johanna a good trip. At the same time I considered whether she could have murdered Elina in hopes of framing Leevi for the crime. It sounded fanciful, but since nothing about Elina's death made sense, why not? There was something ritualistic about a woman frozen in the forest, something both insane and sacrificial. Maybe Elina had been the offering that Johanna believed her God required for recovering her children.

Or maybe I had read too many bad psychological thrillers.

Palo resumed his hysterical glancing around as soon as we drove through the gates.

"You're wound up pretty tight," I finally said. "You should take a little time off and get away somewhere so you don't have to worry about Malmberg."

"How am I supposed to get time off?" Palo asked irritably.

"Go to a doctor . . . or a shrink. Getting a death threat like this is stressful. Anyone can see that."

I glanced at Palo, and from his expression I could tell the idea didn't sit well with him. And I understood. The Finnish police force still followed the old code: officers weren't allowed to experience emotions beyond anger, irritation, jealousy, sexual desire, and the occasional surge of joy when a family had a baby boy or Finland won the Ice Hockey World Championships. Fear wasn't on the spectrum. Everyone was afraid sometimes, but you didn't dare show it.

I was used to hiding my own fears even better than the men because everyone assumed I'd be the first to feel afraid. Maybe I had succeeded too well at concealing my fears, even from myself. Maybe that was the reason I wasn't particularly concerned about Malmberg.

"If I went on vacation, I'd just think about it more," Palo said. "At work I'm safer. Where else would I always have a cop with me? Although maybe you and I shouldn't be together, since he wants both of us."

"Maybe," I agreed, just as a call came in over the radio. Ström was on the line. He'd found two eyewitnesses for the garbage dump murder. According to their statements, a stout blond man in his thirties had killed Lindström. When presented with photographs, they identified Madman Markku Malmberg.

"Bastard killed his own father!" Palo moaned in horror.

"Have there been any other sightings?" I yelled into the radio.

"No, none. He has enough contacts to hide as long as he wants if he has the sense to keep his head down. Just remember Larha," Ström said, referring to another fugitive case two years earlier in which the killer Ilpo Larha had managed to evade capture for three weeks before dying in a bloody standoff with police. I was sure the malice in Ström's voice was intentional. I was furious. Anyone else in the department would have tried to reassure us. Anyone else would have said they were checking with Malmberg's contacts and would have him in custody in a couple of days.

But not Ström. Ström knew full well what a serious miscalculation we'd made in assuming Malmberg was going after his father's murderer. Instead, he had killed his father himself. I didn't know how many other enemies Malmberg had, but I was sure of the two names at the top of his hit list now.

Palo and Kallio.

That was when I started to be afraid.

8

As I drove home, I knew I had to tell Antti about Madman Malmberg. He would wonder why I was carrying a weapon anyway.

"How dangerous is he?" Antti asked after sitting quietly for a few seconds staring out the window across the dark fields.

"Dangerous enough," I admitted. "But he's also an escaped convict with a new murder charge dogging him. He'll probably stay out of sight instead of hunting Palo and me."

"Couldn't you get a security detail or something?"

"We don't have the resources for that. And his threat was made six months ago. Malmberg might have forgotten about the whole thing by now," I said. I was trying to convince both of us.

"This feels lousy coming right when I'm suddenly worrying about two people's safety." Antti tried to smile. "Speaking of which, when are we telling our parents and friends the good news?"

"Let's wait a few more weeks. Early pregnancy is always risky. Most miscarriages happen before the twelfth week."

"I bought some old issues of *Two Plus One* at the library book sale. They should tell us how to care for a baby."

"Antti!" In bewilderment I stared at the stack of magazines. A beautiful mother with an even more beautiful baby graced each brightly colored cover in blissful symbiosis. "Do I have to read those?"

Antti's expression was a mixture of satisfaction and embarrassment. "I've been so stressed trying to get these papers submitted and about the whole beltway construction thing, you've got to let me be happy about this," he said a little apologetically.

"Of course you can be happy."

I sat in Antti's lap and buried my face in his black sweater. The heat of his body was so arousing that I started kissing his neck below the ear, his jaw, his lips, and soon Antti was pulling my shirt up and off. Ignoring Einstein's disapproving looks from the bookshelf, we made love on the living room rug.

Sex left me feeling awake and refreshed, so I picked up Johanna's autobiography and settled on the bed to read. Occasionally Antti interrupted me with a ludicrous quote from *Two Plus One*, but after I shushed him a couple of times, he realized I must be reading something important.

I had always liked autobiographies. Voyeurism must be part of that, my innate desire to invade other people's lives. To me, the most interesting life stories were about perfectly ordinary people. A spate of these had been published in recent years, and now I tried reading Johanna's account as I would any of them—just a description of the life of an unknown thirty-three-year-old Ostrobothnian woman, but it didn't really work. The neatly printed pages with their understated lines told me far too much.

I was born thirty-three years ago in the village of Karhumaa in Yli-Ii County, a little north of Oulu, Finland. At that time the village had an elementary school, a church, two stores, two banks, a health center, and the Farmers' Society Hall, which was also used as a prayer room. The county seat, Yli-Ii, was twelve or thirteen miles away, so people didn't leave the village much. My parents were farmers, as were their parents before them. I had three older brothers and after me came one more brother and then my little sister, who is ten years younger than me. Six children actually wasn't very many in our village. Many families had ten children or more, because at least ninety percent of the people in the village are Conservative Laestadians. Our religion forbids contraception and abortion. A large number of children is considered a blessing from God.

Despite the strict religion, I remember my childhood being happy. There were lots of children in the village to play with, and I learned to bake and do farm chores. Because I was the oldest girl in the family, the role of mother's helper naturally fell to me. By five years old I could milk a cow, and by seven I was cooking right alongside my mother. I was ten when my little sister was born, and I remember being the proudest child in the world because Father didn't think we needed anyone to take over the housekeeping while Mother was recovering because I could handle everything.

I have good memories of elementary school too. Because I could already read when I was five, they put me in school a year earlier than usual. Our teachers were strict and sometimes heavy handed, but as I was a good, obedient student, they never had any reason to scold. I did have one problem though: my hair. My curls were so tight my hair would never stay in nice, clean braids. I received constant reminders about my curls falling out of my braids, but cutting my hair was out of the question too. Early on I realized there was something worldly and evil about curly hair, but I can also remember letting my hair down sometimes when I *was alone and enjoying its weight on my shoulders and the way it tickled my face.*

I got onto the academic high school track mainly because the new school system was coming the next year, which would have meant my next required grade was moving to the middle school in Yli-Ii anyway. I remember getting the best scores in my class on our entrance exams, an achievement I was secretly proud of. I awaited middle school with a mixture of enthusiasm and dread. On the one hand, I was thirsty for more learning and excited about new subjects and teachers, but on the other hand I was afraid of having to interact with sinners at my new school. The summer before middle school was full of warnings from family and community members. When I first started school, my oldest brother was already in tenth grade, my second brother, Simo, was repeating the eighth, and my third brother was in seventh grade. Simo being held back was a source of shame for the entire family. I can still remember my father's face when he heard about it and the beating Simo got.

I imagine my brothers were told to make sure I behaved myself in school. Actually, we all watched out for each other. That was always a part of life in our village. The bus took us to school at five to eight and left for home at three fifteen. We didn't have much time left to sin. In the early years, most of my teachers were in the faith too, so things like watching television in school or dancing weren't a problem yet.

But the school had a library kept by one of the Finnish language teachers—not my Finnish teacher, who was very religious, but another one who was about thirty years old and must have been selected for his position by mistake. Either that or he was the son of the headmaster's best friend, but he had certainly abandoned the faith of his fathers. The library had plenty of religious children's and young adult books, but it also had nonfiction and classics, and now and then Mr. Yli-Autio would bring in modern books too. Only the students who weren't in the faith had the courage to check out those books.

I remember my last year in middle school—my seventh year in school altogether—especially well. On Wednesdays school ended at two o'clock, but the library stayed open until our bus left. I would spend that blissful hour from two to three sitting and reading forbidden books. Mr. Yli-Autio had noticed my love of reading and gently led me away from the Anni Swans and Lucy M. Montgomerys, which I remember being off-limits too even though the characters were always going to church, to the modern young adult novels. Those had lots of things I couldn't understand, like people who kissed each other without being married, and girls who had babies even though they were single. I didn't understand how you could get a baby without a husband.

Gradually I began to see that there were many things in the world I didn't have a clue about yet. The hardest thing was realizing that the people everyone in my village called sinners or too worldly could be nice and interesting too. There was another girl in my class who was a bookworm. Anne's dad was a doctor and her mother was an artist. Of course we became fast friends. She always wanted to save the world, which included shaking up all of my narrow views and luring me into sin. My parents didn't look favorably on our friendship, but they didn't presume to say no when a man like Anne's father called them to ask whether I could stay after school one Friday for a sleepover at Anne's house. We were in the ninth grade then. By that time I had developed into a woman. I was wearing a bra and had gotten my first period, both of which I was trying desperately to hide from my father and brothers. Trying to keep womanly things like that secret feels pretty crazy now since

the women in the village were always walking around with big bel-
lies and there was a birth about once a month.

   At Anne's house I wore makeup for the first time in my life and
put on a pair of Anne's jeans when we went out on the town that
night. Anne's parents also seemed to think it would do me good to
get a little distance from my community's traditions.

   . . . He said he had noticed me years before in church and
thought I would be the girl he would make his wife.

I stopped reading and quickly flipped through the pages in my
hands. Obviously one or two pages were missing. How vexing.
I wanted to know what happened during Johanna's first night
on the town. Had she left the pages out on purpose or had she
destroyed them entirely, maybe due to feelings of guilt or shame?

   The need to sleep was suddenly overpowering. Antti was
already snoring softly next to me, a picture of a baby against
his cheek. I threw the magazine to the floor and carefully set
Johanna's story on my nightstand. I only listened to the creaking
of the house for a few seconds before falling deep into a snow-
scented, fluffy white world in which Madman Malmberg had
never existed.

At work the next morning, I finally managed to arrange a meeting with Niina Kuusinen, and after handling a couple of routine
matters, I was ready to dive back into Johanna's autobiography.
Apparently the preacher Leevi Säntti had come on the scene.

He said he had noticed me years before in church and thought I
would be the girl he would make his wife. I had dreams of going to
medical school after my matriculation exams. My admiration for
Anne's father was probably part of it. My parents wouldn't hear a

word about my plans, even though I had the highest test scores in five subjects. Calculus was the only one I didn't get a perfect grade in. My parents recommended home economics school or secretarial college, but neither interested me.

I have to admit I was a little infatuated with Leevi too. He was eight years older than me, so twenty-six, good looking, and a stylish dresser for someone in our village. He always looked polished. His father and grandfather were famous preachers and had amassed a significant fortune. The Säntti house was one of the nicest in the county. Leevi was already off to a good start as a preacher and had plans to start a family as soon as he finished building his own house next to his parents'. He said he chose me because I was the right age and beautiful in the eyes of God. Of course that flattered me. Other than one crush in school and Anne's father, no one had ever called me beautiful.

We were married two weeks after my high school graduation. The whole village attended the wedding, along with Laestadian brothers from all over Northern Ostrobothnia. I was proud to become the wife of such a well-known, respected man, and I felt like a queen that day. My dress was spotless white and close-fitting, and I managed to do my hair so a few curls peeked out from under my veil. I didn't dare wear the lipstick Anne had given me, even though I wanted to.

I was completely unprepared for what happened that night though. As a strict believer, my health teacher had sidestepped our sex talk by saying that was only something for after marriage. My mother said it was my husband's job to teach me. I'd read random things in books and magazines, and I had pieced some of it together, but reading is different from experiencing something

*personally. In retrospect, I realize Leevi was actually quite expe-
rienced sexually. He hadn't bothered to save himself for marriage
the way I had.*

*I wasn't prepared for the pain, the blood, or the shame of hav-
ing someone touch the parts of my body I hadn't dared even to
let my own mother see for years. The same thing kept happening
night after night, and after a few weeks I learned to tolerate my
husband's sexual needs. I must have gotten pregnant during the
first week we were married. My first baby, Johannes, was born in
March, one week after my nineteenth birthday. In November, I
was pregnant again, and from then on my life has been mostly
pregnancy, nursing, and caring for my children and the house.
Leevi is away a lot preaching, and although my mother, my sister,
and my mother-in-law have helped a lot in caring for the family,
I haven't had any trouble with extra free time. Usually I collapse
into bed at night completely exhausted from the ruckus of the day.*

*After my fifth child, Matti, was born, I made a discovery that
is hard to write about. Matti was a big baby, almost ten pounds,
and getting him out tore me down there pretty badly. As I was
rinsing the scars, I discovered that spraying water on specific parts
felt pleasurable. I discovered the sin of masturbation, which I've
never confessed. Apparently the sin started affecting me, because I
began having more and more rebellious thoughts. When I turned
twenty-five, I remember wanting to run away for the first time. I
daydreamed about taking the bus to Oulu, buying makeup and
new clothes, eating food someone else had cooked, and sleeping
in a bed someone else had made, between sheets washed by someone else. But of course I never ran away. I was too attached to
my children. On the surface, I looked like an industrious, humble
preacher's wife who was raising her children to walk the paths of
righteousness too. I felt horrible punishing my children for normal*

curiosity about their own bodies and suppressing their imaginations. I never wanted to make them as ignorant and repressed as I was.

My eighth pregnancy was hard. I was anemic and had some dangerous bleeding. My ninth pregnancy was risky from beginning to end. My womb was worn out from the strain of so many children back to back, and I was in constant danger of uterine ruptures. In 1994, I spent more than two months in the Helsinki Women's Hospital. It was there that a whole new world opened up for me.

I had never been away from home for more than a week, and I missed my children terribly. Still, it was amazing to rest and have people wait on me. No one was monitoring everything I did. I could read whatever I wanted and even watch TV. During that time I broke a lot of our religion's commandments, but I also learned the most amazing things about the world, like that the wonderful feeling that came after rubbing myself down there was called an orgasm.

Giving birth to Maria almost killed me, and the doctor at the Women's Hospital told me my uterus couldn't handle any more pregnancies. If I did get pregnant, the baby and I would probably both die. She was horrified when I refused to have my tubes tied and turned down an IUD and birth control pills. But she said she respected the religious convictions Leevi and I had. Leevi thought we had to submit to the will of God, but I had started to doubt that. My doubt aroused strong feelings of guilt and distress in me sometimes, but I didn't know how to talk about it with anyone. I tried to refuse sexual intercourse with Leevi, appealing to the danger of a pregnancy, but he replied that a woman's place was to obey her husband and that God was mindful of us.

Last October, I discovered I was pregnant again. It was like a death sentence. Of course Leevi wouldn't hear of terminating it. He knocked me to the ground when I suggested it, and I remember hoping that the beating would cause a miscarriage. But that didn't happen.

When my own doctor confirmed the extreme danger of the pregnancy, something snapped in me. I didn't want to die. I didn't want to leave my little children. I loved them too much. I found myself hating Leevi and my religion. When I was at the Women's Hospital, I had heard about a women's therapy center. I called their psychologist. She said I had every right to an abortion and promised to give me a place to say if I couldn't return to the village after doing it.

I knew that Anne's father had a private practice in Oulu. I left my children with my sister and didn't tell anyone where I was going. That was a first too. To my relief, Anne's father remembered me and understood my situation. He arranged a referral to the hospital immediately. He seemed to understand that I had to act fast while I still had the courage to go through with it. I would have wanted them to sterilize me too at the same time as the abortion, but that would have required my husband's consent.

The abortion was an awful experience. I knew I was committing a horrible sin, murder. I was sinning against my religion and my husband. Maybe I was looking for punishment, because I went home and told Leevi, who beat me in front of the children and threw me out. I barely managed to grab a coat. Fortunately Anne's father had promised to help, and he lent me the money to travel to the Rosberga Institute.

The weeks here have been hard. My husband won't let me see my children, and I miss them. I have a hard time bearing the burden of my sin, but I go on living because I know my children need me. They are the reason I'm doing this. There has to be a way I can get them back.

After Johanna's account ended, I sat for a while at my desk. I was so angry I felt physically ill. Although I already knew the broad outlines of Johanna's life and was aware that there were people who still lived like this even in Finland, I was infuriated. Between the lines of Johanna's narrative, it was so easy to read the humiliation, the emotional and physical violence, and her foreignness in her own skin. I abhorred religious fanaticism. My own relationship with God was courteous but cool. We left each other alone.

Someone knocked at my door. I knew it was Taskinen just from the precision of his knock: three raps of identical force, evenly spaced. I told him to come in.

"Hi, Maria. How's your year starting out?" Taskinen said with false heartiness. I was sure this was going to be something bad.

"I'm OK," I said. "The Elina Rosberg death is still my top case. I'll probably have to head up to Karhumaa north of Oulu to interview a suspect. One of the Christmas guests at the house claims her husband was in the area at the time Rosberg disappeared. I'd like to check his alibi."

"Couldn't the local cops handle it? Or the National Bureau out of Oulu?"

"I'd like to handle it myself." Only after saying this did I realize just how curious I was to see Johanna's village and meet the Säntti family, especially the patriarch.

"It's just about your security . . ." Taskinen pursed his lips and rubbed his nose, looking uncertain.

"Do you mean Madman Malmberg? He's not going to follow me to Oulu."

"We don't have any solid intel on Malmberg's location right now, but yesterday there were two bank robberies, one outside Hämeenlinna and another north of Tampere. Based on the camera footage, one of the perps might be Malmberg. The MO is similar to the Soukka Post Bank case. And I guess Ström told you and Palo that Malmberg killed his own father."

"Has that been confirmed?"

"The eyewitness reports seem reliable, although we're talking about winos here. Malmberg found his dad with two drinking buddies and then stabbed him ten or more times before using a saw. The other two drunks took off running. They didn't report it to the police because they thought we'd blame them. In prison Malmberg talked about breaking out so he could settle old scores. Apparently he mostly talked about killing his father."

"And Palo and me, right?"

"He did threaten you, along with the prosecutor and the judge. I think we should take this seriously. You know Malmberg. It wouldn't surprise me at all if you and Palo were in real danger."

I opened the top drawer of my desk and pulled out my revolver in its shoulder holster. "I do have this. It won't stop crossbow bolts or pipe bombs, but it's good against knives. If there's time."

"Palo is wound really tightly. He suggested that the two of you should work apart for the time being." Taskinen's eyes told me that he understood the reasoning behind Palo's suggestion. As a pathological misogynist, Malmberg would probably go after me first.

"What if I take the night train up to Oulu, assuming my witness is available?" I asked.

"We'll see," Taskinen replied and asked a few more questions about the Rosberg crime scene and the progress of a couple of my other cases, but I had the feeling he was less worried about the investigations than about evaluating my mental state. As a result, I played it cooler than I actually felt. Just me here, one of the guys, no need to worry.

Still, when I left to interview Niina Kuusinen, I took extra care adjusting my shoulder holster under my blazer and even thought briefly about grabbing a bulletproof vest. Luckily my car was safe in the garage downstairs. Even so, I kept imagining once I drove away from the station how Malmberg could have snuck a bomb under it during the night. Fortunately I made it to Tapiola to meet Niina Kuusinen in one piece.

The Espoo Music Institute, where Niina worked as a teacher, was located in the Cultural Center, in the heart of Tapiola. The institute was still on Christmas break, but Niina had said she would be practicing on the third floor, in the Grieg room. I frequently visited the library in the building and occasionally took in a concert or a play, but the classrooms upstairs were new to me. I had to wander around for a while before I found my way—mostly by sound—to the right place. Clarinet playing came from the Mozart room, and a piano trio was practicing in the Beethoven room, but from the Grieg room flowed a gloomy Chopin polonaise, which cut off midbeat when I knocked on the door.

A traditional upright and a full grand piano, the lid closed, had been squeezed into the tiny room.

"So you still want to ask me about Elina's death?" Niina blurted before I could even open my mouth. "Haven't you solved it yet?"

"So far all we know is that she died of exposure and that when she died she was in a state of confusion brought on by a mixture of alcohol, sleeping pills, and antibiotics. She was probably unconscious. Did you give her whiskey with Dormicum mixed in?"

Narrow fingers with large knuckles covered her mouth in a childlike gesture as her almond-shaped eyes widened. "Whiskey? What whiskey?" Niina's voice was hoarse, like she had a cold.

She had stood up to let me in the door, but now she sank back onto the wide piano bench. Her dark hair fell over her shoulders onto the keyboard. For a moment her face was hidden behind the curtain of hair until she swept it back.

"I don't have any idea what you're talking about. Did someone kill Elina with poisoned whiskey?" she said.

"Not quite." I sat down on the other piano stool across from Niina. The room was so cramped that my knees almost touched her slender thighs in their black corduroy pants. "Why did you go to Rosberga for Christmas, Niina?"

"What does that have to do with Elina's death?" Niina plunked a few discordant notes on the piano and then kept talking when I didn't answer her. "Why did I go? I was lonely. My dad was in France. He spends all his winters there since Mom died of cancer three years ago. I hate Christmas, all the fake peace talk, the idyllic family crap. All it's about is giving people stuff. That's it. I hadn't planned to do anything over the holiday, but the loneliness hit me. Elina once said I could always come to Rosberga. So I took a taxi over there."

The image I had of Elina Rosberg while she was alive was not that of a mother hen gathering the whole world into her bosom, but I could still imagine Elina sincerely inviting Niina to stay and asking Aira to set a sixth plate at the table and put clean sheets on the bed. But welcoming as she was, Elina wouldn't have made a fuss over Niina.

"So you knew Elina well enough to go to her house for Christmas without an invitation?"

"Well enough . . . I've been to a few of her courses. A body image seminar last fall was the first one. The classes at Rosberga are very . . . very intense. You always get to know other people really fast. I was at the emotional self-defense course too, the one you came to talk at in December."

"Oh." Usually I remembered faces, but apparently Niina had succeeded in hiding in the crowd well enough that she hadn't caught my attention. "What drew you to Elina's courses?"

"Elina. She was an amazing therapist. I started individual sessions in December too, but . . ." Niina shrugged. The casual gesture made her mass of hair tremble.

I wondered what Niina was seeing a therapist for, so I took the liberty of asking.

"Depression. Abandonment complex. Lack of a healthy self-image. It started when Mom died. Everything happened so fast: when they diagnosed her with cancer, it had already spread to her liver, pancreas, spleen, and lungs. Three months later it was all over. My world just fell apart. How did Kari, my old therapist, say it? The stars spiraled out of their orbits and the whole world looked different."

A therapist who talked about stars spiraling out of their orbits. It made me think of Madman Malmberg. Then I remembered that Niina had tried to discover Elina's whereabouts by looking at her horoscope. Maybe the expression was just a figure of speech from an enthusiastic astrology buff. I asked Niina about her previous therapists. Maybe one of them could tell me whether Niina was potentially aggressive.

"First I saw the psychologist at the health center here in Tapiola, but he was kind of dull. He just listened and nodded but never gave me any answers. Then I went to the Student Health Service: same thing. After that I got mixed up with Scientology for a while. That was the summer after Mom's death. I didn't have any money and wanted to sell some of the stock I inherited from her to pay for my first course with them, but Dad stepped in. Thankfully. Those guys are a bunch of crazies."

I nodded, thinking of the many insincere do-gooders who preyed on the sick and lonely by promising beauty, health, and money. How people found their bliss was all the same to me. Let them believe in benevolent beings in UFOs or healing rocks, just so long as they didn't try to manipulate and scam other people too. About ten years before, I'd made the mistake of taking a Scientology personality test. Based on their test they said I was in urgent need of "auditing." Fortunately I had the sense to decline that honor.

"Then I found astrology at the Spirit and Knowledge Fair," Niina continued. "I've always been interested in horoscopes. I think they make a lot of sense. They aren't bogus like some people think. They're a way to take control of your life and help other people. I have my own call-in number now and do readings for people. That's a kind of therapy too. But I'm not nearly as good as Kari. He has a degree in psychology too."

"Kari who?"

"My last therapist before Elina. Kari Hanninen. He's an astrotherapist. He combines astrology and brief therapy." That sounded suspiciously like Malmberg's therapist. I had seen the man in court, and he seemed seriously full of shit, a first-class manipulator. In fairness, his analysis of Malmberg's mental state had lined up pretty well with the statement from the psychiatrists who conducted the official examination. Hanninen, however, gussied up his own diagnosis with all kinds of astrology

BS. Because Malmberg was a Scorpio, by nature he harbored destructive energy. This, combined with a difficult childhood, had ensured his development into a psychopath. I had been a little surprised that the defense had called on Hanninen to testify, both because of his diagnosis and how crazy he sounded.

"Why did you leave Kari Hanninen for Elina?" I asked.

"Well, because Kari only does brief therapy, and our ten sessions were already done. He did offer to be available for me and to help me interpret star charts if I needed."

I wondered whether the Finnish Psychological Association allowed someone who practiced such a unique brand of therapy on its list of recommended providers. Maybe Kari Hanninen would be worth a phone call once I got back from Johanna's village.

"I guess I need to look for a new therapist now," Niina said quietly. The sorrow in her eyes was genuine. "Elina's death was a little like losing my mother again. I guess that's what I was looking for in her, a mother figure to replace the one I lost."

According to my calculations, Niina was at least twenty years old when she lost her mother. Maybe losing a parent was traumatic no matter how old you were. The relationship between a child and a parent was lifelong—or even longer, I guessed, since it lasted until both parties were dead. My own future flashed before my eyes again, immediately followed by fear of what I was getting into. Fortunately my job was to ask people about their business rather than having to think about my own.

"Since we talked last, have you thought of anything that might help us figure out what happened to Elina?" I asked.

Shaking her head, Niina repeated the same account of the events of that Boxing Day evening. The only new thing she said was that she'd listened to Bach's *Christmas Oratorio* on her headphones lying in bed before going to sleep. She seemed interested in discussing what might have happened to Elina, but perhaps more eager to learn what the police knew than to help solve the case.

From the Cultural Center, I walked to the nearby mall and bought a ticket for the sleeper train to Oulu. Maybe the local cops could give me a ride to the village of Karhumaa. I'd have to call and ask. The idea that Milla and Aira were mistaken and Elina had actually met with Leevi Säntti seemed more appealing by the minute. I knew I was seriously biased—I could just imagine the slick traveling preacher duded up in his shiny suit threatening old ladies with hellfire if they didn't stop watching their soaps.

Niina Kuusinen was hard to figure out though. Tarja Kivimäki thought Niina's problems were just for show, but to me, Niina seemed genuinely messed up. Hopefully the stars would bring her brighter times.

I had barely made it back on the road in my car when my cell phone rang. I didn't usually drive and talk at the same time, but I answered anyway. Maybe they'd nailed Malmberg.

"It's Ström. You don't need to worry about Malmberg anymore. We know where he is. He's barricaded himself in an abandoned cabin in Nuuksio, and he has a hostage. He grabbed Palo on his way back from picking up sedatives from the doctor."

9

Nuuksio was no longer quiet. The main road wasn't closed, but a uniformed police patrol—a couple of guys from our department—guarded the lane leading to the cabin where Malmberg was holed up. They only let me through after I explained exactly why I was there.

The cabin was deep in the forest on the bank of a small pond. It was only about a mile from Rosberga Manor. Why was Malmberg in Nuuksio? Did he know the owner of the cabin?

There were fewer police cars at the cabin than I had assumed there would be and no hovering helicopters or military vehicles. But almost everyone had a weapon out. I saw Ström, Taskinen, and Pihko in the crowd. Ström was smoking and Pihko was wearing a helmet. I asked the nearest uniformed officer for permission to approach them. The cop, a nervous-looking kid, led me to them along a path formed by cars and sandbags. Taskinen was on the phone in a heated conversation. It seemed to be related to bringing in more backup. When he saw me he came over. For a second I was sure he was going to hug me, but then he froze and turned back to his call.

"Do you want a vest and helmet?" Pihko asked without saying hello.

I nodded, and he went to get them. I asked Ström what happened.

"Taskinen ordered Palo to see a doctor. I guess he thought Palo needed some sick leave. He's been totally panicked over this Malmberg thing. But the doc says Palo didn't want a break; he asked for sedatives. Malmberg must've followed Palo when he left the police station. Apparently he broke into Palo's car and was waiting in the backseat when Palo came out of the doctor's office. He told Palo to drive here, and then they called us."

"Has anyone talked to Palo? Are you sure he's still alive?" I asked.

"He was fifteen minutes ago, and we haven't heard any shots. Hopefully his heart can handle this. He had a pretty bad arrhythmia a couple of years ago." Ström was trying to adopt his usual cold, cynical, who-gives-a-shit tone, but it wasn't working. I could hear the rage and fear under his façade. He was smoking an unbroken chain of cigarettes, although he was having trouble holding the lighter. Pihko brought me the bulletproof vest and helmet, which I put on.

Malmberg had chosen his hideout well. The single-story log cabin was situated along a narrow forest road. Someone had cut the brush back from the pond so that the view was unobstructed, and there were clear lines of sight from each window. To the left of the cabin was a sauna with a window that faced the road as it curved away toward the base of a craggy, forested hill. A good shooter could cover someone moving toward the cabin from almost any direction.

Still, Malmberg's position was hopeless. Why had he drawn attention to himself by taking a hostage? Was revenge really the main thing he was after?

"Has he made any demands?" I asked Ström.

"The usual. Money and a car. He says he has a cache of weapons and explosives in the cabin. He might be serious. He's been out of jail long enough to stockpile them."

"Sure," I said. "But he killed his father with a saw, not a gun. And he doesn't have much of a history with gun crimes. Usually he uses a knife or his fists. But that may not matter in this situation. Do we know who owns the cabin?"

"An elderly couple from Helsinki. We're trying to reach them now. We haven't found any connection between them and Malmberg, but you know places like this. They're usually empty during the winter, so breaking in is easy."

Having finally finished his phone call, Taskinen walked over to us. His eyes looked anguished; the gray was several shades darker than usual. The skin on his face was stretched like a mask and lacked all color despite the cold air.

"Maria. You didn't need to come," he said, extending his hand and touching me on the shoulder like a shy teenager.

"Where else was I supposed to go? It's just the luck of the draw that it isn't me in there instead of Palo," I said.

Finally saying out loud what I'd been thinking the whole drive over, I started to crack. I wanted to cry and scream, but the cold had frozen the tears deep inside me. Something was constricting my throat, preventing the sound from escaping. Only my legs weren't frozen. They had turned as soft as newly fallen snow and could barely hold me up.

"Maria? Are you OK?" Although Taskinen's face was close, his voice sounded far away. He grabbed my shoulders, trying to calm the uncontrollable shaking that had me in its grip. The visor of my helmet fell over my face, and I didn't bother to lift it when I pressed it against Taskinen's shoulder. His embrace felt almost desperate, and I realized he needed human touch right now as much as I did.

The sound of vehicles approaching interrupted the moment, and we both looked up. Something red and shiny appeared behind the blue-and-white police vans. A fire engine—two, in fact.

"I don't know if it's smart to pile so many troops in here. I'm afraid the situation will only get worse if we have helicopters flying around and Special Forces climbing in the trees. Not to mention TV and the newspapers." Taskinen groaned when he noticed the news van trying to squeeze through the road barriers.

He picked up his phone again. "Didn't we agree to keep the media at a distance for now?" he snapped and then turned to me. "Luckily I won't have to decide. The big boss men will be here soon. But we don't need another Huohvanainen or Larha. We were all at Hirsala when that happened, Ström, Palo, and me. You wouldn't believe how fast things went to hell. And this time we've got one of our own in there."

"But what were we supposed to do in Hirsala?" Ström demanded. "Were they just supposed to let Huohvanainen go on shooting at cops? Were they supposed to let him get away? I'm so goddamn sick of listening to bleeding hearts criticizing cops for doing their jobs!"

Ström's familiar bluster made me feel somehow safe. It shifted things back into their usual place so that the world looked almost normal again. I felt my leg muscles begin working and my voice coming back.

"The most important thing is to get Palo out of there in one piece. Who's leading the operation?" I said.

"The county police have already claimed jurisdiction. Since you're here now, you could stay with them once they show up. You interrogated Malmberg with Palo, so you know him a little and how much he hates the two of you. They should probably include you when they plan how to proceed." Taskinen hesitated a moment and then added: "If you're up to staying."

"Of course," I said. "But I have to call Antti before he hears on the radio that Malmberg took one of us hostage."

Although we'd met during a murder investigation—Antti had been one of the suspects—and he was used to my police routine by now, he still struggled with the danger involved. Antti knew I threw myself into my work and that I sometimes took risks I shouldn't. Antti was frequently more afraid for me than I was for myself. That was obviously the case this time. He was furious when I told him what was happening.

"Get the hell out of there!" he yelled. "Doesn't he want to kill you too? Let me talk to Taskinen right now!"

"I won't be in the line of fire," I said calmly.

"You can't do anything there!"

"I know. But I'm not leaving until someone kicks me out. Which will probably happen. They'll call in SWAT and the Guard, and then they won't have much use for us regular cops." I was surprised by how bitter I sounded. I guess all the negative talk in the past few years about itchy police trigger fingers had affected us all.

I was a newly minted academy grad when two SWAT team members opened fire during a hostage situation in Mikkeli. No sooner had that brouhaha died down than the Larha and Huohvanainen incidents happened, and then the poor kid in

Vesala who pointed a toy gun at the police when they tried to arrest him for robbing a taxi driver. People had accused both sides of being too trigger happy.

Around the same time, the army had started admitting women and the government was filling the sky with expensive new fighter jets. Gun clubs and mock combat training for civilians were suddenly in vogue. I wasn't the only one who wondered if all of this was connected, if society was turning more violent in general. When I was a teenager, the boys were writing long epistles to avoid the draft. We were part of the generation that actually believed the slogans we shouted at peace marches. A lot of my friends thought I'd gone over to the dark side when I enrolled in the police academy, but even I never could have predicted the obsession with guns and the military in recent years.

Ström had once asked me whether I would have gone into the army if I'd been young enough. I wasn't sure how to answer, although of course I should have expressed a clear, pointed opinion. Although I probably wouldn't have joined. I guess I didn't think participating in stupid things thought up by men had much to do with the fight for equality. And my militarism only went about as far as jogging to "Rock the Casbah." But here I was freezing in Nuuksio now, wearing a bulletproof vest and a helmet and wondering whether I could shoot the fugitive who had kidnapped my colleague.

County Police Commissioner Jäämaa arrived, and although Taskinen had brought him up to speed on the phone, he wanted to review the course of events again. Apparently the detective chief superintendent from the Ministry of the Interior was of the opinion that because the situation had a direct bearing on the credibility of the entire nation's police force, they should initiate a large-scale operation to get Palo out alive. I knew what those grandiose words meant: the SWAT team, helicopters, and maybe even armored personnel carriers. Everything that Taskinen had feared.

"How've you been keeping in touch with Malmberg?" Commissioner Jäämaa asked.

"He called us on Palo's cell phone. He hasn't responded to any of our return calls, but there's nothing stopping you from trying again," Taskinen replied. Beneath his official tone lay a thread of anger. I suspected he was having a hard time handing over command.

"We reached the daughter of the couple who own the cabin," Taskinen continued. "She said her parents spend the winter in Spain, so they may be hard to contact. According to her, the cabin has a fireplace and an oil stove that should be operational. There's no electricity, but there are candles and a couple of flashlights. The daughter says the pantry is stocked with cans of food. We haven't seen any smoke from the chimney, so Malmberg must be using the stove for heating."

Unlike the Hirsala hostage situation, we couldn't cut the electricity because there wasn't any. Dark would be coming soon, and the county teams were already setting up floodlights. The smell of coffee wafted from an open car window, and to my astonishment I realized I was hungry.

Taskinen related Malmberg's background to the county commissioner, who said he'd already been in contact with the central prison. Malmberg's threats of breaking out and exacting revenge had come up several times, the commissioner said.

"Malmberg had a therapist. Would it be worth contacting him?" I asked and couldn't help mumbling, "We don't want to repeat all the Hirsala mistakes."

"Who are you?" Commissioner Jäämaa asked rudely.

Taskinen told him before I could open my mouth, and the commissioner said he would like to have a word with me in his car. But first he was going to try to contact Malmberg.

"Be our guest," Pihko groused once the commissioner was out of earshot. "Does anyone else need grub? I'll get it. Isn't there a store on the highway?"

"Pick up a microwave and extra long johns while you're at it," Ström said.

Standing in the middle of the forest waiting for something to happen felt unreal. Waiting had always been hard for me. I was used to acting, often without much forethought. I couldn't help speculating about what I'd be doing right now if it were me in there instead of Palo. But it was pointless. I only knew the broad outlines of the situation, not details such as how Malmberg was armed. But I did know that he was acting alone. It was just Malmberg and Palo in the cabin. And it was all too easy to imagine how scared Palo was. He was a cop, so he knew how situations like this usually ended. From watching TV you might think it was a simple matter of sending a sniper scampering down the chimney to tap the bad guy between the eyes.

Was Malmberg smart enough to use Palo's knowledge of hostage procedures to predict what was coming his way? Palo had been at Hirsala too. He knew the massive operation this would touch off. And the situation was even worse here than at Hirsala. There was no way Malmberg was as good a shot as the perp in that case, but he had a hostage.

A runner from the county commissioner interrupted my musings. I was being summoned. The commissioner's car was warm, and I couldn't turn down the coffee he offered.

"This time Malmberg answered," Commissioner Jäämaa reported. "He probably saw where the situation's heading. He demanded a speaker phone. Obviously he won't let Sergeant Palo talk with us unless he can hear what we're saying. We're going to move now." Jäämaa sipped his coffee while I warmed my stiff hands on my own cup and listened to my stomach growl. "So, Sergeant Kallio, you're the other officer who worked the Malmberg case. He was convicted based on the investigation you and Sergeant Palo conducted."

"Yes, sir. The evidence was ironclad, so the case was pretty straightforward."

"But he still threatened to kill you both?" the commissioner asked.

"Yes. To be honest, sir, I would have assumed he would start with me." Almost unconsciously I was adopting Jäämaa's formal way of speaking. It made it easier, as though we were talking about someone else, not me and Palo.

"Why would he have started with you?"

"His main convictions were for robbery and rape, sir. Even during the robberies he always assaulted a woman, just for the fun of it I guess. And when we interrogated him, my presence clearly irritated him."

I remembered again Malmberg's light-blue eyes and the ice in them, and I remembered Pentti Lindström's body mangled by a saw and the terror in Palo's voice when he heard the moose in the forest.

"Sergeant Palo actually took a backseat in the interrogation. It was easier for me to harass Malmberg and get him to slip up. He had a habit of bragging about what he'd done, which made our job much easier."

"Can you offer any insight into what Malmberg is trying to achieve here? The situation doesn't seem terribly promising from his perspective."

"I don't understand his plan, sir. I would have expected him to just kill me and Palo in cold blood. Maybe he thought his chances of getting away with it were so bad he might as well attract as much attention as possible. And we don't really know whether he has accomplices waiting somewhere."

"Or maybe he just wants to die and make sure he takes at least one policeman with him," Jäämaa said coldly. There had been talk of suicide by cop in the Vesala toy gun shooting too. The theory was that the kid didn't have the guts to shoot himself so he manipulated the police into doing it for him. I didn't know what the truth was, and I still didn't know what to think of the cop in that case or why he chose to shoot for center of mass instead of the legs. He must have feared for his life.

"You've worked with Sergeant Palo a good deal, correct? Can you evaluate how well he'll cope with a situation like this?"

I hesitated. "He's been extremely tense about this death threat, sir. Now his worst fears have come true . . . Oh, have you informed his family?"

"I'm told Detective Sergeant Taskinen tried to contact his wife. Listen, Sergeant Kallio, I'd like you to remain here for the time being. We may need you in the negotiation. What was it you were saying about Malmberg's therapist?"

I told the commissioner what little I knew about Kari Hanninen, and he said he would send someone to look for him. It was miserable having to climb out of the warm car back into the biting cold wind blowing off the pond. Fortunately Pihko was just coming back with a bag of food.

"You should've brought some sausages and we could have a campfire," Ström said with a humorless grin before shoving a cold meat turnover into his mouth. I settled for rye bread and cheese spread.

"Hey, what's going on over there," Pihko said suddenly. One of the county sharpshooters had circled the far side of the pond and was starting across the ice toward the cabin. Instinctively, we shifted to watch him as he moved out of view.

"He's got the phone Malmberg asked for," I said.

"They've probably got someone ready to pop him the second he shows his face," Ström said, then reconsidered. "Except of course he'll send Palo out to get it."

We circled around up into the trees to get a view of the porch. We knew we were in the line of fire but assumed Malmberg had better things to do than shoot randomly into the woods if he wanted to stay in control of the situation. When the officer arrived in the yard outside the cabin, the door opened. Out stepped Palo.

An odd whistling came from Pihko. We couldn't see Palo's expression—all we could see were his hunched shoulders and shuffling steps as he walked toward the phone the officer had left in the yard. We could also see the rifle barrel pointed at Palo's back through an almost nonexistent crack in the cabin door.

"Goddamn it! Get to the windows and fill the bastard full of lead! What the fuck are they waiting for?" Ström cursed as Palo disappeared through the door.

"They can't just butcher him. There's TV cameras watching," Pihko pointed out.

"Damn them to hell! What are we saving that bastard for? Why the fuck are my tax dollars supposed to give him three hots and a cot for the rest of his life? They're always talking about cops with itchy trigger fingers, but what about the bad guys? It's fine for some recruit to walk onto his army base, steal an assault rifle, and start shooting up his neighborhood, but watch out when a cop hurts a hair on the little shit's head. The media has a field day then."

"Maybe they're just playing for time. It's almost night. Larha fell asleep eventually," I said, trying to calm Ström down as I waved the others out of the line of fire.

"But what if you were in there instead of Palo? What would you want us to do then? Sit out here with our knitting while you had a gun to your head?" Ström asked.

"Why don't you go talk to the commissioner about it," I snapped back.

Just then Taskinen broke away from the larger group and walked over to us. "Jäämaa talked to Malmberg and Palo just now. Malmberg's threatened to shoot Palo unless we deliver a getaway car and five hundred thousand marks within the next two hours."

"And Palo?" I asked.

"Scared. He had his handcuffs with him when Malmberg grabbed him. Malmberg's using them to chain him to the fireplace. Jäämaa says Palo pleaded with us to give in to Malmberg's demands. He was begging for his life."

Ström's face tightened, and I wondered how he would act in Palo's place. Eventually he'd beg for his life too, especially after seeing Malmberg's father's stomach sawn open.

"No one is forcing you and Pihko to stay," Taskinen said coldly, addressing Ström.

Night had started to fall, and the first floodlights were turned on. Red-gold wisps of cloud shone in the sky over the pond. Huddling deeper into their coats, neither man responded to Taskinen. Ström's nose glistened red, his giant pores gaping like dozens of angry mouths. Someone waved Taskinen back over to the command post.

"It's so goddamn cold," Ström complained after a moment of silence. "Are they setting up a tent over there or what? Maybe we could get in and warm up. Look . . . They're chasing off the reporters. Good. Maybe something's going to happen now."

A line of civilian cars and media vans really was being ushered back toward the main road, although the wind carried the sounds of angry protests. I wondered whether the cabin might have a battery-operated radio so Malmberg could enjoy his fifteen minutes of fame. Maybe that was the whole point. Palo would be famous too. I hoped no one mentioned my name in connection with the case.

Taskinen walked back over, his face even more tense than before, if that was possible. "Someone just found a body near Hämeenlinna, shot in the back with a rifle. Based on the blood-stained cash found on the body, they're assuming he's the other guy who pulled the bank job up there. His name was Jouni Tossavainen, and he just got out of prison down here. Footage from the bank should confirm the ID. And, yep, you guessed it, he was in the same cell block as Malmberg."

No one responded. Things were suddenly becoming too intense. The sound of a helicopter approaching from the south distracted us. Soon there were two circling the pond.

"Jäämaa contacted the ministry," said Taskinen. "They're in charge of the operation now. The choppers have snipers in them. They're going to let Malmberg sweat for a while before making contact again. They're also getting ready for the possibility that Malmberg will make a run for it using Palo as a shield. And considering dropping a gas canister down the chimney if—"

A crackling series of gunshots interrupted Taskinen. We all hit the deck automatically. Ström ended up collapsed on top of me. The stench of his aftershave made me retch. I lifted my head just enough to see that the shots were coming from the right-side window of the cabin. It seemed random and stopped after about ten seconds.

I quickly tried to construct the scenario from the sound of the shots. Had Malmberg been shooting out the window, or had the shots targeted someone inside the cabin? Was Palo still alive?

After a few minutes, we worked up the courage to stand. A light flickered inside the cabin. Malmberg must have lit a candle. It would be dark soon.

I realized I had to pee. Keeping carefully outside the line of fire, I walked into the dark of the forest to relieve myself. Luckily I was carrying some tissues. From there, the area now starkly demarcated by the floodlights resembled a military encampment. Here and there I could see a flashlight or the burning tip of a cigarette. Armed men tramped back and forth speaking into their phones. The helicopters had pulled back after the gunfire, but their maddening thump-thump-thump still echoed from a little farther south. I wondered if any other women were here. Maybe a female officer was out directing traffic, but I knew these situations tended to be opportunities for the all-male command and the special operations groups to play with their toys. Never mind that a man's life was at stake.

When I got back, everyone was ordered to take up some sort of defensive position, because the arrival of the helicopters had infuriated Malmberg. He was threatening to start shooting again unless they were called off. Apparently Malmberg was still talking to Jäämaa—at least I could see the tape recorders still running in the command center. Just then I noticed a couple of fleet-footed figures all in black break away from the shadows and sneak behind the cabin. I assumed they were trying to get a bug into the wall of the cabin so they could listen to Malmberg's and Palo's movements, and maybe even their conversations.

Apparently they were successful, because after a few seconds the team returned to the safe side of the barricade. Someone started forming us up into more organized groups. Although Pihko, Ström, and I really shouldn't have been there, no one bothered to send us away. Everyone understood Palo was one of ours. I also had Commissioner Jäämaa's authorization to be present in case they needed me.

Pihko and I tried to stay undercover as best we could while we watched the forces being assembled. Ström, who was unarmed, marched to the supply truck to get a rifle. When he came back, he told us that they'd spoken to Palo again and that although he was physically unharmed, he was starting to crack under the pressure. With that, Ström snuck closer to the cabin, as if to make sure he got the first shot off when Malmberg showed himself.

"What are they up to?" Pihko asked, shifting his weight from one foot to another in an effort to stay warm. His condensed breath encircled him like a cloud, momentarily concealing his face.

"Seems like a two-pronged approach," I said. "They're playing for time, but they're also reminding Malmberg there's a lot of us out here. If those mics are as sensitive as I think they are, they'll be able to hear when Malmberg falls asleep. And then they strike. That could take a while though, maybe even days."

"Are you going to stay the whole time?" Pihko asked.

"I'm already so frozen, I should probably head home to sleep if Jäämaa will let me," I said. "Is any of that bread left? I'm hungry again."

As I ate more rye bread with cheese spread and drank some orange juice, I listened to Pihko speculate about what would happen next. His vision was less bloody than Ström's, but he too clearly wanted revenge. I had just finished eating when Pihko asked if I was glad it was Palo in there instead of me.

The question was so stupid I had to clear my throat before I could answer. "Of course I am. And Palo would be happy if it were me in there instead of him."

A flashy red vintage Chevrolet pulled into the floodlights, distracting me. "Hey, what's happening over there?"

I couldn't make out the features of the man who stepped out of the car, but I could see his jacket flapping in the wind and the thick blond hair that fell to his shoulders. It gave him a sort of lion quality. I'd seen him somewhere before.

"Who's that?" Palo asked.

"I think it's Kari Hanninen. The astrologer therapist who treated Malmberg."

The previous spring I had stumbled across a TV debate between the leaders of the Skeptics Association and a group of occultists, Hanninen among them. Antti's kisses had proven more interesting than the show, so we'd turned it off. But I'd seen enough to remember the confident way in which Hanninen had said he'd succeeded in combining the science of the occult with the sciences of the soul, astrology, and psychology.

We watched Hanninen disappear into the command center tent, which was set up a few hundred yards from the cabin, and then went back to freezing. I knew I needed to leave soon. No matter how much I wanted to, I wasn't going to be any help here. And I had to pee again.

I was just heading back into the woods when Taskinen called me to the command post. Apparently they needed help profiling Malmberg.

Inside the command center a warm stove glowed. I stepped close for a moment to thaw out a little before making my way over to Taskinen and Jäämaa's table. With them was the man I assumed was Kari Hanninen and a couple of suits I didn't recognize. Near the back wall of the tent, two tape recorders were running, and behind them were two men wearing headphones. They really could hear inside the cabin.

Commissioner Jäämaa introduced me. "This is Sergeant Kallio, one of the Espoo police officers who handled Malmberg's original case. Kallio, this is Captain Koskivuori from the Ministry of the Interior, Deputy Warden Matala from the Helsinki Central Prison, and Dr. Kari Hanninen, who was Malmberg's therapist. Please, have a seat."

Hanninen pulled out the chair next to him for me. His hand intentionally grazed my back as I sat. Close up he looked like an over-forty former rock star. He instantly turned on the charm. Apparently it was an automatic response to any woman, because my helmet hair and runny red nose hardly made me flirt-worthy.

"Our goal here is to figure out what Malmberg is after, and how to predict his behavior. We also need to address which tactics are most likely to get him to surrender, or at least release his hostage," Commissioner Jäämaa continued.

Someone brought me coffee and a ham sandwich. I had just finished eating it and was walking the commanders through Malmberg's criminal past when we heard gunfire again.

"Malmberg is shooting!" someone cried. "We have a line on his head, should we take it?"

"Not in the head. Too risky. Just take cover." Koskivuori didn't even think about his reply. After a few seconds, the shots ceased.

Before we had time to continue our discussion, Malmberg called the command center. "You have one more hour to bring me that getaway car. Then I blow up the cabin. But I really don't think Palo wants to die. He even shit his pants to prove it. These charges are big enough you'll be warm and toasty out there when they go off."

Malmberg's expressionless, slightly hoarse voice echoed from the speakers set up in the tent. By the time he finished listing his demands and repeated his threats, desperation had leaked into it. I was starting to work out that something bad really was going to happen when the hour was up. Finally he told Palo to speak.

"Please, give him the car. Let him go unless you want people to die. Jyrki, if you're still there, tell them I have a wife and six kids—" Palo was crying.

Taskinen's eyes swept past mine to fix on Jäämaa's. We all knew the demand for the car was empty. Malmberg was aware that we'd put a tracker on it and he'd never get away. Of course he'd take Palo with him. But moving from the cabin to the car would be a huge risk for Malmberg, no matter how he used Palo as a shield.

Next to me, Hanninen was waving anxiously that he wanted to talk to Malmberg. When Malmberg returned to the phone, the handset was handed to Hanninen.

"Hi, Markku, it's Kari Hanninen here." Hanninen's voice was a deep and hypnotic purr. It sounded absurd, especially directed at another man. "You've gotten yourself into a bit of a tight spot, Markku. I don't think you want to die though. And the stars say it isn't your time yet."

I listened spellbound as Hanninen's coaxing voice worked to tame the beast. He clearly knew how to talk to Malmberg. Malmberg's blustering calmed, and eventually he even agreed to negotiate with Captain Koskivuori. After several minutes on the phone with Koskivuori, however, he still refused to talk about releasing Palo. Palo would be going with him in the getaway car. Malmberg asked to speak with Hanninen again.

"And what if we trade places and I come with you?" Hanninen suggested. Bravely, I thought. Every eyebrow around the table went up: there hadn't been any talk of a trade.

"This cop is worth more than you," answered Malmberg. "The only person I'd be willing to swap Palo for is that cop bitch, Kallio."

A chill washed over me.

"She's here, would you like to speak with her?" the idiot Hanninen replied. Now I turned to ice.

The others around the table started waving their arms and shaking their heads, and Jäämaa quickly took the phone. "Dr. Hanninen has no authority to arrange trades. Let's talk some more about the car."

"I want to talk to Kallio," said Malmberg.

"I don't think—"

"I want to talk to Kallio. Or do you want me to start shooting Palo's toes off? They're right here."

Everyone in the tent was staring at me.

I wasn't sure I'd be able to speak a single word, but I took the phone. "This is Sergeant Kallio. Hi, Palo. I'll see you soon."

"Too bad you parked your car in such an open place today," said Malmberg. "I couldn't risk breaking in. I was there at the Cultural Center this morning. I saw you. You know it's you I really wanted. You're probably a better cook than Palo."

"Could be." My voice was stuck in my throat and I didn't know what to say. The whole conversation was a gamble, and I was furious at Hanninen for revealing my presence. All it did was complicate things.

"What would you say if I promised to let Palo go on the condition that you take his place? I've always liked women more than men. We could have a lot of fun together. What do you think, Kallio? Should we go for a little drive?"

10

Captain Koskivuori didn't let me answer. He snatched the phone from my hand while Commissioner Jäämaa dragged Hanninen away from the table to enlighten him about what you did and didn't say during telephone negotiations with psychopaths. Malmberg refused to talk to Captain Koskivuori again and hung up after repeating that we had one hour to bring him a car.

Taskinen caught my eye, and I forced myself to smile and shrug.

"I know you'd go in there, but we aren't going to let you," he said.

"No, I wouldn't," I replied, thinking of the child living inside of me. "He would kill me even more surely than Palo."

"You should head home," said Taskinen gently.

"You're right. Hopefully my Fiat will start in this cold. But first I'm going to have a few words with Hanninen. It's about the Rosberg case."

Jäämaa and Hanninen seemed to be arguing, but I could only make out snatches. Captain Koskivuori was conferring with a gas expert. Given that they'd installed the mics undetected, they thought they had a good chance to throw a tear gas canister down the chimney, but the risk was that Malmberg would just shoot Palo when he realized what was happening.

The sound of the helicopters was growing louder again. I went to the door of the tent to see. One of the choppers tried to sweep in above the cabin but had to retreat when a series of shots exploded from a window. Buckshot rattled against its rotors.

"He has a sawed-off shotgun," someone shouted.

The tent door rustled behind me and Kari Hanninen appeared at my side. After offering one to me, he lit a cigarette.

"I'm sorry about what happened in there. I knew a female cop would cause a pretty strong reaction in Markku—that's what I was hoping for. I would have succeeded if your colleagues hadn't butted in."

"You think it would be a good idea to swap me for Palo?"

"Of course not! How much do you know about Markku Malmberg? He doesn't like women."

I said I knew that.

"Do you know where that comes from? His mother. She watched for years while his father abused him sexually. She even participated sometimes. She was a real monster. Markku has never had a normal sexual relationship with a woman."

"A bad mother made him a thief and a killer?" I couldn't keep the scorn out of my voice, although Hanninen's insight did help me understand why Malmberg had lopped off his father's penis with the saw.

"They're complicated processes," said Hanninen. "Markku is a person for whom everything in life has gone wrong, systematically from day one. But we still have a moral obligation to care about him. He has the right to live, as does his hostage."

"I agree, although I put more weight on the hostage's life," I said. "On another note though, once this is over, I'd like to talk to you about a separate case. Or I should say another patient of yours who is mixed up in a case."

"Patient information is confidential."

"I know. But this is a murder," I said. "As I understand it, you also knew the victim—your colleague Elina Rosberg."

"Oh, you want to talk about Niina! Is she OK?" Hanninen's tone suddenly turned more serious, and his brown eyes looked concerned. It was easy to believe that Hanninen really cared about his patients and that the mantras he repeated in his manipulative voice were intended to make them happy, but there was still something that felt off to me.

"She's one of several persons of interest at the moment. That's all. Is your number listed?"

"Here, I'll give you my card." Hanninen dug through the pockets of his long, antique-finished leather coat. This guy definitely had style, a sort of relaxed masculinity mixed with empathy. I'm sure it worked well on his female patients.

"That isn't smart," Hanninen said, handing over the card just as the helicopters moved in on the cabin again. "Markku wants to feel he's in control of the situation. Those helicopters are only going to make him lose his cool."

"What do you think we should do?" I asked.

"Talk to him as much as possible and wait for him to realize he isn't going to get away. Convince him to surrender or at least give up his hostage. I'm still willing to take his place. Markku won't hurt me."

Buckshot sprayed the rotors of the helicopter again. Inside the command center one of the men wearing headphones yelled something to Captain Koskivuori, and I rushed back into the tent. I was sure Malmberg had shot Palo.

But no. It was just the operator saying that Malmberg and Palo were both losing it. Malmberg was alternating between firing at the retreating helicopters and shooting blindly behind the cabin. Everyone in the back took cover. The noise was insane.

From the tent I saw the helicopters hovering over the cabin, apparently enticing Malmberg to shoot out the north window. While he was doing that, the SWAT team was climbing up the south side of the cabin. The noise of the helicopters covered their movements. The whole thing looked reckless to me, but what did I know? I was just a regular cop.

Captain Koskivuori was shouting orders into the phone, and more than a dozen rifle scopes were trained on the cabin as the gas charge went down the chimney. Half of the SWAT team dropped from the roof onto the porch. One helicopter descended almost insanely low, and someone in it started firing on the cabin too.

One of the guys with the headphones shouted, "Palo says there are no explosives!"

The sound of the hovering helicopters almost drowned out the exchange of gunfire. I instinctively started running toward it, but someone grabbed my coat sleeve. Suddenly it was completely still. The shooting stopped, and both helicopters disappeared behind the trees. The person holding me released my sleeve. I recognized Ström's aftershave without looking at him.

One of the SWAT team members appeared, shouting for an ambulance, but the paramedics were already on their way. I hadn't realized how many photographers and TV cameras were in the woods, but now they descended on the cabin like tigers smelling a fresh kill.

Captain Koskivuori's voice echoed from a megaphone: "The operation is over. Markku Malmberg died during the exchange of fire. Unfortunately, he seriously wounded Sergeant Palo."

"Goddamn!" breathed Ström. I didn't say anything.

"Wait. I'll go ask what he means by 'seriously,'" Ström said.

I watched the cameras approaching their prey and heard the sound of safeties clicking back on and the buzz of voices around me as if I wasn't really there.

When Ström came running back, his eyes told me everything: Palo was already dead.

At that moment it didn't matter that I detested Ström. He was my brother and we were experiencing exactly the same emotions. We wrapped our arms around each other. Within seconds Pihko and Taskinen were in the same heap. We all cried—some of us silently. I howled. I couldn't bear to watch when the covered stretcher finally came out of the cabin.

Other than to attend the crisis therapy meetings they organized for us, I didn't go back to work for the rest of the week. Maybe it would have been easier to be at work, but either way, the days were hell and the nights were worse. Because of the baby, I could only take a sedative the first night.

Fortunately Antti was able to take the rest of the week off too. Sex turned out to be the best therapy. Antti was surprised when I wanted to make love the same night I returned from the hostage scene in Nuuksio. But I always felt alive when I made love, and experiencing something through my body gave my mind a rest. Antti said he'd always thought women's sexual desire decreased when they were pregnant, but so far I'd smashed that myth.

Over the next few days, Antti answered all the phone calls for me, turning down interview requests and calming our parents and friends. I wasn't able to talk about how I felt. One night I dreamed I was in the Cultural Center parking lot opening the door of the Fiat. Out collapsed Palo's and Malmberg's bloody corpses.

I heard Taskinen went back to work the very next day. Ström, on the other hand, treated his depression in the grand tradition of most Finnish men—by going on a multiday bender. During the therapy session on Friday afternoon, I wasn't sure whether his shaking was a result of a hangover or trauma. On Friday they told us that Malmberg was quicker to shoot than they'd expected. He shot Palo instantly when he realized the gas canister had come down the chimney. The sawed-off shotgun made a mess of Palo's torso. He didn't die immediately, but nothing could have saved him.

Malmberg was a different story. It was impossible to tell which bullet killed him. Apparently he'd shot himself in the head with a pistol at the same moment he shot Palo with the shotgun, but his lower body was full of SWAT team rounds. Clearly the investigation was destined to be a long one—even if the families of Palo or Malmberg didn't sue. The media spent several days in a tizzy over the incident, but then a famous politician was pulled over for drunk driving on Epiphany, providing the papers with new headlines.

Eva Jensen called that night to see how I was recovering. When she complained about how boring the third trimester was, I suggested we go for a walk the next day, Sunday. The weather forecast called for sunshine, and I wanted to start easing back into work. Wasn't that what they told riders: when you fall off the horse, you have to get back on as quickly as possible?

After Eva's call, I flopped back down in front of the TV to watch figure skating. A massive Canadian male figure skater was throwing triple axels to a movie soundtrack. It helped me shut out the ghosts of Nuuksio for a few minutes.

Eva came over Sunday morning. She said she could walk as far as I wanted as long as we went slowly. We walked across the frozen field toward the side streets leading to Central Park. Even though the ground was slick, Eva said she'd rather walk in the open than along a busy road inhaling exhaust fumes. The sun shone a dull winter yellow, and the fluffy clouds promised the dry weather would continue. Bullfinches were polishing off the last of the rowanberries. A rabbit scurried under a bush. Eva's swollen belly barely fit under her cape-style coat, and her slender arms and legs looked comical compared to it.

"So how are you doing?" she asked once we made it across the field to a group of houses and a freshly graveled lane.

I shrugged. "About once an hour, I ask why I get to be alive when Palo is dead. Otherwise I'm fine."

"Do you feel guilty about being alive?"

"Of course. But I know that's normal. It was such a little detail. Malmberg was after me, but I happened to park in a more visible place. It bothers me that everything turned into such a mess at the end."

I had avoided reading the newspapers and their denunciation of the police's handling of the situation, but at some point I'd have to face that reality. I'd asked Antti to save all the articles people were writing and to tape the news for me to watch when that time came.

"By the way, do you know Malmberg's therapist, Kari Hanninen?" I asked Eva. "I had a few minutes to chat with him before all hell was unleashed."

"Yes, I've met him a few times," she said. "If you're looking for enemies of Elina, there's at least one for you. Elina didn't approve of Hanninen's astrotherapy thing. Or, actually, it was more because he tried to sell it as real science. Which I don't think it is either, of course."

"It does sound weird," I agreed.

"In a way, Hanninen and Elina were competing for the same clients: self-aware, feminist-leaning women. Plenty of women like that take astrology and tarot reading completely seriously. They believe both are based in ancient female wisdom that male-dominated religions and the so-called hard sciences have tried to suppress."

"But Elina didn't think so?"

"I guess she thought it was dangerous telling people they aren't responsible for their own decisions and letting them blame cards or stars."

"Did Hanninen and Elina have any public run-ins?"

"Yep. They were students around the same time. I've heard rumors they were involved romantically. But that all ended when Elina kept getting better test scores than Kari."

I laughed, remembering my own college boyfriend, Kristian. The same thing had happened to us: the poor boy couldn't handle me getting better grades. Now Kristian was writing a dissertation in law school, and I was risking my life as a cop.

"A couple of years ago, they had a huge blowup when Elina demanded the Psychological Association censure and maybe even kick Kari out for mixing science and occultism," continued Eva. "In the end he got off with a warning, but Kari's relationship with the association has been cool ever since—to say the least."

"Elina stole at least one client from Kari. I'll have to ask her whether she knew about the conflict between them. But I don't want to talk about Kari Hanninen. I'd rather hear about Elina. You said she was your therapist too."

"Yeah, going through therapy yourself is part of the training for anyone who wants to be a therapist. When I applied to the program, it wasn't that long since homosexuality had been removed from the diagnostic manual as a mental illness! Finding a therapist who didn't consider the idea of a lesbian doing this work repulsive wasn't easy. Elina was a real find in more ways than one. She also taught me a lot about the job."

The wind was blowing sharp crystals of snow from the branches of the fir trees; they raked our faces like a stiff bristle brush. A magpie took flight from the top of a tree but couldn't stay aloft for long, settling instead on a branch high in a birch tree fifty feet away. It swayed there, cawing something that sounded like magpie cursing. I had once listened to Einstein arguing with a magpie sitting in a tree. One of them howled and the other cawed. I'd been completely sure they understood each other.

Down the road, a man who looked like a retired sea captain was dragging a bushy, snow-colored Samoyed away from the trunk of a tree. The dog clearly had found the most interesting scent in the world and wasn't willing to leave it for anything. Although I'm generally what you'd call a cat person, I've always loved big, furry dogs. I couldn't pass the Samoyed without scratching him behind the ear. Instantly he smelled Einstein on my boots and turned to sniff first me and then the scent of golden retriever on Eva's clothes.

"Elina was a great therapist," Eva continued once we turned down the lane toward Espoo Central Park. "She was always present, and she really listened. When our therapy relationship ended and we became colleagues, we got to know each other better. We were never really friends though because Elina was so reserved. She didn't talk much about herself, her feelings, or her life. She mentioned Joona Kirstilä occasionally, and it was clear he was important to her, but that was it."

"Could you imagine Elina committing suicide?"

Eva shook her head, and her wide mouth pursed in doubt. "What was the actual cause of death?"

"A drug and alcohol interaction left her unconscious, which led to hypothermia and death. It's hard to say whether anything in the case was premeditated." I considered mentioning the letter Aira had found in her purse. Because I still wasn't sure it was genuine, I decided to keep my mouth shut.

"That's a pretty chancy way to kill yourself. It seems more like a cry for help, like she was expecting to be found. But that doesn't sound like Elina. She wasn't the suicide type even though there was something about her . . . Like, I don't know, hidden rooms under her calm public persona where she locked away all her sorrows. Sometimes she would crack those doors, but only for a second."

"What did you see through the doors?" I asked.

"A tension between a need for solitude and a need for connection. Elina didn't have any family except Aira. I had the feeling she wanted a child but also couldn't quite face the idea. Her relationship with Joona was typical. They were close, but she didn't want to be too close."

That description sounded familiar. I had been the same way. Actually, I still was. Part of the reason I married Antti was because he understood and shared my need for solitude. A child would change that. A child would always need someone around. Since Palo's death, I'd started thinking about my maternity leave as a break from work, a time without murderers and desperate attempts to squeeze half-truths out of people. Yes, with a child things would be different, but maybe in a good way.

Although just a few days earlier I'd ordered Antti to keep the news about the baby to himself, I suddenly found myself telling Eva. "We're actually expecting too."

"Congratulations! We wondered a little why you drove to the New Year's Eve party. What week are you?"

"What is it now . . . Eighth, I guess. I'm due at the end of August. It was a pretty big surprise because I had an IUD. I haven't really wrapped my head around the whole idea yet."

"That's a lot of stress all at once—a coworker dying and a surprise pregnancy," Eva observed.

"You're telling me. But maybe that's exactly what this whole cruel system is about: birth and death side by side." I shook my head. "Geez, I'm sorry. I don't mean to sound so melancholy. Should we head back?"

I walked Eva to her house in Mankkaa. Kirsti was horrified that her wife had slogged nearly six miles so close to her due date, but Eva cheerfully dismissed her worries. I said good-bye to them and decided to walk the last mile and a half back, hoping Antti would have a meal ready when I arrived.

Like Eva, I didn't feel like walking along the busy main road, so I started weaving down the back lanes. Suddenly I stopped. A man stood leaning against the fence in front of a row house, compulsively picking stray hairs from the shoulders of his coat. Pertti Ström. But he didn't look like the Ström I knew. This man's shoulders were slumped in exhaustion and his head hung down. His whole bearing was utterly resigned, which was totally at odds with Ström's typical self-confident, boorish personality. I stood there watching him, wondering whether I should go talk to him. Then it struck me. Why on earth was he leaning against a fence in Mankkaa looking like he was waiting for someone? He lived two miles from here. Was he waiting to interview a witness? But it was Sunday, and I was relatively sure Ström had the day off too.

Nervously he glanced at his watch. Then the door to the row house opened and a boy of about seven peeked out.

"We'll be there in a minute, Dad. Jenna can't find her swimsuit."

Ström's shoulders instantly rose to their usual arrogant level, and the gruffness of his voice was familiar as he yelled into the house behind the boy, "Don't even try it, Marja. Give Jenna the swimsuit!"

Jenna, Marja, and a boy about seven years old . . . It clicked into place. Ström was waiting for his kids. What was the boy's name? Jani? I'd caught a glimpse of the children's pictures in Ström's wallet once when he bought me coffee after an important arrest. Imagining Ström having warm feelings toward anyone was a stretch—although of course he was attached to his kids. Then I remembered the way Ström had cried with me over Palo's death.

Now it became clear that Ström's relationship with his ex-wife was worse than his relationship with me: their conversation about when the kids should come home had turned into a shouting match. "Eight at the latest. They have school tomorrow!"

"What the hell? If we go to the meet, we won't be back until nine at the earliest! They're big kids now. They can handle staying up a little late one night! Come on, Jenna, let's go already!"

"You aren't the one who has to wake them up tomorrow morning! If Jenna can't find her swimsuit, she just won't go swimming."

Finally Jenna came out, triumphantly dangling a pink bathing suit from one finger. Seeing Pertti Ström's features in the face of a ten-year-old girl was amusing. Then, embarrassed about spying on a colleague's private life, I slipped behind the nearest house.

On Monday morning, everything seemed almost normal at work. Only the picture of Palo, which had been cut out of a newspaper and taped with a black border to Palo and Pihko's office door, served as a reminder that everything had changed. Pihko was nowhere to be found, and Ström wasn't around either, but Taskinen was sitting behind his desk, his face ashen and strained. The smile that appeared when he saw me was surely the first of his day.

"Back to work?"

"I had to come in eventually. What's new?"

"Nothing major. We need to divide Palo's cases between us. I doubt we'll be getting a replacement anytime soon. Be ready for an interview about the hostage incident later this week. It's going to be a big mess."

"You're telling me. I'll keep working on the other Nuuksio case for now. And I'll probably head up to Oulu tomorrow night."

"Kari Hanninen, the psychologist, sent his regards and said he would always be at the disposal of such an enchanting female specimen." Taskinen could barely get the words out without laughing. I mentally forgave Hanninen his irritating comment. At least it had made Taskinen laugh.

I was just about to pick up the phone to ask Dispatch for Leevi Säntti's number when the ringer beat me to it.

"Tarja Kivimäki, Finnish Broadcasting. Hello. I see you're back at work after this second shocking incident in Nuuksio."

"Yes. Do you have any new information about Elina Rosberg?" I said.

"Unfortunately not," she answered. "I imagine you've had other things on your mind lately as well. That's what I'd like talk to you about, Maria. I can call you Maria, can't I? Well, anyway, *Studio A* is doing an in-depth report about all the shootings over the past few years. We'd like to interview you, and I'd be the one to do it."

"But you don't work for *Studio A* anymore," I said.

"I've been thinking about moving back. I'm getting tired of doing the news, and there are a few reasons I'd like to get away from reporting on politics."

"I don't think I can," I said. "First, I'm not really excited about talking about my coworker's death publicly, and second, you're still technically a person of interest in an open case I'm investigating."

"Am I? Could we at least meet? Dinner, tonight. I'll buy."

"No, you won't. As I said, you're still a person of interest. But OK, we can meet. Name the time and place."

When I hung up the phone, I felt like a blood-sucking parasite. I had no intention of giving Tarja Kivimäki an interview. But I did intend to trade for information, and that would be easier done at a dinner table than in an interrogation room.

Next I called Leevi Säntti, who was fortunately at home and not on the road preaching. I introduced myself with as much authority as possible and hoped Johanna hadn't told him that I was the one who'd recommended her lawyer.

"What are you calling about? Has my . . . um . . . wife murdered someone else?" he said.

"What do you mean someone else?" I asked, although I knew exactly what Leevi Säntti meant.

"She murdered our child by having an abortion. And this is what it's led to. Once you step onto the path of sin—"

"Mr. Säntti, your wife is only one of several persons of interest in the case. I'd like to meet with you in Karhumaa."

"Of course. I understand how police procedure works." Leevi Säntti's phone voice was intentionally pleasant and manipulative in a similar way to Kari Hanninen's.

Ending the call, I knew I should phone Hanninen too, but I couldn't force myself to do it yet. Over the past few days I'd spent hours wondering whether Palo and Malmberg would still be alive if the police commanders had listened more closely to Hanninen. Whenever I thought about it, anger began rising from beneath the agony. I wanted someone to blame for Palo's death, someone I could scream at, someone to punch and kick. It didn't matter that Malmberg had fired the shot that killed Palo. I had been killed there too—if I had been in the cabin in Palo's place, the same thing would have happened to me and my inch-long baby.

When I went down to the cafeteria for lunch, people stared at me as if I were a freak. I had sometimes heard my suspects talk about this: anyone involved in a dramatic death, whether directly or not, bore a mark that aroused simultaneous disgust and curiosity. Of course, it was worse for suspects than witnesses or police officers, but still.

At last a female patrol officer came over to chat, dragging a couple of others to the table, so I didn't feel so isolated anymore. Still, I knew I was a living reminder of the side of our work we preferred to put out of our minds.

Fortunately I had a routine to follow after lunch. The work that had piled up the week before still had to be dealt with, and I had meetings to arrange and reports to type up. But whenever I came upon a case Palo and I had worked together, I felt like pushing it aside. With the restaurant break-in, I was almost out of my chair and on my way to ask his opinion when I remembered he was gone.

How did Pihko feel? Had HR already cleaned out Palo's desk? Had the family pictures pinned to the cubicle divider been removed? Had they taken his things from the closet and emptied the box that housed his famous medicine cabinet? I didn't want to look yet.

Managing to squeeze in time after work to stop by home to change clothes, I set off for Cucina Raffaello, where I was to meet Tarja Kivimäki. On the bus, I caught myself eying a tightly secured baby stroller. The baby, only a few months old, was sleeping peacefully. Its father, a thin, long-haired guy tattooed down to his fingertips, kept adjusting the blankets and picking up the pacifier. He looked strangely familiar.

At the next stop, a heavy guy who seemed mildly drunk stepped onto the bus carrying a clinking plastic bag. He greeted the tattooed father animatedly.

"Hey, Nyberg! Shit, dude! I haven't seen you since you got out. What are you doing in Espoo?"

"I got a wife and daughter here. And don't yell so loud. You'll wake the baby," Nyberg said.

The rotund man lifted an unsteady finger to his lips and whispered that he was going to sit in the back so he wouldn't bother the baby. The sack clanged dangerously against a railing as the man tottered toward the rear bench.

He didn't stay quiet for long though. "Did you hear those pigs shot Markku Malmberg? That dude was crazy as shit. I was there that time he smashed one of Soininen's fingers in the weight room."

Nyberg didn't answer. He just dug a pouch of tobacco out of a pocket and started rolling a cigarette. When a cry from the stroller interrupted the ritual, the father rushed to comfort the baby. With her quiet again, he quickly returned to his task, then shoved the unlit cigarette in his mouth.

"Hey, driver, is the next stop Tapiola? That's where I get off," the man with the bag announced. As he stepped off the bus, he noticed the cigarette hanging from Nyberg's mouth and rushed back aboard to bum it. Strangely, the driver and other passengers didn't seem to mind the two minutes it took them to exchange the cigarette and reminisce about how good the coffee had been in prison. Maybe the men's previous address had something to do with their reticence.

When I arrived, Kivimäki was already sitting in a rear booth with her tape recorder on the table. As I ordered a glass of mineral water, I realized I wasn't the slightest bit hungry. In fact, I felt somewhat nauseated.

"So have you recovered from last week?" Kivimäki asked with false perkiness.

"No. Have you recovered from Elina's death?" I replied.

"I guess you're right. Do you mind if I tape our conversation?"

"What are you going to use the tape for? I didn't agree to an interview."

Tarja Kivimäki drew a deep breath but didn't have time to reply before the waiter returned to ask if we were ready to order. I ordered a bland shrimp pasta. Maybe that would go down. Nothing with meat or tomatoes sounded good.

"Let me tell you about the program," Kivimäki said after ordering jambalaya and a Mexican beer. "Our goal isn't just to cover the Nuuksio hostage drama but to investigate the tendency of the police to use their weapons more generally, starting way back with the Mikkeli incident. Of course Hirsala and Vesala, and the Tampere Police Academy case."

"Why do you want to interview me?"

"It's well known Malmberg first tried to break into the car of another police officer but had to settle for Sergeant Palo. The identity of the other officer wasn't hard to find out. I was hoping you'd participate in a little thought experiment: how would you have wanted the police to act if you'd been in that cabin?"

"Are you doing a documentary or something sensational? I don't think I'm interested in that kind of speculation."

"No? Then you think the situation was handled in the best possible way? You don't have anything critical to say?"

Of course I had plenty to say. But I didn't have the energy to go down the rabbit hole of that kind of postmortem. In a way, it sounded tempting to pour all my grief and anger and fear through the television screen into the living rooms of half of Finland. But Palo wouldn't have wanted that. I guess I'd finally learned the code: cops don't shit where they eat.

"Isn't it unethical to stay silent if you see something wrong?" said Kivimäki.

"I think it would be unethical to interview me when you're involved in a homicide investigation I'm working on."

"Someone else could interview you."

"Forget it. Why are you going back to *Studio A*? I doubt they'll let you hide behind the camera."

"A lot of reasons. One is that I can do longer, more in-depth investigative pieces than I can as a news reporter. And personal reasons too. I guess you could say they have to do with ethics too."

The waiter brought our salads, and I filled my mouth so I wouldn't have to say anything. Getting me to criticize the police command for Nuuksio certainly would make a good story: a female in a police force dominated by men seeing the mistakes more clearly than any of them. I was used to putting myself on the line in my investigations, but I wasn't ready for that kind of attention. After I swallowed, I said as much to Kivimäki.

"Too bad. I thought we could help each other," said Kivimäki.

"How?" I asked.

"I haven't wanted to betray Elina's trust because she only told me. But I've thought about it and realized it could possibly be the motive for Elina's murder."

As usual, I spoke before I thought it through. "So you're saying you'll tell me the motive for Elina's murder if you get your interview? And you're the one lecturing me about ethics!"

I stood up, pushing my salad plate out of the way and into Kivimäki's beer bottle, which fell over.

"You're welcome to come discuss the motive for Elina Rosberg's murder at the Espoo Police Station. How about Thursday at ten? And be on time. If you aren't, I'll have a warrant issued for your arrest for concealing evidence and hindering a police investigation. Enjoy your jambalaya!"

11

When I burst out onto the street, I was pelted with sleet. Under normal circumstances, I would have headed for the nearest bar to throw back a couple of quick shots of whiskey. As a pregnant woman, I had to settle for venting my frustration on an empty Coke can lying on the sidewalk. Although it was perfectly possible Kivimäki was bluffing, I intended to follow through with the Thursday interrogation. Same difference whether she was or not. I hadn't liked her from the beginning, and the idea of grilling her felt great.

I had more than half an hour until the next bus, so I headed over to the Ruffe Pub to get out of the weather. Deciding to paint the town red, I ordered a nonalcoholic beer. As I scanned the place for a seat, I found that my work day wasn't quite over yet. There was Joona Kirstilä sitting at a window table with a pint of dark Kozel and a laptop in front of him. I considered whether I should bother him. The computer appeared to be turned off and Kirstilä was just staring into his glass.

I had unfinished business with Kirstilä. That morning a report had been waiting on my desk confirming that Kirstilä had been on a bar crawl in Hämeenlinna with his friends, but not on Boxing Day, on Wednesday the twenty-seventh.

If it had been a normal work week, I could have believed Kirstilä mixed up the days, but I doubted even he could confuse a holiday with another day. Kirstilä had claimed he last saw Elina before Christmas, but it was looking more probable that he was in Nuuksio on the twenty-sixth.

So I took my not-quite pilsner and marched over to Kirstilä's table. He glanced up from his glass and nodded. It was easy to see he wasn't exactly sober. His brown eyes looked young and bright, but even the relaxation of intoxication couldn't smooth the lines around his mouth.

I sat down in the empty chair.

"How's it going?" I asked when I couldn't think of anything else to say.

"It isn't really. My words seem to have died with Elina." He nodded toward the blank screen of his laptop. "Luckily there's plenty of booze. Have you found out anything?"

"We have. You weren't in Hämeenlinna on Boxing Day, Joona. You didn't go until the next night. We have at least ten witnesses."

"I'm here to get drunk, damn it, not interrogated!" Kirstilä's shout was even louder than the Green Day blaring. The customers at the nearby tables glanced at us curiously.

"Calm down," I said, standing up. "I can leave if you want. I'll call tomorrow and tell you when to come to the police station."

I was still in a bad mood from my meeting with Kivimäki. Tormenting Kirstilä felt like kicking a puppy, but I couldn't just leave things there.

"Do I have to? I hate that place. I'd guess I'd rather talk now."

I sat back down, although I knew our conversation wouldn't carry any official weight. Kirstilä was drunk, and I was alone. But I still had time until the bus, and the sleet outside was only getting worse. Few places were as desperately ugly as the Helsinki Bus Depot in a storm. The Ruffe's blue and green and violet stained glass distorted the scene outside, turning the windows of the six-story redbrick Union of Agricultural Producers and Forest Owners building across the bus plaza into ornate polygons and painting the muddy buses beautiful pastels.

Kirstilä emptied his Kozel and waved to the bartender for another. Obviously he was a regular, because the waitress brought his glass to the table and said she'd put it on his tab. The poet downed a quarter of the pint before speaking.

"I guess I got the days wrong. It must have been Wednesday when we went out drinking," he said hesitantly.

"So how did your Christmas actually go?" I asked. "You came back from Hämeenlinna to say hi to Elina or something?"

"Yeah. I missed her."

Kirstilä brushed his thick hair away from his face and pulled a crumpled cigarette pack out of his pocket. The last cigarette was almost broken in half. He had a hard time getting the match lit, and finally I grabbed the box and did it for him. The cigarette smoke nauseated me even more than usual, and I turned away quickly. A little incidental second-hand smoke wasn't going to hurt my baby, and I couldn't exactly wrap myself in plastic for nine months.

"Christmas always makes me maudlin," Kirstilä said. "All the family nonsense and peace on earth and goodwill toward men. It felt kind of stupid to spend Christmas with my parents and my sister when I don't even like them, and the only person I really cared about was seventy miles away. I called Elina that night and asked her to come over to my place. She said she couldn't because she had something to do, so I suggested I come to Rosberga. I had to take a taxi, but Elina promised to pay."

Elina met Kirstilä at the gate. Her head cold was horrible, but she'd told him she wanted to get out of the house for a while, to "air out her brain." Kirstilä got the impression that Elina's Christmas had turned out to be unexpectedly exhausting.

"I started talking crazy. It was probably all the sentimental Christmas nonsense that made me say it. I asked Elina to move in with me, but she said no. She said she was at a place in her life where she couldn't even think about making any big changes."

That fit with Milla's story. But how did Aira get it into her head that Joona Kirstilä was going to leave Elina? It sounded like the opposite.

"So Elina wanted to continue your relationship the way it was?" I emptied my glass and immediately wanted another. Well, not really. I wanted a real beer. But my superego wouldn't hear of it.

"Yeah. We ended up fighting about it. I thought Elina would be pleased that I couldn't stand being away from her on Christmas. Childish. It's just . . . I mean it was so damn hard with Elina living so far away and always having a house full of women. What if I just wanted to see her some night when we didn't have plans? What was I supposed to do then?" Kirstilä pursed his lips, and his expression reminded me of my two-year-old nephew, Saku, when his mother told him he couldn't have something he wanted. "I shouldn't've complained. Now I don't have Elina at all . . ." Kirstilä started crying, tears dripping into his beer.

"How did you get back to Helsinki if the buses weren't running? By taxi?"

"No, I stayed the night in the little house. I didn't leave until morning," Kirstilä said tiredly, wiping his eyes.

"What? You were at Rosberga all night?"

"Yes. That's the horrible thing about it all." Kirstilä's eyes teared up again. "Elina didn't want me to stay. She wanted me to take a taxi back to the city. Finally she gave in, but she said she wanted a night to herself because she was so sick. I waited until one o'clock in case she came back anyway."

"Did you hear anything that night?"

"No. I fell asleep after emptying a bottle of wine I found in the cupboard."

My bus would be arriving shortly, and the next one wasn't for an hour. I felt bad leaving Kirstilä alone, but I had to go. Standing up, I saw that a pretty young woman at the next table appeared to have recognized him and kept glancing over. Maybe he would find comfort sooner than he thought.

But apparently Kirstilä wasn't finished yet. "We parted on slightly cool terms," he whispered, wiping his face with his red scarf. "I called her at one o'clock, just before I finished the wine and fell asleep, but she said she couldn't talk to me because she was in the middle of a conversation with someone. And in the morning"—Kirstilä swallowed—"in the morning I was so pissed off that Elina hadn't come back that I took the first bus into town. Now all I do is wonder. If I'd pushed and demanded to be with her, she would still be alive." Kirstilä's last sentence dissolved into sobbing.

I'd been pulling on my coat as he spoke but now I stood frozen. "With who?" I almost shouted. "Who was Elina talking to?" All of the women in the house had denied seeing Elina again after she came back from her evening walk.

"She just said she'd tell me later because it had to do with me too. She sounded sort of like . . . like she was drunk. But I guess by then I was too."

I had to rush to my bus, so I told Kirstilä I'd interview him again later in the week. So Elina hadn't been alone that night! Which meant that one of the Rosberga women was lying.

There was no way I could break away and get to Rosberga Manor the next day. I had inherited a couple of cases from Palo, and although I was trying to concentrate on them, I still found my mind wandering. Suddenly I was in Nuuksio again, near the cabin surrounded by trees, listening to the noise of helicopters and gunshots, all ending in dead silence. At lunch I sat with Pihko, and when we returned to our department, I asked to see Palo's office.

The desk was exactly as before except Palo's messy case notes had been taken away and redistributed to the rest of us. A thick, dark-blue cardigan hung from the back of Palo's chair. When I touched it, I smelled the scent of his cough drops and deodorant.

"Every morning when I come to work I'm surprised he isn't here," Pihko said softly. "His wife is supposed to pick up that stuff tomorrow. I just hope Lähde doesn't move Ström in here next."

"We have to get a replacement," I said. "When are they opening up the position? One of my friends is taking the NCO course right now. You don't know Pekka Koivu, do you? He'd fit in great. I worked with him in Helsinki."

My friend and former partner Pekka Koivu had left Joensuu and its race brawls behind and was currently sitting in a classroom just a few miles away taking a course for noncommissioned officer candidates. We'd been talking about going out for a beer after Christmas, but of course there wasn't time for that now.

When Koivu called after hearing about the Malmberg incident, I got the feeling he had a new girl up to bat.

Pihko's phone rang. To our mutual surprise, it was Taskinen, who apparently needed me in his office ASAP. In his office I discovered the Espoo chief of police, with whom I'd never had the honor of speaking. I was sure they wanted to talk about the schedule for the preliminary investigation into the hostage drama. Taskinen motioned for me to sit but avoided my eyes, instead staring past me as if some new, fascinating painting had appeared on the wall above my left ear.

"Sergeant Kallio, I just received an extremely testy phone call from someone high up in the Ministry of the Interior," the chief of police began. He was nearly at retirement age, and I'd heard that he rose through the ranks like a meteor during the Kekkonen years. Back in those days, when the Soviet Union still cast a long shadow, plenty of cops were willing to look the other way if the price was right. The strain of lunch meetings spent greasing palms and sauna nights at exclusive seaside villas boozing it up with corrupt politicians was visible in the chief's stout frame and the broken blood vessels of his face. His expensive-looking dark-blue suit only served to accentuate the impression of banality. You didn't buy suits like that on a policeman's salary. Internal Affairs investigations had come close to him several times, but the police chief's reputation was still miraculously intact. Some thought that might have something to do with the current minister of the interior also having been one of President Kekkonen's young protégés and an old friend of the chief. I imagined that the big shot at the ministry who'd called was none other than Interior Minister Martti Sahala.

"I'm assuming it has to do with the Nuuksio hostage incident," I said crossly. Was the minister of the interior now going to tell us what to say in our interviews?

"No, it had nothing to do with the Nuuksio incident, although there will certainly be plenty to say about that when the time comes. This was in regard to the unexplained death that also happened in Nuuksio a couple of weeks ago. As I remember, the name of the victim was Elina Rosberg."

I was taken aback. "Why was the Interior Ministry calling about that?"

"The minister demanded that you stop groundlessly threatening witnesses with arrest," the chief said.

"What?" I suddenly realized that it had to be about Tarja Kivimäki and our altercation the previous evening. But what did that have to do with the minister of the interior?

"I assume you remember your conversation with the reporter Tarja Kivimäki last night at a restaurant called Raffaello? You threatened to arrest her unless she came in for an interview at a time you dictated unilaterally."

"Sergeant Kallio has been through a lot lately. It's completely understandable if she got upset," Taskinen said. He still wasn't looking at me. I had never seen such intense embarrassment on anyone's face. Taskinen and the chief of police had clashed over several white-collar crime investigations during the past year, and from what I'd heard, their relationship had gone from cold to frigid.

"If Miss—excuse me—Mrs. Kallio is incapable of discharging her duties properly, she should take some sick leave," said the chief.

"Tarja Kivimäki tried to bribe me. She promised to reveal a motive for Elina Rosberg's murder if I gave her an interview for her TV program. She admitted to concealing crucial evidence in a homicide investigation. What was I was supposed to do?" I asked.

As I stared at the police chief's multiple chins, I remembered what Tarja Kivimäki had said about her change of employment: ethical considerations had made working as a political reporter difficult. Was the name of one of those "ethical considerations" Minister Martti Sahala? What the hell did Tarja Kivimäki see in him? The man was a five-and-a-half-foot sound-bite machine who'd grown up surrounded by potato fields. Was it the power that turned her on? Sahala had been called the shadow prime minister more than once. He wasn't much over forty, but he had already been on the national political scene for almost two decades and had held three ministerial portfolios.

"You aren't a little girl anymore, Mrs. Kallio," replied the chief. "A police officer needs the eye of a psychologist. Sometimes small concessions can be useful."

I counted five police chief chins before I lost the battle to keep my mouth shut. "Don't the same rules apply to Interior Ministry mistresses as the rest of us?"

I should have known that would be too much for the police chief. The screaming fit was pretty dramatic. The content of it was more or less that I should ask for some time off before he gave me a permanent holiday. Taskinen and I sat like two cowed children who had managed to burn down the family sauna playing with matches.

"Jyrki, I trust in the future you'll take more responsibility for your subordinates' tact," the police chief finally snapped. He didn't shake our hands before rolling out the door, slamming it behind him.

Taskinen looked at me for the first time and took a deep breath. "OK, now tell me what this is all about."

I tried to keep my cool as I told him, but I saw that my irritation was infecting him too.

"Kivimäki must have been really offended to put such big wheels in motion," he said after hearing my version.

"That woman is going to be here at ten on Thursday or else. I know how to play this game too," I said. "The tabloids would just love to hear about a government minister shielding his mistress from a murder investigation!"

"Maria, calm down! Don't make your life any harder than it already is."

"If Kivimäki really does have something to tell us about the motive for Rosberg's murder, I'm going to squeeze it out of her even if it means going through the high heels Martti Sahala keeps in his closet for special occasions." My rage dissolved into giggles, which only worsened at the thought of how Martti Sahala would look stripped to his skivvies during an assignation.

Taskinen watched me giggle hysterically for a few seconds and then grabbed a bottle of mineral water from his cabinet. "Drink that and try to get a hold of yourself. Are you sure you don't need more time off?"

"Of course I do," I said once I was able to speak. "So do you and Pihko. And I want to vomit just thinking about the chief. But don't worry. I'm not going to lose it. I'm taking the night train to Oulu, and I promise to behave myself. And when I get back on Thursday morning, Tarja Kivimäki will be waiting for me here."

"Without you doing anything?"

"Exactly. I think she's aware that she can't afford not to come, despite her bigwig boyfriend."

Taskinen looked as if he almost believed me. I wished I did. Marching to my office, I tried to pick up the pieces of my day, but even staring at Geir Moen's leg muscles didn't help. I had to force myself to dial Elina Rosberg's lawyer's number.

The will didn't contain anything in particular. There were a few bequests to organizations like the Finnish Feminist Association and the Red Cross Disaster Fund. Otherwise all the property would go to Aira Rosberg. Joona Kirstilä didn't even rank a mention.

I hadn't really expected to find a mysterious heir, but I was still disappointed. At least my conversations with Kivimäki and Kirstilä had kept alive my hope of making progress with the case. At the same time the skeptic in the back of my mind reminded me that Kirstilä might be lying about Elina's late-night visitor just to turn suspicion away from himself and that the motive Kivimäki had promised might be a hoax.

I called Rosberga Manor, and to my good fortune Johanna answered.

"Hi, it's Maria Kallio from the Espoo Police. How did your visit home go?"

"Thank you, well. I got back yesterday. I could hardly stand to leave the children once I got to see them. Only Johannes, my oldest boy, stayed away."

"Did you see your husband?" I asked.

"No. He and Johannes were at Leevi's parents' place the whole time I was home. If I just had a place to live, I would've taken the children away with me right then, at least the smallest ones."

"How long do you intend to stay at Rosberga?"

"Aira promised I can stay here until I get things worked out. I need to find a job and an apartment, although I think that'll take a miracle."

What was Johanna living on now? Where was she getting money? Had Elina lent her some?

"Elina's body still hasn't been turned over to us. Aira needs to organize the funeral," Johanna continued.

I'd forgotten that too. Palo's death had screwed up a lot of things.

"Maria, I found out that Leevi wasn't home on Boxing Day. He told everyone he was going somewhere to give a sermon." Johanna's voice was agitated. It occurred to me that Elina could have gone out for walks with Kirstilä and Leevi Säntti, although that didn't seem likely.

"That's why I called you. I'm going to talk to Leevi tomorrow."

"What? Are you going to arrest him?" Johanna breathed.

"There's no reason for that yet. But I do intend to talk to him. Thank you for your autobiography, by the way. It was interesting, but I think a couple of pages were missing."

"That stuff from when I was in school doesn't have anything to do with my situation now."

I felt two-faced talking with Johanna as a friend. Of course I wasn't going halfway to the Arctic Circle just to check on Leevi Säntti's movements. I was also going there to ask about Johanna. There was something so strange and unhinged about Elina Rosberg's death, I had a sense that at least one person involved was mentally disturbed. Johanna was a perfect fit for that role.

The phone rang again. It was the officer at the desk downstairs. I had a visitor. "He says he doesn't have an appointment. His name is Kari Hanninen, and he's a therapist. Do you want me to send him up?"

I didn't have the time or energy, but Hanninen was a good excuse to go get some coffee. I said I'd come down and get him. In the elevator, I looked at myself in the mirror: my eyes looked green-black from exhaustion, my skin was paler than ever, and the winter had wiped the freckles from my nose. My hair could have used a new bottle of red dye. Under my green sweater, my breasts looked bigger, but the waist of my jeans didn't feel tight. Almost the opposite.

Hanninen's cowboy boots, Levi's 501s, and black bandanna tied around his neck only added to the aging rock star effect. When he saw me, it was as if he hit an internal charm button: a new glint flashed in his coffee-colored eyes, his mouth with its thin upper lip spread into a wide smile, and laugh lines filled his cheeks and the corners of his eyes.

"Sergeant Kallio. I'm so happy you had time to see me. I happened to be driving by and stopped in to see how you were doing. You said you wanted to talk to me."

"I need a cup of coffee," I said. "We can talk in the cafeteria."

Hanninen followed me, then pulled out my chair as though we were on a date. I wasn't used to that kind of treatment, at least not at work. Here I was just one of the boys and carried my own gear and put on my own coat.

We talked about Malmberg first. Hanninen was angry about what had happened, and I had heard from colleagues that he'd used some pretty strong language about the police in interviews. I wasn't surprised, knowing he'd genuinely cared what happened to Malmberg, even if he'd unwittingly made the situation worse.

"Markku was clearly a very disturbed individual," said Hanninen now. "But do we have the right to just run in and kill people? Even someone like him? All those guns and helicopters . . . Anyone would have gone crazy from that level of intimidation. Not to mention someone with a death wish. What would the situation have been if Markku's hostage hadn't been a police officer?"

"Well, maybe they would have rushed things less," I agreed. "But really I wanted to talk to you about Niina Kuusinen. Do you mind if we move up to my office?"

The coffee had given me heartburn, and being around Hanninen felt oppressive. He was permanently connected to Palo and Malmberg in my mind.

"Theoretically professional ethics don't allow me to discuss my patients," Hanninen said once we were sitting in my office. "But maybe I can be a little flexible since you seem to be smarter than the average cop."

"You knew Elina Rosberg personally, didn't you?" I asked.

"I knew her really well at one point. We even dated for about a year while we were in college—twenty years ago now. I hadn't thought about it until I heard Elina had died."

"I've heard rumors of a skirmish between the two of you involving the Psychological Association."

Hanninen's eyebrows went up, and he shifted more comfortably in his chair, stretching his long legs in front of him and clasping his hands behind his head.

"Is that what this is about?" he asked in amusement. "You don't really want to talk about Niina; you want to talk about Elina and me. Are you short on suspects, Sergeant Kallio?"

I didn't answer. I stared back at Hanninen's pleasantly wrinkled face, noticing that there were black circles around his eyes, as if he'd been awake for days.

"I can tell you about Elina Rosberg if you want," Hanninen said. "Isn't part of police work doing profiles of suspects and victims? Elina thought she was always right. She looked at the world through a very narrow lens. Usually women are more open than men to new things like astrology. But not Elina. I'm sure she was a perfectly good therapist. I have no beef with that."

According to Hanninen, the conflict with the Psychological Association was more a matter of narrow-mindedness on the part of Elina and a few other psychologists than his use of questionable therapeutic methods. As a result of the dust up, KELA, Finland's public health insurance agency, had reevaluated whether it would reimburse for the therapy Hanninen provided, and a couple of years ago it had removed him from their lists.

Hanninen must have realized that I would discover the repercussions of his dispute with Elina if I asked the right person. Madman Malmberg had been one of Hanninen's last state-covered therapy patients. He didn't hide his pride as he related that Malmberg chose him as his therapist because he hadn't seemed like a candy-ass.

It was clear Kari Hanninen loved talking about himself. I wondered if he was as good a listener. He said that after the KELA decision, he'd increasingly focused on his work as an astrologer. People trusted him because he was also a trained psychologist.

"Astrology unties knots," he said. "It helps people see things in their lives that they wouldn't recognize otherwise. I never tell people that the stars demand this or that, or that they don't have any options."

"Why did you tell Malmberg the stars said it wasn't his time to die yet?" I asked only because this idiotic comment had been bothering me since I'd heard it.

"It was just a way to get Markku to calm down," he said. "Even if it was meaningless. I wasn't—"

I didn't want to rehash the hostage situation with Hanninen, so I rudely interrupted him and turned the conversation to

Niina Kuusinen. "Kuusinen said she went into therapy after her mother died. I'm sure you can talk about that without breaking confidentiality."

"Niina was very attached to her mother. A typical Cancer. She lived a very sheltered life, the only child of a wealthy family and all that. Her mother wanted her to be a pianist, but Niina didn't have the self-confidence. Because of Niina's father's work, the family lived in France for a long time. That's probably why she felt a little rootless here."

"She studied at the Sibelius Academy?" I asked.

"Yes. She graduated as a music teacher last spring. Hopefully she won't have to work in a school. Giving private lessons is a much better fit for her."

I thought of how shy and jumpy Niina was and wondered whether she might have feelings for Kari Hanninen. And why did Niina really switch from Hanninen to Elina? Hanninen didn't say anything about brief therapy. Was Niina dissatisfied with him?

"Kuusinen told me that Elina's death felt like her mother dying all over again. Could she have been projecting her feelings about her mother onto Elina?"

Hanninen smiled at me in the way adults smile at children who ask silly but adorable questions. "Police psychology is so quaint! Elina wasn't even old enough to be a mother figure to Niina. And she wasn't the right type at all. Niina's mother was the archetypal old-fashioned housewife, gentle and attentive. Of course it's true that patients frequently project feelings onto their therapists. It's actually part of the process."

"Did Niina Kuusinen need sedatives? Sleeping pills?" I asked.

"That definitely crosses over the confidentiality line."

I knew I wasn't going to get much more out of Hanninen if we started skirting the edges of patient privacy. "Why did Niina break off your therapy relationship and start seeing Elina?"

Again the amused smile that implied Kari Hanninen didn't think I was nearly as clever as I imagined. "Who told you she broke off our relationship? It just changed form. I still read Niina's astrological charts, with her, actually, since she's become so proficient. She does readings herself now to bring in a little extra cash. KELA paid for the psychotherapy she was getting from Elina . . . I've heard some criticism of late concerning Elina's ultrafeminist approach to her group therapy and seminars. What is it they say about glass houses and casting stones?"

"It sounds like you really hated Elina," I said. "Did you send Niina Kuusinen to be her patient to spy on her?"

Now Hanninen laughed out loud. "Don't you wish! On the contrary, I thought Elina's approach would be a perfect fit for Niina's mother issues. But I see what you're getting at. I'm sure you'll be delighted to hear that I don't have an alibi for the night of the twenty-sixth. I was home alone in my apartment."

I blushed and saw that Hanninen noticed, which bothered me. As usual, I'd gotten overly excited and run with an idea that was probably ludicrous.

The department secretary knocked on the door. She had a report on Rosberga's incoming and outbound calls over the Christmas holidays. I'd asked for it ages ago.

I wanted to look the report over in peace, which meant getting rid of Kari Hanninen. But he just lounged in the chair across from me giving no indication of leaving.

"What's your sign, by the way, Sergeant Kallio?" he asked suddenly. I didn't like the way he was eying me. "I would guess one of the dualistic signs. Gemini . . . No, maybe Pisces."

"Why is that significant?" The last thing I wanted was to admit to Hanninen that he was right. I really was those two fish eternally swimming in different directions.

"I'd love to do a reading for you sometime. Free of charge of course. Just tell me your precise date and place of birth."

I smiled uneasily. What would it hurt? I didn't believe in any of that nonsense anyway. Or maybe I did. Why else would I care if this man studied my "celestial nature" or fate? Maybe I was just bothered by the idea that after reading my horoscope he would think he knew me. His teasing smile finally made me give in. I told him the place, time, and date of my birth. Maybe it would get rid of him.

The strategy worked. He jumped out of the chair and said he'd get right to work and have my birth chart ready by the end of the week. I wondered whether he would bring it to me personally but didn't ask.

After Hanninen left, I tore into the phone LUDs. I already knew about most of the calls. Tarja Kivimäki had called her parents in Tuusniemi on Christmas Eve, and Niina Kuusinen had called to announce her arrival on Christmas Day. Joona Kirstilä called several times, from both Hämeenlinna and Helsinki, and his claim about the one o'clock phone call was accurate. But before that call was an absolute bombshell: why had Elina received a call at eleven from Leevi Säntti's cell phone?

1 2

The rhythmic rocking of the train was a good cradle: I fell asleep within fifteen minutes of departure and didn't wake up until morning, just a little before we arrived in Oulu. I barely had time to use the bathroom, wash my face, and throw on some makeup.

The train swayed just as I was putting on my mascara, giving me a nice thick brown streak down my nose. It took some hard scrubbing to get it off because I'd forgotten to bring makeup remover with me. There was a reason I usually didn't do my makeup until I had some coffee, but I'd have to wait until the Oulu railway station for that.

Ten years had passed since I'd last been to Oulu, for a rock festival with some friends. I didn't remember much of the city, but I knew the police station was close to the train depot. An officer there would accompany me out to Karhumaa, Johanna's village. I'd made the request after learning Leevi Säntti had called Elina's personal phone from his cell the night she died. I wanted to conduct an official interview.

The coffee and cheese sandwich I got from the station café were tolerable and helped me clear my head before I found my way to the police station. The desk officer announced my arrival to Officer Rautamaa, and in a few moments a six-foot-tall blond woman about my age dressed in winter uniform coveralls marched over to me.

"Hi, I'm Minna Rautamaa," she said, shaking my hand. "Weren't we at the police academy together for a while?"

"Yeah, we were," I said with surprise. "I think you left early to go on maternity leave. But your name wasn't Rautamaa then, was it? That's why I didn't realize I knew someone here."

"My maiden name was Alatalo," she said. "And that baby is already twelve, if you can believe it. Shall we go?"

I remembered my disappointment when Minna Alatalo's pregnancy had forced her to drop out of the academy. She was the only other woman in my class, and after she left I felt like an orphan.

The sun hadn't fully risen, and a frigid wind kept the city shivering. In many homes Christmas lights still burned even though Epiphany had already passed. Minna drove at a steady fifty-five as she told me about life as a cop and a mother of three. She had an application in for the NCO course. Now that her youngest was in school, she had more time for her career. I briefly related what I'd been doing since the academy and then moved on to explaining why we were meeting with Leevi Säntti.

"The case was in Nuuksio, right?" Minna asked. "Isn't that the same place where the hostage incident happened last week? Wasn't the cop who died from your department?"

"He was in my unit actually," I said quickly and then turned back to the Elina Rosberg case. Minna cast me a brief glance but had the sense not to pry.

"How old is Johanna Säntti?" Minna asked once I'd filled her in.

"About thirty-three."

"She must be the same Johanna Yli-Koivisto who was in my class in high school. She was from Karhumaa and got married to a minister of some kind. I don't really keep up with religious stuff, but Leevi Säntti's name is familiar. I think he's one of the main leaders of the Laestadians around here."

"So you knew Johanna in school! Tell me about her."

"She was quiet. A really good student who always had perfect grades and got crazy good scores on her college entrance exams. We didn't run in the same circles though. The Laestadians kind of kept to themselves. I guess they weren't allowed to spend time with us normals. But I do remember one thing about her. It was probably during our first year in high school. Johanna was pretty even though she tried not to show it by dressing in weird sack dresses and keeping her hair up in a bun all the time. But that didn't—"

A logging truck came toward us around a snow-covered curve, and Minna broke off to quickly do an evasive maneuver. The car slid for a while before she got it back under control.

"Flippin' heck. That guy was going at least fifteen over!" Minna huffed. "We should go after him, but I'm not really interested in rally racing in this snow."

"I hear you," I said. "When I was younger I had the energy to jump on every little thing. So what was this about Johanna in school?"

Minna told me about Jari Kinnunen, the class bad boy who had fallen for the beautiful, quiet Johanna Yli-Koivisto during their freshman year. Jari would try to talk to Johanna between classes and he sat next to her in the cafeteria. He even brought her chocolates and wrote her love songs.

"Do you keep up with rock music?" asked Minna. "Have you heard of a band called Brain Drain? Jari's their guitarist."

I did know Brain Drain. They played a fun brand of retro punk. I had assumed the band members were much younger than me.

According to Minna, Jari was the last person Johanna would have gone out with. At first she seemed irritated by all the attention. But as the fall wore on, Johanna started to thaw. To everyone's surprise, she showed up at a Christmas party at Minna's house, even though her brother made it clear she couldn't stay long and he would pick her up by ten.

At school that day, Jari had bragged to his friends that he would finally wake his Sleeping Beauty that night. And that's exactly what happened. When Johanna's brother came to pick her up, she wasn't in the living room, where the rest of the class was chatting and getting drunk.

"He found them kissing in my little brother's room, surrounded by all his car tracks and hockey sticks and stuff. Just kissing, mind you. Completely innocent. But Johanna's brother totally flipped out. First he hit Jari and then Johanna, and the language he used . . . I didn't think religious people knew swear words like that. In the middle of it, he yelled something about Johanna whoring again. Then he dragged her out to the car. Jari wanted to go after them, but the rest of us convinced him that fighting her brother would just make things worse for her.

"The next Monday at school, Johanna was quiet and didn't say a word about what had happened. She wouldn't talk to Jari at all. The last class of the day was gym, and although Johanna tried to hide in the corner of the dressing room, the other girls saw that she was covered in bruises.

"In hindsight we should have done something." Minna sighed. "But we were so used to the religious kids living their own lives, we thought it was best to leave her alone. Then in the spring Jari quit school anyway because he got a spot in a touring tango band. Johanna didn't participate in prom or our graduation ceremony, and when she came for our college English test, she was wearing an engagement ring. I think she wanted to go to medical school, but instead she got married."

We had arrived in the town of Ii, where the road turned east along the Ii River toward Karhumaa and Yli-Ii. In the summer the riverside road would probably be a fun bike ride. Gradually the sun began climbing in the sky. Its slanted rays made the snow sparkle in a kaleidoscope of colors. I looked out at the landscape rather than the road until a wave of nausea hit me so hard that I had to ask Minna to stop the car so I could open the door and puke.

Of course Minna guessed immediately that I was pregnant. With the experience of a mother of three she began sharing nausea prevention tips. I looked for a service station where I could stop to rinse my mouth before we arrived in Karhumaa, but there weren't any. In the end I asked Minna to stop again about half a mile outside the village. I filled my mouth with snow from the side of the road and waited for it to melt. Just like when I was a kid, at first it tasted fresh and clean, and then oily and gritty.

The village was small and had only one main road. Our directions were good, and we easily found the Säntti home about a mile past the center of the village, right along the river. Evidently the lot had been lopped off from the land belonging to the farmhouse farther along the bank. The Säntti home, like all of the houses in the village, looked spacious, as if every builder had been preparing for a family of twelve, but it was more attractive than the others: a white brick rambler that had to be more than three thousand square feet. In the driveway stood a classy dark-gray Volvo sedan and a minibus of the same make. Of course a minibus was the only kind of vehicle the Säntti brood could fit in. Cross-country skis and kick sleds stood in the yard in a row. The frilly curtains in the windows looked as if they had been cleaned yesterday. Contrary to my expectations, the house didn't look the slightest bit dreary. The man who opened the door and stood waiting for us was different from what I expected too.

Although Leevi Säntti's voice on the phone had been controlled and pleasant, I had still imagined a short, round man with his greasy hair parted down the middle, 1960s-style glasses, and high-water pants.

In reality Leevi Säntti was six feet tall with broad shoulders and short, neatly groomed brown hair that had definitely seen some styling product. His facial features were pleasant, and he was wearing dark-blue corduroys and a casual blue-and-brown mottled sweater over a light-blue striped dress shirt. He didn't look a day older than his age of forty-one.

He invited us into a roomy entryway with a handsome row of cabinets. From farther inside the house came the sounds of small children. Suddenly a three-foot-tall, towheaded little girl appeared at the end of the hall, pointed at me, and, proud of her newfound skill, said, "Auntie. Auntie."

The child couldn't be more than two, so she was probably Maria, Johanna's youngest. I felt like running over and sweeping her up in my arms, but before I could do that, a girl of about six came to get her.

"We should go in my office, where we can talk without interruptions," said Säntti. "I don't want the children to hear the police asking about their mother. At least you came in a civilian car."

"This is just a routine visit," I said reassuringly. On the way to his office, I managed to catch a glimpse of a traditional-looking living room and a children's bedroom complete with guardian angel pictures and bunk beds.

"I'm actually just a part-time minister. My main job is at my father's sawmill," Säntti explained as I looked curiously at his bookcase with its rows of religious texts and woodworking manuals. "I actually need to be at the mill this afternoon, so we should get down to business. Maija-Leena will be in shortly with coffee."

There was something about Leevi Säntti that reminded me of Kari Hanninen. It wasn't his pleasant appearance or soft-spoken speech, which forced you to lean in close to hear him. I couldn't put my finger on what the characteristic was. I doubted Leevi Säntti believed in astrology.

"Do you have any objections to me taping this conversation?" I asked.

When Säntti shook his head, I continued. "Elina Rosberg, whose home your wife Johanna has been staying at since she left here, died recently under mysterious circumstances. I'd like to talk to you about your wife's mental health. She has experienced some very difficult things. The decision to have an abortion and to leave her family, even temporarily, couldn't have been easy. Do you think she might have snapped?"

"Do you believe in God, Sergeant Kallio?" Säntti asked.

Although the question was off topic, I decided to answer anyway. "I don't think I know what I believe. Why do you ask?"

"With Johanna I wouldn't talk about mental illness but rather defying the will of God," said Säntti. "The Bible forbids murders like abortion, and it gives clear instructions on a wife's subservient position to her husband. It's also very clear that a mother belongs with her children. I don't know my wife anymore. Her brothers remember how during her school years she transgressed the will of God several times, but for years she's been a good mother and obedient wife. Given her behavior, I don't know whether she's possessed or not. She already killed one person—and I think she very well could have killed another."

"Did you hold Elina Rosberg responsible for your wife's abortion?" I asked.

"What do you mean?" Leevi Säntti seemed genuinely surprised, although I had no doubt he understood what I was getting at.

"Elina Rosberg encouraged your wife to have an abortion and offered her a place to stay," I said.

"I didn't know that." A defensive note had entered Säntti's baritone voice. "I just thought Ms. Rosberg operated some sort of women's shelter."

"A shelter? For battered women?" I asked, probing.

"What are you insinuating?"

"I'm not insinuating anything. I just want to know what your understanding was of Elina Rosberg and the activities of the institute she operated."

Just then the door opened and a slender young woman entered carrying a tray. I assumed it was Maija-Leena Yli-Koivisto, Johanna's sister. The likeness between the two was striking, although Maija-Leena didn't look nearly as sad or exhausted as her beaten-down sister. Despite the grandmotherly dress she wore, she was a very pretty young woman.

On the tray with the coffee was rye bread with *pulla* that looked and smelled homemade. Minna glanced at me as if encouraging me to eat to ward off the nausea. After setting down the tray, Maija-Leena wordlessly left. I wondered whether I might be able to interview her after Leevi Säntti left for the sawmill.

The bread tasted like summer at my uncle Pena's farm. I'd eaten almost a whole piece before anyone spoke again.

"I know the events of the past months have been difficult for Johanna, but they've also been difficult for me," Leevi Säntti finally said. "No matter how hard I try to believe that God knows what he's doing, I still commit the sin of doubt. The baby Johanna killed was my child too. Why did God want to punish me by killing my child?"

"The baby probably would have died anyway, along with your wife," I said.

"The Lord has performed greater miracles. Perhaps he would have preserved Johanna and the child if we'd had the humility to bend to his will and put our trust in prayer."

I looked at Leevi Säntti in disbelief. I realized suddenly what it was about him that reminded me of Kari Hanninen. Both of them turned on their personal charm full blast when they talked about the things they knew their listeners would have the hardest time believing. Säntti was probably a charismatic preacher.

"Why didn't you take your wife back after the abortion?" I asked.

"Even if this worldly society accepts it, abortion is a very serious sin. Of course the children need their mother, but they're better off growing up without a mother than under the direction of a godless sinner like that."

Minna shifted uncomfortably, and her elbow bumped the recorder, sending a stack of papers tumbling to the floor. I was glad for the interruption, which gave me a second to gather my thoughts and calm down. Trying to change Leevi Säntti's mind wasn't my job, and I wouldn't have been able to anyway. But it was hard to stay quiet and just listen.

"Our religion does not condone divorce, but Johanna intends to go through with it anyway," he continued. "Because of the children, I've tried to keep an open heart. I even allowed Johanna to sleep under my roof last week despite my fears that she would poison my children's minds. Even though she doesn't have a home to offer them, she wants them for herself. She"—here Säntti spread his arms, and for a moment I thought he was imitating Jesus on the cross—"wants to destroy me and my family."

"So you aren't going to give her the children?" I said.

"No, not without a fight. And I have God on my side."

I couldn't say whether I believed in God, but I knew I didn't believe in a vending machine deity who gave you what you wanted as long as you remembered to fold your hands and bow your head at regular intervals. And I really didn't respect a God who thought the mother of nine small children should die rather than have an abortion to save her life. I realized I was getting angry again. I'd probably be asking Leevi Säntti if he'd ever heard of condoms if we didn't wrap things up soon.

"You keep hinting that you think it's possible your wife murdered Elina Rosberg. Do you have any idea what her motivation would have been?"

Leevi Säntti looked at me with extreme sadness. "You just said that Ms. Rosberg encouraged my wife to have an abortion. Perhaps Johanna finally started feeling contrition and decided to kill her tempter."

I sighed. With that logic Johanna would be skulking around Oulu bumping off the hospital staff that had performed the abortion. But Säntti's suggestion made me think. Was this the insanity I kept sensing about Elina's death? Johanna was definitely unbalanced.

"Where were you on the night of the twenty-sixth?" I asked.

"Me? Probably here at home. Or no—actually, I think I was away . . . Just a minute." Säntti pulled out an executive day planner.

"There was a revival on Boxing Day in Vihti, and I was asked to speak. I drove there," he finally said.

"Vihti? That's not more than twenty miles from Nuuksio. Where did you spend the night?" I asked.

"At the home of a brother in Vihti."

"Did you happen to stop in Nuuksio?"

"What would I have done there?"

"You could have gone to meet your wife . . . or Elina Rosberg. You called her that night at eleven o'clock. What did you want to talk to her about?"

Säntti glanced toward the heavens, and I wondered whether he was pleading to his God for help.

"I didn't call her," he finally said, looking me straight in the eye.

"Doesn't your religion say that lying is a sin? You did call. Elina Rosberg's personal phone, not the house phone your wife used."

"And what if I wanted to talk some sense into that woman? What if I asked her to send my wife back?"

"At eleven o'clock at night on the day after Christmas?" I asked dubiously.

Leevi Säntti returned my gaze but was saved from answering when the door suddenly swung open and a boy of about three toddled in. He stretched carefully to close the door and then ran to his father.

"Daddy, did Mommy come in that car?"

"Simo, I don't know how many times I've told you that you aren't allowed in Daddy's office when he's working. No, Mommy didn't come in that car, just these nice ladies. Now run back to Auntie Maija-Leena."

Pretending not to hear his father's command, Simo stood and stared at us. Minna's police uniform seemed particularly interesting to him. Leevi Säntti shifted uneasily, and I got the feeling that in the presence of different people he would have ordered his son much more sternly. Finally the boy climbed into my arms, which was a surprise since I've never been the type to attract little kids.

"Our mommy don't live here anymore," Simo explained. Each *r* came out as a *w*. "She just comes visit. Mommy did sin and that why she not live with us anymore."

The word "sin" sounded ludicrous coming out of a three-year-old's mouth. I wanted to tell Simo that his mother missed him, but I didn't want to confuse the child any more. His breath smelled of rye bread, and the skin on his cheeks was warm and smooth like a nectarine that had been lying in the sun. Leevi Säntti stood up and opened the door, calling for Maija-Leena to come get Simo. The young woman came at a half run, three preschool-aged girls at her heels. All of them looked alarmed.

"Come along, Simo. You can help Johannes and Markus clean your room," Maija-Leena coaxed. I had a hard time imagining what enticement there could be in an offer like that, but the boy obediently climbed down from my lap and scampered off into the hall.

With Simo gone, Säntti continued. "I admit the time of the call was odd, but I just happened to be near a phone and assumed people like her tended to stay up late."

"What exactly did you want from Ms. Rosberg?" I asked.

"I wanted her to talk some sense into Johanna so she would either come home or give up her demands about the children. She wants them for herself, but she doesn't have a home for them, an income, or anything," he said. "She isn't going to get the children anyway. She left them, and she's mentally unbalanced. There's no point in her demanding them because God is on my side."

I felt like saying he should probably still hire a lawyer but kept my mouth shut.

"Ms. Rosberg wouldn't help me," Säntti said coldly. "When I said that Johanna could come home if she repented and asked for forgiveness from me, our church, and God, she hung up."

I probably would have too. But *had* Elina hung up? What if despite the ban on men, Leevi Säntti went to Rosberga? What if Elina met him at the gate, and then under the influence of her drugs passed out in Säntti's car? Säntti had seen an opportunity to get revenge and dragged Elina into the woods to die. The fiber analysis from the material found on Elina's body—what little there was—had probably come back by now. What if it matched Säntti's car or clothing?

I asked Säntti for the name of his friend who lived in Vihti. Säntti claimed he'd arrived there around twelve thirty, which would exclude him from the pool of suspects. But we would check.

I also asked for Johanna's parents' address. It turned out her mother had died a few years earlier.

"The moment she killed her baby, she was dead to her father and brothers. I doubt they'll be willing to talk to you," Säntti said.

"We'll see. But first I'm going to talk to her sister," I said.

Säntti's expression turned even more disapproving. "Maija-Leena won't be able to tell you anything I can't. You can just ask me. Then you can leave when I do."

Getting Säntti to allow us to stay in his house after he left for work took some negotiation. He finally asked that we wait until

Maija-Leena put Maria down for her nap and Elisa was home from school to watch the older kids before we interviewed her. This would take some time, so in the end we left when Säntti did, to visit Johanna's relatives, with the promise that we wouldn't return for an hour.

"You must really suspect Johanna if you came all the way up here to ask about her," Minna said as we drove slowly toward the Yli-Koivistos' farm, where Johanna's father lived with her oldest brother and his family and her youngest brother, who was still single. The middle brother, named Simo like his nephew, had moved north to Kemi.

"It isn't just about that," I answered briefly. I wasn't really sure what it was about. I just felt the need to know more about Johanna's life in this tiny religious community.

Johanna's oldest brother had a brood almost as big as his sister's, so I expected the Yli-Koivisto home to be full of life. The main house, painted a dark red, harkened back to the 1800s, and a handsome, well-cared-for stone barn sat on the other side of the farmyard. There were no cars outside, but fresh tire tracks led to the three-car garage.

No one came to the door even though we knocked a couple of times and even rang the doorbell—in the countryside a sure sign that a stranger was visiting. After checking that the barn was locked and no lights were on in the house, we left. Maybe the Yli-Koivistos were home, but they clearly didn't want to talk to the police.

The house Johanna grew up in was a little off the beaten track, and when I glanced at it once more in the rearview mirror, I realized how dreary and withdrawn the dark colors made it look. No wonder Maija-Leena Yli-Koivisto preferred to live in her sister's more modern home. When we returned, she was bustling about

as comfortably as if she were the lady of the house. I remembered
Johanna's comment that Leevi had already chosen Maija-Leena
as her successor if she were to die in childbirth. What would happen now that Johanna was filing for divorce? I didn't know if
Conservative Laestadians were like Catholics and didn't marry
divorcées. Would Maija-Leena still serve Leevi then?

The moment Maija-Leena began speaking, I realized she was
in love with her sister's husband. She talked about Leevi Säntti
as if he were a demigod. She wouldn't criticize him in any way.
Johanna had known that abortion was a sin. God would have
taken care of her and the children. I wondered how Johanna felt
knowing that her entire family had been prepared to condemn
her to death. It suddenly occurred to me that both Johanna and I
had been in mortal danger recently. Johanna had saved herself. I
was only alive out of sheer luck.

"The children are better off without Johanna," Maija-Leena
said. "Her visits just confuse them, and even Maria has been restless at night. We can explain to the older ones what's going on,
but the little ones don't understand." Maija-Leena was sewing
buttons on a dark-blue dress that was about the right size for a
six-year-old. A meat loaf was browning in the oven, and bread
dough was rising on the counter. Eleven-year-old Elisa was in the
other room reading aloud to the younger kids from a book about
a little lost lamb.

"Do you like your sister?" I asked.

Maija-Leena glanced up from her sewing, then looked down
quickly, as if to conceal what her eyes might say.

"She's a lot older than I am," she said slowly. "When I was little, I looked up to her. She was so nice, and she always had time to
play with me. Their wedding was so beautiful. The whole village
said Johanna was blessed to get such a good man. In high school

I was surprised when she suggested I go away to college and complained that she hadn't been able to. She had a nice house and lots of healthy children! What else could she want? I think she's been having worldly thoughts for longer than any of us knew. She's planted them in Anna's heart too, so Leevi has to banish them with the rod."

"Does Leevi Säntti hit his children?" Minna asked casually. We didn't look at each other, but we both knew that evidence of parental violence would be a powerful weapon on Johanna's side in a custody battle. Maybe in Karhumaa they called it discipline, but fortunately Karhumaa law didn't hold sway everywhere.

A child started crying somewhere.

"That's Maria waking up from her nap again," said Maija-Leena. "I have to calm her down. You should leave. The older children will be home soon. I don't want them to see the police here asking questions about their mother."

We had to content ourselves with what we had. I also needed to catch my train. As we pulled out of the Säntti driveway, we saw the school transport taxi stopping on the other side of the road. Out of it climbed a girl of about thirteen whose wild blond curls, pulled back in a ponytail, were unmistakable. Anna Säntti had inherited her mother's hair.

"Minna, stop!"

I jumped out into a snowbank before the car came to a complete halt and yelled after the girl. "Anna! Wait!"

The girl turned, and I saw hope in her expression. It disappeared when she saw that her mother wasn't with us. Still, she started over to us, a young lady striding tall in a dark-green coat that looked like it had been her mother's.

I told her who we were and asked if there was a café in the village where we could talk briefly.

"There isn't a café here. People drink their coffee at home."
The girl's eyes were more grown-up than her age of thirteen, and
her body was already that of a woman. "We can just drive. If you
turn toward Viittakorpi, it makes a loop."

I moved into the backseat next to Anna. Her face was a mixture of Johanna and Leevi Säntti. Her features were attractive,
like her mother's, but also had the firmness and radiance of her
father's.

"I can't be long or Maija-Leena will wonder where I've run
off to. I'll probably have to say the taxi was late. Is it my mom
you want to talk about? Uh-oh, Grandpa!" Anna ducked down
as we passed a stooped man coming from the other direction on
a kick sled.

"Your mother's father?" I asked.

"Yes. He'd be angry if he saw me riding with strangers. At
least you're women."

"Do you miss your mother?" I asked.

There was pity in Anna's smile, as if it were the stupidest
question in the world. "Of course. All of us except Johannes want
to go with her, but she doesn't have a house yet. I want out of
Karhumaa. I want to go where I can wear jeans and watch TV
like everybody else. Do you know when my mom's going to be
well enough to come get us?"

"Your mother is a lot better already. Didn't she say so when
she came to visit?" I said.

"She did. And she looked different. A lot younger, and she was
laughing again like before Simo and Maria were born. Johannes
said Mom is a whore now because she lets her hair down and
wears pants. But he's an idiot."

Why was I driving around the snowy countryside with Anna Säntti? What did I think I was going to get from a thirteen-year-old girl? Evidence that one of her parents was a murderer?

"Maija-Leena is trying to teach the others, especially Maria and Simo, to call her Mom, but I always tell them she's their aunt, not their mother. Mom will come get us soon. But it's hard to tell them what's going on . . . about the abortion and everything. Mom only told me because I asked and asked. How do you explain that to a six-year-old?"

My next question made me feel like a jerk, but I asked it anyway. "Have you heard your father threaten your mother or the woman your mother was living with, Elina Rosberg?"

"Oh, the one who died? I heard Dad talking to Maija-Leena about how God is testing them by letting Mom live after committing a sin like abortion. I think Dad wants to marry the stupid idiot! And he's always talking about how religious people need to stand up against doctors who do abortions, like in America. If there's one thing Dad knows how to do, it's talk." Anna's tone was cruel. "Since Mom left, he's always watching me. At night he comes into my room to check if I'm in my bed like I'm supposed to be."

I drew in a sharp breath. This was starting to sound even worse than I thought. A popular preacher sexually abusing his children?

"What does he do?" I asked.

"He doesn't do anything. He just looks at me. It's creepy. He always pats Elisa, and he whispers that he's glad she's still a little girl and not a woman. But hey, I need to get home. I can't stand the questions whenever I'm late."

We turned back. Anna again assured me that other than Johannes, all of the Säntti children wanted to live with their mother. I didn't dare ask more questions. Interviewing a minor without a parent or a social worker present was a sensitive matter. All I could do was take the material to my lawyer friend, Leena. The court had to listen to the children too.

"So that was Old Man Yli-Koivisto on that sled, was it?" I said to Minna after we dropped off Anna. "Do we have time to stop by there again?"

"Not if the train is on time," she said. "Call the station and find out. I have the number here."

Before I could dial the number, my phone rang. Taskinen's voice kept breaking up, but I still got the message: Aira Rosberg was in the ICU, and it wasn't certain she would survive. At around ten the previous evening she had apparently been attacked as she came home from visiting friends. When Aira got out of her car to open the gate, someone bashed her over the head with the thirty-pound bear statue that stood guard over the entrance to the Rosberga property.

1 3

I wanted to jump on an airplane, but the afternoon flight was full with three standbys, and the evening flight wouldn't be much faster than taking the train back to Helsinki. Besides, what could I do in Espoo right now anyway? Aira was unconscious, and they didn't know whether she would ever wake up.

It was Johanna who'd found Aira, Taskinen explained when I called him back from the train. She'd been watching TV in the library and realized when the program ended that she hadn't heard Aira come in. She peeked in Aira's room and on the security monitor happened to see a car standing outside the gate. When she went down and saw Aira lying in the snow, she called an ambulance. The ambulance crew called the police even though Johanna thought the statue had fallen on its own.

Or so she claimed.

"But isn't that possible?" I yelled at Taskinen through the train phone—I couldn't get reception on my cell.

"No, the statue was too far to the side," he said. "We tried it several times to check."

"How's Johanna holding up?"

"Pretty well, I guess, judging by the way she chewed out Ström when he interviewed her. She's with Aira Rosberg at the hospital now."

"Chewed him out?" I asked.

"Ström isn't the only one who thinks she looks like a good suspect. He just isn't very good at hiding his suspicions. Strange case. Here I was thinking we should put the Rosberg investigation on hold, with nothing new indicating it was even a crime, then this happens . . . Aira Rosberg must have known something dangerous."

"I've always thought that. I'll go over to Rosberga first thing in the morning. Did Johanna Säntti get permission to stay at the house for the night?"

"I'm not sure."

"And of course there isn't a guard there. I think you should send someone over to watch the place and tell her she might not be safe. I'll go myself tomorrow night," I said.

"No, you will not! I'll handle this. Calm down, Maria. You're obviously too wound up about this."

I couldn't calm down. Sitting on the train doing nothing was incredibly frustrating. I tried to call Antti and then dialed Tarja Kivimäki's number. She wasn't home, so I had to talk to the machine again.

"This is Sergeant Kallio. Unfortunately I have to cancel our appointment tomorrow at ten." I paused briefly to give her a moment to celebrate thinking she had scared me off. "I have to go to Rosberga because someone tried to murder Aira Rosberg. Let's change our appointment to Friday at ten."

I spent the rest of the journey in a half stupor, trying to fall asleep in my seat, images flitting through my head like a surreal movie.

What did Aira know? I'd had the feeling all along she was struggling with herself about whether to tell the police something she knew. It was almost as if she wanted to protect Elina's killer. Maybe that was why she created what I'd come to believe was a fake suicide note. Who was she trying to protect? Only one possibility came to mind: Johanna Säntti.

Although it was almost midnight, Antti was at the station to meet me after working late at the university.

"Hard trip?" he asked, taking my arm as we walked outside and headed for the bus stop.

"No, the trip was fine. I just got some bad news while I was there." Briefly I related how we now had an attempted homicide connected to the case.

"Then you aren't going to have time for anything but work." Antti sighed. "That freeway-opposition meeting is tomorrow at five. I was hoping you'd have time to come."

"I doubt it. But go ahead and forge my signature on all of the petitions and stuff," I said.

As we reached the bus station, the biting wind nearly froze me through. Antti complained about the lack of shelters. He was clearly having a bad day. Only half listening, I thought about Aira. Was she still alive? I decided to wait until I got home to call the hospital; we were boarding now, and I didn't want to disturb the rest of the passengers by yelling into my cell.

"I don't know if there's any point anymore," Antti said dejectedly as we settled into our seats. "I mean trying to stop the freeway. The plans and money are all ready to go. How far out in the woods do we have to move to be safe from them paving the whole place? And we don't even get any say. Some city bureaucrat or developer just decides we need more asphalt and that's it. No one can do anything about it."

"Then fight, man!" I grinned at Antti, and his image, reflected in the bus window, tried to respond in kind.

"What happened last week was pretty hard for me," he finally said. "I was scared I'd lose you . . . and the baby. I'm still a little numb."

"Me too," I admitted. "And I don't want to slow down long enough to think about it unless I absolutely have to."

We sat together for a few minutes in silence. Finally I looked out the window. "Should we get off here and walk?" I said. "I've been on the train the entire day. It'd be nice to move a little."

We exited the bus about a mile from home. The snow muffled the sounds of the city, which glowed with a strange light, and frozen crystals crunched under our feet as if the snow was a thin crust over the earth. Next year at this time we'd be pulling a five-month-old baby in a sled behind us. That felt so far away, and suddenly the picture-perfect family scene made me want to gag.

Maybe that was what turned me off about pregnancy—the incomprehensible glory of motherhood, the expectation that somehow I was supposed to turn into this soft, warm, understanding person. I resented the idea of being a housewife with extra matronly pounds and curlers. OK, stereotypes were made to be subverted, but a child was still a child, and someone had to take care of it or it would actually die.

I thought of my taste for whiskey and the physical torture I routinely put myself through when I ran. I thought of the woman who dictated her own schedule and enjoyed losing herself in work. I thought of Antti, whose head was full of mathematical theories most of the time when he wasn't making love to me.

Whether I liked it or not, we were going to be parents. And parenthood would be easier for Antti than for me. To be a good dad all you had to do was show up at the birth, change the occasional diaper, and teach the kid to ski once he or she could stand. Still, I hoped the pastel parenthood I saw in *Two Plus One* would stick to us like chewing gum on a shoe and not come off until our kid received a graduation cap.

When we reached our yard, Antti turned to look at me. A grin lit up his face.

"My snow woman," he said softly, brushing the end of my nose with his mitten. The condensation from my breathing had turned the hair around my face white, and the snow falling from the tree branches covered my hat and shoulders.

"At least I'll eventually melt," I said, thinking of Elina.

I called the hospital before going to bed. No significant changes in Aira Rosberg's condition. She was still unconscious, and they weren't sure of the extent of her brain injuries. Her internal organs were functioning properly. Other than the head trauma, she wasn't really hurt. At the end of the call, the doctor told me he was cautiously optimistic that she would pull through. I wondered how Johanna was doing at Rosberga. Would she be turned out on the street or allowed to live there with Aira gone? Surely it was good that someone was there to watch the house?

The next morning I went straight to the hospital. I didn't expect to interview Aira or even be allowed to see her, but I hoped the doctors could at least update me on her condition. I realized I'd have to reschedule the next couple of days because of Aira's uncertain prognosis, which reminded me that I was going to be questioned about the Nuuksio shooting incident the next day, Friday afternoon. It put me in a bad mood. I already knew how the interviews and subsequent legal proceedings would end. One of the cops giving orders in the field would be sacrificed, while the men who'd really led the operation would never be accused of anything.

My little Fiat looked as if it were drowning in the crowded parking lot of the enormous hospital. Stepping through the exit doors, I realized that in seven months' time, this hospital would swallow me too. It was not a comforting thought. I'd dreaded hospitals ever since I'd had to lie on my back in one for two weeks as a fourteen-year-old because a hungover surgeon had botched my tonsillectomy and the bleeding wouldn't stop. The doctors and nurses had treated me like a nuisance and forced me to eat sickening macaroni gruel.

To me, hospitals felt less like places where they took care of you than places where they forced you to do things. They didn't treat you like a person; they treated you like a leaky tonsil incision, an inflamed appendix, or a broken leg. Was the maternity ward also like that?

At the information desk I had to explain several times who I was before the receptionist would tell me where I could find Aira and the intensive care unit. Colored lines led along the halls to the different units. For me, they led to an elevator.

More red tape was waiting for me in the ICU. I had to first explain my reason for being there to a nurse assistant and then to a nurse specialist. Only after that did I get to talk to the doctor treating Aira. Dr. Mikael Wirtanen, the department head, was so friendly that I assumed it was calculated. It's always harder to pressure a pleasant doctor into giving permission for questioning.

In Aira's case, it was out of the question anyway.

"She's conscious, but very confused," he explained. "She doesn't seem to remember what happened at all. She's also in a lot of pain, so we have her on some strong medication. So far it's difficult to assess how permanent her injury is. Ms. Rosberg is seventy years old, and at that age recovery is much slower than in someone your age, for example."

"How much will her emotional state affect her recovery?" I asked. "Her niece, who was very close to her, died suddenly a couple of weeks ago. That's two major traumas in a short time."

"Everything affects everything. Unlike some of my colleagues, I strongly believe that a person is a psychophysical entity," said Dr. Wirtanen. "Fortunately Ms. Rosberg is in good shape overall for her age."

I considered whether Aira's life was still in danger. If the same person who drugged Elina and left her for dead hit Aira with the bear statue, the MO seemed to indicate they were most likely to strike at night when there was no one around. The ICU was always crawling with people during the day, but what if the assailant snuck in after hours for a second attempt?

Fleetingly I wondered who would inherit Aira's property if she died. I knew real cases weren't like those in an Agatha Christie novel, but I couldn't help imagining Joona Kirstilä as Aira's illegitimate son come to claim his inheritance. I gave a snort of disbelieving laughter, and Dr. Wirtanen glanced at me in surprise.

"Can I see Aira?" I said quickly. "Even through the glass."

"Do you know her other than through your work?" the doctor asked.

"I'm also investigating Elina Rosberg's death, but I knew Aira before that." It felt like an eternity since my lecture at Rosberga Manor. That had happened in another world, a world in which Palo was still alive and I didn't know about the baby hiding in my belly.

"Seeing her won't tell you anything, but OK. Come on."

The top half of the room's door was glass, and I peeked through it cautiously, as if afraid Aira would see me. But she didn't see anything. Her closed eyes were sunk deep into her head, and her high cheekbones protruded like stumps from the moss on a forest floor. Her mouth hung open like a swampy pond, dead and disconcerting. I wondered again what that mouth had refused to divulge. Aira looked lifeless and alone surrounded by the vibrantly flashing machines. At least she didn't seem to need a ventilator anymore. It had been pushed against the wall.

"She might regain consciousness for longer soon, or she might not," Wirtanen whispered.

"But will she live?" I asked.

"I think so. But it's too early to say whether she'll recover fully."

I mentioned to Wirtanen that Aira might still be in danger, hoping he'd take the hint to be more vigilant. When I got to the station I'd look into whether we could send over a guard. Wirtanen promised the hospital would notify me if any changes occurred in Aira's condition, and I shook hands with him as I left.

A very pregnant woman entered the elevator with me. Why was she in the hospital before the birth? Was something wrong? I'd heard stories about women who ended up on bed rest for months because of preterm labor. I'd go crazy if that happened.

Outside, I stood breathing the fresh air for a while before I got in my car. On the radio, the DJs were bantering. I hoped they would play something upbeat. As if the radio announcers had heard my wish, immediately after the Pet Shop Boys' "Go West" came the Rehupiikles' ridiculous but catchy rural Finnish take on the 1960s anthem about going to San Francisco wearing flowers in your hair. My left hand automatically started drumming the steering wheel. Antti was horrified by my taste in music. What appealed to me most was mindless pubescent rock like Popeda and Klamydia. The only rock albums I had that Antti actually listened to were old ones by David Bowie and Pink Floyd.

At the station, I traded my Fiat for a police car and picked up Pihko. Then we set off on the now-familiar route toward Nuuksio and Rosberga. I really didn't know what I was looking for, but I still felt compelled to go.

Pihko asked about my trip to Oulu and told me what Johanna had said about Aira's injury during her interview. Aira must have lain at the gate for nearly two hours before Johanna found her, because a good amount of snow had fallen on her. Ström's questioning had started out fairly objectively, but at the end he asked Johanna bluntly whether she had waited for Aira, knocked her over the head, and then conveniently "found" her two hours later.

"Then Ström said something like 'Wasn't it a shame that Aira didn't die from the blow or freeze to death like her niece?' and 'wasn't it too bad Aira had thought to wear a coat?'" said Pihko. "The Säntti lady was so timid during the interview Ström was lucky to get a yes or no out of her, but when he said this she got so angry so suddenly I almost fell out of my chair. She screamed 'Why would I kill Aira Rosberg? She's the only protection I have in the world!' Ström was completely flummoxed. Puupponen was in there with us taking notes, and he about died laughing. He hates Ström almost as much as you do."

"What? Why would I hate Pertti Ström?" I asked innocently. It was only in storybooks that shared sorrow permanently smoothed over conflicts. Since our brief moment of grief at Palo's death, Ström had been just as big a bastard as before. I was relieved he was tied up with Taskinen on another case today, leaving me with Pihko for a partner.

Slipping and sliding, the car somehow made it up the hill to Rosberga. Strangely, the gate was open. Why? I thought Forensics was done investigating at Rosberga. Glancing at the wall where the bear statue once stood, I tried to estimate how high it was.

I definitely wouldn't have been able to reach the statue without standing on something. But for anyone over six feet tall, it wouldn't be too much of a stretch. What did that mean?

The courtyard was deserted, but someone had recently shoveled the drive and a path to the door. The Russian-made Lada I was driving suddenly slid nastily on the slick ice in previous tire tracks in the snow. Fortunately I managed to get the car stopped six inches from a snow bank.

"Want to bet the snow tires on this thing wouldn't pass a safety inspection?" I said with a sigh as I climbed out of the car. The front door of the house wasn't standing ajar like the gate. I had to ring the doorbell three times before Johanna answered it.

"I'm sorry it took so long. I was on the phone," she explained, but there was none of her old shyness in her apology. "Canceling all of these courses is such a mess. But someone has to handle it with Aira in the hospital."

I had always been fascinated by the makeovers women's magazines did, changing a plain-Jane into a beauty queen. Johanna was now the "after" version. She was wearing jeans and a sweater instead of a frumpy old lady dress, and her curly locks cascaded down her back, looking somehow blonder than before—maybe Johanna had risked highlighting the color the Almighty had chosen for her. Even her posture was different.

"I met your family yesterday," I told Johanna. "Anna is a wonderful girl, and the little ones are so cute."

Sadness flashed across Johanna's face, but anger quickly swept it away. "Yes, they are, and I'm sick of waiting to get them back. I've filled out rental applications with the housing offices in Espoo and Helsinki, but both say they only have a few apartments as big as we need and they've all got huge waiting lists. We could fit in a two-bedroom if we had to, but some stupid law won't let us! I don't have the money to pay a deposit on the private market. Then there's the problem that I'm still listed as a resident in Karhumaa. I have to change my permanent residence to Espoo before anything can happen. Until then I can't apply for welfare here, and I probably won't be able to get unemployment anyway as long as I'm married to Leevi because of the income limits."

Johanna's words poured out in a flood much like her daughter Anna's had. Had the Johanna I met at Rosberga before Christmas been crippled by depression? Had she been medicated? What had changed in her? Or maybe the quiet Johanna had been the real one and now we were seeing the manic murderer.

"Where are you getting money from now? Do you have savings?" I asked, although it really wasn't any of my business.

"Elina loaned me five thousand marks. I haven't had to spend anything. I don't pay rent here, and Aira buys the food. But I can't live like this forever. As soon as Aira's well again, I need to start kicking ass," Johanna proclaimed.

Once I recovered from the shock of hearing Johanna swear, I changed the subject to Aira, asking Johanna the same questions Ström had asked her the day before and receiving the same inconsequential answers. Johanna had apparently been watching *Law & Order*, which was completely new to her, as was every other television show. She hadn't seen or heard anything. She didn't know who Aira had spoken to most recently, but the phone had been ringing constantly with questions about the future of Rosberga.

Meanwhile Ström and Pihko had already questioned the two former coworkers Aira had met the night she was assaulted. Those results had been scant as well. According to the women, Aira had been quieter than usual, but they assumed it was a result of Elina's death.

The attack on Aira was just as mysterious as Elina's killing. Trying to make some sense of it, I walked into Elina's and Aira's rooms again. Aira's bedroom had bare walls and only a few framed photos on the bookshelves, including one of Elina and another of a man and woman approaching middle age and dressed in World War II-era clothing, who I assumed were Aira's parents.

Elina's sitting room seemed frozen in time. I pulled a photo album off a shelf. Inside were pictures of Elina posing with high school friends, with her parents abroad in London and Paris, and with Aira somewhere with sandy beaches and palm trees in the background behind Elina, who looked exhausted. That picture was probably twenty-five years old. In it, Aira looked very much like Elina before her death.

The last photo in the album was an enlargement from some sort of company party. A teenage Elina wore a light-blue evening gown and posed on her father's arm, looking every bit the precocious belle of the ball. Several men in tuxedos stared at her as if she were carved out of marble. I went through the album a couple of times trying to find pictures from the India trip, where Aira claimed Elina had come down with a uterine infection, and this made me remember I still hadn't called her gynecologist. I had considered myself to be working as fast as ever after returning from sick leave, but now I saw how many things were slipping through my fingers. Maybe the boss was right. I needed more time off. But only after the Rosberg case was solved.

Even after several passes through the album, I didn't find any pictures from India or a single one of Elina as an adult. Why? Maybe she'd just stopped putting her photographs in albums. Not everyone wanted to remember their lives that way. For them, their memories—those flashes of experience engraved in the mind—were enough.

I looked out the window at the clearing that led down the hill. The trunks of the willows glowed red, and blue tits flitted around the yard, searching for food. But the peaceful landscape felt fragile. More than one ghost was haunting Nuuksio now.

I went back into the hall. "We're not getting anything here. Let's go," I said to Pihko. "Can you drive? I have to make a few calls. Do you have to get back to the station or can you come with me on some other interviews?"

"I have a meeting at two, but that's not for a while." Pihko avoided my eyes. "I actually prefer not being in our . . . in my office with Palo's stuff still there."

Pihko slammed the car door shut as if to show he wasn't a sissy even if he did admit to having feelings. Fastening my seat belt, I called Information and asked them connect me to Dr. Maija Saarinen, Elina Rosberg's gynecologist.

Elina had only been Dr. Saarinen's patient for a few years, switching practices after her previous gynecologist retired. Dr. Saarinen had noticed the shape and scarring of Elina's cervix too, and had been given the same explanation about question-able gynecological surgery performed in India.

"Although I did wonder . . . I'm not sure if I should say this, but . . . I wondered if it might be something else entirely."

"What? A pregnancy?" I asked.

"Yes . . . Before abortion was legalized, women sometimes did it themselves or found a quack to do it for them. That would cause similar scars. But there was no mention of anything like that in her old records, and a woman of her generation could have a legal abortion. She wouldn't have had to find someone in a back alley."

"Where can I get hold of your predecessor?" I asked.

"Unfortunately you can't. She died a year ago."

Dead end after dead end! That's all this case was!

When had Aira said Elina was in India? About twenty years ago? Wasn't Elina dating Kari Hanninen around that time? What if Elina had aborted their baby on her own . . .

Hanninen's answering machine picked up after one ring. I didn't bother leaving a message.

"Where are we going anyway?" Pihko asked. We had just reached the Turku Highway intersection.

"I don't know. Drive over to that gas station while I make another call."

It wasn't even noon yet, so it was no surprise that Milla Marttila sounded irritable.

"Didn't I say not to call me so early?" she snapped.

"So why do you keep your phone plugged in? It's easy to unplug, you know," I answered.

"What the fuck do you care?" She paused. "So what do you want?"

"Where were you the night before last between ten and midnight?"

"Why?"

"Someone tried to kill Aira Rosberg."

"Aira! What the hell! How?"

"Hit her over the head. She's still in the ICU but out of the woods now. Where were you?" I asked again.

"I was at work from eight until four. Go ahead and ask anyone at Fanny Hill. They open at seven. If that's all you want, I'm going back to sleep."

"Will you be at work tonight?"

"Yeah," Milla replied and slammed down the phone.

I had better luck with Niina Kuusinen. She was at home in Tapiola, and she wasn't planning on going anywhere. So we headed south. Another gas station along the way advertised a burger called the Hawaii 5-0, made with slices of ham and pineapple, so we stopped to wolf down a few and then continued to Tapiola.

The Kuusinens lived in an upscale apartment complex designed by a famous architect. It seemed strange that a twenty-five-year-old woman still lived with her father, but apparently he was retired and spent most of the winter in southern France. Niina didn't ask why we'd come. Dressed in thick violet tights and a black sweat shirt, she opened the door and stared at us for a moment with her large, almond-shaped eyes before motioning us into the living room.

When light was streaming through the tall windows, the room was probably more cheerful, but now the silver-gray drapes were pulled shut and the overall effect was gloomy. The same silver-gray color was repeated in the rococo furniture. I hoped Pihko and I hadn't tracked any slush onto the light-gray rugs.

An arrangement of flowers, candles, and photographs sat on a lace tablecloth on a baby grand piano. The largest picture showed a frail woman with dark hair, smiling weakly. Next to this were a couple of childhood portraits, probably of Niina. The almond eyes were impossible to mistake, even though Niina's hair was much lighter when she was a child. The man in the pictures had to be Niina's father. Niina clearly took after him more than her mother. They had the same tall, slender frame, high cheekbones, and almond-shaped eyes.

"Do you know why we're here?" I asked.

"Probably because of Aira." It was obvious Niina was fighting to keep her voice steady. "Johanna called me yesterday. I just got back from the flower shop. I sent Aira some roses. She's going to get better, isn't she?" Niina asked breathlessly.

"She should," I said. "She's in and out of consciousness. What do you know about what happened to her?"

"Me? Only what Johanna told me. Someone attacked Aira on her way to the house. Maybe it was a robber who read about Elina's death in the paper. I don't know." Niina shook her head, causing dark strands of hair to slip over her face like a glossy veil.

"Where were you the night before last between ten and midnight?" I asked.

"Me? At home. I was doing readings, the ones for pay I told you about. I went to sleep right after twelve. Why?"

"Do you have a car?" I asked.

"My dad's Volvo. But I hate driving in the snow," Niina blurted. She looked at Pihko as if seeking support. "I got my license in France, but they don't have ice like here."

Apparently unable to endure more questioning, Niina stood up, walked to the stereo, and put on a CD. The piano music that trickled from the speakers was unfamiliar to me. It seemed to calm Niina down.

"How are you doing, Niina?" I asked. The empathy in my voice wasn't completely fake. Even if Tarja Kivimäki had claimed Niina exaggerated her problems, I sensed Niina wasn't doing terribly well.

"I have a really bad square between Mars and Saturn right now," she said. "But since I saw it coming, I've been able to prepare for it. It will pass soon, and then I'll have an easier aspect starting."

"Well that's good," I said dryly.

"And you're a Pisces! Kari told me you asked him to make you a chart. He says you have a moon in Aquarius. That was the only thing he told me about your chart though," Niina added quickly.

"Are you seeing him as a client again?" I asked. I was amused to hear the new life in her voice when she talked about the astropsychologist.

"No. I was just asking him for help with a difficult chart."

"So you were alone on Tuesday night? Can anyone confirm that you were here? Did anyone call you or anything like that?"

Niina didn't seem to like that the conversation was shifting from astrology back to what happened to Aira.

"No one called me," she said irritably and then added in a softer voice, "But I called Kari about that horoscope at around eleven thirty."

"And you're claiming you made that call from home?"

In reply, she stood up and motioned for us to follow her.

If Milla Marttila's bedroom resembled a bordello, then Niina's office was like a magician's cave. Constellation-patterned fabric covered the walls and windows, and behind the desk hung a huge round diagram that Niina said was her own astrological chart. The shelves were crammed with astrology books, mostly in French and English.

Niina turned on her desktop computer and loaded an astrology program. I didn't know anything about astrology, so I couldn't follow her when she began explaining how it worked, but Niina's intent wasn't to give a demonstration. She said she just wanted to show us that she couldn't do her charts anywhere but in her office. From what little I could understand, I had to believe her.

"How long did you live in France?" I asked as she switched off the computer and led us back into the hall.

"From when I was born until I turned eighteen. Mom and I moved here after I passed the matriculation exams. I thought the Sibelius Academy seemed like an interesting place to go to school, and Mom wanted to come back to Finland, as if . . . as if she knew she didn't have much time left." Tears appeared in her almond eyes. When Pihko noticed them, he opened the front door as if to escape.

I was more callous. "Why did you stay in Finland after her death?"

"I was still in school. And anyway . . . I get along better here than in France."

"Even though your dad spends most of his time there?" I asked.

"Maybe because of that," Niina snapped, but then instantly realized she had revealed too much. "Dad drinks a lot," she said more softly. "It's a typical reaction for a Cancer to the death of a spouse. I understand, but I can't stand to look at him."

Outside, the roads were still deadly slick. I was driving again. I drove a lot for work, rain or shine, and I usually had no trouble handling a car, but the Lada was like an ice skate. Even my Fiat was safer.

"And these are supposed to be designed for Siberia," I muttered as I tried to take off from an intersection and the tires just spun. I was so soaked with sweat by the time we made it back to the station that I had to towel off in the ladies room. Thankfully I always kept an extra shirt and bra in my office. As I changed, I noticed my nipples looked strangely dark. I remembered reading somewhere that this was part of pregnancy too.

At two thirty the hospital called. Aira Rosberg was conscious and doing well given the circumstances. There was only one problem: she couldn't remember a single thing since Christmas Eve.

1 4

According to Dr. Wirtanen, short-term memory loss resulting from a head injury was nothing out of the ordinary, especially given that the events she had forgotten were so traumatic. He thought it was likely her memory would return with time, at least partially.

"Pressuring her won't help," he said to me on the phone. "I'd prefer you didn't question Ms. Rosberg until next week at the earliest. The officer you sent is guarding her, but we aren't telling her that."

"Good. Supervision could be necessary if any of the following people come to visit." I reeled off the names of Milla Marttila, Niina Kuusinen, Tarja Kivimäki, Joona Kirstilä, and Johanna Säntti.

"Mrs. Säntti? She's here right now. Do you really think she could be a danger to Ms. Rosberg?"

I sighed. I didn't know how to answer. The Hawaii 5-0 was giving me heartburn, and I had a strange craving for buttermilk.

Finally I said, "Please ask the guard to just keep an eye on Ms. Rosberg and any visitors. It's an unusual situation."

After I hung up I sat in my office thinking about the case. I wanted to bug Aira's room, but there was no way I'd get permission. Too bad the guard couldn't actually sit in her room and listen in. Maybe we could recruit a few of the department's young female officers to dress up as doctors and nurses? I could pretend to be an orderly . . .

Ström barged in to remind me that we had an interrogation in five minutes, interrupting my increasingly crazy train of thought. The new case was just a drunken brawl, depressingly familiar and mostly harmless—no one had died. Plus it was obvious that the guy who had whacked his buddy over the head with a bottle already had a huge hangover, and even with a few stitches in his head, the victim was still riding his buzz, as were most of the witnesses gathered for questioning.

Keeping Ström from losing his temper was almost harder than figuring out the sequence of events leading up to the attack. When we finally managed to get all of them out of the station around three, we found the rest of our unit besides Taskinen gathered in the break room. The mood was dejected. Pihko was collecting money for a wreath for Palo's funeral. He asked me to write the card.

"Ask the boss," I said. "I'm no good at that kind of thing. By the way, can anyone pull some overtime tonight? It'll be after eight."

Instantly everyone looked mutinous. The Espoo Blues were playing the Jokers that night, and the match would be televised. Ice hockey was always a point of contention here at the station. In addition to fans of those teams, our unit had followers of HIFK, the Tampere Axes, and even KalPa from up north. When asked, I always said I just cheered for the best-looking team but that watching hockey was boring because the men wore too many clothes.

"What's the job?" asked Puupponen, a KalPa fan from Kuopio.

"I need a couple of guys to go with me to Fanny Hill. It's a strip club in Kallio. We need to interview one of the dancers."

In an instant a shouting match replaced the funereal mood, and suddenly I had my pick of volunteers. Eventually they were winnowed down to Ström and Puupponen, the latter because he was nowhere near his overtime limit and the former because even though I didn't really want to take Ström along, he was less likely than the younger guys to go gaga at the sight of bare breasts.

I had completely neglected exercise for the past few weeks, so after work I headed to the rec center in Tapiola. My abs and back muscles would be stressed by pregnancy over the next several months, and lifting weights or running usually helped clear my head. Sometimes exercising even seemed to allow questions to answer themselves. But even though I did a double dose of crunches, worked my biceps and triceps, and spent ten minutes on the abductor machine, this time it didn't work. My head was empty of ideas. My certainty that Elina's death was murder was fading. Maybe the person who hit Aira was just a thief who thought Rosberga was empty? Or maybe Aira staged it. Wasn't there a novel with a plot along those lines?

"Hey, Maria." Just as I was thinking this, my old friend Makke showed up on the machine next to me and tried to convince me to go out for a beer after the gym. I managed to sidestep the invitation by saying I had to work. This wasn't really a lie, but it made me realize that I wasn't going to be able to conceal my pregnancy for long. No one was going to believe I had made a

New Year's resolution to give up drinking, and my first trip to the OB/GYN was next week. This was really happening.

But at least pumping iron did put me in a better mood. When I arrived home from the gym and found Antti not there, I suddenly remembered the antifreeway meeting. I would have had time to go after all. I shook my head as I thought of him. Was there any windmill one of us wasn't willing to take a tilt at? Give it a year and I would probably be protesting about day-care subsidies with my baby strapped to my chest.

For the evening I dressed as unattractively as possible in black jeans and a nondescript gray blouse. I left my hair down and only wore a little makeup, some mascara and powder to conceal the paleness of my face. Looking in the mirror, I was hoping to see a tough police officer staring back, but as usual there was just the same nervous girl. I never understood why people wanted to look younger than they were. In my profession, girlishness was just about the worst thing for your credibility.

I wasn't exactly thrilled about going to a strip club, especially not with Ström and Puupponen. Puupponen was nice enough, a redheaded, freckled kid from Savo, like me. He got along with Ström even worse than I did. The fact that he had volunteered to go out on a job with Ström was a little surprising. Maybe the draw of Fanny Hill was too overpowering.

When Ström picked me up at a bus stop near my house, I saw that Puupponen was already sitting in the backseat. As we drove, I gave them more details about what we were going to do: ask Milla Marttila about her movements the night before last and confirm her alibi, if she had one. We'd probably have to get permission from the manager to interview his employees during work hours, but I wasn't particularly worried about that. Usually the owners of strip clubs wanted to stay in good with the cops.

"Now don't go lecturing the customers about feminism in the middle of their night out," Ström warned me once I'd finished outlining my plan of attack.

"Crap. I forgot my crochet hooks. I'll have to remember next time," I replied, my voice dripping acid. Ström snorted as he pulled our Saab cruiser onto the sidewalk in front of the club, muttering something about how he wasn't going to go scavenging for a parking spot. The bouncer at the door stared at us, especially me, but let us in when Ström showed his badge and asked for the manager. The bouncer told us to wait at the bar for a minute.

I had been to a strip show at a bar in my home town once, also on duty, but that had mostly been comical. What I was seeing now was bewildering. It was early, but there were already numerous groups of men apparently unwinding after business meetings. Most of them wore suits while the cocktail waitresses serving them were topless. The only women who were fully dressed besides me were the shift manager and a woman sitting with a group of men speaking Russian and looking very lost. I tried to spot Milla in the gaggle of topless girls wearing fishnet stockings but couldn't find her. Maybe she was stripping for someone.

The bouncer returned and motioned us to follow him up a stairwell hung with red velvet and large mirrors. Our images were reflected dozens of times as we passed. The same decor continued in the hallway upstairs, with doors punctuating the red velvet walls. It looked like a hallway in a brothel, but the doors probably just led to the private strip show rooms. Music came from a couple of them.

I almost burst out laughing when I saw the owner of the club, Rami Salovaara. For once someone fit the stereotype in my head.

He was short, obese, and very red-faced. He was bald on top, and his long comb-over wasn't quite able to cover the shine. His mustache, on the other hand, was in full bloom. Under a wide nose, it bristled across his entire lip.

"So what do the Espoo Police want at my club?" Salovaara asked, making no move to stand up to shake our hands. Not that it bothered me. I didn't really want his grubby mitts touching me.

"We're here about one of your employees, Milla Marttila. We need to verify her whereabouts a couple of days ago," I replied.

"So it's Milla, is it? What kind of trouble takes three cops to come pick her up?" Salovaara glanced at a monitor sitting on his desk, which showed what was going on downstairs. Were there cameras in the strip booths that Salovaara used to monitor his employees' activities?

"We just want to confirm that she was here working and not out trying to commit a homicide," I said. "We'd like your permission to interview some of your employees during the evening. Do you have shift logs for the night before last?"

"The club manager'll have them. She's the slightly more dressed, wrinkly woman downstairs. Do you really suspect Milla of murder?"

"That actually isn't any of your business," I said coldly, remembering how this man had treated Milla when she was raped. "Puupponen, will you check those rosters and make sure Milla was at work?"

"I'm not obligated to allow you to harass my staff during working hours," said Salovaara. "If the police need to interview my employees, they should do it when they're off the clock."

"For that we'd need a list of your employees, their addresses, and their telephone numbers," I shot back.

I didn't know exactly how the private stripping side of Fanny Hill worked, but more than once I'd heard rumors about other strip clubs skirting the pimping laws by setting the girls up on what they called intermittent work schedules. Because selling themselves wasn't a crime, the girls' official work ended when a customer watching a perfectly legal private stripping session decided to pay for more. What the girls did in their free time outside of the club wasn't the owner's business. After tending to her client, usually in an employer-provided apartment nearby, the girl returned to the club to continue her official work day. The only way anyone could intervene would be by appealing to the Working Hours Restriction Act, but so far there wasn't any precedent for that. But a bunch of the girls living in the same apartment owned by the club would be an obvious sign of a brothel operation. I also had serious doubts that all of the Russian dancers at Fanny Hill had their papers in order.

Puupponen returned with the shift roster before Salovaara could even respond. According to the list, Milla had been at work on Tuesday night, although given how close she lived to the club, she could easily have said she was taking a client back to her apartment and then slipped away to Rosberga.

"So what's it going to be? Should we interview the staff who worked Tuesday night now, or are you going to give us those addresses?" I said, turning the screws.

Salovaara weighed his options carefully.

"If you give us permission, we'll get all the interviews done tonight," Ström said. Up to this point he had been strangely quiet. "It'll be painless. We won't even need everyone's full contact information."

I knew Ström was negotiating, but his willingness to side with Salovaara's circumvention of the law infuriated me.

"If Marttila is guilty—let's say of attempted murder—aiding and abetting could lead to jail time, especially if the person in question has a police record already," I snapped.

I hadn't checked Salovaara's record, so I was taking a risk, but it worked. He grunted something I couldn't quite make out, but then he gave us permission to question the staff just so long as we didn't mess with his business. As we headed to the door, Salovaara suddenly addressed me.

"By the way, Sergeant Kallio, if you ever get tired of police work, come see me about a job. We have a shortage of curvy redheads. Your breasts are about the right size too and probably don't sag much yet. Our customers like a woman who knows how to take charge. A black leather corset and a whip would be just the thing for you."

Ström caught his breath and started moving toward the club owner, but I managed to reply before he got his hands on him. "Thanks, but no thanks. I prefer to choose who sees me naked. Let's take you for example: Bald is beautiful, tubby, so what exactly are you trying to hide with that comb-over? And that mustache. Is it compensating for something else you lack? Are you having trouble getting it up even with a pro now? Sorry, pal, but it shows just looking at you. Thanks for the help though!" I closed the door after us with exaggerated care, catching one last glimpse of the man's face, which looked something like a tomato now.

"You're just making friends left and right these days," Ström said to me in the hall. "You might want to watch it with that one though."

"What do you mean?"

"The chief spends a fair amount of time here. We came here after the Christmas party, and he knew all the waitresses by name. And I'm sure you noticed they don't have shirts to wear name tags on."

I shrugged. "The chief and I are on a collision course anyway. I really don't have the energy to care. I'm going to look for Milla. You two find the women who were working with her that night!"

I was irritated that I'd lost my cool but couldn't help chuckling at how well I'd given it back to the club owner. As I was starting down the stairs, a door behind me opened and a man stepped out zipping up his fly. Glancing at me with a look of alarm, he hurried past. I turned back and peeked into the room he had just exited. It was dim inside, but I recognized the woman who was pulling on her panties. Milla Marttila was easy to find after all.

"Hi, Milla. Could I have a word?" I asked.

"Well, well, look who we have here. Did you come for a show? I thought you were more into guys. Aren't you married?"

"Come off it, Milla," I said. "Your boss gave me permission to interview you about Tuesday night."

"What's to talk about? I was at work from eight to four." Milla refastened her bra, which still exposed her nipples. Goose bumps covered her pale skin. "Wait here while I grab some more clothes," she said and disappeared through the door.

I sat down in the only chair in the room, a black leather recliner. Next to it was a small table with a box of Kleenex and a package of extra strength condoms. In front of the armchair was a stage about six feet by six feet. It was just the right height so that someone sitting in the armchair could stare right at the dancer's labia. The red lights emphasized the cavelike effect of the black-walled room. Next to the door were buttons that I assumed controlled the lighting and music. I wondered how it felt to dance on that stage and to be the man watching but not touching.

Milla reappeared in "more clothes": a satin kimono embroidered with flowers. It was almost the same kind I had at home. I had never thought of it as sexy before. Milla sat on the edge of the stage across from me and lit a cigarette.

"You say you were here all night, but the problem is we don't have much reason to trust you yet. You and Officer Haikala were never able to find the guy you said you slept with the night Elina died. What time did you take your lunch break Tuesday night?"

"My what?" Milla snorted. "Nobody here eats during work. It makes your tummy bulge. Mine is already round enough as it is. A lot of men prefer the bony type."

Milla's eyes were painted with thick black eyeliner, and her lips and nails were black as well. Maybe it was her version of mourning.

"Two of my colleagues are interviewing your coworkers right now. Then we'll know," I said.

"What actually happened to Aira? I was so groggy when you called."

As I told Milla what happened, I saw the surprise in her eyes.

"Who would want to attack Aira? She's such a sweet person!" Milla said the word "sweet" perfectly seriously. "You think Aira knew too much about Elina's death or something?"

"Maybe. I'd also like to know who's mentioned in Aira's will."

"Not me!" said Milla. "I'm sure you'd be happy if I was behind all this, because the media wouldn't care. I'm not famous like Elina's poet boy or that fucking reporter, and I'm not from a rich family like Niina."

"What kind of family are you from then? You mentioned incest at the course where I met you."

Milla took a last puff of her cigarette and then stubbed it out absentmindedly on the edge of the stage and let the butt fall onto the dark-red carpeted floor. With the heel of my boot I put it out properly. Milla looked at her black toenails in their red sandals and didn't say anything for a minute.

How was Milla's previous life any of my business? But I was curious in the same way I'd been curious about Johanna's life. When I met Milla the first time, I thought she wanted out of being a stripper—and apparently a prostitute. Maybe I thought I could save her.

"My family. Ha!" she finally said. "They're still living out in Kerava. My parents had bad luck. They couldn't have kids no matter what they tried, so they finally adopted me. I think I'd been with them two months when Ritva, my adoptive mother, realized she was pregnant. They ended up with three sons of their own. Ritva spent so much time taking care of her little treasures that she forgot all about her husband's needs. Luckily he had me. I started wearing a bra at ten, and that's when he figured I was a woman."

"You mean he started taking advantage of you sexually when you were ten years old?" I asked.

"Well, that's a pretty fancy way of putting it. 'Taking advantage sexually.' He didn't actually screw me since I have such a pretty mouth and quick hands. On my graduation day I finally told Ritva and the rest of my family what a fucking awesome dad I had. I haven't been home since."

Nausea and anger struggled within me. But I'd wanted to hear about Milla's life, so I deserved it. How did therapists handle hearing this kind of thing? What did Elina say to Milla when she revealed this? Or Johanna? I never knew what to say.

"The sad thing is, the shitheads kept dragging me down. I did well in school, even when I had a hard time paying attention because my dad had me up the whole night before. I got into the literature program at the university on my first try. Awesome, except the people in the financial aid office had the idea that all parents still support students under the age of twenty. So I started looking for a way to make money the only way I knew how."

Milla's round toes with their black nails looked like frozen potatoes. Was there any point suggesting that she press charges against her adoptive father? The abuse had ended several years before, but I didn't think it had exceeded the statute of limitations. But how would she prove he'd done it? Milla's parents must have had a respectable façade or else they never would have been able to adopt in the first place.

An adoption . . . Milla was in her early twenties. Just around the time Elina was dating Kari Hanninen. What if . . . No, the idea was too far-fetched. Still, I couldn't help asking.

"Have you ever found out who your real parents were?"

"What the hell for? Why would I want to know about them? They didn't want me. These men do though, and that's enough for me."

I remembered Tarja Kivimäki's sarcastic comment about the homeless cats Elina collected. Milla was a very lost kitten, one who always kept her claws out just in case. Elina's death had happened at the worst possible time for Milla, given her rape experience. I would definitely check on Milla's real parents though, even if the adoption papers would likely only list the mother. Could that be Elina Rosberg?

There was a knock at the door and I jumped. Was it a new customer for Milla?

No. It was Ström. He gave Milla a look that was about as friendly as the one he gave the drunks we'd interviewed that morning.

"Ms. Marttila here is a talented liar," he said. "From what I hear, your shift the night before last didn't actually start until ten thirty. According to the schedule, you were supposed to start at eight, but you traded shifts with someone named Tatiana. So where were you?"

The look Milla shot back at Ström wasn't any friendlier. "That's what Tatiana says, is it? She doesn't know Finnish or English well enough to tell Tuesday from Wednesday. Or does a big pig like you know Russian?"

"Where were you Tuesday night, Milla?" I asked.

"Tell that idiot to get lost," Milla said, indicating Ström. "I'm not saying anything with him here. He should go ask Tatiana for a lap dance while we chat. No Russian language experience required."

I nodded at Ström to leave, and luckily he had the sense to comply. Or maybe the girls downstairs were just a bigger draw. Milla's tough-girl routine was wearing on me. It was as though she was goading me to smash through the act, to order her to cut the crap.

"Well, go ahead. What happened Tuesday?"

"I . . ."

I realized that Milla's eyelids were fluttering, and black streaks were running down her cheeks toward her jaw.

"I just couldn't do it. I called the apartment where all the Russian girls live and asked if someone could work my first couple of hours. Last weekend was so hard, and Mondays the club is closed. I was just . . . tired."

"Why don't you stop doing this?" I asked.

"For a cop you're so naïve! Is quitting somehow going to magically fix my life? Maybe I should go back to school and marry some Prince Charming? Don't make me laugh."

Milla pulled a clump of Kleenexes out of the box. Her face looked almost comical smudged with black. "These guys even own my apartment. I wasn't willing to shack up with a bunch of other girls like the Russians, but the club still pays the bills. How would I get a new apartment? Don't say in the dorms. I'm too antisocial for that."

I still couldn't find the right words. Only empty advice. Quit the job. Go to therapy and deal with your childhood. Press charges against your father. Instead of saying any of that, I just continued the interview.

"So were you at home Tuesday night?"

Milla shook her head. Black lipstick smeared her jaw, and her nose was red under her white face powder.

"How the hell am I supposed to explain it to you! You're a cop, not Elina. Sure, I was home, no witnesses. Or maybe I was at Rosberga and whacked Aira over the head because she knew I killed Elina. What the fuck does it matter now?"

"It does matter." I rose from my chair and tried to find a way to touch her that felt natural. Touching wasn't allowed in this room—only looking, emotionally and physically stripping the other person bare.

"I know I'm not Elina," I said uncertainly, timidly putting my hand on Milla's shoulder. "But there are other people besides Elina who can help."

Just then the door flew open, this time without a knock. Rami Salovaara poked his head in. "Milla, they want you downstairs. You have a dance at fifteen to—Goddamn it, go clean yourself up! We agreed these interviews weren't going to get in the way of business." These last words were directed at me.

"We're actually finished here. Thank you," I said, unsure whether I was irritated or relieved by the interruption. I'd been on the verge of offering to fix Milla's life, despite having plenty on my own plate.

After thanking Milla for her time, I went downstairs. Puupponen and Ström were standing at the bar with glasses of beer in front of them. The main evening show had begun. The svelte, underage-looking girl gyrating on the stage seemed of particular interest to Puupponen.

"I can take the car back if the two of you want to stay and enjoy the view," I said with a smirk.

"So we're not going to arrest her?" Puupponen asked in disbelief. "We know she was lying."

"I wish it were that simple." My eyes swept the room. The stares I was getting made me uncomfortable. I realized I was violating the club's division between well-dressed men and undressed women, a reminder that I had no business in this place.

Suddenly I noticed another person who didn't look like he belonged here, although Milla had mentioned he'd shown up before. There was Joona Kirstilä sitting at a rear table. He looked like an orphan in the sea of strip club regulars in their suits and ties.

"Seems we have a friend here," I said to Ström, who picked Kirstilä out after a brief search.

"Elina Rosberg's boyfriend. So this is where he goes looking for comfort?"

"Let's go ask. We can kill two birds with one stone and ask where he was Tuesday night."

"Seems strange a pansy like that has the stones to come here," Ström snorted.

"So going to strip clubs is a display of masculinity now? I always heard these places were a release for repressed guys who stare at titties instead of committing rape," I said loudly as I weaved my way through the tables. "Evening, Kirstilä. We keep running into each other in bars."

The drunk eyes that stared up at me couldn't seem to figure out what I was doing at Fanny Hill. Then comprehension dawned. "Is this some kind of raid?"

"No, that's another department. Do you think there's a reason for a raid though?" I asked.

He didn't seem to understand my question. Maybe there was too much poetry in his head. Grabbing a chair from a nearby table, Ström sat down next to Kirstilä. I remained standing like a waitress waiting for an order.

"Hot chicks, huh?" The feigned chumminess in Ström's voice was new to me. "What would your late girlfriend think if she knew you went to places like this?"

I didn't expect such a quick reaction from Kirstilä. Shooting out of his seat, he socked Ström in the nose and started running for the door. I took off after him, knocking over a couple of chairs and beer glasses as I went. I managed to get a grip on the tail of his coat, but he wrenched himself free. He didn't make it past the bouncer though. Like a true professional, he simply grabbed Kirstilä with his left hand and then wrapped his right arm around his throat. Dainty and short as Kirstilä was, he looked like a child swallowed up by six and a half feet of brawn.

"What the hell's going on here?" Rami Salovaara came running. He must have seen the scuffle on his monitor. "We didn't say anything about questioning customers! You're disturbing my business."

I wished I could leave. Just walk out the door while Ström, Salovaara, and Joona Kirstilä sorted out the mess. I wanted to take a taxi home and crawl under the covers next to Antti. Drop this case where none of the clues led anywhere. Every thread we found was just a piece of the same endless ball of dirty gray yarn.

"Your customer struck an officer. He also just happens to be one of the suspects in our investigation." Crap, I was going to have to arrest Kirstilä. Ström would demand it. Knowing him, he'd probably press charges and I'd have to testify.

But Kirstilä's punch had been pretty pathetic. It hadn't even bloodied Ström's nose, which had been broken several times before. Puupponen was grinning behind Ström's back. It was obvious he considered Kirstilä a friend now.

"I think our little poet pal is going to be spending the night in the cooler," Ström said with an unpleasant smile for Kirstilä, who had gone limp in the bouncer's arms. "Are you going to come quietly or do I need my cuffs?"

Kirstilä didn't answer, and I motioned for the bouncer to let him go. As we walked out, Kirstilä between my partners and me behind, I glanced back for a second. There was Milla Marttila, her makeup fixed, standing on the stairs with a horrified expression on her face.

1 5

The mood in the police car was downright jolly. Puupponen drove without speaking, while Ström gingerly held his nose in the front seat. I was sitting in the back with Joona Kirstilä. Ström wanted to drag him straight to jail in Espoo.

Assaulting an officer in the line of duty was a crime, of course, but Puupponen and I thought Ström was making too much out of a little jab, especially since he had provoked Kirstilä. On the other hand, Kirstilä wasn't much help—he was so drunk he passed out as soon as we got in the car.

Just as we were leaving Helsinki, he woke up: "You can't take me to jail. I have to go feed Pentti."

"Who the hell is Pentti?" Ström snapped.

"Pentti is a cat. Does Pentti have water?" I asked.

Kirstilä nodded.

Silence fell once again.

On the Turku Highway, Kirstilä started complaining about nausea. Puupponen flipped on the flashers and stopped at the side of the road. Kirstilä barely got the door open before he lost his dinner on the shoulder. The vomit smelled of beer and sausage. Suddenly I felt nauseated too. I tried not to breathe through my nose, but my stomach was doing somersaults when we arrived at the station.

I expected things to be quiet up in our unit, but it turned out to be anything but. As soon as the elevator doors opened, we could hear someone agitatedly speaking Somali and Taskinen raising his voice.

The hallway looked as if it held a whole extended Somali family. Most of them were men, but there were also a couple of women in full burkas and some small children.

"What the hell's going on?" Ström asked Taskinen, who looked impatient.

"Arson. Somebody threw a Molotov cocktail through this family's living room window. That's what we're trying to get to the bottom of here. Can any of you help? Or do you have an arrest?"

"You go, Puupponen," Ström said before I could open my mouth. A wide-eyed little boy ran into my legs and tripped. Setting him back on his feet, I tried to comfort him, but one of the women in the black burkas snatched him away. I thought I heard a muffled apology through the fabric. The contrast between topless waitresses and fully veiled women was so stark that the Islamic dress didn't bother me a bit, even though it usually felt threatening to me.

"Let's get Kirstilä handled quickly. Jyrki needs our help," I said to Ström.

The Somali men stared disapprovingly at Kirstilä, who stank of vomit. As our first order of business, I sent him to the men's room to wash up.

"Should I go along and make sure he doesn't hang himself with that red scarf of his?" Ström asked.

"That's all we need! Right now all I want to do is get out of here," I let slip without thinking.

"What?" Ström turned back from the restroom door, but then he noticed Kirstilä doing something more interesting. Ström rushed inside yelling, "What do you think you're trying to stuff down that toilet?"

The sound following his question was clearly that of a person crashing against the commode. Ignoring the silhouette of a rooster on the door, I burst in after Ström. He had his arm around Kirstilä's neck.

"Now I wonder what that could have been," Ström said, jerking his head toward the toilet.

Lifting the lid, I cautiously peeked into the bowl. Fortunately the only thing floating in it was a clear plastic baggie about three inches square. There was something brown inside it.

"Looks like hash. Is this why you were trying to get away? Joona?" Kirstilä was squirming in Ström's arms, still looking very inebriated.

Jackass, I thought, not really knowing which of them I meant. If Joona Kirstilä had simply answered our questions at the club about what he was doing Tuesday night, we wouldn't have nailed him for possession.

"Looks like our friend here is going for a full rap sheet," Ström said spitefully as he released the smaller man. "Resisting arrest and possession of an illegal substance. How about that homicide charge? And then there's the attempted murder of Aira Rosberg up for grabs."

Instantly Kirstilä looked more sober. "What happened to Aira?"

"Yeah, yeah. Don't even try. You hit her over the head on Tuesday night. Isn't that right?" Ström said.

One of the Somali men opened the restroom door but quickly retreated when he caught sight of me. I burst out laughing. I couldn't help it. The day had been too long and too full of bizarre crap. I didn't have a single drop of willpower left to stop it.

"What's so funny, Kallio? Get out of here," Ström said, but his words just made me laugh harder. Kirstilä slumped against the wall with unseeing eyes.

Finally I calmed down enough to suggest that we go to my office for the questioning. Ström fetched coffee for himself and Kirstilä and cocoa for me while I set up the recorder. Kirstilä drooped on the sofa under my pinup collection, his long black overcoat pulled tight around him. The coffee seemed to rouse him a bit. My cocoa was lousy. I suspected Ström had only put half a pouch of powder in it.

I asked Kirstilä where he was on Tuesday night.

"Tuesday night?" Kirstilä said, bewildered. "You mean the night before last? How am I supposed to remember that? I was probably at a bar. Maybe Cosmos . . . or Corona . . . Yeah, first the Cosmos and later the bar at the Santa Fe. They threw me out around one, and I guess I went home . . ."

"Who were you with?" I asked.

Kirstilä mentioned the names of a couple of other famous poets who had been at the Cosmos. I asked if he was spending every night now sitting in a bar.

"The words won't come," he said sadly, tossing back the rest of his coffee and reaching for a cigarette. His hand stopped mid-motion as he remembered the no smoking rule.

"And you think you're going to find them at a titty bar?" Ström said cruelly. "Nothing there looked all that poetic to me."

Kirstilä just shook his head. He wouldn't talk about the hash either, other than to say he'd bought it from some guy the night before. "I don't remember if it was at the Corona . . . or maybe the Ruffe."

If it were Puupponen with me instead of Ström, I would have suggested letting Kirstilä go, but I didn't feel like arguing with Ström. Instead, I promised to try to be in right at eight the next morning to question Kirstilä again.

I could barely keep my eyes open as I drove slowly home through another snowstorm. A rabbit dashed across the road, and my headlights caught a skier out challenging the blizzard. At first I thought it might be Antti, but the skier was too short and stout. At home all the lights were on and the house smelled of fresh bread. Einstein ran to meet me in the entryway and Antti followed with a grin. I'd expected to find him discouraged after the Ring II freeway meeting, but he practically glowed.

"Hey, darling. Still alive after a long day?" Antti wrapped his arms around me. His long hair smelled like pine tar and the wind. His sweater was covered with flour.

"Barely. That bread smells great. I'm starving to death."

"Kirsti called about an hour ago. She and Eva had a little girl, and everybody's healthy."

Such good news after such a hard day instantly made the tears flow. Ninny. I never used to cry when someone had a baby.

"Everything went well?" I asked as Antti led me toward the warm bread waiting in the kitchen.

"I guess, although they said it took almost twelve hours. They're going to spend the weekend in Tammisaari. You remember they were going out there for the birth, right? If you have time, we could go see them on Saturday. I think we could use a break from the city."

After four pieces of bread, all my body wanted was a hot shower. It was zero dark thirty when I finally collapsed in bed between Antti and Einstein. In my dreams, bare-chested girls nursed kittens.

The next morning, I tried to make up for the effects of so little sleep by dressing nicer and doing my makeup more carefully than usual. My abs were tender from the previous day's hard training, and I felt sort of strange. My body wasn't just my own anymore. Someone else was living in it. Someone who didn't demand much space yet but still sent a bitter coffee burp back up my throat. Someone whose sense of smell had replaced my own and who could pick out gasoline or cigarette smoke anywhere. Someone who needed a lot of sleep to grow, which made me tired too. Someone who made me cry over the smallest emotional thing.

Soon that someone would start to grow in earnest, and then my waist would spread and I wouldn't fit in my skin or my clothes. And finally, less than a year from now, that someone would come out of me and be a separate person but still completely dependent on me for years.

I looked at my powdered face in the mirror and saw that someone's eyes behind my own—that someone I didn't even know yet. Suddenly I felt a joy that almost made me ashamed. I quickly wiped a tear from the corner of my eye and left for the station anticipating another hard day. On the way, I dropped Antti off at a bus stop in Tapiola.

Old Mankkaa Road was in chaos. A semi with a trailer stood blocking the road. Apparently it had slid at great speed down the slippery hill and rammed into an oncoming van. I didn't want to know what had happened to the driver of the van, but I couldn't tear my eyes away from the light-green sheet metal crushed under the semi. The man who was being bundled into the ambulance was apparently the truck's driver, not the van's.

After sitting in gridlock for fifteen minutes, I tried to call Ström, but my stupid piece of junk phone wouldn't work. Why the force couldn't just buy decent cell phones for everybody was beyond me. It was already past nine when I finally reached a driveway where I could turn my little Fiat around to backtrack and go another way. When I made it to the station, Ström wasn't around. Dispatch said he was with Haikala in interrogation room number three.

When I marched in, the room was empty. I finally found Ström in the break room.

"I thought you slept in. You need a lot of rest in your condition," he said. "I handled the Kirstilä prelims with Haikala."

"Where is he now?" I asked, intentionally ignoring Ström's reference to my "condition."

"I let him go. He was so wound up about getting two charges against him."

"You're effing kidding me!" I said. "I wasn't done with him yet. At least you checked his alibi for Tuesday night?"

"Haikala's calling right now." Ström shoved the last piece of his Danish into his mouth and then stepped close to me and whispered into my ear with exaggerated intimacy, "So when are we going to lose you? When does your maternity leave start?"

"What the fuck are you talking about?" I snapped, pulling my arm out of Ström's ostensibly solicitous grasp and striding off toward the elevator. Ström followed me, just getting a leg in before the doors closed.

"You probably won't be coming back to this unit though," he continued.

"And why not? The kid has a dad too," I huffed, although I knew it was stupid to actually confirm Ström's suspicion that I was pregnant.

"Taking care of a little kid doesn't work with shifts like ours," he said, strangely serious now. "Trust me, I know. Sometimes I went weeks without seeing Jani and Jenna other than at the breakfast table. It wasn't exactly fun."

The elevator came to a stop, and I made a beeline for my office, ignoring Ström, who strode after me but stopped when he saw that someone was waiting for me in the hall.

I'd been right. Tarja Kivimäki had shown up. It wasn't quite ten yet, but there she was, standing in front of my door in a shiny red pantsuit that looked riotous against the pale-gray walls of the police station. Kivimäki had been to the salon since I'd seen her last: her boring brown bob was now shorter, blond, and curly.

"Good morning," I said and opened the door. This was going to be a private conversation. I would only call in a witness and turn on the recorder sitting on my desk if I sensed she had something really important to say about Elina's murder.

I hoped she would start talking. I knew I was wading in deep snow. I already had one reprimand hanging around my neck thanks to Tarja Kivimäki, although I really didn't want to bring that up with her.

But that was exactly what she wanted to talk about.

"Martti didn't call your boss, did he?" Kivimäki asked. Her concern seemed almost genuine.

"Martti?" I asked just as innocently. But I really didn't feel like keeping up the charade. "If you mean Interior Minister Martti Sahala, then, yes, he did send his greetings. I would have thought such a high official would have other concerns than the behavior of a single police officer."

"I was pretty upset that night." Tarja Kivimäki tapped the surface of her briefcase with her red nails, which were so shiny she must have painted them that morning. "Actually... Actually, Elina's death has been much harder for me than I've been willing to admit. I might have exaggerated your threats a bit. Martti takes everything so seriously."

"So you're in a relationship with the most respected member of the government? I have to say I'm a little surprised. What brought you two together?"

Maybe it would be better to play friends with Tarja Kivimäki. You tell me your secrets and I'll tell you mine. We did share a similar background—the trauma of growing up in a one-horse eastern Finnish town.

"Martti is a completely different man in private from the way he is in public. He isn't really stiff at all," Kivimäki said, pointedly looking at me to let me know she was referring to his reputation. "So that's my big secret. Not many people know about it. Elina was one of the few. Of course a lot of people would love to have something like this to use against Martti."

"Does his wife know?" I asked, purely out of curiosity. Personally I was such a hopeless liar that I would never be able to keep another man a secret from Antti. Or the fact that I was expecting a baby, apparently. I couldn't believe I had let it slip to Ström. The whole department would know before lunchtime.

"I don't know," Kivimäki was saying. "Why tell her when our relationship isn't a threat to their marriage? Martti's family lives five hours away in Kokkola, and he spends all his free time there."

"But the relationship is hurting your work because you had to leave the news," I pointed out.

"Well, I think I've always been objective, but reporting on the actions of an administration that the man I love is a part of is problematic ethically. Anyway, I'd been in the newsroom for six years. I was getting bored with it. Don't you ever get sick of your work?"

Now it was my turn to start making confessions. "Of course. That's why I keep changing jobs. I also studied law and worked in a legal firm for about a year. And then one summer I was deputy sheriff in Arpikylä. How long have you been with Sahala?"

"A couple of years. Martti was interior minister in the previous government too, so that's how we got to know each other. Sometimes I wonder what my parents would think if I told them about our relationship. They're still waiting for wedding bells. Anyway, Martti belongs to the wrong party for them."

I couldn't help smiling at Kivimäki. There was something both irritating and magnetic about her. Maybe her will to walk her own path—even when it meant breaking trail through knee-deep snowdrifts—reminded me of my own. But I couldn't show that I was actually starting to like her.

"By the way, where were you Tuesday night between ten and midnight?" I asked.

The change of subject caught Kivimäki off guard, but then her expression relaxed.

"Oh, you must mean Aira! That's why . . . Actually, that's why I decided to come see you. I don't like being threatened, but I understand your position. When Elina disappeared, I wasn't completely sure what happened, but now with Aira . . . She's going to recover, right?"

"Hopefully. You didn't answer my question."

"Tuesday. I'm sorry, Maria, but I was at work. The late news was doing a report on the dustup in the National Coalition's parliamentary faction about the energy policy. I was interviewing the chairman. I left work for Tapiola about eleven thirty."

At night you could make it from the Finnish Broadcasting studios in downtown Helsinki to Nuuksio in less than half an hour, but I didn't say that.

"When we met at Raffaello you said you'd thought of something that could be the motive for Elina's murder. No more hinting. Just tell me."

Kivimäki set down the briefcase she had been holding in her lap as if she was playing for time. I had the feeling she had rehearsed what she was about to say.

"I don't know exactly what all this means, but . . . Well, OK, let's start from the beginning. Elina didn't really drink much, and usually she only drank whiskey. About a year ago, last January, we were hanging out at my apartment. I'd bought a bottle of Laphroaig just for her, and suddenly she was throwing it down by the glass. I'd never seen her drunk before. We'd been talking a lot about me and Martti and her and Joona, and about how neither of us wanted a commitment—you know, a 'normal family life' with screaming children and men's socks on the floor. I drank a bit too much whiskey too, so I don't remember everything perfectly, but at one point Elina said she had the chance to start a family once when she was younger but gave it up. I asked what she meant, but I don't really remember the answer. But I got the impression that Elina had been pregnant at some point in her life."

"When? Did she give birth?" I felt my abdominal muscles clench as if they were trying to crush the block of ice that had suddenly dropped into my stomach. Could this be the source of Elina's cervical scarring?

"Well, see, that's what I don't remember. But I do remember the impression that it was a long-term relationship, even Elina's one great love. At first I thought she was talking about a child with Joona, but I'm pretty sure she was talking about someone from a long time ago. Have you talked to Elina's doctor?"

Absentmindedly I nodded, wondering whether Taskinen had already given permission to move Elina's body from the morgue to the funeral home. Probably. It had been more than two weeks since her death. "Did Aira plan to bury Elina next weekend?" I asked.

"Yes, the funeral's scheduled for Sunday. Aira and Johanna were organizing it. I don't know what will happen, with Aira in the hospital. I guess they'll hold it anyway."

I'd never seen a report from Dr. Kervinen in Pathology, so he must have forgotten to schedule the specialist I requested. But if Elina hadn't been buried yet, we still had time, even if that meant a trip to the mortuary. I would have to talk to Taskinen.

Tarja Kivimäki and I talked for a few more minutes, but although she tried, she couldn't remember exactly what Elina had said. It was all so ambiguous.

"You sure you won't give me an interview for *Studio A*?" Kivimäki asked as she opened the door to leave. When I declined again, she let the matter drop and just wished me good luck trying to solve Elina's murder and the attack on Aira.

After she left, I thought about what she'd told me. She had been open and cooperative during the whole interview, but I still wondered about her. Was she lying about Elina's pregnancy? And if so, why? To deflect attention away from herself? But why would she kill her best friend?

Taskinen confirmed that Pathology had sent Elina's body to the mortuary. I spent the rest of the day trying to find out when Elina was being buried and whether I could find a qualified gynecologist to look at her body. I was lucky. Johanna Säntti had called the mortuary the day before and asked for a delay in the funeral. The funeral director had been put out, but apparently Johanna possessed some of her husband's rhetorical gifts, because despite the inconvenience for the mortuary, she convinced them to push the funeral back a week, when Aira might be well enough to attend. I also managed to schedule a gynecology specialist for Monday.

Doctor Wirtanen also called with an update on Aira. She had been conscious all morning, but she was still tired and unable to remember much. Cursing the upcoming weekend, which would interrupt any momentum we were gaining, I said I'd drop in to see Aira on Monday at the latest. With any luck, she would be ready to answer questions by then.

"You said that Ms. Rosberg was suffering from temporary short-term memory loss. Can something like that be faked?" I asked Dr. Wirtanen before hanging up.

"Sure, of course, but probably not for very long. Do you mean Ms. Rosberg might be pretending not to remember in order to protect her attacker?"

"Either to protect or avoid." By now I was relatively sure someone had tried to kill Aira Rosberg because she knew how her niece had died, but I didn't want to reveal too much to Wirtanen. Instead, I said, "We can't rule out the possibility that she's faking the memory loss. She's a trained nurse and I believe she used to work with the elderly. She knows how complicated human memory is."

"I know you're a police detective and your job is to suspect people, but that sounds a little far-fetched to me," said the doctor. "But who knows? I'll bear this in mind and keep my eyes open."

I was looking up Milla's information in the population registry when Puupponen knocked frantically at the door. "Do you speak French, Maria?"

"I studied it in high school, but I'm pretty rusty."

"We have a crowd of immigrants who only speak French. Their Finnish is terrible, and we can't find an interpreter anywhere. Could you help for a minute?"

"Is it the Molotov cocktail thing again?" I asked.

"No. Moroccan students who got in a fight at a university dorm last night," he said.

"Students who don't know Finnish or English? That sounds suspicious. I'll be right there, but I have to be at Internal Affairs for an interview at two."

Quickly I checked Milla Marttila's government records. There was no mention of an adoption. According to her records, her parents were Risto Juhani Marttila and Ritva Marjatta Saarinen. I knew the adoption would be recorded somewhere in the database even if it didn't come up automatically using a basic search. I needed Milla's birth certificate to get more information, but I didn't have time to make the request right then.

My half-forgotten French wasn't much help, but I still spent fifteen minutes trying to sort out the brawl. One of the Moroccan students was seriously injured, but the others claimed the incident was a harmless showdown between two clans and really just part of their culture. I was happy I had an excuse to leave it to Taskinen and Puupponen. I was looking forward to taking a break on the train ride into Helsinki before being questioned about the botched cabin raid.

Actually, it wasn't much of a rest. Although I hadn't been actively trying not to dwell on Palo's death, I must've subconsciously kept my head filled with the Rosberg cases to avoid the issue. On the train I had nothing to do but think, and unfortunately it was Palo and Malmberg who crowded my mind. The therapist had advised us not to repress our grief and fear, so I didn't fight it, but I certainly didn't feel rested when I walked out of the station.

My interview with Internal Affairs was being held at my old workplace, the same building where I had solved my first murder a few years earlier. I had questioned Antti during that investigation. The idea that I'd once suspected him of murdering his best friend was surreal now.

The corridors smelled the same as they had then, and some of the walls on the Finnish Broadcasting Company side of the building were still under repair after the bomb attack in the fall. I was tempted to peek down my old hallway, but I didn't want to bump into Kinnunen, my old boss. I'd heard he still had his job despite all the hours in the day he spent drinking.

In the restroom, I checked my makeup and added a little more waterproof mascara while repeating that I wasn't going to cry in front of the review board. As far as investigations went, my situation wasn't that bad. No one was accusing me of anything. I was just one of the pieces the review board needed for putting together a picture of what happened on that night in early January. Still, the picture would be incomplete and distorted because Palo and Malmberg could not tell us what had been in their minds.

The board was on schedule: at two minutes to two, an officer stepped out of the meeting room. At one minute past two, he asked me in.

The setup was as formal as it could possibly be. The lighting was bright and artificial and the room was a blinding white. Sitting in a row at a long table along one wall were five stiff-looking men. The clerk, also a man, had his own table to the left of the examiners. One of the officers motioned for me to take a seat in a relatively comfortable-looking armchair facing the long table.

When I sat down I realized my legs didn't reach the floor. Male policemen were generally at least eight inches taller than me, so this was nothing new. Still, I felt like a rag doll propped on the edge of a bed.

The review board introduced themselves. They were high officials from the police hierarchy and the Ministry of the Interior. Before beginning the actual questioning, they expressed their condolences about the death of my coworker. Everything was controlled, orderly, and correct. It was clear they were going to ask about facts, not opinions. They knew I hadn't had an official role in the hostage operation; I was only there because of my relationship with Palo and Malmberg.

The goal of the board was obviously to demonstrate that Malmberg had been a dangerous psychopath whose behavior was impossible to predict. And that was why the use of force and the SWAT team's surprise attack had been justified. I answered as truthfully as I could, although the leading questions of one of the lieutenants irritated me. Kari Hanninen probably would have had fun with this board. I didn't.

"You and Sergeant Palo handled Markku Malmberg's case last year. Why did he hold such a grudge against the two of you?"

In other words, what had we done wrong in Malmberg's case?

"You worked with Sergeant Palo for a little over a year. What was he like as a partner? How capable was he in emergency situations?"

Had Palo maybe fumbled the situation? Could they blame him for his own death?

"Palo was afraid," I answered curtly. "So was I. There was no one available to guard us. I've heard civilians who've received threats like this talk about how frustrating it is when the police can't do anything before a crime actually occurs. Now I understand them better."

"How do you think the situation should have been handled?"

You could have given us guard details, I thought angrily, or hunted down Malmberg more actively, or secured the prison better. Or you could have written to Santa Claus and asked him to protect all the good girls and boys.

Frustrated, I swung my dangling legs and glared at the five cautious men who didn't actually want to get to the bottom of the incident. All they wanted was to sanitize the reputation of the police. I realized suddenly that this case could go on for months. My baby could well be born before they came to any conclusions, and whatever they decided, someone would be dissatisfied. I had joined the police force to serve truth and justice, and when I couldn't find that in policing alone, I went to law school. And here I was still forcing myself to believe in those ideals, even if the shine had worn off in places. If I lost that, if I stopped believing, I'd have to quit.

The interview lasted less than an hour, but by the end I was exhausted. I'd spent the whole time walking a tightrope, trying to find a balance between the answers they were looking for and my own feelings. And in the end, what I said wouldn't really matter. Palo was dead; his funeral was on Tuesday. Maybe we could have saved him by stalling Malmberg, maybe not.

Outside the train window the world was gray. The lights along the tracks shone through my reflection in the glass. I suppose that was how everyone saw the world, filtered through themselves, overshadowed by whatever was going on inside their own heads. Through those filters, one person saw a justification for murder, another for beating immigrants, a third for setting foxes free. I just had to find the people who looked through themselves and saw a reason for killing Elina and attempting to kill Aira.

1 6

Several years had passed since I'd last held a newborn. The Jensens' seven-pound-eleven-ounce girl felt so insubstantial in my arms. She weighed half as much as our cat.

"Relax, babies are surprisingly durable," Kirsti Jensen said with a laugh. The baby rested peacefully in my arms, her mouth making tiny sucking motions. Our weekend jaunt to Tammisaari was turning out to be a nice idea. Although the small country town was hibernating, walking down the narrow streets lined with wooden houses felt almost like being abroad. Compared to Jorvi Hospital in Espoo, the facility in Tammisaari was small and homey—and didn't smell like death. The family room was full of life. Along with Eva, three little Jensens were sitting on the double bed. Antti was rocking in a rocking chair, and Lauri and Kirsti were giving competing versions of how the birth had progressed. Jukka Jensen had gone to the cafeteria to get ice cream for everyone.

I had never been the type to coo over a tiny newborn, and Eva's baby's wrinkly, sour-smelling face had a strange dignity that made me want to speak with deference. I realized I was starting to grow accustomed to the idea of having my own baby.

After half an hour with the Jensen circus, we drove east to Inkoo to Antti's parents' cabin in the woods. We hadn't seen them in ages. A couple of years earlier, they had sold their house in Tapiola and now rarely visited the metro area. We'd decided not to tell them about the baby just yet, although my father-in-law looked at me inquisitively when I declined the glass of wine he offered. They were discreet people though and didn't pry. My parents definitely would have started asking uncomfortable questions in the same situation.

"Should we tell them about baby Sarkela now or wait a bit longer?" Antti asked as we sat in the sauna after taking a quick night ski out on the frozen waters of the Baltic Sea.

"What do you mean baby Sarkela? What makes you think the baby's going to have your last name?" I teased, although I hadn't even considered the naming issue yet.

"Well, because you always know who the mother is, but you can never be sure of the father," Antti said with a grin. "The baby is going to be more bonded to you anyway, whether you have the same name or not."

I admitted that Antti's logic was sound, and Sarkela was a significantly rarer last name than Kallio, but we decided not to set anything in stone just yet. When we got out of the sauna, Antti's parents were still watching the same endless talk show on TV. It was about alternative medicine. My mother-in-law was interested in the subject, and she had asked curiously about Eva's birthing experience because Eva had spent most of the time it took her cervix to dilate floating in a bath of warm water. For a few seconds I listened to the lecture on how medical schools used to treat even acupuncture as flimflam before I decided to head to bed and read. A familiar voice from the TV stopped me in my tracks.

"I don't think traditional medicine should shut out things like astrology or homeopathy so quickly," the voice said. When I looked at the television again, Kari Hanninen's charismatic face almost jumped off the screen. I changed my mind and sat down next to Antti's mother on the couch to listen to Hanninen's presentation on how astrology and psychoanalysis could work together.

"The occult sciences and medicine have the same goal. We all want to help people. But while medicine, psychology, and psychiatry often forget the patient's emotions and just focus on physiology—deadening feelings with drugs—astrology tries to help people understand themselves and treat themselves right. Star charts can help you see all kinds of things in a person, such as a predisposition for alcoholism. I would never tell someone that the stars had fated them to be an alcoholic and that they couldn't do anything about it. But I can look to the stars for healing power."

The women in the studio audience clapped. You couldn't deny how convincing he was. Even when he'd talked to me about Madman Malmberg, a vicious murderer, he had really seemed to care what happened to him. Still, I regretted giving him my birth date. I didn't actually want to know what he saw in my horoscope—or imagined he saw.

The talk show host must have been reading my mind. He said to Hanninen, "In your work you've met all kinds of people and faced some pretty incredible situations. Markku Malmberg, the man who killed himself and a police officer earlier this month in Nuuksio, was one of your patients. Can a star chart show you things like a future career in crime or a violent death?"

Hanninen laughed at the question. "Astrology doesn't actually tell the future. But yes, you can see violent tendencies and specific times of potential crisis in a person's life."

"Did you see that in Markku Malmberg's star chart?" asked the host.

"Yes, clearly. But the end result didn't have to be Markku and the police officer he abducted losing their lives. To use the old cliché, it wasn't written in the stars." Hanninen's smile was just the right amount of sad. He brushed his thick hair off his forehead. Antti had taken my hand when the conversation turned to Nuuksio.

"How much advice do you dare give your clients?" asked the host. "For example, if someone comes and asks you about what profession to choose or who to marry, do you answer?"

"Of course. But the ultimate responsibility is always with the person himself. I'm truthful if a chart shows that two people aren't right for each other or if someone isn't a good fit for a job, such as being an actor. But I also always try to look for alternatives. I don't like abandoning people to their problems."

The interviewer moved on to a crystal healer, but every now and then the camera panned back to Kari Hanninen, who was sitting comfortably and seemed to be exchanging significant glances with several girls in the front row. Then the show switched to a tango singer bleating a sappy love song, and Antti and I retreated to the kitchen to make some tea. We didn't talk about Kari Hanninen and astrology until the next day as we were driving home.

"The fact that you don't want Hanninen to make a chart for you actually means you believe in horoscopes," Antti said to irk me as he passed a tractor creeping along the side of the road.

"No it doesn't! I just don't want him thinking he knows me because he knows my sign—oh my God!"

That last exclamation was caused by a BMW speeding toward us. It veered back into its own lane only seconds before it would have demolished our poor little Fiat. Though I should have been used to the number of kamikaze drivers on this country road between Inkoo and the freeway to Espoo, I was so frightened I almost didn't notice my phone ringing. It was the station.

"Hi, Maria, it's Akkila. You said to call if the hospital had any news. There's a message here that says Aira Rosberg is starting to get her memory back."

"What? Thanks. I'll head straight there." I ended the call and asked Antti to make a detour and drop me off at the hospital.

"Back to work?" Antti asked with resignation in his voice.

"I won't be long. I can walk home if I need to," I said.

"Oh no. I've got a book with me. I'll wait for you in the lobby. Or do you think they'd let me see the maternity ward? I could compare it to the one we just saw in Tammisaari."

I grinned. "You don't look very pregnant."

The doctor on call in the ICU said Aira was doing so well they were moving her to the recovery ward the next day. The return of her memory wasn't exactly what I had hoped for though. The doctor said Aira remembered Elina's disappearance, but not that she'd been found dead. No one had told her yet. I managed to talk the doctor into letting me see her for just a few minutes.

Aira was awake and half sitting up in bed, but she still looked older and smaller than I'd ever seen her at Rosberga. When she noticed me, a slightly uncertain smile spread across her lips, but then recognition flared in her eyes.

"Sergeant Kallio. How are you? You came and spoke at the institute a few weeks ago."

"Hello, Ms. Rosberg. How are you feeling?" I asked, keeping things a little more formal since she'd apparently forgotten she'd been using my first name.

"My head hurts sometimes, and I can't quite remember some things . . . I guess I fell . . . I must have been looking for Elina. Has anyone found her yet?"

I shook my head. Lying was hard, but telling her Elina was dead wasn't my job. A dark shadow passed across Aira's face, and she shook her head, bewildered, when I asked her where Elina might have gone.

"I thought she was with Joona . . . Joona Kirstilä, her boy-friend. They were supposed to go to Estonia together, to Tallinn. Have you been to Rosberga? Maybe they've come back."

With Joona to Tallinn? I'd never heard anything about this before. Or was Aira mixing things up, maybe remembering the previous Christmas? I had to ask Kirstilä. Maybe Aira was fak-ing. Her pale-blue eyes looked sharp. But I wasn't a doctor.

"She hasn't come back," I replied. "Do you remember any-thing about your own accident? Where did you fall?"

Aira Rosberg shook her head again. "Remembering hurts," she said in the helpless tone of an old woman. It sounded strange coming from her, despite how fragile she looked. "It gives me headaches."

Just then a nurse knocked on the glass. It was time for me to leave. I wasn't going to get anything out of Aira now, and my questions might even hinder her recovery.

"Ask Elina to come see me when you find her," Aira pleaded as I opened the door. Her voice was small and reedy. I nodded as a lump filled my throat. How was Aira going to react when she learned Elina wasn't coming? Why did she have to experience the worst anguish of her life twice?

I tried calling Joona Kirstilä, but he didn't answer. Maybe he was out looking for his lost words in some bar again.

I spent the rest of my night mending my old black graduation dress. Because we didn't wear uniforms at work, we had all decided to wear civilian clothes to Palo's funeral too. The dress was torn under the arm from some long ago overenthusiastic dancing. I'd had it for a good ten years, and it was probably time to retire it. I had a bad habit of getting attached to clothes and then wearing them until they were literally falling off my body.

Looking at my closet, I caught myself wondering how many of my dresses would still fit me in the summer and came up with a big fat zero. The thought of maternity clothing was so unpleasant I decided to rebel and grabbed a "near beer" from the fridge. At least it gave me the comfort of that familiar taste.

The next morning a report was waiting on my desk with details about the tire tracks Forensics had found outside the gates at Rosberga the night of Aira's attack. Since we couldn't go around inspecting everyone's car tires, maybe we could get permission to look at the tires of cars owned by people who frequented the house in order to rule them out. Like a madwoman, I plowed through the urgent paperwork that had piled up on my desk, hoping to make time for this. The next day was going to be a complete loss, I knew. I had an appointment with my OB and then there was Palo's funeral.

After lunch I tried calling Kirstilä again. He sounded hungover. Between his cat, Pentti, meowing angrily into the receiver and Kirstilä's tubercular hacking fits, I could barely understand what he was saying. I finally realized he was telling me that he had no idea what trip to Estonia Aira was talking about.

"I'm not going to jail for that hash, am I?" Now it sounded as though Kirstilä was opening a can of cat food.

"Doubtful," I said, although I probably shouldn't comment. "Nowadays you can get off without being charged if the amount is as small as what you had. But get yourself a lawyer. Hitting an on-duty cop is a pretty big deal."

"So you bastards just get to say anything you want to me and I don't have any right to defend myself?" Kirstilä was sounding more alert. Maybe he'd opened a bottle of beer along with the cat food.

"Sergeant Ström does have a bit of a mouth on him," I admitted.

"I bet he hates any guy with long hair, and my being a poet just makes it worse," Kirstilä said, sounding like a sullen, bullied schoolboy. Still, his description of Ström was dead-on—his ability to look at the world through such narrow blinders was astonishing, condemning everything unfamiliar to him right down to the Chinese food they occasionally served in the station cafeteria.

"Speak of the devil . . ." I muttered to myself as Ström appeared at my office door.

"That Molotov cocktail case," he said.

"Yeah?"

"Taskinen and I are handling it. We already have some suspects, the same skinheads who've been causing trouble all over. Pretty pathetic, going at foreigners that way. At least they could stand up and fight face-to-face."

"Cut the crap. What do you need me for?"

"We need to question the mother of the family. She can't be in the same room with other men without her husband present,

but we can't legally have him there. You wanted multicultural-
ism, and now you've got it. It won't take long."

"OK. Give me five minutes."

Lifting my finger from the mute button on the phone, I discovered Kirstilä had hung up. I still had one more question to
ask, but it could wait.

Mrs. El-Ashram was wearing a full burka and answered
my questions in muffled monosyllables. Talking to a woman
while barely able to see her eyes was odd. I'd just been accusing
Ström of racism, and now I found myself wondering about Mrs.
El-Ashram. Did she really want her daughters walking around
fully veiled too?

The sudden urge to drop all the routine questions about the
attack on their home and satisfy my real curiosity about these
"foreigners" was disconcerting. Even more disconcerting was
how much Mrs. El-Ashram reminded me of the way I'd felt reading Johanna's autobiography. I liked to think of myself as tolerant
and open-minded, but I drew the line at wife beating, burkas, and
female circumcision. Early the previous fall I had been assigned a
difficult case. A school nurse and elementary school teacher had
filed a criminal complaint about the abuse of an eight-year-old
Somali girl. The girl was out of school for a week without any
explanation and then started bleeding in the middle of class. It
turned out the girl's mother and aunt had circumcised her in the
family bathroom.

I spent weeks going around and around with the district
attorney, the refugee authorities, and social services about
whether to press charges. Two weeks later the tabloid headlines
were all about anti-immigrant riots in Joensuu and a psychotic
Somali killing a Finnish schoolgirl in Tampere. After that, we
quietly shuffled the case off to Child Protective Services. I had

often wondered if it was the right thing to do and if I would have intervened more aggressively had it been Finnish parents abusing their children that way.

Somberly I resumed questioning Mrs. El-Ashram and listened patiently to her answers before bringing her back to her husband. Then I returned to my office and made a call to Milla's mother.

I had spent a lot of time thinking about how to approach Ritva Marttila since it didn't seem appropriate to ask her over the phone whether her daughter was really hers, and if not, why the adoption wasn't recorded anywhere.

Ritva Marttila's manner of speaking was brusque, like Milla's. But were their voices similar? I wasn't sure. "Milla? Yes, we have a daughter by that name, although she hasn't shown her face at home for years. What's she done now?"

I intentionally left her question unanswered. "Is Milla Marttila your biological daughter?" So much for tact.

"Biological . . . What do you mean?"

"Is she your and your husband's daughter, or was she adopted?"

"What the hell are you talking about? Of course she is. What kind of lies has she been telling you? What else has she been lying about? I can show you her birth certificate if I have to."

"Does Milla have a habit of lying?" I asked.

In answer I received a confused account of what a horrible brat Milla had been, always accusing her father of terrible things. Although Ritva Marttila had just confirmed the population registry's information that she was Milla's mother, I wasn't ready to believe that everything Milla had told me was a lie. But it wasn't my job to go digging into the Marttilas' family past any more than I already had. Unfortunately, wives tended to believe their husbands more than their children when accusations of incest came up—no matter what the truth was.

"What has she done now?" Ritva Marttila asked again.

"She's mixed up in an unexplained death," I replied.

"So she's moved on to murder now? One of our neighbors said he saw her working in a strip club. Is that true?"

"Why don't you ask her yourself? I can give you her number," I offered.

Ritva Marttila replied by slamming the phone down in my ear. That was motherly love for you. I remembered one of my friends who also had a difficult childhood once saying that all children hate their parents. She said there wasn't a parent living that hadn't screwed up something, even if they meant well. What was the little critter floating around in my belly going to think of me and Antti in twenty years? Would he or she remember parents who lived for their work and never had any time for their child? I was starting to get afraid again, so I moved on to searching the computer databases for information on everyone I thought might have any connection to Elina Rosberg's death.

In theory, I was thinking that Milla could be Elina's child—the ages lined up, but Joona Kirstilä couldn't be her father. There were other possibilities, although the whole thing could just be about money. Elina was extremely wealthy, and Aira was her only heir. What if Aira had had a child . . . ?

I had already been through Aira's records once, but I went back to them now. There wasn't any mention of a child, but at a rough guess of their ages, she could have been the mother of any of the suspects, other than perhaps Milla. I could probably rule out both Sänttis, since they had spent their whole lives living in the same tiny village. Aira would have been forty-five when Niina Kuusinen was born, so she could just barely be Aira's daughter. But Niina bore such a strong resemblance to her father when he was younger that I had a hard time believing she wasn't her parents' offspring. However, Tarja Kivimäki, Joona Kirstilä, and Kari Hanninen still all fit the time frame.

Of course, none of their records showed any indication of an adoption, but it was possible that the adoption was handled under the table. I had heard of such cases. Tarja Kivimäki's parents must have been over forty when she was born. I tried to picture Tarja and Aira side by side on my mental overhead projector. Was there any similarity in their features? Had Elina and Tarja gotten along so well because they were actually cousins? Or was it Elina and Joona?

Or was the truth even more complicated—what if Elina was Aira's daughter? Or . . . maybe I had just read too many mystery novels. Still, it would have been interesting to know whether Aira had ever given birth. Who was her doctor? I found myself dialing the familiar number for the ICU. But when a nurse answered, she informed me that they had moved Aira to another ward because she no longer required special monitoring.

Theoretically that was good news. In practice though, it meant increased danger: in the ICU, Aira had been under constant watch. Getting onto a floor of the hospital that was less vigilantly monitored was significantly easier for an outsider. Was Taskinen still in his office? I'd have to stop by and ask about getting another guard assigned to Aira since my authority hadn't been enough to keep someone there past the first forty-eight hours.

My boss's door had lights outside to indicate whether he was busy, but unless they were red, we all knew we could just walk in. Now the lights were off, but I knocked anyway. At the muffled "come in," I entered and found Taskinen at his desk with the phone receiver in his hand, the dead line beeping audibly. His face looked wilted like an old potato. There were more creases than ever around his eyes.

"Bad news?" I asked cautiously. Taskinen didn't talk much about his private life, so I didn't know if he had a seriously ill mother or something.

"I was just talking to Palo's wife. The first one," Taskinen added. His attempt at a smile was like a remnant from the time when Palo's three wives and numerous children from his different marriages had been a common topic of banter around the unit. "Palo's oldest daughter is expecting—or *was* expecting—a baby. She was three months along. She lost it over the weekend, and they're saying the shock of her dad dying was part of the reason."

"Jesus." I couldn't think of anything else to say.

Taskinen continued, as if to himself, "I couldn't think of anything to say either. There just aren't words for this. I'm supposed to give a eulogy at the funeral tomorrow. All I can think of are clichés. Do you know what keeps going through my head?"

"What?" I asked, wary of the agitated tone of Taskinen's voice.

"Jokes. Bad jokes. Like I'm the best man doing a wedding toast."

I knew what Taskinen meant. Our brains did the strangest tricks in the effort to fight off sorrow.

"How did your interview go on Friday?" I asked.

Taskinen shook his head as if snapping himself back to reality. He finally hung up the phone. We compared our experiences with Internal Affairs. It was obvious we both wanted to talk. Trying to predict the outcome of the Internal Affairs investigation was as good a topic as any. Both of us were willing to put money on Koskivuori being the administration's scapegoat this time.

"That might be hard," Taskinen replied when I asked him to arrange another guard for Aira now that she was out of the ICU, but he promised to try. "Oh yeah, Pihko said you might have a recommendation for filling Palo's position. It opens up the first of March."

I told Taskinen about my old colleague, Pekka Koivu, who was just finishing his NCO course and didn't want to go back to the Joensuu race wars.

And I was just about to tell Taskinen that I was also going to need a stand-in for about a year in the not-too-distant future when the door opened without a knock and a very beautiful young woman poked her head in. Actually, Silja Taskinen was just a girl of seventeen, but figure skating had given her a poise and femininity rare for someone her age. Just before Christmas I had been to an ice show where Silja played Sleeping Beauty. She was widely considered one of Finland's most promising skaters, and I knew Taskinen stretched his paltry police salary in order to send her to Canada several times a year for training.

Taskinen was taking Silja to a skate shop, so we agreed to see each other the next day at church. I was happy Silja had interrupted our conversation. I still wasn't sure I wanted to tell Taskinen about my pregnancy yet.

Before leaving for home I dropped by the lab to look again at the robe and nightgown Elina had been found in. It seemed the scrap of satin fabric I'd discovered on the path was from the hem of her robe. So Elina had left the house by walking along that longer route rather than across the field. But we still didn't know whether she'd been walking or was being dragged when the fabric ripped; the alternating snow and rain had frozen everything too solid.

Pulling on latex gloves, I took the clothes out of their plastic evidence bags. Was that still a hint of rose I smelled? No, I was just imagining things because I'd seen a bottle of rose talc in Elina's bathroom. Both the robe and nightgown were ripped on the upper back and the bottom, matching the abrasions on Elina's body. But whether they had been caused by someone dragging Elina on her back or because she fell downhill and slid on the snow wasn't clear.

The robe and nightgown had been such pathetic protection against fifteen-degree weather. The synthetic fabric actually would have made her colder. Why would anyone go out dressed like that? And without any shoes on?

And why was Elina under the spruce tree? Had the killer expected snowdrifts to cover the body so that no one would notice her? Or was it Elina herself who had decided to become a snow woman?

1 7

With my office blinds drawn, I pulled on my tight black dress. Palo's funeral was starting in half an hour. Ström and Pihko were waiting outside for me, both looking strange in their dark suits and ties. My phone rang just as I was shoving my work jeans and sweater into the closet. I briefly considered whether to answer, but then couldn't stop myself from grabbing the handset.

Aira Rosberg's voice still sounded old and frail, but she was obviously well enough to use the phone.

"You didn't tell me Elina was dead," she said accusingly.

"I didn't want to wake your memories before you were ready. Do you remember now?"

"I remember Elina died. But I don't really remember how I ended up here."

"You don't remember who hit you?"

"No. But I'm ready to answer your questions. The doctor gave permission too."

"You mean today?" I wasn't sure how long Palo's memorial and burial service would run. I thought quickly. "I can come by this evening, if that works for you."

Ström shoved his head through the doorway just then, completely ignoring the fact that I was on the phone. "What is it with women always making everybody wait!" he yelled.

Pulling a face at him, I said good-bye to Aira and grabbed my heels before rushing out the door. We couldn't be late. The funeral was starting at twelve, and every police station in Finland would be observing a minute of silence in memory of our fallen comrade.

The chief of police was just shoehorning himself into his car when we entered the motor pool garage. Fat chance he would've bothered coming to Palo's service if Palo had just died of a heart attack at home. But today all the big police muckety-mucks and even a few reporters would be in attendance, so he'd been forced to make the effort.

As we drove off, I stared out the window. The weather was a hopeless slush again, the fresh snow that had brightened the landscape for a couple of days now splashed to the side of the roads in an ugly gray glop. My shoes were wet because I'd broken through the ice over a puddle while walking to the obstetrician's office.

Early that morning I'd woken up from a nightmare about blood flowing between my legs and Madman Malmberg's eyes covered in ice. After that I'd tossed and turned, nuzzling against Antti and listening to Einstein jumping around the house, apparently hunting the moles wintering under the floorboards. Palo's funeral and my first real pregnancy checkup had me in knots.

Although my friends all had nightmarish stories about Nurse Ratched types doing their exams, my own nurse turned out to be a perky young woman who seemed to think pregnancy was the most natural thing in the world. She didn't lecture me about anything, not my job or even that I'd admitted drinking the occasional glass of wine on the intake questionnaire. Everything was normal and the fetus and I were doing fine. It still felt a little unreal holding the blue-and-white accordion paper that would record all of the changes in my body from month to month.

Ström, who had taken the driver's seat as if he owned it, fiddled with the radio, scrolling past Radio Finland and a classical station. On RadioMafia, they were playing "Stairway to Heaven," which felt at once corny and touching. The parking lot in front of the church was jam-packed, and Ström had to park half in the snow.

Tapiola Church usually looked like a gloomy concrete bunker. Not exactly the most inviting house of worship. But now candles illuminated the crude walls, and the mass of humanity crammed inside radiated warmth. Everyone from the department was sitting in the front of the chapel. Squeezing between Taskinen and Ström, I looked curiously at Palo's relatives sitting in the first row on the other side of the center aisle. Which of the women were his wives? Palo's youngest child wasn't even in school yet. She was probably the little girl wiggling in the pew looking like she wanted to go and see if Daddy really was in the coffin up by the altar.

The organ started playing the chorale from Bach's *St. Matthew Passion*. Looking at my hands, I felt empty and insubstantial. If I hadn't been wedged between two men, I probably would have floated off the bench toward the ceiling of the church, rising through the concrete blocks, past the tops of the pine trees ringing the building, to somewhere far away, where Palo had gone. The hymn was the most formal one they could have chosen, "Bless and Keep Us, Lord," also known as "The Finnish Prayer." I sang loudly and a little off-key.

Next to me, Taskinen had a beautiful, soft baritone, and even Ström growled something resembling the song. It would have been easier if the pomposity of the music had continued in the sermon, if Palo's funeral had passed easily as an extravagant official ceremony we could all observe as outsiders, maybe even cracking a smile at Palo's unintentional elevation to hero status. But the pastor's remarks were thoughtful and emotional, addressed to Palo, his family, and his coworkers.

"Juhani Palo became a victim because he did his job well. It feels senseless. It feels unjust. And yet many of Juhani Palo's colleagues have probably had moments of guilty gratitude that this violence didn't land on their doorsteps. And why wouldn't we think that? Why shouldn't we thank God we're still alive?"

Folds of skin stood above the collar of the county police officer sitting in front of me, and the back of his hair was cut unevenly. I tried not to listen to any more of the priest's sermon, because the tears were flowing. One had already reached the tip of my nose. No one was stopping me from crying. Of course you could cry at a funeral. It was part of the deal. Taskinen fished a handkerchief out of his pocket, and for a second I was afraid he would hand it to me, but he used it to blow his own nose. None of us wanted to even glance at each other. It was as though we were ashamed of our grief and our fear that it might be our turn next to lie in a coffin, deaf to our comrades' sobs masked as coughs.

There were so many mourners that the presentation of wreaths took a long time. Six children—Palo's ex-wives each brought their kids separately to the casket. The young woman scarcely more than a girl crying inconsolably must have been Palo's eldest daughter, the one who miscarried after hearing of his death.

Flanked by his adjutants, the chief laid the department's official wreath. His words of condolence were almost presidential. I'd tried to wriggle out of our unit's wreath detachment, but the guys had demanded I accompany Taskinen and Pihko. I didn't even hear the tribute Taskinen read—I was just trying to hold it together. As we left the casket, we nodded to Palo's tearful family in the front rows. Standing before them, I found myself wracked by guilt.

Other than the protracted presentation of the wreaths, the funeral was simple. The organist only played the two chorales, and the hymns were impersonal. I didn't know whether Palo even believed in God. We didn't talk about things like that.

The memorial luncheon was held in a banquet hall in a hotel next to the church barely big enough for the funeral guests. Taskinen was nervously rehearsing his eulogy while Pihko, Puupponen, and a couple other guys from the unit headed for the hotel bar. I said I didn't really feel like drinking when they invited me to come along. Ström and I ended up together at a table in the corner, staring out the window at the frozen fountain outside and not saying anything.

"Which of those are Palo's kids?" I finally asked, nodding toward a table in the middle of the banquet hall where at least one of Palo's wives was sitting surrounded by a group of young people dressed in mourning. Ström's silence felt too heavy, strangely connecting us. I wanted to get him talking because I knew he would say something irritating before too long that would break the odd feeling of camaraderie that had formed between us.

"Wait . . . The two little ones are from his current marriage. And the woman in her twenties is his oldest daughter. The guy with the beard must be her husband. No! What the hell?"

As we watched, the chief of police pushed his way through the crowd into the middle of the room, obviously intending to deliver a speech. Ström didn't like people in general and was as disgusted by the chief as I was.

"The other guys had the right idea going for a beer," he growled.

The chief would be retiring in just over a year, and the competition to succeed him was already fierce. Taskinen was one of the possible names that had come up, but his lack of interest in politics would probably hamper his advancement.

"Policing is a profession with greater than normal risks," the chief proclaimed as if announcing something groundbreaking. "Sometimes the job even demands a life. The situation Juhani Palo ended up in was difficult, and we have no way of saying whether it could have been handled differently. Each and every one of us recognizes the enormity of Palo's sacrifice . . ."

Clichés, clichés, clichés. I grimaced at Ström and he grimaced back. Fortunately the chief didn't go on for long. After he finished, one of the county police commissioners got up and repeated basically the same stuff, just with more tact than the chief. I wondered how the family felt, having their grief stolen from them and turned into public property. Palo was no longer someone's spouse, father, or friend, just a name on the memorial to police officers fallen in the line of duty.

Next a young boy introduced himself as Palo's son. In a voice trembling with anxiety he thanked us for coming and invited us to help ourselves to the buffet. As he spoke I saw the bigwigs slipping off to the coatracks; apparently the official part of the funeral was done. Palo's youngest daughter dragged her mother toward the smorgasbord, announcing in a ringing voice that she wanted juice and cake.

Just then I remembered that I hadn't heard back from the gynecologist who examined Elina's body the day before.

"Do you have your phone with you?" I asked Ström. I'd left mine at work, afraid I'd screw up the settings and it would start ringing in the middle of the service.

Ström handed me his, strangely without a single question, and I ducked out to the lobby. No luck. After thinking for a few seconds, I left two numbers, Ström's cell phone and my office phone at the station. I had to go back there before heading to the hospital anyway.

Returning to the banquet hall, I found that the family had already taken their turn at the buffet table and it was time for the rest of us to eat. Pihko and Puupponen were already helping themselves, but I wasn't the slightest bit hungry.

As I passed Palo's family, his youngest widow stopped me with her gaze. I was still searching for something appropriate to say when she blurted, "So you were the other officer Malmberg was hunting?"

I nodded, forcing myself to meet the sorrow and accusation in her eyes.

"Hopefully you stay lucky." The woman's voice was flat but loud, and another woman, Palo's first wife, sitting at a table nearby, stood up and approached us.

"Don't worry, Eila. I'm not going to make a scene," Palo's third wife said to her. "But I'm not going to pretend either. Of course I wish Malmberg had grabbed her instead."

What could I say to that? I nodded lamely and choked back my tears until I could get a few yards away. Fortunately Taskinen appeared at my side asking if his tie was OK because it was his turn to speak. Straightening his already irreproachable knot gave me an excuse for the momentary human contact I needed apparently as badly as he did. Then I slipped back into the chair next to Ström and returned the phone.

"My name is Lieutenant Jyrki Taskinen, and I was Sergeant Juhani Palo's supervisor in the Violent Crime and Repeat Offender Unit. Up until last week we never worried about coming to work even if we happened to be a little under the weather. Whether it was a cold coming on, a self-inflicted headache, or a sore shoulder from the firing range, there was always someone who had the right medicine."

Taskinen's introduction was such a stark contrast to the previous speeches that complete silence fell over the room.

"We all poked fun at Palo for the pharmacy he seemed to be running out of his office. But just yesterday I could have used something for a headache. And then I realized that my head hurt because the person who always gave me medicine was gone. It's easier to talk about needing a pill than the man I worked with for more than ten years."

Taskinen told more stories about Palo, stories that made us cry and laugh at the same time. Listening to him speak, I found myself thinking about Palo but also about how I'd never realized before just how much I liked my boss. If the circumstances were different, I think I would've been in danger of getting mixed up in my first workplace romance.

After he finished, Taskinen went to shake hands with the family.

"Is that blond kid Palo's son too?" I asked Ström, who had been uncommonly quiet all through Taskinen's speech.

"Let me think . . . Yeah, Toni's last name is Palo, but if I remember right, he's from Hannele's—Palo's second wife's—first marriage. Or, actually, I don't know whether she was married before."

Just then Ström's cell phone started ringing. Luckily the general hubbub was loud enough that no one noticed.

Ström answered and handed it to me. Opening the door to the balcony, where a couple of people were smoking, I stepped outside to talk.

The gynecology specialist sounded agitated. "Elina Rosberg definitely gave birth at least once, but it was a long time ago."

"How long?"

Sleet pelted my face like a cold rag. My nipples felt frozen the instant I stepped out onto the balcony.

"Hard to say with any accuracy, but I'd guess about twenty years ago. There wasn't any mention of it in her records, which was why I wanted a second opinion before I called you."

"And the scarring?"

"There is record of an operation conducted under less than ideal circumstances sometime in the mid-seventies. The scarring is probably from that. That would have allowed her to claim she had never given birth, but a good doctor should have noticed . . ."

"She may have had some sort of tacit understanding with her doctor," I said. "Thank you. We may need your statement in court."

Turning off the phone, I stared through the sleet at the building block shapes of the Cultural Center across the water. Elina had given birth to a child. And what had Ström just said about Palo's son? Something Antti said in the sauna in Inkoo also came back to me.

Suddenly the picture started to come into focus, although I wished I could have another look at the snapshots in those photo albums at Rosberga Manor. But when I really concentrated, I could recreate them on the screen in my head. A high-school-aged Elina, looking wan and tired, standing with Aira against a backdrop of palm trees. A flock of admiring young men staring at Elina at a company party.

Of course. That was it! And Aira must have known all these years. That's why she had protected Elina's killer!

Maybe Aira was in danger after all . . .

Returning to the banquet hall, I forced myself not to break into a run. I found Taskinen and Ström at the buffet. Both turned, expecting a few words of praise for my boss's speech. Instead, I blurted that I had to go to the hospital.

"I know who killed Elina Rosberg and why," I explained. "First I just have to make a few calls and talk to her aunt. Then I think I'll have enough evidence for an arrest."

"When is this going to happen?" Taskinen's voice contained little enthusiasm. For him, the Rosberg case had been buried long ago under the loss of Palo.

"Preferably today," I said. "I'll need someone with me."

"OK," Ström and Taskinen said at the same time. Instead of choosing one of them, I arranged for both to meet me at four thirty at the station. Then I grabbed a ground beef turnover and a pastry filled with rice and egg for the road and rushed off to the taxi stand outside. I realized I still had Ström's cell phone, so while I was in the taxi I called the head offices of SF Lumber. After a few seconds of confusion, the receptionist was able to confirm a fact I'd been wondering about. After that, I still had time to call the international phone directory service before the driver dropped me off at the front doors of the hospital.

I ended up racing around half the hospital before I found Aira. She was sitting in her bed flipping absently through a women's magazine. Most of her fragility had disappeared, and the fat gauze bandage wrapped around her head had been replaced by a thinner one.

She even smiled when I walked in. "Sergeant Kallio . . . Maria. Hello."

"Hi, Aira. How are you doing?"

"Better all the time, although thinking about Elina hurts. But my head isn't splitting the way it was."

"Do you remember everything yet?"

Fear flashed in Aira's eyes, but she drove it away. She didn't answer.

"It doesn't actually matter as long as you remember the past," I said. "Elina died because of her past, isn't that right?"

Aira was silent for a moment. "How much do you know?" she finally asked.

"A lot. But a few things I still don't understand. For example, why have you been dropping hints about Joona Kirstilä the whole time? What do you have against him?"

Aira didn't reply, just shook her head as if she didn't know the answer herself. Maybe the reason for her accusations was simply that she knew Kirstilä was innocent and thought that meant he'd get off if he was arrested.

"Why did Elina's killer try to kill you? Did you threaten to tell the police? You knew what was going on from the beginning, didn't you?"

"I never would have told. But she didn't believe me. She's . . . she's unbalanced. I don't think she meant to kill me. Hitting me was just a reaction."

"So you remember what happened?" I asked again.

Aira didn't look at me as she nodded.

"So why don't I tell you what I know about the events, and you fill in the holes," I suggested. I wanted to make this as easy as possible. I felt sorry for Aira. She'd lived her whole life through and for other people and had almost died for it.

"Do I have to testify against her?" Aira asked.

"I'm hoping for a confession," I said.

"Tell her I forgive her. I was partially to blame for what happened. I was the one who came up with the plan all those years ago. Apparently I was wrong. My decision had such destructive consequences."

Then we started telling each other why Elina died. I had guessed the facts, but Aira was better able to describe what led to the events, so I let her talk.

When we finally finished, Aira's face was as gray as stone, but her eyes had regained the natural serenity I had seen in them the first time I met her at Rosberga.

"I'm making things easy for you," Aira said. "They're all going to be at the house tonight preparing for Elina's funeral: Johanna, Tarja, Niina, Milla, and even Joona, I believe. Go tonight and you'll find the rest of your answers.

1 8

"So you've got a whole room of suspects waiting for us?" Ström said with a snort as he turned off the highway toward Nuuksio. "Sounds very whodunit."

"Exactly. I'll go through the suspects one by one, starting with the least guilty. Whoever's left is Elina Rosberg's murderer."

"Is that Kirstilä shit going to be there?" Ström asked. "I thought men weren't allowed."

"I guess enough cops have traipsed through the house that the whole idea has gone to pot." Actually I wasn't very happy about having a big revelation scene at Rosberga, but I wanted to wind the case up. And it might be good for everyone to be there. Elina's death had changed all of them, and maybe they'd now be able to go on with their lives.

The gates of the mansion were locked. Apparently the opener wasn't working, because Tarja Kivimäki came to let us in.

"Three police officers? Nothing's happened to Aira?" she demanded before I was even out of the car. In addition to Elina's car, Kivimäki's red Volkswagen and Niina Kuusinen's father's Volvo were in the courtyard. Although Niina claimed to hate winter driving, she had driven to Rosberga in a sleet storm.

"Aira's fine," I said. "We have something to talk about with the rest of you."

Inside, the kitchen was warm and inviting. Niina, Milla, and Joona Kirstilä sat around the table. Johanna busied herself making more tea when she saw us, although I said we wouldn't be staying long. Ström and Taskinen were quiet. They knew who we were here to get, but they let me do the talking.

"Aira sends her greetings," I finally began, but I didn't look at anyone. "I spent a long time with her today talking, and she confirmed something I already knew. The identity of Elina Rosberg's killer."

"Killer? So it wasn't an accident?" Kirstilä said hoarsely.

"In a way I think it was an accident. I don't think the purpose was to kill Elina, at least not at first. The whiskey and Dormicum were just meant to put her to sleep. The killer didn't know about the antibiotics Elina was taking and didn't have a clue erythromycin enhances the effects of sleeping pills and keeps them from being flushed out of your system. But the object wasn't for Elina to freeze to death, right?"

Now I looked at them all, pale-faced Kirstilä, Niina fiddling with her hair, Milla who stared back brazenly, and Johanna measuring out the tea.

Tarja Kivimäki was the first one to speak. "Bad luck. No one jumped up and screamed no."

"I guess I'll have to be more direct then. How did Elina end up in the forest, Niina?"

When Niina heard her name, she flinched as if I'd hit her. Milla, who was sitting next to her, breathed in sharply and whirled, aghast.

"Why the hell did you kill Elina?" Milla's tone was harsh, and she raised her hands aggressively but stopped when Niina spoke.

"I didn't mean to kill anyone! I just wanted her to suffer. I wanted to leave her out in the cold the way she left me."

"What are you talking about?" Tarja Kivimäki's voice was incredulous. I decided it was better to let the others handle the conversation. Niina would open up to her friends much more easily than to me.

"Elina was my mother," Niina hissed. "My mother, who abandoned me right after I was born and pretended not to know me when I showed up here even though she knew exactly who I was!"

"Your mother? But you're at least twenty-five! Elina must have been a baby when you were born!" Milla said.

"Elina was sixteen." I took the floor and explained what Aira had told me about Niina's birth.

Niina's father, Martti Kuusinen, had worked for Elina Rosberg's father in the late 1960s at SF Lumber, one of the largest wood processing firms in the country. At the time Kuusinen was twenty-five, already married to his college sweetheart, Heidi. Kuusinen soon became a favorite of Elina's father, Kurt Rosberg, who had always been disappointed not to have a son of his own. Kuusinen visited the mansion frequently, and fifteen-year-old Elina fell head over heels in love with him. Elina was an early bloomer, tall and beautiful. Aira, who had returned to Rosberga around that time to care for her sick sister-in-law, was the first to discover Martti and Elina's relationship. She immediately told her brother, but the damage was already done. Elina was expecting Martti Kuusinen's child.

At first Elina probably didn't even realize she was pregnant. And by the time Aira found out, it was too late for an abortion. To top it off, Martti Kuusinen's wife was also expecting. Kurt Rosberg was furious and fired Martti from his company. I remembered Aira's exhausted face and faltering voice as she told me about Niina's birth and the horrible spring preceding it.

Elina's mother was very sick, and the girl was in a deep depression. Aira wasn't sure what Elina expected to happen. Maybe she thought the father of her baby would leave his wife and marry her. She wouldn't even speak to her own father because he had fired Kuusinen. Aira was the only person Elina would listen to, and finally Aira came up with the plan. The baby was due in October. Instead of going to school in the fall, Elina would go abroad for the birth and then give the child up for adoption.

Then Martti Kuusinen found a job in the south of France, the same position he still held. Heidi, his wife, didn't want to move away from Finland to a country where she didn't even know the language, but her husband convinced her to go. The irony of fate was that both of Martti Kuusinen's children were due to be born within two weeks of each other.

Aira wasn't exactly sure about the details of what happened next, but one night Kuusinen returned home from work and found his wife lying unconscious in a pool of blood. She'd gone into labor two months early, and there was no way to save the child. It would have been a little girl.

Kuusinen wrote to Aira and suggested that he and Heidi raise the baby Elina was carrying as their own. In a way it was a good solution, and Aira was able to talk Elina into it. In early August, Aira accompanied Elina to France. Elina went willingly—her pregnancy was already becoming too obvious, and her father had barred her from leaving the house.

The months in France were torture, Aira recalled. It was terribly hot, and Elina spent half her time acting crazy over Martti Kuusinen and half the time hating him. And Heidi Kuusinen could have used professional counseling after the death of her baby and learning that a schoolgirl was expecting her husband's.

Martti Kuusinen never reported the death of his wife's child to the Finnish authorities. Of course the French doctor who treated her knew, but Aira assumed Kuusinen handled that with money. The Finnish authorities also never knew that Elina was pregnant. She hadn't visited a maternity clinic here, so her condition was never recorded.

Martti Kuusinen was the one who came up with the idea of presenting Elina as his wife at the hospital when she went into labor. Although Heidi was eight years older than Elina, the pregnancy had been difficult and had aged Elina enough that no one suspected anything.

Elina gave birth half drugged. In the end they had to drag Niina out with forceps. Elina refused to see her baby at all, and two days after the delivery she left the hospital. Aira and Elina traveled to Paris, where Elina spent a week recovering, and then they both returned to Finland. After Christmas Elina went back to school. The Kuusinens stayed in France. There was no further contact between Elina and Martti Kuusinen. No one ever asked whether Elina missed her daughter, and Elina never mentioned her again.

That was where Aira had ended her story. In hindsight, she added, it would have been easier if they'd given the baby to strangers, but on the other hand, Martti Kuusinen was Niina's father.

Niina hadn't moved or made a sound during my story. It was time for us to leave, but before I could say as much to her, Tarja Kivimäki spoke up.

"Niina, when did you learn Elina was your mother?"

Slowly Niina turned to face Kivimäki, her eyes full of tears. Now that I knew to look, I saw the similarity between Niina, Aira, and Elina—their high cheekbones.

"My mother . . . Heidi left me a letter I was supposed to open only after she died. In it she said she'd been struggling for years over whether to tell me and decided in the end I needed to know my real mother's identity. What good was that supposed to do me! I wish she'd never told me! Maybe Mom thought I wouldn't miss her as much when she died, but she was wrong. I never had any mother but her, and it never even occurred to me that she might not be my real mom . . ."

Niina's sobs made it hard for her to speak, but she couldn't seem to stop talking. "Dad told me the rest of what Mom didn't say in her letter. I couldn't understand how he could've done what he did, and our relationship basically ended that day. Elina never contacted him again after leaving France. But I was her child. How could she abandon me like that?"

"Elina was sixteen when you were born. She couldn't have been a mother to you," Tarja Kivimäki said gently.

"Why not? Her family had money. They could have hired a nanny so Elina could still go to school. Elina didn't want me, so she got rid of me!" sobbed Niina.

"Did she say that to you?" Joona Kirstilä had been frozen all this time. "She told me the exact opposite. She said no one would let her keep her baby and she didn't have any say."

"You knew?" Niina and I asked at the same time.

"Not that it was you. Actually, I suspected Milla was her daughter . . ." Kirstilä glanced at Milla, and a faint smile flitted across his lips. "Elina just said that she had a baby when she was really young and her family made her give it away."

"That's right! Of course Elina didn't talk about me," Niina said angrily. "I spent years wondering whether I wanted to meet a woman who hadn't shown the slightest interest in me. She must have heard about my mom's death—there were big obituaries in the papers. Wouldn't that have been a good reason to come meet me? But she didn't."

The anger in Niina's voice was disturbing. I was sure Elina's version would have been very different. She probably hadn't wanted to interfere with Niina's life.

"In the end I decided to meet my real mother," said Niina. "In the fall I signed up for her emotional self-defense course. When I met her I told her my name, but she didn't react. I was just like anybody else coming for a class."

"Kuusinen is a pretty common name," Tarja said. "And Elina might not have even known your first name."

"Yeah, she probably wasn't interested enough in me to find out." Niina paused for a moment. "At the course I wasn't able to talk to her much, so I decided to become her patient. We met once a week, and our first therapy session was three weeks before Christmas. In the first one I told her so much about my parents that she had to guess who I was. But she didn't say a word. She just sat and listened. Can you believe that?"

"Use your head, girl! Elina was a professional. She could see you were bat-shit crazy and you'd only get worse if she dropped a bomb like that on you. 'Oh really, well actually I'm your real mother.' Seriously? And *you* were the one who started the charade." Milla was furious. "Why didn't you just tell her you knew? Was it Christmas when you finally told her? Is that why you came here?"

Niina's face was blank. All expression had gone with the tears. "It was that night. On Boxing Day. I met her in the hall and told her I had something I needed to talk to her about. She gave me a funny look but told me she didn't have time right then. She wanted to walk with Joona first! That's when I started getting angry. Elina must have guessed what I was going to tell her, but she didn't want to hear it! I'd brought her a bottle of whiskey because I overheard her at that course telling someone, probably you, Milla, that Laphroaig was her favorite. I crushed up a package of Dormicum and dissolved it in water. That's all the plan I had. I meant to show Elina that I could kill her . . . if I wanted to. But such a small amount wouldn't actually kill her."

Niina's tears had dried, and her voice was steady as she told us how she went to Elina's room after the movie ended that night. Elina was already in her nightgown. They'd barely started speaking when a call from Joona Kirstilä interrupted them. While Elina was talking to Joona, Niina mixed Elina a drink.

"Elina tossed the whole glass down in one gulp after she got off the phone. I guess she needed a pick-me-up and that's why she only tasted the whiskey. Then I kind of got mixed up. I knew the medication worked fast. I—I told Elina I knew she was my mother and ran outside and through the back gate. I couldn't stand being inside the house."

Elina followed, without shoes or a coat. Niina ran headlong across the field, losing Elina when she reached the forest. For half an hour she ran in the cold, and when she recovered her senses and returned through the main gate, she assumed Elina was already back. She went to her own room and waited for Elina to come to her, but that never happened.

Milla swore. "Why didn't you wake us up, you idiot!"

Niina didn't answer. There weren't any answers.

We would probably never know what really happened, how Elina ended up where the skier found her body. The drug interaction must have hit her suddenly and she fell and slid down the icy bank on her back. I didn't want to think about the cold or what she was feeling as she ran after Niina in the snow.

In any case, it seemed clear Niina never meant to kill Elina. At most she would be charged with negligent homicide in Elina's death and battery or attempted murder for attacking Aira.

Aira had told me that she had called Niina earlier that day and asked her to come to Rosberga for the night. Aira had planned to tell Niina that she knew the truth and wanted to help her.

Niina had just arrived when Aira returned from visiting friends, and she met Aira's car at the gate. But when Aira greeted her and started telling her what she knew, Niina became enraged and hit her with the bear statue.

"It happened so fast," Niina said, crying again.

"I think we'd better go now," Taskinen said as her sobs filled the silence. "Ms. Kuusinen, you'll need to come with us. We'll contact the rest of you later for questioning."

"Are you taking me to jail?" Niina wailed. When none of us answered, she started sobbing again.

Ström glanced irritably at Taskinen. I took a step toward Niina, but Johanna, who had remained quiet all this time, got there first. Wrapping her arms around Niina, she comforted her the way she would a small child. Eventually Niina was able to collect herself enough that Johanna could persuade her to get her things and go with us. Tarja Kivimäki promised to arrange for a lawyer, and Milla and Joona begged us to please treat Niina gently.

Niina didn't say another word, barely acknowledging the others' good-byes. Even in the car she sat silently next to me. I didn't know what to make of her. Where had such rage toward

Elina come from? Or had the rage come after the fact, as a way of channeling her guilt onto someone else?

Taskinen had to stop at the intersection at the main road to wait for cross traffic before he could turn left. That was when Niina moved. She hadn't buckled her seat belt, and she was out of the car in an instant, dashing toward the lake. Taskinen and I were both runners, so normally we wouldn't have had any trouble catching her. But our funeral clothing hindered us. I was still wearing a long winter coat and my tight-fitting dress, and Taskinen had on slick-soled leather shoes. Taskinen took a flying leap out of the car and ended up splayed on his back in the middle of the road. By the time he was up and running, with me following him, Niina was already out on the ice.

Ström yelled something after us, and then we heard the car engine being gunned. Apparently he planned to drive around the lake to cut Niina off. Hopefully he was also calling for backup. As I ran, I hiked up my skirt, and when Taskinen fell again, I caught up with him. Ahead of us Niina was a dark figure disappearing into the night.

"What the hell does she think she's doing running across the ice? There's nowhere to hide," I said, panting.

"She probably isn't thinking," Taskinen replied. "She might just think she can lose us in the darkness. Woah!" Taskinen almost tripped in an ice fisherman's borehole. "Hopefully there aren't any bigger holes out here!"

Niina was visible again as a silhouette in the lights shining on the far shore. She had slowed down, as if looking for a suitable place to climb the rocks that lined the bank. The phone in Taskinen's coat pocket rang. It was Ström. He was on the ice now and had called for reinforcements. Suddenly from around a bend in the lake, far beyond Niina, the glimmer of Ström's flashlight came into view.

"We can see you and Kuusinen," Taskinen panted into the phone. "Take it easy. She isn't any danger to us. The most important thing is to catch her before she tries to do something to herself."

The ice under me made a nasty cracking sound that stopped me in my tracks. At this point in the winter, the lake ice should have been solid. I hadn't even thought to question it. Niina was now close enough that I could yell to her.

"Wait, Niina! This won't work. You can't get away. Don't make things worse for yourself!"

Yourself, yourself, yourself . . . The word echoed off the cliff on the opposite shore. Seeing how close we were, with Ström coming from the other direction, Niina looked around in panic. She must have noticed the hole in the ice a few yards away just as Taskinen and I spotted it. Someone had been keeping a swimming spot open through the winter. By now I was so close I could see the expression on Niina's face as she dashed toward the black water.

"No!" I screamed. Taskinen and I charged after her, but he slipped again on the ice and landed hard on his face. Out of the corner of my eye I could see his smashed lip leaking blood, but there was no time for first aid because Niina launched herself at the hole without a second's hesitation. The thin sheet of ice covering it shattered as Niina's body splashed into the water, making an enormous crash in the stillness of the night. Rushing from the other direction, Ström scooted himself to the edge of the ice at the same moment I did.

Niina shot to the surface, reflexively gasping for air, but immediately put her head under again. If she managed to swim under the thicker ice, that would be it. I started pulling off my coat.

"The hell you are!" Ström bellowed, shoving me so violently that I slid back at least six feet. Then he stripped off his coat and jumped in the water. As I crawled on my stomach back to the edge of the hole, Taskinen appeared next to me. From somewhere far off I heard voices. The water churned in the hole, and Ström's head came up, grotesquely red.

"She's here," he gasped.

Still on my stomach, I grabbed Niina's wrist, but instead of letting me help her up on the ice, she tried to pull me into the black water. Her almond eyes looked into mine as coldly and lifelessly as Madman Malmberg's had. The weight of Niina's limp, water-soaked body dragged me forward. The fingers that grasped my wrists were cold and the nails were sharp. The ice cracked beneath me, and I could feel the frigid water creeping onto the surface. I realized I was screaming. My sleeves were already wet, my arms sinking into the icy embrace of the lake.

Then Taskinen grabbed my ankles, and slowly I felt myself sliding away from the edge. Splashing and grunting, Ström heaved Niina onto the ice. All I could do was hold her thin wrists as she struggled. Her long dark hair felt like icy octopus tentacles on my face.

When Taskinen scooted next to me and grabbed Niina under the arms, she was too stiff to thrash anymore.

Ström wasn't in great shape either, although he was able to pull himself back out of the hole. Thankfully we were no longer alone. Help was coming from the house on the shore, and two uniformed officers were approaching across the ice.

"Call an ambulance!" Taskinen yelled.

Blood was still running from his mouth, and he tore off his coat and wrapped it around Niina, who was sobbing in fits. Ström kept lifting his feet as if afraid he would freeze in place. I wanted to give him my own coat, but what good would that do when it was also wet and about five sizes too small for him?

After what seemed like an eternity, the other cops brought blankets from their car to wrap around the shivering Niina and Ström. Niina couldn't walk, so the officers carried her to the nearest house to wait for the ambulance, which finally came and took her away. Ström, who had peeled off his wet clothes and borrowed some police coveralls a couple of sizes too small, claimed he didn't need a doctor, just a few rum toddies and a head of garlic. When we couldn't coax him into going to the hospital, Taskinen and I drove him home.

"Thank you, Pertti!" I forced myself to say as Ström was getting out of the car in front of his house. When I was preparing to jump into the lake after Niina, I'd forgotten I was pregnant. But Ström clearly hadn't. You can do a lot when you're pregnant, but winter swimming probably isn't recommended.

"It's high time you learned to look before you leap," Ström replied, teeth still chattering. But his tone was significantly less mocking than usual. Taskinen listened to our oddly meek exchange with a confused look on his face. Fortunately he didn't ask any questions as he drove me home. In fact, neither of us spoke. Even with the car heater blasting the whole way, I was still so cold I thought I would never thaw.

19

The next day found me sitting in the hospital at Aira's bedside again. I'd briefly met with Niina beforehand because there were a couple of holes in her story about the night of Elina's death. Niina was in a sedated haze, but she was able to talk with me for five minutes before drifting off again. That was enough.

"Will they let me see her?" Aira asked. "How long will she be here?"

"A few days. And you?"

"They say I'm going home tomorrow. Are you coming to Elina's funeral on Saturday?"

"I imagine so," I said, although two funerals in one week felt excessive.

Just then Johanna walked in with a bouquet of yellow roses in her arms. She wore a red sweater over a new dress in a red flower pattern. Even her lips bore a hint of artificial red. If only the uncertainty would leave her eyes, she'd be stunning.

Johanna greeted us and asked about Niina. I told her how the previous night had ended.

"Have you thought about my proposition?" Aira asked Johanna once she had finished lamenting Niina's fate.

"I have. It's a great idea. I'll have to ask the children, but I think they'll agree. I'm sure they'd love living at Rosberga."

"You and your kids are moving in? That's fantastic," I said. Even with everything else going on, I hadn't stopped trying to find an appropriate home for the Säntti brood. I'd also informed my lawyer friend Leena what Minna and I had learned on our visit to Johanna's village, and she had turned the screws on Leevi Säntti. Now Johanna told me that there wouldn't be any custody hearing, and any of the children who wanted to live with their mother could.

"It's high time we had some children in the house," said Aira happily. "Between Johanna and me, we shouldn't have any problem driving them around to school and activities."

I could easily imagine her nurturing the Säntti children, spending the rest of her life serving others as she always had. I guess that was one way to live, and no worse than a lot of others.

Aira had also told me she would help Niina any way she could. She said she'd already asked the family lawyer to handle Niina's defense and arrange for her to be recognized as Elina's daughter. I knew there was no way the law would allow Niina to inherit from Elina since she had caused her death, but the situation might be different with Aira's estate.

I didn't have the heart to tarnish Aira's hopes about Niina. If I was any sort of judge, the girl was going to need psychiatric help for years to come. And the charges arising from Elina's death weren't easy to predict given how complicated the case was.

From the hospital lobby I called Kari Hanninen on my cell phone.

"Oh, hi!" he said sincerely. "I was just thinking I should call you and say that your chart is ready."

"I can come get it right now, if that works for you."

"Sure. I just woke up, but come on over. I could use some conversation with my morning coffee."

Hanninen's apartment on the island between Espoo and Helsinki smelled like fresh bread and café au lait. He was wearing jeans and an unbuttoned flannel shirt. His eyes were significantly brighter than my own. I'd seen the dark bags under them in the elevator mirror.

Hanninen poured coffee into enormous mugs and pulled a sheet of croissants out of the oven. He had my astrological chart spread out on the table and explained it as he sipped his coffee. Under the chart were printouts of interpretations, but Hanninen seemed to enjoy telling me what I was like and what I could expect from life. My eyes did go a little wide when he mentioned a big change coming in August, but thankfully he didn't go into more detail. I had to admit he was convincing. When he claimed I had a tendency to act first and think later, I remembered Ström's words from the night before. I also recognized a tendency in myself to withdraw into my own world even though I was interested in other people's lives and emotions. But still— did Hanninen really say anything he couldn't have concluded from the several times we'd met?

"Living with you isn't easy," Hanninen said. "You don't know how to live on other people's terms or at their pace. You always want to walk your own road."

"So I wouldn't make a good mother?" I asked, feigning lightheartedness.

"I wouldn't put it that harshly. Maybe more that it'll be hard for you to make that commitment."

"Do you believe a bad mother can ruin a child's life?" I asked.

"What do you mean?" Hanninen's voice turned more cautious.

"Well, Niina Kuusinen for example."

"What about Niina? She didn't have a bad mother. Maybe a little too protective is all. Niina was never allowed any independence."

"I'm not talking about Heidi Kuusinen. I mean Niina's real mother, Elina Rosberg. You knew about that, didn't you? Did you hear about it back when it happened, or did Niina tell you later?"

Hanninen didn't reply. He just started buttoning his shirt.

"We arrested Niina yesterday. She told us what happened at Rosberga on Boxing Day. Congratulations on an amazing job of manipulation. You intensified Niina's mommy complex even though you masked it as therapy. What were you trying to get, Kari?"

His confidence restored, Hanninen looking straight at me again. "Oh, is that what Niina's saying? Don't you see? That's just how she is. She always has to blame someone, whether it's her parents or the stars. Now she's trying to turn me into her scapegoat. That's typical in a therapy relationship. She's transferring all of her anger at Elina onto me."

"But you're still morally responsible for what Niina did. If I had to guess, I'd say you encouraged her to take revenge on Elina. Revealing the hidden love child of a famous feminist therapist would have been a juicy story for any tabloid."

"Moral responsibility . . . That's a hell of a slippery concept."

I could tell Hanninen thought he had the upper hand again. His smile was positively triumphant. "It's sad Niina did what she did. This has been a tough start to your year. Maybe you should think a little harder about moral responsibility before blaming me."

Standing up, Hanninen grabbed a cigarette and lighter, opened the window, and sat on the sill to smoke. Although he considerately tried to blow the smoke outside, the stench still drifted into my nostrils. My hair would stink for the rest of the day.

"Elina's death isn't just about moral responsibility," I said. "After hearing Niina's story, I kept wondering how Elina ended up on the side of that ski track. Niina's version had them running in completely different directions. And where did those scrapes on her back come from? Then I realized. Niina must have called you after she came inside."

His phone records had been waiting for me on my desk that morning, I explained when he denied it. "You went to Rosberga. Maybe you found Elina alongside the road, cold and unconscious, and you realized that killing her would be the best revenge for all the trouble she caused you. You dragged Elina into the woods and left her there to die. You would have let Niina take the blame."

Hanninen threw his cigarette butt out the window before he replied, now in a tone full of pity and sympathy. "You must really need a vacation. I didn't have anything to do with Elina's death."

"Then why was your car seen on that road around one thirty on the morning of the twenty-seventh? Your red Chevy is hard to miss. And this teenage kid who lives out there just happens to be a car buff, so he was sure of the make and model. He even remembered the license plate number, but that wasn't hard." Hanninen had registered his Chevy a couple of years earlier with a vanity plate that read KAR-199.

I hadn't expected a confession, and Kari Hanninen didn't offer one. He just laughed and said that driving to Nuuksio wasn't a crime. I didn't have enough evidence to charge him with anything.

"Oh, don't you worry. We'll find what we need," I told him as I left.

I had to make myself believe that, because otherwise nothing about my job or the world would make any sense.

I felt so emotional that I didn't dare get behind the wheel of my own car yet, so I aimlessly wandered the streets for a while. Watching a two-year-old screaming in his stroller, his mother pushing him along with her face set in irritation, I wondered what went wrong to turn innocent young children into Hanninens and Malmbergs. Hanninen's horoscope was probably right. Becoming a mother wasn't going to be easy for me. Frequently I became so entangled in other people's business that I ignored my own issues. I was only ten weeks along. It wasn't too late yet to terminate my pregnancy.

Thinking that made me snort. There was no way I was doing that now.

I would have to learn from all the Millas and Niinas I had met in my life to try to at least avoid the failures I'd seen. I knew I wouldn't always succeed, that I'd make some mistakes—possibly with results I wouldn't know about for decades. But I was feeling more ready to accept the challenge.

My walk had deposited me into a small park where kids squealed with delight as they slid down a frozen hillside on their behinds. Watching them for a moment, I tried to imagine that joy in my own child's face. Then I pulled out my phone and dialed Antti's number.

"Hi. It's me. Let's go to lunch," I said.

"Sure. How soon?"

"Fifteen minutes. I'll pick you up at your office."

Marching back to the Fiat, I set off into the traffic of downtown Helsinki. The winter sun made the world a little brighter, already hinting that in two months' time it would drive the snow away with its warmth. At the end of the bridge, I switched on the radio. Kollaa Kestää was singing "A Farewell to Arms":

Today I'm gonna stand up on my own feet,
Today I'm goin' out in the world, to walk on my own road,
Today I want to see for once what's beyond these four walls.

Joining in on the chorus, I decided to believe the words of the song at least until the end of the day.

ABOUT THE AUTHOR

© Tomas Whitehouse, 2011

Leena Lehtolainen was born in Vesanto, Finland, to parents who taught language and literature. As a child, she made up stories in her head before she could even write. At the age of ten, she wrote her first book, a young adult novel, which was published two years later. Besides writing, Leena is fond of classical singing, her beloved cats, and—her greatest passion—figure skating. She attends many competitions as a skating journalist and writes for a Finnish figure-skating magazine, *Taitoluistelu*. *Snow Woman* is the fourth installment in the bestselling Maria Kallio series, which debuted in English in 2012 with *My First Murder* and continued in 2013 with *Her Enemy* and *Copper Heart*. Leena lives in Finland with her husband and two sons.

ABOUT THE TRANSLATOR

Owen F. Witesman is a professional literary translator with a master's in Finnish and Estonian-area studies from Indiana University. He has translated more than thirty Finnish books into English, including novels, children's books, poetry, plays, graphic novels, and nonfiction. His recent translations include the first three novels in the Maria Kallio series, the satire *The Human Part* by Kari Hotakainen, the thriller *Cold Courage* by Pekka Hiltunen, and the 1884 classic *The Railroad* by Juhani Aho. He currently resides in Springville, Utah, with his wife and three daughters, a dog, a cat, and twenty-nine fruit trees.

Made in the USA
Monee, IL
12 April 2024